Never Say Goodbye

Susan Lewis

Never Say Goodbye

CENTURY

Published by Century 2014

2 4 6 8 10 9 7 5 3 1

First published in Great Britain in 2014 by
Century
Random House, 20 Vauxhall Bridge Road,
London SW1V 2SA

www.randomhouse.co.uk

Addresses for companies within The Random House Group Limited can be
found at: www.randomhouse.co.uk/offices.htm

The Random House Group Limited Reg. No. 954009

ISBN 9781780891743

A CIP catalogue record for this book is available from the British Library

The Random House Group Limited supports the Forest Stewardship
Council® (FSC®), the leading international forest-certification organisation.
Our books carrying the FSC label are printed on FSC®-certified paper.
FSC is the only forest-certification scheme supported by the leading
environmental organisations, including Greenpeace. Our paper procurement
policy can be found at www.randomhouse.co.uk/environment

Typeset in Palatino by Palimpsest Book Production Limited,
Falkirk, Stirlingshire
Printed and bound in Great Britain by Clays Ltd, St Ives plc

I'd like to dedicate this book to everyone who has
been in Josie's or Bel's position

Chapter One

'So what do you think that's all about?' Josie Clark murmured, almost to herself, as she put down the phone.

'All what?' her husband wondered from behind his latest copy of *Exchange and Mart*. It would be a flipping miracle if they could afford a new car, second-hand of course, but there was no harm in looking.

Josie's lively violet eyes flicked in Jeff's direction. Though she couldn't see his face, her own was partially reflected in the mirror hanging over their faux-brick fireplace, and what she could see were small, delicate features, with a pixyish chin and nose that seemed to belong more to a child than a woman of forty-two years. Her crowning glory, as her dad used to say, was the mop of honey-red curls that shone and tumbled about her head as though they had a life all their own.

'That barnet of yours is the envy of half the women I know,' her neighbour, Carly, regularly complained. Not that Carly's hair was bad, it just wasn't naturally blonde, and in truth it didn't have all that much verve in it either. However, on Friday nights when she went out with the girls, her artful handling of it ensured that no one would ever have guessed how many extensions, pieces, pins and lacquer sprays were holding it all up.

At five foot two Josie could never be described as tall, but then neither could Jeff at five-five. What he was though, or certainly in her opinion, was the best-looking bloke in Kesterly-on-Sea. Or on their street, anyway. Probably on the whole estate, because not a single one of the blokes she knew, young or old, looked a bit like Tom Cruise when they smiled, nor could they make her heart skip a beat the way Jeff sometimes did. That was really saying something after twenty-two years of marriage, which didn't mean they hadn't had their ups and downs along the way, because heaven knew they had. In fact, there had been a time when she'd seriously feared they wouldn't make it, but she didn't allow herself to dwell on that too much now. No point when the other woman, Dawnie Hopkins, had moved up north after it had all come out about her and Jeff. That had happened five years ago this Christmas, and had totally spoiled the holiday, that was for sure. In fact, Christmas had never really been the same since, given all the painful memories that seemed to pour down the chimney instead of seasonal cheer.

Last Christmas had been the worst, though not thanks to Dawnie this time – in the circumstances Josie might have actually preferred it if her ex-best mate had staged an unexpected return. No, the source of their upset last year had been Ryan, their eighteen-year-old son, whose gift for getting into one scrape after another after another had surpassed itself so spectacularly that Jeff would no longer have the boy's name spoken in his hearing.

Oddly, the crisis of Ryan's trial and imprisonment had seemed to bring Josie and Jeff closer together for a while, probably because it had given them more to think about than how much damage the shenanigans with Dawnie had done to their marriage.

She still couldn't help wondering if Jeff ever regretted staying.

She didn't ask, it wouldn't do any good, not only because she was nervous of the answer, but because she herself had banned Dawnie's name from being spoken inside number 31 Greenacre Close. This was their home, a tidy little semi at the far end of a cul-de-sac, next to a lane that ran through to the playing fields behind, and they didn't need to sully its fresh, lemony scent with stinky reminders of a so-called friend's betrayal. (Josie would never admit this to another living soul, but she actually missed Dawnie more than she'd imagined she would, though she supposed it wasn't all that surprising given they'd been best mates practically since birth.)

Just went to show, you could never trust anyone, even those closest to you, which had been a very painful lesson for Josie to learn when she herself was so loyal she didn't even like to change a dental appointment.

The real light of her and Jeff's life was Lily, their twenty-one-year-old angel of a daughter, who was currently at uni doing a BA honours degree in history and politics! Imagine that! No one, from either of their families, had ever done so well, nor, come to that, had anyone else on their street. However, Lily was special; everyone said so, and had been saying it for most of her blessed little life. She sparkled and laughed and made everyone feel so good about themselves that love just came cascading back at her like a rainstorm of stars.

'She's her mother all over,' Dawnie always used to say, but Josie didn't think she'd ever been as lovely as Lily. True, she enjoyed a good laugh, and she wasn't backward in offering a kind word when one was needed, but she didn't have the same inner glow, or the innate belief in goodness that constantly shone out of her daughter.

Maybe she'd had some of it once, but definitely not any more.

Now she had scars on her hopes and shadows over her dreams, though to look at her, or talk to her, no one would ever know it. She simply went about her days in her usual cheery way, with a duster and polish in her hands on Mondays and Wednesdays, a teapot and frying pan on Thursdays and Fridays and, until recently, a telephone headset plastered to her ears while she engaged in a spot of telemarketing at the weekends. (Living where they did, on the notorious Temple Fields council estate, there wasn't much in the way of swearing, cursing and death threats she hadn't heard before, but not until she'd taken this last job had she ever been on the receiving end of it. Honest to God, the things some people said when you rang them up out of the blue . . . She'd never repeat their abuse, not even to Jeff, who, it had to be said, had some choice phrases himself for when his taxi broke down. And best not get him started on the kids who treated his back seat to a tactical chunder after a

3

skinful on a Friday night, because that really wasn't pretty, for anyone.)

The telemarketing had ended up proving a waste of her time, since she'd never made a red cent out of it, so these last couple of weekends she'd been enjoying a bit of time to herself. Just as well, given the commitment she had for every other Saturday, and nothing was ever to get in the way of that.

She had to wonder if it was why her reflection was showing a woman who was worried, stressed, even drawn. Strange, since she wasn't aware of feeling anything in particular at the moment, apart from mildly intrigued to know what was behind the call she'd just taken.

So, should she run upstairs now to make herself a little more presentable ready for the visit? A quick rub of foundation, brightened by a couple of dabs of blusher and several waves of the magic mascara wand? She didn't usually wear make-up on her cleaning days, and since today was Wednesday she hadn't bothered when she'd got up this morning. Jeff always said, in his usual gruff way, that she didn't need it, she was lovely au naturel. He didn't often lace his compliments with fancy French phrases, mainly because that was the only one he knew, but on the rare occasions he remembered it, it pleased her no end, especially in the light of all they'd been through.

'Have you got any bookings today?' she asked, going through to the kitchen to put the washing machine on for a second spin. One was never enough these days, a warning that the old tub was probably about to break down. Joy! Another expense they couldn't afford.

'Mm?' Jeff grunted.

'That was Lily on the phone,' Josie called out. 'She and Jasper are on their way over.'

Sounding surprised, he said, 'In the middle of the week? To what do we owe the pleasure?'

'She wouldn't say, but she wants to talk to us both, so if you've got any fares . . .'

'Nothing so far,' he admitted despondently. 'I'll go over to the cab office later and check out what's what. Are you putting the kettle on?'

'If you like.' After doing the honours, she went to stand in the doorway between the kitchen and living room, taking a moment to enjoy their new wallpaper with its smart grey stripes and floral border. They'd got it for a third off at the B&Q end-of-season sale, and it didn't really matter that there hadn't been quite enough, because no one ever looked behind the sofa so who cared if there was a bare patch there? What was important to Josie was the fact that it really was quite similar to the paper in the extremely elegant drawing room at John Crover-Keene's. This was one of the big houses on the other side of the hill that faced down over Temple Bay, where she cleaned on Mondays and did the laundry on Wednesdays. She used to do for a couple of his neighbours until they'd asked her to stop coming after the unfortunate business with Ryan last year. Mr Crover-Keene wasn't like them. He was sweet and considerate and understood completely that she wasn't to blame (actually she probably was, in a way, but it was really good of him to take such a kindly view). Sadly, he was hardly ever at home, since the Close, as his house was called, was really only a weekend place for him, so it was usually empty when she went flitting about with feather dusters and vacs.

Imagine having all those bedrooms – six in total all with their own bathrooms – a separate laundry room, a kitchen as big as the downstairs of her whole house, acres of landscaped garden with a tennis court, pool and fabulous view of the bay, and the place wasn't lived in all the time. What it must be like to be that rich and single. She didn't really envy him though, because he always seemed quite lonely to her in spite of all the friends who came for weekends. She often thought of this when money was tight for her and Jeff, which was most of the time these days; at least they had their health, and their kids, and each other.

Well, they certainly had Lily anyway, who'd rung a few minutes ago to say she was on her way home to have a chat with them. And Jasper was coming too. Josie liked that name, it made him sound as though he came from a classy family, which actually he did. Jeff thought it was a bit pansyish, though he was fond enough of the boy.

Jasper and Lily had been going out together since their first year at UWE – University of the West of England – and as far as Josie knew Jasper's Kent-based family were as smitten with Lily as their youngest son clearly was. She just hoped Lily didn't end up going over to the south-east to live once she graduated, though of course she'd never say that to her. After all, she couldn't be tying her to the West Country for ever, though if they were able to find some work in Bristol or Exeter, the nearest big cities, that would be lovely. Neither was too far away, about an hour on the train, a bit longer in the car, and they were really happening places, as Lily kept telling her.

Actually, Josie had been spending a little more time in Bristol these last few months. After going to see Ryan at the prison she and Lily shopped and chatted, drank wine in harbour-front cafés and took in all the culture Lily could cram in before Josie had to catch a train home. It was just how Josie imagined her life might have been had she been able to go to uni, though back then she'd never even considered it an option. Certainly it wasn't something her parents had encouraged. Actually, her dad might have if he'd lived long enough to see her scoop up five As and four Bs in her GCSEs, but he'd had a heart attack one Saturday afternoon at the football when she was fourteen, and hadn't even made it to emergency. By then her parents had been divorced for almost ten years, so her mother, Eileen, hadn't felt the loss anywhere near as deeply as Josie had. In fact, she'd uttered something horrible like 'good bloody riddance' when she'd heard the news, and hadn't even bothered coming to the funeral. Jeff had been there, of course, and loads of her dad's mates from around the estate, who'd all expressed how sorry they were that old Bill had gone and popped off at such a young age.

It was quite typical of her mother to make herself scarce at such a harrowing time, since she'd always been more about Eileen than she had about anyone else. Her dad hadn't been like that. When he wasn't drunk, which admittedly wasn't often, he always showed an interest in her education, and every time she earned herself some good grades he'd taken her for a pizza to celebrate.

'Bet you'll be a high-powered lawyer, or even Prime Minister, one of these days,' he used to tease her.

'Well done, it's what school's for, to keep you out of trouble,' was about the most Eileen could manage as she got ready for a hot night out, or to work a double shift at Tesco.

Since there was often a lot of trouble on the north side of the Temple Fields estate, it was a constant worry for those on the south side that the druggies, thugs and hoodies who kept Kesterly police in business would surge over the border formed by the busy high street on some sort of teenage recruitment drive. It rarely happened that way, mainly because the south-side youths all too often took themselves north in search of adventure.

Josie herself never went much further into the estate than the high street, and if Jeff was ever called to an address in the Zone, as they sometimes called it, he made sure he kept all his doors and windows locked until he was safely out again. In his opinion taxi drivers should be allowed to carry guns into those streets, which Josie calmly agreed with since it could never happen. Her mother, was forever telling Jeff he should arm himself with a baseball bat at the very least, since he never knew what sort of lowlife he might be picking up, whether on the estate, or anywhere else come to that.

Eileen for mayor!

Deciding the impromptu visit from Lily and Jasper called for a change out of her cleaning clothes at least, Josie was heading for the stairs when Jeff's mobile started to ring.

'If that's a call-out,' she said, 'can you try to be back within the hour? Lily should be here by then.'

Signalling that he'd heard, he clicked on the line and sang out a cheery 'Hello, Jeff's Taxis, any time, anywhere.'

Wondering why that still made her smile when she'd heard it a thousand times, Josie continued up to their bedroom, trying not to notice that the stairwell and landing could do with a lick of paint, or that the hem was hanging loose on one of the curtains. She'd been asking Jeff for weeks to get it down so she could sort it, but he still hadn't got round to it, and even if she were able to brave the ladder, which she wasn't due to the awkward position of the window, she still wouldn't be able to reach the rail.

That was Jeff Clark for you, heart of gold, do anything for anyone, any time, anywhere, but he never seemed to get round to things at home. Unless it was for Lily, of course. He'd climb mountains, swim rivers and play the clown for his precious girl – indeed he'd done all three over the years in a bid to help her raise money for various causes, and Josie was sure Lily hadn't finished with him yet. It could well be the reason she and Jasper were on their way here, to try and talk Jeff into joining a sponsored cycle ride to Land's End, or cross-dressing for a jog along the Somerset-Devon coast road. There was no end to the schemes Lily and Jasper got involved in, or to the charities they seemed to support, and Josie only wished she and Jeff could afford to back them with a bit more than a fiver or a tenner a time.

'Pickup from a works Christmas do tomorrow,' Jeff informed her as he came into their bedroom, the *Kesterly Gazette* in one hand, a pen in the other. Josie knew he was on the lookout for a new car to replace their Opel Estate, which was spending more time in the garage lately than it was on the road. She wouldn't ask how they were going to afford it, since she knew already it'd have to be on the never-never, and he'd be no happier than she was about getting any further into debt.

Still, when needs must, and thank goodness he'd found a way of earning a living after the builders' merchants where he'd worked for the past fifteen years driving a forklift truck had closed. Jobs were in short supply around these parts, and he'd hated being on the dole – it had really brought him down having to live off the state. He was a man with a lot of pride, and the fact that he'd always paid his taxes and was entitled to some help when times were hard hadn't made him feel any better. His redundancy would have come in handy, if it hadn't all gone along with their savings – and their son.

'Are you going back to Crover-Keene's later?' Jeff asked, plonking himself down on the bed and stretching out his legs. Since the room wouldn't fit a king-size it was only a

8

double, but with neither of them being exactly big they managed just fine. Josie wouldn't have minded a bit more wardrobe space though, or a second dressing table so Jeff could have one to himself, but there was barely enough room to edge round the bed as it was, so definitely no chance of fitting anything else in.

'No, I've finished for today,' she replied, kicking off her baggy old trackies and fishing out a pair of George jeans. Eight pounds ninety-nine at Asda, a real bargain and they didn't make her bum look big. Not that it was, particularly, but she was definitely wider in that department than she'd like, and it seemed no amount of exercise or dieting would shift it.

Liposuction.

Dream on.

'Does your boss know you're skimping on your hours?' Jeff teased, putting his hands behind his head as he watched her change.

'Actually, he told me to,' she replied, zipping up the jeans and tugging off the thick woolly jumper she'd had for a birthday, or was it Christmas, about ten years ago. It still did perfectly well for when she was cleaning, or working a shift at the Seafront Caff, especially at this time of year. 'He's hosting a drinks party on Saturday night, he said, so he'd rather I went in before to make sure everything's ready for his guests. *And*,' she continued meaningfully, 'he's asked me to help serve and clean up after, so that should give me an extra couple of hours.'

'That's good, and you know where to call if anyone's looking for a taxi. Except I don't expect that posh lot would want to get into anything less than a Merc.'

'Your Opel is a shining example of its breed,' she assured him. 'No one could keep it cleaner, or take more pride in its luggage space.'

Jeff's expression was wry as he said, 'Or want to kick its ass harder when the bloody thing breaks down. Anyway, what's all this about with Lily, do you reckon?'

'She just said they were on their way and they'd tell us everything when they got here.'

He frowned. 'Everything?'

'That's what she said.'

'I hope they're not about to announce he's got her up the duff,' he commented, as Josie headed off for the bathroom for a quick lick and promise. 'He'll have me to answer to if he has.'

'He'd be so scared if he could hear you,' she mocked.

'So he should be, because they're way too young to be tying themselves down with kids. If you ask me they shouldn't even be living together, but no one ever bothers asking me.'

Josie laughed. 'I don't recall you objecting when we went up there to help them move,' she reminded him.

'I'm sure I said something, but as usual no one was listening. They haven't even graduated yet,' he rambled on, as she came back into the bedroom, 'and how are they ever going to get themselves top jobs if they've got a baby at home?'

'If their jobs are that good they could probably afford a nanny,' Josie pointed out. 'Anyway, I can't imagine it's going to be about that. Lily's as keen to travel and see the world before settling down as he is, and she's on the pill.'

He scowled. 'Do I need to have the reason for that in my head?' he demanded.

Knowing he was roasting her, she tossed a towel at him and pulled on a pale blue turtleneck that she quickly decided was too tight, and abandoned in favour of a black velveteen tracksuit top. 'My guess is,' she said, bundling the laundry into the basket, 'they're either wanting to involve us in some new charity stunt, or they've come up with some sort of plan for Christmas. Maybe Jasper's family are going to invite us over there for the day, so we can all be together.'

Jeff's eyes widened. 'Do you reckon?' he responded, sounding dubious and impressed. 'I'd be up for it if they did, wouldn't you?'

No, actually, she didn't think she would, she liked doing Christmas here in their home, but what she said was, 'Let's wait to find out before we start getting our hopes up, shall we?'

*

'Mum! Dad!' Lily cried, bounding down the garden path as radiant as a sunbeam in her white fur jacket and red woollen hat. 'You're both here, great! Especially you, Dad.'

Smiling wryly as Lily embraced her father so hard it might have been a year rather than a week since they'd last clapped eyes on each other, Josie turned to Jasper and pulled him into a hug. 'How are you?' she asked warmly. She had no problem understanding what Lily saw in this lad, since he was, as Carly next door would put it, the complete package. Tall, dark, with the looks of a rock star, and from a dead posh family, he had the kind of drive and personality Josie could only dream of for Ryan.

'Come in, come in,' Jeff was insisting. 'We don't want to be letting the heat out. What's all this?' he asked, as Lily thrust a Sainsbury's bag into his hand.

'You'll find out,' she informed him, going to hug her mother. 'Are you OK?' she asked, frowning. 'You look a bit tired.'

'I knew I should have put some make-up on,' Josie sighed. 'Go on through. Fire's on, make yourselves cosy. Can I take your coat, Jasper?'

Shrugging off his Barbour, he handed it to her and went to stand over the three brightly burning gas bars, rubbing his hands to warm them. 'You know, I so love this room,' he announced, as though he didn't say it every time he came. 'It feels just like home.'

Considering how different it must be to his parents' place, Josie was, as ever, touched by the compliment. 'Well, you're always very welcome,' she assured him.

'As long as you're treating my girl right,' Jeff added as a warning.

Rolling her eyes as Lily poked her father, Josie took the coats back into the hall and hung them over hers and Jeff's. No overnight bags had come in, so they presumably weren't staying, unless they hadn't completely unloaded Jasper's Audi Roadster yet. Not the kind of car that found its way into this little cul-de-sac very often, and Josie knew that part of Jeff was proud as Punch for it to be outside their garden gate. The other part never stopped worrying that the wheels might be missing by the time Jasper went out again.

'Shall I make some tea?' she offered, going back into the room to find Jeff in his usual chair and Lily perched on the arm.

'I'll help,' Lily cried, springing up. 'You stay here, Jaz, and have a nice little chat with Dad.'

'Bossy or what?' Jeff commented as Lily hooked her mother's arm and walked her into the kitchen.

Eyeing her daughter as she closed the door and put an ear against it, Josie said, 'What are you up to?'

'Ssh,' Lily responded softly, putting a finger to her lips. 'I want to hear this.'

'Hear what?'

Beckoning her over, Lily cracked the door an inch and made room for her mother to join in the eavesdrop.

'What are they saying?' Josie asked, moving Lily's strawberry-blonde curls out of her face.

'Nothing yet,' Lily whispered. She turned to her mother, eyes so bright she might just burst into some sort of rapture. 'He's about to ask Dad . . .'

'What the bloody hell?' Jeff suddenly blurted.

Alarmed, Lily spun back to the door and peeked through. 'Blimey,' she muttered, and sailing back into the room, she exclaimed, 'You're not supposed to go down on one knee to *him*, Jasper!'

Jasper's cheeks were crimson. His eyes went to Josie who was trying not to laugh, then back to Jeff who was having a job containing himself too. With a sheepish grin, he said, 'Seems I've screwed it, and now I feel a total prat.'

Trying to be helpful, Josie suggested, 'Shall we go out and come in again?'

Clambering to his feet, Jasper glanced at Lily as he replied, 'I know you were listening anyway, so you might as well stay.'

Clearly thrilled, Lily went to perch on the chair opposite her father's and reached for Jasper's hand as he came to stand next to her. At six foot one he was the tallest person they'd had in the room for a while, and hoping he wasn't able to see over the back of the sofa to the bare patch, Josie positioned herself strategically, watching as he fixed solemn dark eyes on Jeff.

'Mr Clark,' he began earnestly, 'I'm sure you've guessed what this is about already, but just so's we're clear, I've come here today to ask your permission for Lily's hand in marriage.'

Though it had been obvious where this was going, Josie couldn't stop a gasp of elation, and as Jeff cleared his throat, attempting to sound grave, she could tell he was brimming with pride.

'Well, first of all I thought we'd done away with the Mr and Mrs business back in the summer. We're Josie and Jeff to you, son . . .'

'Or Mum and Dad?' Lily piped up mischievously.

Jeff narrowed her a look. 'Josie and Jeff will do for now,' he informed her. 'I haven't given my permission yet . . .'

'But we know you're going to.'

'Oh do we?' he retorted archly. 'You shouldn't take so much for granted, young lady. I need to find out what this lad's prospects are, if he can keep you in the style to which you've become accustomed . . .'

'*Dad!* This is Jasper you're talking to.'

'I'm aware of that, but he needs to know that you have certain standards . . .'

'Mum!' Lily cried. 'You have to stop him.'

'I only wish I knew how,' Josie replied, stifling a laugh – and everything else she was feeling that she'd never dream of revealing in this joyous moment.

'I think I know what you mean, Jeff,' Jasper interrupted hastily. 'Lily's always been loved and fantastically well taken care of and treated to nothing but the best, so I want to assure you that I'm ready to pick up the mantle.'

Jeff flicked a glance at the fireplace. 'Is that necessary?' he asked.

Groaning at the joke, Josie said, 'Take no notice of him, Jasper. Of course you have our permission . . .'

'What?' Jeff protested. 'It was me he asked, not you, and what I want to know, my lad, is this: Have you got her up the duff, because if you haven't I don't understand what all the rush is. Mind you, if you have, I shall be showing you the door.'

'What is he like?' Lily complained, dropping her head

in her hands. 'No Dad, I'm not pregnant, and there isn't any rush. It's just that we know we want to spend the rest of our lives together . . .'

'You're twenty-one!' Jeff expostulated. 'How can you possibly know anything? You haven't even been out into the big wide world yet . . .'

'Excuse me, who's at uni in this room?' Lily challenged. 'And exactly how old were you and Mum when you got married?'

'That's not the point . . .'

'It's absolutely the point. You knew your minds when you were our age, so why should it be any different for us?'

'What I'm telling you is that we thought we knew a lot of things back then that time has proved us wrong about. Isn't that right?' he challenged Josie.

Though it was on the tip of her tongue to ask if Dawnie Hopkins might feature in his thinking somewhere, Josie said, 'I think we've always been certain of how we feel about each other, haven't we?'

The flush that crept up from his collar showed that he'd got her meaning. 'OK, we've never been in any doubt about that,' he conceded, 'but maybe we wouldn't have had children so young if we'd known what hard work you can be.'

Lily broke into one of her more dazzling smiles. 'You know very well that your life wasn't complete until I came along,' she informed him playfully.

'And my pockets weren't empty either, nor was my hair grey or the bags under my eyes big enough to bring the groceries home in.'

'You still wouldn't be without me.'

Jeff regarded Jasper helplessly. 'Are you sure about this?' he asked, as though he really couldn't believe he'd be so insane.

Grinning all over his face, Jasper nodded. 'I'm sure,' he replied, tightening his hold on Lily's hand. 'More than sure, if that's possible.'

Jeff sighed. 'Then I wish you good luck, son, because you're getting yourself a handful there, take it from me.' His tone softened as he added, 'You've also got a star prize and I should know, because I got one of my own when I was your age, and Lily's nothing if not her mother's daughter.'

'Oh Dad,' Lily gushed, throwing her arms around him. 'That's such a lovely thing to say, about me, and about Mum.'

Relieved no one was paying her too much attention, Josie joined in the hugs and tried to make herself think only of what she needed to say next.

Thank goodness for tea.

'No, no,' Lily objected. 'We've brought champagne. That's what's in the bag.'

Jeff's eyes widened.

'Well, it's a special occasion,' Lily pointed out. 'So I thought we should toast it properly.'

Shaking his head, as if such extravagance was beyond his comprehension, Jeff looked to Josie for some sort of guidance.

'I'll get the glasses,' she declared, and finding herself keen for a sip of something she didn't have very often, she headed for the dresser where they kept the flutes they'd won at bingo on holiday in Dawlish when Lily was ten and Ryan was seven.

'So, here's to you two and a happy future together,' Jeff declared when the glasses were full. 'I still don't know why you have to do it . . .'

'Dad!'

'Jeff!'

'All right, all right, I was just saying, that's all.'

Taking over, Josie said, 'Congratulations to you both. I think you're very lucky to have found each other, and we're lucky too, because we'll get to have Jasper as a son-in-law.'

Apparently thrilled with the toast, Jasper and Lily clinked her glass, did the same to Jeff's and drank.

'So when's the big day?' Jeff wanted to know. 'Not too soon, I hope.'

'Actually,' Lily replied, glancing at her beloved, 'we were thinking of next summer.'

Jeff's eyes went straight to Josie's. 'And they're not rushing?' he queried ironically.

Concerned, Josie said, 'This is your final year. Wouldn't you rather wait until you've graduated and perhaps decided what you want to do after . . . ?'

'Whatever we do,' Lily interrupted, 'we know we want to do it together, so what difference does it make when we tie the knot?'

A lot, if your father and I have to pay for it, Josie managed not to say, while knowing it was exactly what Jeff was thinking.

'We thought we could have the ceremony at St Mark's where you and Dad got married,' Lily ran on eagerly, 'and the reception at Kesterly Golf Club in that huge room overlooking the sea. Jaz is going to ask his brother to be best man, and Dad you'll give me away, but you're not allowed to cry or it'll make me cry too and I don't want to turn up at the church with mascara down my face. Oh Mum, just think how wonderful it's going to be, shopping for dresses, choosing the flowers and the menus. We're up to about eighty people so far, but I know you and Dad'll want to invite lots of your friends too, so you can decide how many we should be.'

Still taking care not to blurt out her biggest concern, Josie said, 'Well, it sounds as though you two really have been making plans. And what about your parents, Jasper? Have you broken the happy news to them yet?'

'No, we're planning to drive over there at the weekend,' he told her. 'We wanted to share it with you first, so I could ask for Lily's hand – and make a total prat of myself in doing so – and be sure you were cool with it all.'

Josie looked at Jeff. 'I think we're cool, don't you?' she prompted.

'Very cool,' he agreed, in a way that told her he was probably in need of a lie-down now the potential cost of it was starting to sink in. 'And your parents,' he went on, 'do you think they'll be . . .'

Please don't let him say willing to pay.

'. . . happy to hear you're getting married?'

Jasper didn't look in any doubt of it as he turned his lovestruck eyes to his equally lovestruck sweetheart. 'They're going to be thrilled,' he assured them.

Looking slightly less than, Jeff asked, 'And what if they want you to get married over near them?'

Knowing this was a desperate hope that the Cunninghams might weigh in for at least part of the bill if it was happening on their doorstep, Josie said, 'We don't have to make any concrete decisions now. We can . . .'

'Oh, but we ought to go and see the vicar to find out what dates are available,' Lily jumped in quickly. 'You know how booked up they get at St Mark's with it being in such a pretty location, and at the golf club. We might find out they can't fit us in until the year after next anyway, but at least we'll be able to make plans once we have dates.'

Feeling Jeff grasping the straw with her, Josie said, 'This is true, you might indeed have to wait until the year after next, which wouldn't actually be such a bad thing. We'll have had plenty of time to track down the right dress by then, maybe even to have it specially made . . .'

'I'm going to do that anyway,' Lily chipped in. 'There's this brilliant designer who was featured in the *Bristol* magazine. You should see her stuff, Mum. Talk about Jenny Packham stand aside.'

'Who?' Jeff wanted to know.

'Let's hope she's not charging Jenny Packham prices,' Josie quipped.

'Oh, I don't think so,' Lily responded dismissively. 'Anyway, do you want to come and see the vicar with us?'

Josie blinked. 'Now?'

'Why not now? We're here, he's there, or presumably he is . . .'

'What about talking to Jasper's parents first?' Jeff put in. 'They might not take too kindly to being cut out of all the decisions.'

'Oh, they won't mind,' Jasper promised, in a way that reminded Josie of Ryan. What was it with kids that they assumed everything they did was OK with their parents?

'Do you think we should ring first, or just turn up?' Lily wondered, looking at her mother. 'What did you do when you booked your wedding?'

'Oh God, I can't remember that far back,' Josie protested.

'Maybe we should send an email,' Jasper suggested.

'Yeah, if we want to wait a week for a reply,' Lily countered.

17

'We can't all fit into that car,' Josie pointed out.

'Dad can take us in the taxi.'

Knowing what Lily was like once her mind was made up, Josie threw out her hands as she said, 'OK, let me run upstairs and put a face on first. I don't want the vicar thinking we're there to sort out my funeral.'

'Not funny,' Lily called after her as she ran up the stairs.

No, it wasn't funny actually, but Jeff had always been better with the jokes than she had.

She'd got no further than rubbing in a spot of foundation when Lily appeared in the doorway. When she didn't speak, Josie glanced at her reflection in the mirror. 'Everything OK?' she asked.

Lily frowned in a way that Josie wasn't expecting. 'What is it, Mum?' she asked. 'And before you say nothing, remember how well I know you.'

Though Josie's heart twisted, she couldn't help but smile. 'Would that be as well as I know you?'

Lily nodded. 'Something's not right,' she said bluntly, 'and I want to know what it is. It's Ryan, isn't it? You're wondering how we can invite him.'

'Ryan's definitely a concern,' Josie admitted. 'Surely you want him to be there?'

'Of course we do, and he will be if they let him out early.'

Josie regarded her with fond despair. 'You know that's not very likely,' she said.

'You have to look on the positive side,' Lily insisted. 'I'm definitely not giving up hope of him coming home sooner than we think. After all, anything can happen between now and then.'

Josie's gaze drifted. Yes, indeed anything could happen between now and then.

'There's something else, isn't there?' Lily said, coming to sit on the end of the bed so she could see her mother's reflection more clearly. 'I'm guessing you're worried about how much it's going to cost.'

Josie's eyebrows rose. She couldn't lie about that, any more than she could magic the funds out of thin air. In fact, part of her could feel quite angry with Lily for not considering how difficult it would be for her parents to throw a lavish wedding at any time over the next couple of years, when she knew very well that all their savings, and Jeff's redundancy, had been used up on trying to help Ryan.

All the more reason for Lily to have everything she wanted; after all, it had never been their practice to give to one and not the other. So maybe her anger was more towards Ryan.

Lily was nodding knowledgeably. 'I told Jaz you'd see it as your responsibility,' she declared, 'but it's not, Mum, it's ours. We're the ones who want to do this, so we're the ones who should pay.'

Josie regarded her in astonishment. 'And where exactly are you going to get the money from?' she demanded, knowing very well that Lily was no better at existing on her meagre allowance than she and Jeff were on their equally meagre wages. 'The kind of wedding you're proposing could set you back fifteen grand or more.'

'I know, but Jaz came into some money on his twenty-first that will more than cover it. So, you see, it's all sorted. You don't have to worry about a thing, apart from what you're going to wear, and helping me organise it all.'

Avoiding her eyes, Josie smiled past the lump in her throat.

Turning her round so she could see into her mother's eyes, Lily said, 'Why do I still have the feeling that you're keeping something back?'

Because I am, Josie couldn't say. *And I have to, because there's no way in the world I'm going to spoil this special day for you. Or any other day, come to that.* 'You're imagining things,' Josie told her with a smile.

Maybe she was too. It could be that the sore swelling in her left breast that had been there for a while now wasn't the onset of something terrible. There was every chance it was just a boil that wouldn't break, or an inflamed cyst. She'd had cysts before, so there was no reason for this one to be any different, apart from the fact that it was all red and angry. She hadn't found anything online to tell her what it might be, but now she was peri-menopausal, as they liked to call it, her hormones were no doubt up to all sorts of tricks that she didn't begin to understand. So she wasn't worried, really. She probably wouldn't even be thinking about it if she hadn't read a piece in the paper this morning about how many women's lives could be saved if they'd only get tested as soon as something unusual showed up.

She wasn't going to ignore it any longer. She'd ring the surgery tomorrow to make an appointment, which she probably wouldn't get for a week or more, and by then the swelling would no doubt have gone down of its own accord. If it had, she'd cancel her session to make room for someone who really needed it.

'I'm not hiding anything,' she told Lily firmly. 'Now let me get ready, will you? We've got a vicar to see and a wedding to start arranging.'

Chapter Two

'This one! This one! Please Auntie Bel, can we have this one?'

Isabella Monkton looked down at her niece and nephew's upturned faces, and so much love surged into her smile that it broke into a laugh. 'But it's huge,' she protested. 'It'll take us a week to decorate it.'

'That's all right, we'll help,' seven-year-old Oscar promised, turning to his five-year-old sister for support.

'Yes, we will,' Nell agreed earnestly. Her adorable blue eyes were so like her mother's, Isabella's twin sister, that Bel sometimes felt Natalia was looking back at her from wherever she was now. Nell had her mother's silky blonde hair too, and her rosebud mouth. In fact she was a little replica of Natalia, or Isabella, depending which of the twins you were looking at. Whether Nell had also inherited something of her mother's character, only time would tell, Bel guessed, though she was certainly starting to show early signs of it. 'And if we have a really big tree,' Nell was explaining knowledgeably, 'Father Christmas will definitely be able to find us.'

'Mm,' Bel responded, as though assessing the merit of this. 'And I suppose there'll be more room for him to leave presents underneath it, as well?'

Oscar's face lit up as Nell jumped up and down in glee.

Turning to the young lad who'd been wandering up and down the rows of Christmas trees with them, helping to make the choice, Bel said, 'It seems we're going to have this one. Can you deliver?'

'Of course,' he replied, giving Oscar a wink. 'I'll bring it in my sleigh, shall I?'

Nell gasped excitedly. 'Have you got a sleigh?' she cried. 'Auntie Bel, he's got a sleigh!'

'Don't you need snow to drive a sleigh?' Oscar pointed out.

The lad looked perplexed. 'You're right,' he decided. 'So if we haven't had any by the time I'm ready to bring this, I'll put it on the lorry. How does that sound?'

'Good idea,' Oscar agreed. 'Can you bring it today? We don't live very far from here, do we Auntie Bel?'

Loving that they considered her home theirs, and why wouldn't they when they spent so much time there, she said, 'Just a couple of miles. We're on Bay View Road, at the Westleigh end. Do you know it?'

'I sure do,' he responded in his broad West Country burr. 'We've got a few more deliveries scheduled to go up that way today, so I'd say it should be with you by five, six at the latest. Will you be home by then?'

The children's anxious eyes came to Bel.

'We'll make sure we are,' she told them. 'Now, I guess we'd better pay for this eight-foot monster and choose some more ornaments, because I'm sure we don't have enough to fill it.'

'Yes, yes, yes,' Nell cried, already skipping back towards the garden centre's Christmas grotto.

'And you said we could have a hot chocolate,' Oscar reminded her, as they followed.

'And you were going to decide whether you want one here, or down on Kesterly seafront,' she reminded them.

'Here,' they echoed together.

After filling a small trolley with dozens of glittering stars, baubles, angels and lights, and handing over almost two hundred pounds at the checkout, Bel steered her little charges into the crowded cafeteria. Being the first weekend of December, it seemed half the families of Kesterly had decided to brave the chill wind to choose their trees. There was a time when they used to come here to visit Santa in his grotto, but since the scandal that had rocked this small coastal town a year or so ago, the custom had been dropped. Not that anyone believed every man in Kesterly was a potential paedophile, it was simply that sending small children to sit on a strange man's lap no longer felt appropriate to the townsfolk, after the deputy head of a primary school had been arrested and imprisoned for the abuse of his own child.

Coming from the kind of background she did, Bel could only feel thankful that she didn't have to try and talk her niece and nephew out of describing their hearts' desires for Father Christmas. She invariably became fussed when having to explain about possible dangers, particularly of that variety, and her sister, their mother, had never found it any easier. Fortunately the children's father, Nick, was much better at dealing with the sort of questions that generally arose when they were warned that not everyone was good.

'What do bad men do?'

'Where do they live?'

'How do we know if they're bad?'

'What do they look like?'

'Why do they want to hurt us?'

Unanswerable questions, every one of them, as far as Bel was concerned, yet somehow Nick managed.

Spotting a couple leaving the café, Bel made a rapid dash for their table, but wasn't quite fast enough. A plump young woman with a pushchair and three children in muddy anoraks and wellies beat her to it, plonking herself down heavily to make sure Bel knew she'd lost.

'Sorry,' the young woman grimaced, not appearing sorry at all.

Bel smiled thinly and turned away.

'That was rude,' Oscar whispered, slipping a hand into Bel's.

'Maybe she was here before us,' Bel whispered back.

'Oi, you want to teach that kid of yourn some manners,' the plump woman shouted after her.

Bel turned round, certain the woman couldn't have heard Oscar's remark, so what was her problem?

'Her,' the woman cried, pointing at Nell. 'Poked her bloody tongue out at me, she did. What kind of way's that for your kids to carry on?'

Bel looked down at Nell's guilty face and had to suppress

a smile as she took her hand and led her away. She probably ought to have made her apologise, but the woman had the table, didn't she? She couldn't have everything.

And why not? Bel could hear Natalia enquiring. *Some people do, so why can't we?* Back then it had seemed that they did.

'There's a table,' Oscar cried, and diving for it, he hit the chair so fast that he skidded straight across it and landed on the floor the other side.

Chuckling, an old man helped him up, while Nell screeched with laughter, and Bel, laughing too, settled her shopping under the table and gave him a hug.

'Our hero,' she declared, unbuttoning his coat. 'He found us a table and made us all feel jolly again. So, what's it to be? Two hot chocolates and two mince pies?'

'Three,' Nell piped up. 'You have to have one too.'

Bel started to protest.

'Please!' Nell implored. 'Please, please, please.'

Smoothing her silky blonde hair, Bel said, 'Even though I'm not hungry?'

'I'll eat it if you don't want it,' Oscar offered helpfully.

'He would,' Nell assured her.

'I have no doubt of it,' Bel laughed. 'OK, three mince pies coming up. Wait here, don't move, don't take your eyes off me, and don't poke your tongues out at anyone else.'

With sheepish giggles they watched her go to join the line at the counter, until 'Away in a Manger' began playing on the music system and much to the amusement of those closest to them they broke into song.

Smiling and shaking her head, Bel felt their happiness lighting her world in a way only they ever could. She absolutely adored them, and was fairly sure they felt the same about her. Certainly they always loved coming to stay, and when they were with her she made sure to clear her diary so she could spend every minute of every day with them. It was no less than they deserved, and considering how much she enjoyed their company it was certainly no hardship to put her own life on hold. Not that she had much of a life these days, but that was hardly the point.

By the time they'd downed their drinks and devoured the mince pies (she managed half of hers before passing the rest to Oscar) there was no time to stop and view the Christmas lights on the seafront, as promised. They simply drove underneath them, Oscar and Nell squealing and cheering in excitement and waving to children in other cars, before joining Bay View Road which wound up and around the southerly headland, past Kesterly Park and the Aquarium. Their route took them along the stretch known as Fisherman's Walk, where a dozen or more colourful cottages had seen a couple of centuries come and go, until they finally arrived at the more exclusive end of the road. Here properties were mainly gated at the front and enjoyed panoramic views of Westleigh Bay at the back.

Stillwater, Bel's black and white Victorian villa, was no exception. Though it wasn't quite as large as some of the mansions further along the street, it was still far too big for one person, but Bel had no plans to move out any time soon. In truth, she'd never had plans to move in, since she'd bought it as a renovation project, but by the time most of the work had been carried out it had become clear that she needed to stay in Kesterly for the foreseeable future. Her sister, who lived a few miles away in Senway village and who had found Stillwater for Bel in the first place, was sick. She needed help, and being as close as they were there was no way Bel would ever have let her down.

So with her newly renovated property not yet sold, she'd moved everything down from London in order to be closer to her sister and brother-in-law, and of course the children. Now, three years on, she was still in the house, and unless she wanted to make her life even more complicated than it already was, it was where she was going to stay.

Empty, but complicated, that was her world, which should have been a contradiction in terms, but in her case it wasn't.

'Where are we going to put the tree?' Nell cried, as they piled in through the glossy black front door. 'I know! It can go here, in the hall, because it's very, very tall and the ceiling is right up there so there'll be plenty of room.'

'But then you'll only be able to see it from the window

25

in the roof,' Oscar complained, gazing up at the magnificent glass dome that Bel had designed and installed to flood the ebony staircase and whitewashed landings with light.

'That's where Father Christmas lands,' Nell reminded him.

'Yes, but you have to see it through the window, don't you, Auntie Bel?' he objected, 'or people will think we haven't got one.'

'Well, not necessarily,' Bel responded, dropping her bags next to an ornate limestone fireplace where a real fire could burn to welcome guests as they arrived. 'We can always put some lights around the porch to show we're nice and Christmassy,' she suggested, 'and I was thinking perhaps the tree could go in the sitting room, next to the fireplace so Santa won't have a problem finding it when he comes down the chimney.'

'Yes, yes, yes,' they cheered.

'But is the ceiling high enough in there?' Oscar worried.

'If it isn't, we'll just chop a little bit off the top of the tree,' Bel replied. 'I expect we'll have to do that anyway, or the fairy'll be swaying around on the end of a stalk like a silly old drunk.'

Shouting with laughter, they charged across the hall and into the room that Bel loved best in the house. By knocking down several walls she'd created an open-plan kitchen-cum-sitting room that occupied the whole of the back of the property, and installed no less than six arch-topped French windows, each opening on to a spacious flagstone deck and vast flat lawn. At the far end of the lawn was a gate into a wild-flower meadow, and beyond that a ragged cluster of coastal rocks sloped gently down to a pebbled beach. Even on a gloomy winter's day the views from the house were spectacular, taking in a magnificent sweep of the estuary, along with Kesterly's southerly headland and the notorious Vagabond Cliffs.

The room's interior had a wonderfully friendly feel to it, with a grand marble fireplace dominating one end of the room, and a custom-built farmhouse-style kitchen seeming so settled into the other that it might always have been there. In between was a truly eclectic mix of tables, sofas, deep-pile rugs and squishy pouffes that made a perfect rough-and-tumble space for the kids, while a niche close to the fireplace gave room for Bel's desk.

She'd only just got the fire lit, ably assisted by the log-carriers Oscar and Nell, when the bell rang from the front gate. Since they were only expecting the tree Oscar and Nell leapt up and dashed into the hall, and had already pushed the button to release the gates by the time Bel joined them at the front door, surprised by how still they were.

'It's the police,' Oscar stated in perplexity as a marked car drove in through the gates.

Bel's heart turned over. Something had happened to Nick, the children's father. It didn't occur to her to think of her own father.

'What do they want?' Nell whispered.

'I don't know,' Bel replied, watching the car pull up at the bottom of the front steps. *Please don't let it be Nick, please, please,* she begged inwardly. 'Go back in the warm,' she told the children. 'They've probably got the wrong house.'

They simply pressed in closer to her as a young male officer came round from the driver's side, while a woman in a padded coat, who appeared equally young and slightly harassed, climbed out of the passenger seat.

'Can I help you?' Bel asked, as they started up the steps.

'I'm Detective Constable Lisa Peters,' the young woman told her, displaying her ID. 'And this is PC Brad Lowman. We're looking for Natalia Lambert.'

Bel's shock felt physical. Surely she hadn't heard right. 'I . . . um,' she faltered, as the children closed in more tightly. 'Can I ask what this is about?' she managed.

'Are you Natalia Lambert?' the detective enquired.

'No, I'm her sister. Natalia . . .' Bel's arms went round the children. 'Natalia died fifteen months ago.'

The detective's eyebrows rose skywards, but before she could respond her mobile rang. Without excusing herself she clicked on and turned back to the car.

Bel glanced at the uniformed officer, who merely shrugged.

'I'm going to take the children inside,' she told him, and

without waiting for his agreement she led them back to the sitting room.

'Why are they looking for Mummy?' Oscar wanted to know, his tender young face pale with concern.

'I'm not sure yet,' Bel answered, 'but obviously there's been some sort of mistake.' *Or something had happened to Nick and Talia was still assumed to be his next of kin. Please God don't let it be that.*

'Is Mummy still alive?' Oscar asked fearfully.

'I want to see her,' Nell said, starting to cry.

'Sssh, ssh,' Bel soothed. 'We'll get this sorted out, don't worry. You just wait here . . . Tell you what, why don't you finish off your notes to Santa?'

Feeling terrible for abandoning them when they were understandably distressed and confused, she went back to the front door where Lisa Peters had now apparently finished her call.

'Is this about my brother-in-law?' Bel asked, terrified, but needing to know. 'Is he all right?'

Lisa Peters raised a hand, palm forward. 'I don't know anything about your brother-in-law,' she told her, 'but I do need to speak to your sister.'

Finding it hard to think straight through so much confusion and relief, Bel said, 'I've just told you, she died fifteen months ago – and the children inside are hers, so I'd appreciate it if you don't do any more to upset them.'

Lisa Peters had the grace to flush. 'I'm sorry,' she apologised. She glanced at her fellow officer. 'I guess that's that then,' she said, and to Bel's amazement she started back to the car.

'Just a minute,' Bel called after them. 'I need to know what this is about.'

Turning round, Lisa Peters said, 'You might have heard on the news that a girl was found dead in the early hours of yesterday morning.'

Certain the world was going slightly mad, Bel asked, 'What does that have to do with my sister?'

Peters held out a crumpled card. 'We found this in the victim's coat pocket.'

Taking it, Bel's mouth dried as she recognised Talia's

writing, her own name and Bel's address. 'Who is the girl?' she asked hoarsely.

'We haven't been able to identify her yet,' Lisa Peters told her. 'We were hoping your sister might be able to help.'

Bel could only look at her. 'Where . . . How did she die?' she finally managed.

'She was found under the viaduct out past Temple Fields,' Peters replied. 'We'll know more about the cause after the autopsy.'

Imagining the rat-infested, syringe-littered netherworld of Kesterly's down and outs, Bel said, 'Have you tried talking to anyone at the Wayfarer Centre?'

Peters seemed interested. 'One of my colleagues is there now,' she informed her. 'Do you have a connection with the place?'

'My sister used to help out on occasion. It could be that this girl was one of the homeless and Talia told her to be in touch if she needed to.'

'But you say your sister's been dead for fifteen months.'

'Do you know how long the girl had the card?' Bel countered.

Peters's face tightened, showing she didn't. 'Out of interest,' she said, 'how did your sister die?'

Thrown by the insinuation that it might in some way be linked to these enquiries, Bel said, 'She had cancer.'

'I see. I'm sorry. Well, thanks for your help, Mrs . . . ?'

'Miss,' Bel corrected. 'Monkton.'

'We'll be in touch if we need to speak to you again.'

Suddenly stupidly wanting to cry, Bel closed the door and stood against it, listening as the police car drove away. For a few wildly insane moments she'd actually found herself wondering if Talia was still alive, if the nightmare of her illness, the heartbreak of her death had been some cruel figment of her imagination.

Tensing as the bell at the gates sounded again, she pulled open the door, expecting to find the police had come back. It turned out to be the Christmas tree. A godsend, since it would help to distract the children from the shock of wondering if their mother was still alive.

Half an hour later, with no repeat visit from the police

and the deliverymen gone, the tree was proudly positioned next to the hearth, and Bel was pouring herself a large glass of wine.

'Once it's lit,' she told the children, who were gazing up at it in awe, 'it's going to be the loveliest tree in Kesterly.'

'No, in England,' Oscar cried.

'The whole wide world,' Nell insisted.

'The universe,' Oscar one-upped.

'Whatever, we're going to love it,' Bel assured them, 'and that's all that matters. So, who's ready to help me bring down the other ornaments?'

'They're already here, silly,' Nell reminded her. 'We did it this morning. Can I be the first one to hang something up?'

'You're always first,' Oscar argued.

'I'm not, am I, Auntie Bel? You are, because you're the oldest, but I think I should be this time, or it's not fair.'

'Tell you what, why don't we toss a coin?' Bel suggested. 'Winner hangs the first ornament; loser switches on the lights.'

Seeming happy with that they set about unpacking the old ornaments, while Bel, still inwardly shocked and shaken by the police visit, began removing labels and price tags from their day's purchases. She could think of a dozen questions she wanted to ask now, and only wished she'd had the wit to at the time, but it had all happened so quickly.

Maybe she should contact Lisa Peters tomorrow to find out more. Or maybe she should try getting hold of Nick in Peru. But what could he do, apart from share in her shock? And would he really want to be bothered with it while on honeymoon?

Whatever she decided, she wasn't going to let anything spoil this day for the children. They were so happy and excited, and ready now to start filling up on the shepherd's pie they'd helped her to prepare this morning. After that, they were going to cosy into one of the sofas to watch *The Polar Express*.

This evening had to be about them, at least until they went to bed. After that, well, perhaps by then she'd be able to think more clearly about what, if anything, she should do.

'Bel! Can you hear me?'

'Yes, I can hear you,' Bel answered, struggling awake. 'What time is it, for heaven's sake?'

'Uh, it's just after midnight with me, so it must be . . . Eight in the morning with you?'

'Five,' she corrected, glancing at the clock. Wasn't it just like Nick to get the time difference wrong?

'Oh no, sorry. Go back to sleep. I'll call again . . .'

'It's OK, I'm awake now. How are you?'

'Yeah, we're great. Fascinating place. How about you? Are the kids behaving themselves?'

Picturing them snuggled up in their own rooms across the landing, Bel smiled as she said, 'Of course. We got a Christmas tree yesterday.'

'A tree! I bet they loved that. We'll have to get another as soon as I'm back.'

Of course, it mattered much more that they should have one at their own home than it did having one here. 'We can arrange for it to be delivered,' she offered, 'to make sure you don't miss out. Anyway, let me go and get them . . .'

'No, no. Leave them to sleep. I'll catch up with them later. Tell me about you. What's been happening over there?'

'Actually,' she said, more awake now the memory of the police visit had kicked in, 'you're not going to believe this. The police were here yesterday looking for Talia.'

'What!' he exclaimed. 'How can that be?'

After explaining about Talia's name and Bel's address being found on a dead girl, she said, 'They don't know who she is yet, but I'm sure she must be someone Talia met at the homeless shelter. It would explain why she had Talia's name but my address. Do you remember how Talia used to do that to prevent anyone turning up at your place in case the children were there?'

'Yeah, I guess that makes sense,' he concurred, 'but for the girl to still have Talia's details after all this time . . . It could be as long as two years or more since Talia last saw her.'

'True, but if Talia was kind to her at a time when she was at her lowest, it's likely she'd hold on to the details like some sort of lifeline.'

'Indeed, though it still doesn't help explain who she is. How did she die?'

'I don't know, but she was found under the viaduct.'

'Mm, so probably drug-related, and now they're trying to trace her family?'

'I guess so. I'm going to get in touch with the police again later, see if there's any more news. Anyway, tell me about you. How's it going over there?'

He gave an ecstatic-sounding sigh. 'Where to begin?' he responded. 'Actually, I ought to put Kristina on, she's better with the words than I am and I know she'd love to talk to you.'

Wishing he wouldn't, but unable to stop him without causing offence, Bel waited for his new wife to come on the line.

'Bel!' Kristina cried, as though she was Bel's best friend. 'How are you? Have you seen any of the wedding photos yet?'

'Yes, they're lovely,' Bel assured her, because they were. 'Did you get the link? Have you seen them yourself?'

'Yes, we're so happy with them. Aren't they gorgeous of the kids? And there are some beautiful shots of you.'

Nick suddenly came back on the line. 'I promise you, I'll never . . .' he called out laughingly, but whatever he went on to say was lost as the connection failed.

Putting the phone back on the nightstand, Bel lay in the darkness listening to the rain beating the windows, while trying to imagine where Nick and Kristina were now. It wasn't easy to picture their surroundings, since the Sacred Valley of the Incas didn't feature amongst the many places in the world Bel had visited. Nick and Kristina, archaeologists both, had joined a dig for their honeymoon. This was how they'd met, on a project somewhere in Israel, where Nick had gone in an effort to escape his grief after Natalia's death.

Try as Bel might, she simply couldn't understand how Nick had found himself able to marry again so soon. It didn't make any sense to her, when he'd always been so crazy about Talia. How had he got over the loss so quickly, when so much of Talia was still all around them? He hadn't even emptied her wardrobes or cleared away the photographs by the time he'd brought Kristina home to meet Oscar and Nell.

Five months after that, he and Kristina had tied the knot, and now there they were, in the depths of Peru, probably not thinking about Talia at all, while Bel hardly ever stopped. How on earth was she going to accept Kristina into the family when everything about her presence felt wrong? It wasn't that she disliked the woman – under any other circumstances she was sure they'd get along well. Kristina had apparently been good friends with Talia when they'd spent time in Egypt together during their uni days, though Bel had no recollection of Talia ever mentioning anyone of that name back then.

It didn't mean anything; she and Talia had made plenty of friends and acquaintances over the years that the other knew nothing about. They hadn't gone to the same uni, or chosen the same subjects, nor had they shared a home after graduating and moving to London. By then Talia had been with Nick, so they had found a place together, while she, Bel, all fired up about winning an internship at Tate Modern, had splashed out on a studio close to the river at Limehouse.

Though she and Talia had inherited a small fortune from their beloved mother after her untimely death while they were still in their teens, their father had tried to pay for everything back then, because that was what their father did, try to throw money at his daughters. Or, put more accurately, at his guilt. Presumably he thought he was buying off his conscience, or perhaps buying their silence, and Bel supposed that in a way he'd acquired the latter. They never talked about him to anyone; as far as they were concerned, it was as if he was dead. The tragedy of it, at least to Bel and Talia, was that their mother had seemed to love him in spite of his violence. She'd even considered him a doting father, or as doting as he could be given his own torturous past. Bel didn't know too much about that, nor did she want to. She only felt relieved that after their mother's death their father, a prolific and highly regarded artist, had taken himself off to some Pacific island where he could, presumably, indulge his passions more freely without ever having contact with his daughters again.

He hadn't even returned for Talia's funeral, and Bel was profoundly glad of that, since she knew he was the last person on earth Talia would have wanted there.

Her eyes closed as the pain of her sister's loss surged through her in a relentless wave of longing.

Was a day ever going to dawn when she didn't wish for Talia to be alive again, when she wouldn't imagine how happy she'd feel if she could go downstairs and find her preparing breakfast in her usual way?

'Morning Bel,' she'd say, her tousled blonde hair flattened in a whorl at the crown of her head, her blue eyes sparkling with both mischief and empathy. 'Are you OK? Did you sleep well?'

'I think so,' Bel would answer, 'apart from a terrible dream in which one of us had to die and it ended up being you.'

Knowing Talia she'd find that funny, or accuse her of having drunk too much wine the night before, and minutes later it would be forgotten. The past three and a half years would be compressed into nothing; the shock, the fear, the loss of everything that mattered would never have happened.

Why had death reached out for someone so young and passionate as Natalia? What possible good could ever come out of using cancer to take a mother from her small children? No more good than had been achieved by giving her and Talia the father they'd had.

Talia had always been the quieter of the twins, the most thoughtful and probably the easiest to love. Their mother would have denied that, of course, but by the time it had occurred to Bel that Talia possessed qualities she didn't have, their mother had no longer been with them. And she, Bel, was to blame for that.

Since losing them both Bel had become a shadow, an inwardly tormented version of the woman she used to be, unless the children were with her. She loved it when they were around. Life felt worth living then, since they gave her a sense of purpose, a hope and desperately needed feeling that Talia was still close. She knew how selfish that was, that she shouldn't put such a burden on their tender shoulders, but she was careful never to talk about their mother unless they asked her to, nor to let them know how wretched she felt every time their father came to take them home.

Thankfully they only lived ten minutes away by car, and of course she was welcome to visit at any time. Even Kristina was at pains to assure her that the door was always open. Bel couldn't help but admire her for that, since she wasn't sure she'd be quite as generous in Kristina's shoes. On the other hand, it clearly suited Kristina – and Nick – to have a devoted aunt on tap. It allowed them to travel at the drop of a hat, as Nick had done with Talia before the children came along. Bel would always be there, the children were safe and happy with her, so they could focus on raking up the past in far-flung corners of the globe while Bel tried to deal with today, and tomorrow.

Feeling a horrible sinking sensation at the prospect of what her tomorrows might bring, she drew the duvet up over her head and closed her eyes.

'I promise you,' Nick had said just now, but whatever the promise was she knew it would never be the forgiveness she craved; nor the ability to undo what she had done, since it wasn't in anyone's power to change the past.

Chapter Three

'So where are you now?' Jeff was asking.

'Just leaving the caff,' Josie replied, swapping her mobile to the other ear as she made her way along Kesterly's busy seafront towards the bus stop. The wind was bitter this afternoon, whipping the waves up over the rocks, and tearing through the Christmas lights like some avenging fiend.

'Then I'll pick you up,' he told her. 'I'm just turning out of North Road, so I should see you any minute.'

'No, don't worry about me,' she cried, probably too quickly. 'I've got some shopping to do, and I promised Carly I'd meet her for a cup of tea at Yuri's when I get off the bus.' Since Yuri's bakery was next to the cab office on Temple Fields high street, she had to hope that Jeff didn't take it upon himself to drop in and surprise her. It might be a good idea to text Carly, the neighbourhood blabbermouth, to ask her for cover, except then she'd have to explain what she was really doing, and since she didn't want Carly and the rest of the world knowing her business she felt suddenly irritable and frustrated. 'I have to ring off now,' she told Jeff shortly. 'I'll see you at home about seven,' and before he could say any more she ended the call.

Just don't let him be in the cab office by the time she got off the bus, or he'd be likely to see her walking in the opposite direction to the bakery and wonder where the heck she was going. Actually, he'd probably guess, since the only reason they ever ventured north of the high street, apart from when Jeff was picking up or dropping off a fare, was when one of them needed to see the doctor whose surgery was at the Health Centre on Long Walk.

It wasn't easy having secrets, but no one had ever said it was, and anyway it wouldn't be for much longer. She just needed to get this bit of nonsense sorted out, then she could get on with organising Christmas.

After that it'd be full steam ahead for the wedding.

August 11th was the date Lily and Jasper had set when they'd gone to see the vicar the week before last. Luckily, the golf club was able to fit them in on that date too, so the venues at least were settled. Quite what Jasper's parents were making of it all she could only guess at, since Lily hadn't told her yet how the news had gone down. If they hadn't been thrilled Lily was sure to have said so, and since all she'd texted about these last few days was the fantastic dress the designer was creating, Josie had to presume that the Cunninghams were at peace with their youngest son blowing his little windfall on a wedding.

'They're probably seeing it as saving them from having to fork out,' Jeff had commented gruffly.

The fact that he wasn't expected to foot the bill was a bit of a mixed blessing for him, since he felt relieved, of course, given they didn't have a brass farthing to call their own, but Josie knew it was sitting badly with him not to be able to take it on himself.

Another black mark against Ryan, as if there weren't enough already.

Still, the important thing right now, especially for Jeff, was that Lily and Jasper were planning to spend Christmas Day with them and Boxing Day with his folks over in Kent. Had it been the other way round, she knew Jeff would have felt every bit as crushed as she would about neither of their children being at the Christmas table. Of course, being the way he was, Jeff wouldn't have voiced his disappointment in more than a few grunts and sighs, but Josie generally knew what he was thinking, in the same way as she knew that his son was rarely far from his thoughts.

Certainly he was rarely far from hers, or from his sister's, which would be why Lily, in her typically sensitive way, had made sure she would be with them on Christmas Day itself. It was going to be their first without Ryan.

Dismissing the awfulness of that from her mind as she

spotted three rolls of Christmas paper for a quid in the window of the Pound Shop, Josie ran in, grabbed six, tossed two coins at the cashier, and ran out again just in time to jump on the 28 bus. It was easing her conscience a bit, she realised, as she sank into a window seat, to have turned the lie to Jeff about doing a bit of shopping before heading home into a truth.

Now all she had to do was get some presents to go inside the wrapping and a few tags to tie on – luckily they'd set a fifteen-pound limit for everyone this year so as not to break the bank – and they still had to bring their tree down from the loft. She'd been on at Jeff about it for over a week now, but, as usual, he was either too busy to go and borrow a ladder from Alan across the street, or there was something on telly he just had to watch. He'd get there eventually, he always did, and even though they couldn't afford a real tree, which she'd have dearly liked, he'd no doubt pull off his usual trick of popping in the garden centre on Christmas Eve to snap up some real mistletoe, if there was any left, and a wreath with berries and a ribbon for a fraction of the original price.

Forty minutes later, after a tiring stop-start bus ride out to the estate, Josie was settling herself down in the doctors' waiting room. Hearing her mobile bleep with a text she took it out, expecting it to be Lily, but it turned out to be from Mr Crover-Keene.

Sorry, Josie. Should have been in touch earlier to say thank you for helping out Saturday before last. As usual you did a stellar job.

You're welcome, she texted back. *Do you mind if I take Christmas week off, or will you be needing me?*

If he did, she'd try to work it in somehow, not only because they needed the money, but because he'd been so kind to her over the Ryan business that she never liked to let him down.

A message quickly came back saying, *No problem. Not around again till New Year so Merry Christmas to you and your family.*

To you too, she texted back, wondering where he might be spending his time, and who with. Probably Jennifer

Whatever-her-name-was, the latest girlfriend. She'd been down to Kesterly a couple of times now, and if Josie was being honest, she hadn't taken to her all that well. A proper snob was what Jeff would have called her, if he'd seen the way she'd looked right through Josie during the cocktail party. She hadn't even called Josie by name when she'd asked her to circulate with the canapés. In Josie's book that was just plain rude, but she wasn't the only person Josie had come across of that class who didn't seem to have much in the way of manners. Or certainly none they bothered trotting out for the help.

Still, Josie had no desire to make a bosom pal of Jennifer Thingummybob, indeed, she had no intention of thinking about her at all when she had more than enough to occupy her mind. A visiting order had come through from Ryan this morning, so she needed to ring up and confirm that she and Lily would be there the Saturday before Christmas.

Glancing up as someone's name was called, she watched an overweight woman waddle towards the corridor of GPs' offices and wondered if she was on her way to see Dr Moore. The only GP Josie would ever see was Cecily Moore, mainly because she always seemed to make time for her patients, particularly the kids. Jeff totally swore by her, especially after she'd sorted out his spell of depression following the Dawnie Hopkins episode. And the treatment Dr Moore had prescribed for his back when he'd wrenched it last summer had him up and about again in no time at all. Remembering that, Josie made a mental note to mention the backaches she'd been getting lately. Perhaps the same pills and exercises would work for her. More likely a change of mattress was needed, but that was an expense they really couldn't run to.

It was twenty minutes after her scheduled appointment that her name was finally called, and feeling a little queasy all of a sudden she put aside the old copy of *Heat* she'd been flicking through and resisted the urge to walk out the main door. It seemed all wrong to be wasting the doctor's time with her bit of nonsense when there were people out there – actually probably in here – who had much more need of her help.

Feeling the receptionist's watchful eye as though daring her to make a break for it, she walked on down the corridor and was about to knock on Dr Moore's door when Dr Moore herself opened it and greeted her almost like an old friend.

'Josie, this is a nice surprise,' she said warmly. 'Come in, come in. Sorry to have kept you. How's the family?'

'Oh, we're all fine, thanks,' Josie assured her, as the doctor closed the door and waved her to a chair at the side of the desk. She'd probably forgotten Ryan was in prison, or maybe she didn't know. 'And you?' she said. 'Are you keeping well?' It felt strange to be asking a doctor how she was.

'Oh, I mustn't grumble,' Dr Moore replied with a smile, 'though my husband says I never stop.'

Josie smiled too.

'So, what can I do for you today?'

'Well,' Josie began, feeling her insides starting to curl up in knots, 'I've got this . . . Well, I've had a bit of a backache lately, and I was wondering if you might be able to let me have some of the pills you gave Jeff when he was having a problem with his.'

Dr Moore's sweetly lined face was showing only interest as she nodded. 'OK, we'll take a little look at you. Is there anything else?'

Josie felt herself starting to flush. 'Well, um, I had a bit of thrush a while ago, and I think it might have come back, so if you can give me something for that . . .'

Dr Moore made a note and opened her top drawer. 'Shall we have a quick check of your blood pressure before we go any further?' she suggested, pulling out the equipment.

Knowing this was routine, Josie shrugged off her coat and rolled up her sleeve.

'And is there anything else?' the doctor asked as she wrapped the cuff around Josie's arm and tightened it.

Josie shook her head. 'No, nothing,' she assured her. 'Just my back and the other little business.'

Dr Moore nodded, watched the digital readout, declared everything fine there and released Josie's arm.

The inspection of her back, and down below, didn't take long and as usual, Dr Moore was very careful when it came to prodding the speculum where it was designed to go. 'When was your last smear test?' she asked, peering into the darkness. 'Can you remember?'

'I'm not sure,' Josie replied. 'A couple of years ago, I expect. It's only supposed to be every three, isn't it?'

'That's right. I'll just check your records, because if it's about due we might as well get it done now.'

Happy with that, Josie continued to lie where she was with her legs in stirrups and a modesty cover over her knees. She wouldn't much care for being a doctor, she was reflecting, coming face to face with women's undercarriages on a regular basis, and men's, come to that.

'OK, seems you're not due for another fourteen months,' Dr Moore informed her, 'so we won't bother with it now,' and coming to remove the speculum she lowered the chair, stripped off her gloves and waited while Josie put her clothes back on.

'I expect,' she said, as Josie sat down again, 'that the problem with your back is to do with your job. You're still cleaning, are you?'

Josie nodded. 'Not as much now though. I'm doing some shifts in town, at the Seafront Cafe.' There was a good chance the doctor had worked that out for herself, since the greasy scent of all-day breakfasts was probably lingering all over her.

'You smell good enough to eat,' Jeff used to say when she first had the job. These days it either turned him off, or he'd just stopped noticing.

'I haven't been there for a long time,' Dr Moore commented. 'We used to go a lot when the children were young. Anyway, you should take care of how much you're lifting and the way you're lifting it. I'm giving you a sheet of exercises to help strengthen your muscles, and if you can get yourself a Pilates balance board, all the better. They're not expensive, somewhere around twelve to fifteen pounds, I think.' She twinkled. 'Maybe you can put one on your Christmas wish list?'

A good idea, since Jeff kept asking what she wanted. Maybe he could track one down on eBay for a bit less than the asking.

'OK, so here's a prescription to help with the thrush,' Dr Moore continued. 'We'll go the cream and pessaries route for now, but if it doesn't get any better, come and see me again and we'll try something else.'

'Thank you,' Josie said softly as she took the prescription.

Dr Moore's eyes came to hers.

Josie's throat turned dry. The doctor knew. Somehow she'd sensed that Josie hadn't come clean with everything.

'This is, well, it's probably nothing,' Josie stammered, glancing down at her hands, 'but there's this, um . . . Well, I've got a bit of a sore boob. It's not a lump, or anything . . . Well, it is, but I think it's some sort of boil, or cyst . . .'

Keeping her expression neutral, Dr Moore said, 'Why don't you slip off your top so I can have a look?'

Wishing she hadn't brought it up now, Josie did as she was told and lay back on the bed while Dr Moore had a little prod round. 'It doesn't feel quite so tender today,' she said with a shaky laugh. 'That's what happens, isn't it, when you come to the doctor? All the symptoms you thought you had just up and disappear.'

Dr Moore smiled. 'Well, this one hasn't, I'm afraid. It's still there, and I think, to be on the safe side, we should have you checked over by a specialist. You can get dressed again now.'

Pulling the T-shirt over her head, Josie said, 'It's probably another cyst. I've had them before.'

'Indeed you have,' the doctor agreed, 'but this one seems a little different, so I'm going to arrange an appointment for you at the breast clinic.' Fear must have shown in Josie's eyes, because she quickly went on to say, 'I don't want you to start worrying, it's simply a precaution, to be on the safe side, because if it does turn out to be something untoward we want to catch it good and early.'

Josie tried to swallow. 'So you think it might be . . . ?' She couldn't bring herself to say the word.

'Let's just say we want to rule it out,' the doctor responded. 'The clinic's at the Kesterly Infirmary, so you won't have far to go. I'm just not sure they'll be able to fit you in before Christmas, with it being only ten days away.'

The words seemed to hammer inside Josie's skull. *Before*

Christmas? She must think it's something really serious if she's in such a rush.

'Don't look so worried,' Dr Moore said kindly. 'The rules state that everyone with breast symptoms has to be seen within two weeks.'

That sounded like a good rule for those who needed it.

'Here's a leaflet, explaining all about it,' the doctor continued, handing one over. 'If you have any questions after you've read it, give me a call. I'll be happy to go through it with you.'

Josie was staring at it, but for the moment she couldn't seem to take it in.

'Breathe,' Dr Moore smiled. 'It'll be fine, I'm sure. I'll contact the clinic now and they should be in touch with you directly sometime in the next week to give you an appointment. As I said, it's probably not going to be before Christmas, but I'm sure they'll slot you in soon after.'

Realising she should be glad of that, Josie said, 'Thank you. I, uh . . .' She couldn't think what else to say.

Squeezing her hand, Dr Moore told her, 'They have a One Stop facility at the infirmary, so chances are you'll know the results by the end of the day.'

'That's good,' Josie mumbled.

Getting to her feet, Dr Moore went to the door. 'They'll keep me in touch with everything,' she said, before opening it, 'and once again, if you want to talk, or come back and see me before your appointment . . .'

'I'll be fine,' Josie assured her, mentally pulling herself together. 'I'll read this leaflet and turn up when I'm told to. I'm sure it'll all be a lot of fuss about nothing, but as you said, it's better to be safe than sorry.'

'It is indeed.'

Back out on the street Josie took in several lungfuls of chill, snowy air. For a moment she couldn't think where she was going, or what she was supposed to do next. Remembering, she started down Long Walk towards the main road. It was dark out now, with Christmas lights glowing from just about every house, blurring and clearing in front of her eyes, a playful kaleidoscope of cheery colours. She glanced up at a bunch of reindeer on someone's roof, and a Santa starting down the chimney on someone else's.

If Jeff didn't borrow Alan's ladder tonight, she'd go over there tomorrow and borrow it herself.

Realising she was still clutching the leaflet with its big Dean Valley NHS logo at the top, she stuffed it into her bag and took out her phone. Not sure who she was intending to ring, she simply slipped it into her pocket and took out her gloves. The hole in the thumb reminded her that she'd intended to ask Jeff for a new pair for Christmas, but now she was going to ask him for a Pilates board. Perhaps Lily could get her the gloves. She'd spotted two pairs for a fiver in Primark the last time she was in Bristol, with any luck they still had some.

The big question really was what on earth she was going to get Ryan. Lily had already made up a calendar with photos from their childhood marking each month of the coming year, while Josie's mother, his doting nan, was proposing to send him a girlie magazine. Josie was fairly certain the prison wouldn't allow that, but rather than argue with her mother, she'd decided it was best simply to let her get on with it. The last time she was there Ryan had mentioned he'd taken up reading, so a couple of paperbacks might be a good idea. She'd find out what sort of books he was into, then pop in the second-hand shop to see if she could track them down there.

Remembering she hadn't actually arranged her visit yet, she opened up her phone to try and do it now. Since it was past the time they took the calls, she made a mental note to do it in the morning, and put the phone away again.

What day was it tomorrow? Was she supposed to be at the caff or at John Crover-Keene's?

She wondered how her boy was filling his days, stuck there in that dreadful prison. It scared her so much to think of what the other inmates might be doing to him. Her only way of dealing with it was to shut it out of her mind. After all, it wasn't as if he was in for interfering with children, or anything terrible like that. He'd been involved in a burglary that had gone horribly wrong when one of his accomplices had hit the homeowner round the head with a crowbar and fractured the poor bloke's skull. Fortunately, the victim had survived, so the charge had been downgraded to grievous bodily harm for which Ryan had received the maximum sentence of five years. The others, previous offenders from the Zone every one of them, had managed to get away with three years apiece after insisting that Ryan had wielded the bar. Josie believed her son when he swore to her that he hadn't. Ryan had never been violent. Foolish, yes, and easily led, but never violent. The trouble was, he was so afraid of the villains he'd got involved with and what they'd threatened their families would do to his family if he didn't take the rap, that he'd ended up copping to the assault, and nothing Josie, Jeff, or the criminally expensive lawyers could say had persuaded him out of it. (They should have qualified for legal aid, but with all these cuts they hadn't, which was why Jeff's redundancy payout had gone, along with their savings.) What hadn't helped Ryan with the judge was the fact that his mother was a cleaner for the family he'd burgled, which was how Ryan had got hold of the key – and how Josie had ended up losing four good paying jobs on the west side of the hill.

Ryan, Ryan, Ryan, she was sighing to herself as she crossed the main road at the traffic lights to start heading into the maze of their part of the estate. *What on earth's going to happen to you when you do finally come out? Please don't let your life be ruined by this. Make something good come of it, son, for your own sake, if not for ours.*

A sudden, horrible thought struck her.

She would still be around when he came out, wouldn't she?

The shock of even thinking it was so brutal that it took her a while to realise someone was calling her name.

'Hey, Josie, hold up, where's the fire?'

Turning round she saw her old school chum Bob Chapman, waving out from the door of Chanter Lysee, the karaoke bar he managed.

'Hi Bob,' she responded cheerfully. 'How are you? All ready for Christmas I see. Hope all those lights are hotwired into Downing Street. Let them jokers pay the bills, is what I say.'

'You'll get no argument from me on that,' he assured her. 'Bet none of *them*'s worrying about how they're going to put a turkey on the table Wednesday after next. Anyway, I wanted to make sure you're coming for our Christmas special on the twenty-third.' He was pointing to a sign in the window. *Happy Hour all night long, bottle of bubbly to best singer in town.* 'You'd be an outright winner,' he informed her. 'That lovely smoky voice of yours, I keep telling you, you should go on *The X Factor*, make yourself a fortune.'

'Yeah, right,' she laughed. 'The next SuBo, that's me. Or was she on *Britain's Got Talent*?'

'Who cares? So are you going to come? I'll put a couple of tickets aside if you are, on the house, given how you bring in the crowds.'

Laughing again, she said, 'Yeah, you can count me and Jeff in. I expect my mother will want to come too, just please don't let her have the mike when she's had a few. She'll only start murdering "Je t'aime", and she's embarrassing enough without going that far.'

Chuckling, Bob said, 'Three tickets are yours and I'll keep your favourite table. Any chance Lily and her chap might join you? I hear they're getting married next summer.'

Since Josie had broken the happy news to Carly over a week ago she wasn't in the least surprised to find out that Bob already knew, half of Kesterly probably did by now. She just hoped they weren't all waiting for invites, because if they were a lot were going to end up disappointed. 'Yes, she should be home by then,' Josie told him, 'so I'm sure they'll want to come.'

Giving her the thumbs up, he waved her on and as he took out his mobile to answer a call, she fumbled for her own to check who was trying to reach her.

Lily.

'Hello my love, how are you?' she asked, clicking on.

'Yeah, I'm cool. I just wanted to tell you to look at your emails when you get home. I've sent you a link to a stationery website. They've got some seriously cool stuff for weddings and I want to know what you think.'

'Of course, have you highlighted any in particular?'

'Not yet. I want to see if you come up with the same ones I did. You know, like we usually do when we're choosing stuff.'

Josie smiled. It was true, they really did seem to have similar tastes. 'I'll let you know as soon as I've had a look,' she promised. Then, changing the subject, 'Have you sent the calendar to Ryan yet?'

'No, I thought I'd take it in when we go to see him next week. Have you arranged it yet?'

'It's top of my list tomorrow.'

'OK, just let me know. Where are you now?'

'On my way home. We've been invited for a karaoke evening on the twenty-third, if you and Jasper can make it.'

'Yay!' Lily cheered. 'Definitely sign us up for it. It's such a scream, and you and Dad are so brill. Anyway, better go, loads to do. Love you, love to Dad too,' and she was gone.

So what's wrong with that, Josie snapped irritably in answer to the little voice inside her that was asking, what if your appointment turns out to be on the 23rd? *It won't be in the evening, so I'll still be able to go to Chanter Lysee, and even if the news turns out to be bad, which it won't, no way is it going to spoil Christmas for anyone, least of all me.*

Just over a week later Josie and Lily were queuing up with other friends and families, waiting to be let into the prison. If there was a more depressing place on God's earth Josie didn't want to know about it, it was bad enough having to cope with this one. Its old grey stone walls made her think of dungeons and torture chambers, while its towering gothic windows were straight out of a Hammer House of Horrors. Just thank God Ryan was in one of the newer units at the back where each inmate had his own cell and the heating, or so he told her, was a functioning part of the place, unlike it ever seemed to be in the visitors' room.

She'd watched a documentary the other night about young offenders at Aylesbury Prison and now seriously wished she hadn't bothered. She'd hardly been able to sleep after seeing the way those tormented youths beat each other up, attacked the officers, vandalised their cells or went to terrible lengths to self-harm. One poor lad was so

47

fixated on killing himself that he had to be constantly watched and even then they didn't always catch him putting a noose round his neck, or slashing his wrists with the corner of a toothpaste tube. She couldn't begin to imagine how his mother must feel, knowing he was so miserable, so devoid of hope that all he wanted was to end his life.

Maybe he didn't have a mother, or not one that cared. It could be the whole root of the problem.

It was one of the worst parts of being a parent, she thought, as a gate finally opened in the huge blue iron doors to start letting the line through, the constant worrying over what your kids might be up to, or what you, as a parent – a mother in particular – had done to send your child down the wrong road. God knew she'd done her best with Ryan, had loved him the same way she'd loved Lily, and still did, but right through from the time he was born, a month prematurely with a tiny hole in his heart, to when he was six and nearly drowned in the sea off Temple Bay, to all the trouble they'd had with him at school, things had never seemed to go right for him. He always tried his best, but no matter how much effort he put into his lessons, or projects, or even a job after he'd turned sixteen, there had always been someone there to lead him into bad ways. He was too easily influenced was what Jeff always said, and though Josie hated to think that their son didn't have a mind of his own, she had to admit that if he did, he didn't always use it. She'd even wondered in her darkest moments if he was a little bit delinquent, but since none of his teachers had ever come forward with that, and nor had Jeff, she'd kept the awful suspicion to herself. After all, he wasn't stupid, he understood the difference between right and wrong, he just didn't always draw the line in the same place most other people would.

'At least we're out of that wind,' Lily shivered, as they were ushered into a forbidding stone room with no seats or windows, just a noticeboard full of rules for visitors and a couple of security scanners. 'It's still like a fridge in here though,' she grumbled, hugging her faux-fur jacket more tightly around her.

With her honeyed curls peeking out from under a blue bobble hat and her spiky dark lashes curling around her violet eyes she was as pretty as a primrose, Josie thought, and twice as precious.

'It's bloody cruel, if you ask me,' a woman behind them piped up. 'No one should have to put up with these sorts of temperatures, especially when they ain't done nothing wrong. They could at least heat these communal areas.'

'Too bloody mean,' someone else joined in. 'It's inhuman locking people up in a place like this. They should have done away with it years ago.'

'My husband's in the newer unit,' another woman informed them, 'so it's not too bad for him, but he says he hates coming over here for visits. Bloody nice that, innit? I comes all this way and he says he hates the visits.'

As the others laughed, Josie and Lily smiled politely, knowing better than to join in, since these exchanges often ended up turning nasty and neither of them was capable of holding their own with the type of women who came here. The male visitors weren't much better, a mixed barrel of lowlife in the main, with a handful of quieter ones who, like Josie and Lily, knew to keep their heads down for fear of being picked on for no reason, which could happen right out of nowhere.

'Did you bring the calendar?' Josie whispered as they opened their bags ready to load them on to the scanner.

'Yeah, it's here,' Lily replied, pulling it out of her backpack. 'I didn't wrap it, like you said, but I brought some paper and sticky tape just in case we can do it once we're through. It'll be nice for him to have a surprise to open on Christmas Day.'

'Great minds,' Josie smiled. 'I've brought some paper and sticky tape too. Did you think to bring any labels?'

'No, but I've got a pen so we can write on the wrapping. What did you get him in the end?'

'I found a copy of Beckham's autobiography in really good nick at the Book End Store on Fairley Avenue, so that and a three-pack of socks. Nan tried to get me to bring a girlie magazine from her, but I swapped it for a copy of *Shoot* when she wasn't looking.'

Lily giggled. 'She's a riot. Is she coming on Christmas Day?'

'Presumably, unless she gets a better offer. You know what she's like.'

'And what about Grandpa Clark, is he coming?'

'As far as I know Dad's picking him up on Christmas morning, same as usual. We got the tree down from the attic last night, trouble is we haven't managed to find the ornaments yet so it's still standing there as bare as Mother Hubbard's cupboard. I just hope they didn't get thrown out by mistake last year when we packed everything up, or we'll have to go without.'

'What about lights?'

'It's pre-lit, so that's OK. I expect Jasper's family have a real tree, don't they?'

'I'm not sure, but probably.'

'Bit posh, are they, Jasper's family?' the woman behind them cut in. 'What kind of bloody name's that when it's at home?' she shouted for anyone to hear. 'Jasper! I ask you. Sounds like a bloody cat to me.'

Easing herself between Lily and the woman, Josie was preparing to follow Lily through to the other side of the scanner when a siren suddenly began wailing fit to deafen them all.

'OK, ladies and gentlemen, step back into the reception please,' an officer shouted above the din.

'What the bloody hell?' the woman behind them growled.

'What's going on?' someone else demanded.

'All right, you don't have to push!' an angry old woman snapped.

'There aren't going to be any visits today,' the officer informed them.

'What?' Josie cried in alarm, along with several others. 'Why not? What's happening?'

'We've got a security breach,' the officer replied, still ushering the crowd back to the door.

'But how?' she protested. 'No one did anything . . .'

'Not here, in the prison,' he explained. 'Now, pick up your belongings, those of you who've put them on the scanner, make sure you don't leave anything behind or you'll lose it.'

'But we've got Christmas presents,' Lily objected. 'This is our last chance. If we can't give them now, they'll have to go without.'

Ignoring her, the officer said, 'That's it, folks, time to go home.'

'You can't do this,' a balding man in a smart parka coat informed him hotly. 'Prisoners have rights too and . . .'

'Take it up with your MP,' the officer interrupted.

'Please will you take this to my son,' Josie implored. 'It's just a book. It can't do any harm. His name's Ryan Clark . . .'

'Sorry, Mrs, no can do. Now move along please, you don't want to end up on the wrong side of the door when lockdown hits over here.'

Minutes later, crushed, angry and perplexed, Josie and Lily were in the biting wind once more, heading for the bus stop half a mile away that offered no shelter or time-table indicating when to expect the next bus.

'Poor Ryan,' Lily murmured, as she snuggled in more tightly to her mother for warmth. There was only a small crowd with them, since most had arrived by car, and it didn't seem anyone felt inclined to offer lifts into town to those less fortunate. 'Has this ever happened before when you've come?' she asked.

Josie shook her head. 'And for it to happen now, right in front of Christmas . . .' She was so upset she hardly knew what she wanted to say. He'd have been looking forward to their visit, pinning all his hopes on what they might bring for Christmas, savouring every last detail of what they said so he could go over it again after they'd gone. He'd told her in one of his letters that was what he did, and she had to admit she did much the same thing.

He was so lonely, so wretched about what had happened to him, that it could just about break her heart.

'I know, why don't you leave everything with me?' Lily suggested. 'Jaz and I can try to drop it off on Monday morning before we drive down to Kesterly. You never know, as it's Christmas, they might accept it.'

Since it was the only chance they had of getting something to Ryan, Josie had to agree, though handing over the small bag she'd packed especially for him wasn't easy. She had so desperately wanted to give it to him herself, not because there was anything all that special inside, but because she'd have been able to see his face when he took it, watch the way his eyes drank everything in before he broke into one of his dear smiles.

'I'll write to him tonight,' she said. 'He'll understand why we couldn't see him, obviously, but I want him to know that we tried. If I get it in the post on Monday it might be with him by Tuesday.'

Hugging her, Lily said, 'You're the best mum in the world, do you know that?'

Josie glanced along the busy main road, hoping for a sign of the bus.

'You're not listening to me,' Lily chided.

'I am,' Josie corrected, 'but you're talking nonsense as usual.'

'Charming,' Lily teased. 'And there was me trying to cheer you up.'

Feeling a smile pushing up from her heart, Josie said, 'I'm OK, just a bit disappointed. Well, very disappointed, but I'll get over it. You don't think he had anything to do with the security breach, do you?'

Lily sighed, as if having expected the question. 'I shouldn't think so, Mum. He's always telling us how he's keeping his head down, trying not to get involved with anyone else so he can get out early on good behaviour.'

But Jeff was right, Ryan was easily led. 'And he hasn't been in any trouble since he went in there,' Josie responded, trying to bolster herself, 'so I expect I'm worrying about nothing.'

'As usual, but I'm sure I'd be the same if he was my son. It's bad enough him being my brother.'

Always concerned for how badly this business might have impacted on her daughter, Josie said, 'Have you told Jasper's parents about him yet, and why he probably won't be at the wedding?'

'No, but I keep telling you, if he's *really* good he might be out in time.'

It was a happy thought, but still not one Josie could pin much hope on. 'Aren't you worried how they'll feel about you having a convicted criminal for a brother?' she asked.

Lily shrugged. 'Jaz isn't bothered by it, and that's what matters to me. Anyway, his parents are really cool. You wait and see, they're dead easy to get on with and they're really keen to meet you and Dad.'

Feeling slightly anxious about that, not only because of Ryan, but because of the difference in their social standing, Josie said, 'I suppose we ought to set something up.'

'Definitely, we will, as soon as they get back from Singapore. Richard, Jaz's dad, has got offices in Singapore, so they tend to split their time between here and there. Anyway, I honestly can't see him or Miriam, Jaz's mum, turning their backs on us because of a stupid mistake Ryan made. They're just not like that.'

Unable to imagine the Cunninghams taking such a relaxed view of matters, Josie decided it was time to let the subject drop. She could spend the whole journey back to Kesterly worrying about Ryan, and right now it was only fair to focus more on Lily.

By the time the bus finally dropped them at the train station Lily was still in full flow about the wedding, and since Josie didn't have the heart to cut her short just yet, she took her for a cup of tea in the station caff.

'What about you?' Lily cried, when Josie only ordered one.

'I don't fancy one much,' Josie lied. She wasn't going to admit that she only had enough in her purse for her bus fare home when she got back to Kesterly.

Please God let Jeff have a ton of bookings in the lead-up to Christmas, because things were so tight now that she was becoming seriously worried about where it would end. Every last penny of her wages between now and then had to go towards paying for gas, electric and rent, or they were going to end up cut off, or out on the street, which would make a right merry Christmas for them all. At least Fliss, at the caff, had promised her a bonus at the end of her shift on Christmas Eve, and Mr Crover-Keene usually paid a bit extra into her account at this time of year, as well. If they both came good she'd be down Aldi quicker than you could say Rudolph the Red-Nosed Reindeer for the Christmas shop. Actually, she wouldn't go until six p.m. on Christmas Eve, which was when all the prices generally got slashed. She'd grabbed a four-kilo turkey last year for under a fiver, and a ham for two quid and even a bit of smoked salmon for one pound fifty. That was a rare treat for them, smoked salmon, and didn't they all just lap it up for a starter with a slice of lemon and brown-bread triangles?

All being well she'd get lucky again this year. She might even win the lottery if she found a spare pound for a ticket.

Clicking on her phone as it rang, she said, 'Hi love, everything all right with you?'

'Bloody car's gone and broken down again,' Jeff growled.

Oh no, oh no.

'I was halfway up West Bay Hill when the sodding engine just upped and died. Lucky Harry Philips wasn't far away so he could come and take over the fare.'

'So where are you now?' Josie asked, feeling Lily's watchful eyes probing her face.

'Getting towed to Trev's place so he can have a look at it.'

'Then don't let the police catch you on the phone, the last thing we need is a fine.'

'I know, I know. I just want someone to tell me how the bloody hell I'm supposed to earn a living in that old crock when it's about as reliable as your mother's tips on the horses.'

Taking a quick breath she said, 'All right, listen. As soon as you're at Trev's, give my cousin Steve a ring and ask if you can borrow his Mondeo while he's in Spain. He goes on Monday till after the new year, so that should be long enough for Trev to get ours up and running again.'

'Unless we need parts that we aren't going to get over Christmas.'

'Try to look on the bright side. I'll be home in a couple of hours, I'm sure you'll have it sorted out by then. Now please ring off before someone spots you on the phone.'

'Poor Dad,' Lily sympathised as Josie put her mobile down. 'That car really stresses him, and I have to tell you it worries me a lot to think of him driving it.'

You and me both, Josie was thinking.

'You wait till I'm earning,' Lily ran on, 'first thing I'm going to buy is a decent car for you two so you can come and visit us any time you like no matter where we are, unless it's abroad obviously, but then we'll pay for your air fares, or maybe we'll spring for a cruise . . .'

'How you dream on,' Josie chided playfully. 'Let's get Christmas out of the way, shall we, and then you should be knuckling down to study for your finals . . .'

'. . . while you organise the wedding.'

Josie cocked an eyebrow. 'I knew it would all come down to me in the end,' she retorted, 'but don't worry, I'm happy to do it, just as long as you don't keep changing your mind every five minutes.'

'As if! Once I've decided on something, that's it, no going back.'

Laughing, Josie said, 'I'll remind you of that when the time comes. Now I'll leave you to drink that while I go and find out if my ticket'll allow me to get an earlier train.'

As she got up Lily caught her hand.

'Are you OK, Mum?' she asked as Josie looked at her in surprise.

'Of course,' Josie laughed. 'Don't I seem it?'

Lily shrugged. 'You just seem . . . I don't know, not your usual self, I suppose.'

Josie squeezed her hand. 'You know how I get about Ryan,' she said. 'And not being able to see him today . . .'

Though she still didn't appear entirely convinced, Lily smiled and let go of her.

By the time Josie came back to the table Lily was engrossed in sending a text. 'Jaz wants to know how much we owe for the karaoke tickets,' she said as Josie sat down.

'I'm not sure,' Josie replied, 'you can sort it out with Bob on Monday. He wants a list of the songs you're up for, so drop him an email when you get home to let him know.'

Dear Bob, always good for a couple of drinks as well as three or four tickets, but it wouldn't be fair to take too much advantage of his generosity when someone like Jasper could well afford to pay his way. They probably ought to put Bob and his wife on the guest list for the wedding, considering how good they'd been to the Clark family over the years.

Ten minutes later she was leaning out of a train window with Lily standing on the platform waving cheerio and pretending to cry.

'I'll be home on Monday,' Lily reminded her as the train began inching out of the station, 'don't miss me too much till then.'

'I'll try not to, but it'll be hard,' Josie informed her. 'And don't forget to take those things over to Ryan.'

'Promise I won't. Love you, Mum.'

'Love you too.'

'Love to Dad.'

'And to Jasper.'

'Don't talk to any strangers.'

Josie laughed. 'Nor you.'

'Let me know if I can bring anything on Monday.'

'You and Jasper will be plenty.'

'OK. Still love you.'

'Still love you too.'

'Best mum in the world.'

'Best girl.'

Lily winked and blew a kiss.

Josie did the same and stood watching her daughter getting smaller and smaller until the train rounded a curve in the track and she was lost from view.

It's just till Monday, she reminded herself, as she went to take a seat, *so nothing to be feeling so upset about.* And she mustn't allow herself to get worked up over what might be happening at the prison either, since she was sure it had nothing to do with Ryan, apart from the fact that he'd been denied his last visit before Christmas. Hopefully today's visiting order would be valid for after the new year, given it hadn't been used. She'd ring up on Monday to make sure, because if it wasn't Ryan needed to get another to her pronto.

Luckily all visits were at weekends, so she wouldn't have to miss one for her clinic appointment, but having to go the first Thursday in January would mean taking some time off work. She was sorely tempted to try and change that, since it was one of her caff days, which weren't as easy to swap around as cleaning for Mr Crover-Keene. On the other hand, Fliss was usually quite good about her disappearing for a couple of hours when she needed to, provided she gave enough notice. She probably ought to text Fliss now, then she'd know it was done.

Once she'd pressed send she gave Jeff a quick call to find out where he was and how he'd got on with borrowing Steve's car.

No reply, so she left a message telling him to ring back.

If Steve had said yes, she was thinking as she gazed out at the passing countryside, it was going to be a bit of a treat having the Mondeo for a couple of weeks. Even better would be if she could persuade Jeff to take her up to the prison in it. She wasn't going to hold out any hope for that though, since it was the last place he'd want to go even if it meant making life a bit easier for her.

Wincing slightly as she shifted position, she closed her eyes and rested her head on the seat back. She couldn't be doing those exercises the doctor had given her very well, because her back was aching. Never mind, she'd take a couple of painkillers when she got home and while they still had gas in the house, she'd put the fire on and snuggle up cosily in front of *Strictly*. There was a good chance her mother would drop in to watch it with her before taking off pubbing or clubbing or whatever she did on a Saturday night in her too-short, too-tight clothes and dangerous heels. She might look ten, even fifteen, years younger than her sixty-five, but in Josie's opinion she was still way too old to be going about getting pissed and picking up men the way she did. Of course, it was all about loneliness really, Josie understood that, and she felt sorry for her mother, wished she could do something to make her feel happier and more fulfilled. She might have smiled to think of what her mother would have to say to that, had she not known it would come peppered with the kind of cuss words Josie abhorred.

Funny how different they were, hardly like each other at all, either in personality or in looks. While she was growing up Josie used to feel sure she'd been stolen from a well-to-do family down in Kesterly South, who'd one day find out where she was and come to rescue her. She'd even searched back copies of the local papers in the library once to see if any children had gone missing around the time she was born. Tragically, there were quite a few, but none she could reasonably claim might be her. Still, it had kept her going as a child when things had been particularly difficult with her mother, and actually she wouldn't mind losing herself in that little daydream now. It would be a whole lot better than sitting here worrying about clinic appointments and failed prison visits when there was probably nothing to worry about.

Chapter Four

'He's here!' Oscar and Nell cheered as their father's car pulled up at the gates, and leaping down from the window, they dashed into the hall to press the button to let him in.

By the time Bel came through they'd torn open the front door and were running down the steps straight into Nick's arms.

'Wow, what a welcome,' he laughed, swinging them up to his height. 'And look how you've grown, you're as tall as me already.'

Squealing delightedly, they hugged him as hard as they could, planting kisses all over his unshaven cheeks as they told him how they'd been waiting by the window and how they had made mince pies with Auntie Bel and a Christmas cake and some snowman biscuits that they'd eaten all up, but had saved one for him.

Watching from the door, Bel experienced such mixed emotions that she barely knew whether to laugh or cry. She adored them so much, Nick too, and seeing them together would have been nothing but a joy, were it not for the fact that it should have been Talia sharing this moment, not her.

'Bel,' Kristina said, coming to hug her. 'It's good to see you. How are you?'

'I'm fine,' Bel assured her, returning the embrace. The stunning Kristina was as raven-haired as Talia and Bel were blonde, not quite as tall, but certainly far curvier. 'How was the trip?' she asked. 'Did you manage to unearth something amazing?'

Kristina laughed. 'Not really, but it was fascinating. I'm

glad we went,' and lowering her voice, 'as honeymoons go I think I can say it was a success.'

Bel tried to hold her smile. Surely Kristina realised that she, as Talia's sister, didn't need that sort of information.

'Here she is!' Nick cried, coming to sweep Bel into his arms. 'Gorgeous as ever and twice as scrumptious.'

Laughing as she hugged him back, Bel said, 'We ought to go in out of the cold. You won't be used to it, coming from all that heat. Will you stay for lunch?'

'Oh, I think so,' he replied, turning to Kristina.

'I hope so,' she responded, 'if you're sure it's no trouble.'

'We made a lasagne,' Nell declared happily. 'I helped, but Oscar didn't because he was wrapping up your presents. I did the ones from me last night.'

'You did?' her father cried, scooping her up again and carrying her inside. 'Are you going to tell me what you've bought for us all?'

'No, it's a secret. Auntie Bel's going to give them all to Santa and he'll bring them on Christmas Eve.'

'Oh, but that's two days away,' he protested. 'I can't wait that long.'

'He has to, doesn't he?' she said to Bel.

'Absolutely,' Bel agreed. 'Come on through, everyone. There's champagne on ice, in case you feel like celebrating your return, or hot chocolate if you prefer.'

'I'll have champagne,' Oscar informed her.

'Would that be with one straw or two?' Bel responded.

Nell screamed out a laugh.

'She's funny, isn't she?' Nick chuckled, his spectacles steaming up as he nuzzled Nell's neck. Though he looked and often sounded every inch the archaeology professor he was, as a father, and a husband, he was unfailingly loving and attentive. He was popular with his students too, some of whom had applied to Exeter just to be taught by the legend, as some of them called him, or Indiana Jones as the more irreverent preferred.

'I know I've said this a hundred times,' Kristina sighed as they entered the spacious open-plan sitting room, 'but I absolutely love this room. And you've even managed to turn on some sun.'

Glancing to where it was sparkling over the still grey waters of the estuary, Bel said, 'I've only been able to get it for the morning. Apparently, our time runs out this afternoon.'

Smiling at the answer, Kristina took off her coat and sank down on one of the sofas. 'What a fabulous tree,' she commented, eyeing it with what appeared to be genuine approval. 'And so beautifully decorated. Did you two help?' she asked the children.

'Yes,' they chorused.

'And we chose it,' Oscar added. 'When are we going to get one for our house, Dad? Auntie Bel was going to order it, but we weren't sure what size to get. Can we have one as big as this?'

Bel didn't miss the way Nick glanced at Kristina, as he said, 'The ceilings aren't quite as high at the cottage, and I'm not sure we'll have much of a choice now, with it being so close to Christmas.'

'But can we go and look?' Oscar implored. 'The garden centre's open till six.'

'How about tomorrow?' Nick suggested. 'Kristina and I have had a long flight, so we're a bit tired today.'

Though Oscar scowled, he was quickly distracted by the plate of nibbles Bel handed him to pass round.

'I think I'll go and use the bathroom,' Kristina declared, as the plate came her way. 'Nick, darling, before you get stuck into the champagne, remember you're driving later. Unless you'd like me to.'

'We could all stay here,' Nell suggested. 'Auntie Bel's got lots of rooms.'

'And I'm sure she'll be thankful to have them all to herself again for a while,' her father retorted. 'Don't worry, I'll limit myself to one glass,' he promised Kristina.

By the time Kristina returned, looking as fresh as a spring morning, Bel was sitting with Nell in one of the deep-seated armchairs, allowing her the tiniest sip of champagne as they watched Nick and Oscar battling aliens on Xbox.

'Already?' Kristina cried, clearly surprised. 'We haven't been here more than ten minutes. Don't you want to find out what the children have been doing while we were away?'

'Of course,' Nick replied cheerily. 'We can catch up with this later, son. So, Bel, have they behaved themselves?'

'Yes, we have,' Nell informed him. 'I was only naughty once, but Auntie Bel said it was all right, because the lady was horrible anyway.'

Nick looked intrigued.

'It was just a silly thing,' Bel assured him. 'No harm done.'

'She poked her tongue out,' Oscar blabbed.

'You shouldn't tell tales,' Nell cried. 'He shouldn't, should he, Auntie Bel?'

'And you shouldn't poke your tongue out,' Oscar retorted.

Nell immediately poked it out at him.

'Enough,' Nick laughed. 'I'm sure whatever happened, Auntie Bel had it under control. Now, why don't you pop out to the car and bring in the blue carrier bag from the back seat? I think you might find a few interesting things inside.'

As they raced off, Kristina said to Bel, 'They're just small gifts. It was difficult to know what to bring when you've already got so much gorgeous jewellery, and I'm not sure Peruvian wall art is quite your thing.'

Bel's eyebrows rose as she waved an arm about the room. 'As you can see,' she said, 'I'm easy to please, but you shouldn't have been thinking about me while you were there. You were on honeymoon, remember?'

Kristina seemed to glow as she looked at Nick who didn't appear to be listening, so she simply twinkled as she confided to Bel, 'It was sometimes hard to forget.'

Accepting that she'd walked right into that one, Bel dutifully smiled and tried to remind herself that under any other circumstances she'd probably feel very differently towards Kristina. After all, it was hardly her fault that Natalia was no longer with them and what did she, Bel, want, that Nick should lock himself away and wallow in grief? How was that going to help anyone, particularly the children? All it would do was make him as miserable as she was, and that wasn't what she wished for him at all.

She just couldn't get used to seeing him with Kristina, that was all, and the truth was, she didn't want to get used to it.

A while later, with presents of pan flutes, glow necklaces, roly-poly nativity dolls and embroidered purses spread out on the floor, Bel was serving the lasagne, while Nick opened a bottle of red wine. It was a Merlot that he particularly liked, which was why she'd taken it out of the rack, but now she was worried that Kristina would blame her for encouraging him to drink. Not that he made a habit of overindulging, but he could certainly put it away when he wanted to, and for some reason he seemed to be in the mood today.

Perhaps the honeymoon hadn't gone as well as Kristina was trying to make out, though why she, Bel, should deduce that from Nick's eagerness to enjoy some wine she couldn't really say.

'It's OK,' Kristina said softly, as Nick went to fetch fresh glasses, 'I've already decided I'll drive later, so I'll stick with water.'

Feeling bad for always being so ungracious where Kristina was concerned, Bel smiled, and heaped an extra helping of lasagne on to her plate as though to make up for her negative thoughts. Or perhaps it was to try and make her fat?

What ridiculous things go through your head, she chastised herself irritably as she took her place at the head of the table. Nick was at the other end with his back to the view, which didn't feel right, but she didn't want to cause a fuss by changing it so she stayed where she was.

'So, what news about the girl they found under the viaduct?' Nick asked, as the children charged off to wash their hands.

'Oh yes, I'd forgotten about her,' Kristina piped up. 'Have they found out who she is yet?'

'I'm not sure,' Bel replied. 'I went to the morgue, the day after the police came here, but she wasn't someone I recognised.' She shuddered at the memory of the poor girl's bloodless face and matted hair. 'They're pretty convinced she'd been living on the streets for a long time,' she expanded, 'and apparently she had a heroin habit.'

'Was that the cause of death?' Nick asked.

'Mm, it was. I asked them to be in touch if they find her family. Not that there's anything I can say, or do, but I think Talia would want me to make contact, if only to let them know that someone had cared.'

'That's so sweet,' Kristina commented, watching the children return to the table. 'Oscar, will you pass the pepper, darling?' she asked when he was seated.

Passing it for him, Nick said, 'Imagine dying, and no one knowing who you are. It must have been a pretty desperate existence, out there on the streets. I guess they don't even know if she's British.'

Bel shook her head. 'Which, presumably, is why it's proving so hard to find out who she is. Now back to you guys, and your trip. Oh, by the way Nick, I kept an article for you from *The Guardian* about Mes Aynak. I thought you'd be interested to see it.'

'You bet,' he agreed. 'Thanks for thinking of it.'

'I'd forgotten you went to Mes Aynak,' Kristina put in.

'Where is it?' Nell wanted to know.

'Afghanistan,' Nick replied. 'I went there with Mummy and a team of French archaeologists a few years ago. I'll have to find the photos to show you. Now, enough about me, I want to hear all about what you've been up to. I can see from the number of presents under the tree that you've been busy shopping, so how many are for me – and the answer better be *all*.'

'No!' Oscar shouted.

'They're for me,' Nell cried, banging the table.

'Don't do that, sweetheart,' Kristina chided, 'you might knock something over.'

Nell's hands immediately went under the table; her eyes moved to Bel.

Giving her a playful wink, Bel picked up her fork. 'Bon appétit, everyone,' she declared. 'I hope you're hungry, because there's plenty for seconds.'

It was much later in the day, after they'd all dozed in

64

front of the TV and indulged in a mince pie or two, that Nick and Kristina finally began packing the children and their belongings into the car. This was the moment Bel had been dreading. The house was going to feel unbearably empty without them; she could already sense herself wandering around it like a ghost, not sure what to do next. She knew she ought to make more of an effort to be in touch with her old crowd in London, but for some reason she hadn't been able to face them since losing Talia. In fact, she'd hardly seen them since moving to Kesterly, mainly because she'd been so busy doing up this place, and then taking care of Talia and the children. Had she been a better correspondent it might have helped, but she wasn't, and since her old friends had their own paths to travel, life had moved on for them all.

'So what are the plans for Christmas Day?' she asked, as Nick slammed closed the boot of his BMW estate. 'Shall I bring everything on Christmas Eve, as usual?' she added quietly, so the children wouldn't hear.

Nick glanced at Kristina, but she looked away, leaving him to slip an arm round Bel's shoulders and walk her back to the house. 'The thing is,' he said, his breath clouding the air as they went, 'Kristina's parents are keen for us to go to their place, in Cheshire, and with this being our first Christmas together, and as a married couple . . .' He broke off awkwardly. I'm sure you get where I'm going with this.'

Yes, she did, only too well, and she was so shocked, devastated even, that she simply didn't know what to say. What a fool she was. Why hadn't she seen this coming?

'We're planning to leave on Christmas Eve afternoon,' he continued, 'so it depends on you, whether you want to bring the kids' presents before that, or have a belated Christmas with them after we get back.'

She didn't know what to say.

'I'm sorry to spring it on you like this,' he said in the end, clearly feeling more uncomfortable by the second. 'I guess you could always come with us . . .'

'No, no, it's fine,' she cut in quickly, hating the idea almost as much as him feeling sorry for her. 'It's right that you should spend the time with Kristina's family. They'll want to see you, and the children. After all, they're kind of their grandchildren now.'

He grimaced. 'Yes, I guess they are,' he agreed, as if the thought had only just occurred to him. Still not quite meeting Bel's eyes, he said, 'We'll Skype, obviously, and I'm sure the children will ring several times a day. You know what they're like.'

Unable to push any words past the lump in her throat, Bel forced a smile as she nodded.

'So what will you do while we're away?' he asked in a tone that made her wonder how keen he was to go. It would be the first Christmas they'd spent apart in over ten years, though not the first without Talia.

Though she attempted an airy laugh, it sounded ludicrously more like a sob. 'Me? Oh, I'll either invite a few friends down from London, or perhaps I'll go there. I haven't been for ages and it's a good time to take in galleries and shows.'

'That sounds like a plan,' he commented approvingly. 'It'll do you good to have a change of scenery for a while.'

And you'd feel a hundred times better if I did, because it would help get me off your conscience. 'I'll bring the children's presents after they've gone to bed tomorrow night,' she told him. 'That way you can take them to Cheshire with you. They'll really believe in Santa then, if they find them under their new grandparents' tree on Christmas morning.'

His eyes were searching her face. 'Are you sure you wouldn't rather do a belated . . .'

'No, I think it's important for them to have their presents on the day,' she interrupted. 'I'll organise a lunch or something for when you get back. Will you stay in Cheshire until New Year?'

'I'm not sure yet,' he replied. 'We'll see how well it goes, given they're not used to having children around, and Oscar and Nell don't really know them yet. They'll miss you, of course.'

Bel tried to smile, but it wasn't easy. Did he even begin to realise how much she was going to miss them? 'They'll be fine,' she assured him. *It's their mother they really miss,* she wanted to remind him, *and right now I'm the next best thing.* Of course she'd never say it, she didn't even like thinking it, and really shouldn't when that role belonged to Kristina now.

Pulling her to him, he said, 'I still miss her too.'

She wanted to push him away, but couldn't or he'd see how close she was to tears.

'I'll always be there for you,' he said, and pressing a kiss to her forehead he left.

Though Bel knew that waking up alone on Christmas morning wasn't going to be the worst experience she'd ever had, she was aware that it could easily rate up there amongst them if she allowed it to. Which was why, in an effort to rescue herself from an ocean of loneliness and self-pity, she decided to step into Talia's shoes and called the homeless shelter to offer to help out for the day.

'Great idea,' Nick declared, when he and the children Skyped first thing Christmas morning to wish her a merry Christmas and thank her for the presents.

After all the excitement was over and the children returned to the bosom of Kristina's family, he said, 'I'm worried about you. I don't like to think of you on your own.'

'Then don't think about me at all,' she replied. 'I'm a grown up. I can take care of myself, and remember, I know the people at the shelter from the couple of times I went with Talia. And believe me, they need all the help they can get today. In fact, it's making me feel quite saintly to be lending a hand.'

With a dutiful laugh, he said, 'Then give us a call later to let us know how it went.'

'Of course,' she agreed. 'Before you go, is everything working out up there?' *How terrible she was for wanting the answer to be no.*

'Yes, it's fine. Kristina's parents are very easy-going and the children were completely blown away by all the presents under the tree. They've had far too much of course, but we'll sort out some things for the hospice when we get back.'

Since this was what they did every year, let the children decide which of their many gifts they'd like to donate to those less fortunate, Bel said, 'I've been wondering if it's a good idea for them to take the toys themselves this year, or do you think they're still too young?'

He gave it some thought. 'I'll run it past Kristina,' he said, 'see what she thinks.'

How would Kristina know? She's not their mother. She's not even their aunt. As far as Bel was aware she had no involvement in helping others at all. This was something she and Talia had done, ever since losing their own mother; it was a ritual that belonged to them.

What she said was, 'I hope she won't mind if the children decide to donate presents from her or her parents.'

'I'll explain the custom,' he assured her, 'and I'm sure they won't have a problem with it. What time are you expecting to be back from the shelter?'

Having no idea, she said, 'I guess that'll depend on how much they need me. If it's late I'll wait until tomorrow to ring you.'

It was late now, just after nine in the evening, and though she was exhausted after a hectic and challenging day, she felt faintly exhilarated too, which she often did after pouring her efforts into helping others. She'd never been quite as dedicated to it as Talia had, but perhaps she should now try to become more involved. Apart from anything else it was a great way to stop focusing on herself for a while, which she'd certainly have done if she'd stayed at home today. And there truly wouldn't have been any laughs within her four walls, unlike at the shelter, where in spite of their wretched lot some of the unfortunates could be extremely entertaining. They were an inspiration, she found, a true example of how indefatigable the human spirit could be.

There was an enormous amount of tragedy there too, of course, and though she'd never known the girl found under the viaduct whom the police had now identified as Anca, she couldn't help feeling a profound sadness at how lonely and possibly afraid she must have been when she'd died. It turned out that Talia had met her at the shelter, but no one there had seen the girl for some time – in fact not until one of the directors had gone to the morgue to identify her. She was Romanian, apparently. Her body had been flown back to her family a few days ago; the criminal gang that had brought her here was the focus of an ongoing police operation.

What an awful Christmas it must have made for her parents, getting their daughter back that way.

Did they speak any English, Bel wondered. She'd try to find out, and if she could get an address she'd at least send a card.

For now though, she needed to let it go, to accept that she'd done all she was able to for today, and that it was OK to feel safe here at home.

'We each of us come into this world alone,' one of the shelter workers had reminded her, 'and alone is how we travel it, and how we leave it.'

That might be true of most people, of course, but Bel hadn't been born alone. She and Talia had shared their mother's womb, slept side by side in cots, beds, tents, cars, planes and shared drunken teenage binges. Whenever they looked in mirrors they saw the other's face staring back at them; whatever they felt, the other felt it too. Bel had even fallen for Nick at the beginning, though thank goodness it hadn't lasted. The really odd part of that was how guilty she'd felt when she'd realised that she didn't love him the way Talia did. It was nonsense, of course, but for a while she'd found herself trying to fall for him again. In the end it was Talia who'd understood what was happening, and had taken her aside to talk it through. Together they'd come to realise that what Bel really wanted was to be able to share the same kind of closeness with a man that Talia was managing to share with Nick. For her it had never been possible, and she feared it never would.

Not wanting to think about that now, she set it aside and went to open her emails. In spite of it being Christmas Day there were a few, mostly junk, but a couple were round robins from old friends. She didn't read them, but nor did she delete them in case one contained news she needed to know. She'd open them tomorrow, after she'd called Nick

69

and the children, then she'd start searching for properties in need of renovation.

There was plenty she could do to keep herself busy, or more importantly to stop her mind travelling into the kind of darkness that frightened as well as compelled her. She kept thinking that Talia was at the other side of it, waiting for her, unable to move on until she joined her. It really wasn't that she wanted to die, and yet at the same time, on nights like this, she wanted it more than anything.

Chapter Five

Josie had never been partial to waiting rooms. They always seemed to be attached to places she didn't want to be – dentists, courts, prisons – and now here she was at one of the worst, the breast clinic.

What a palaver she'd had trying to find it, walking for what felt like miles, up and down corridors, across squelchy courtyards, through a derelict section (and they were trying to say there were no cuts in the NHS), until finally she'd ended up at the wards over on Blackberry Hill. If she'd known in advance where the unit was located she'd have caught the 44 bus up from town, rather than the 18 which had dropped her at the main hospital gates. Still, she'd know for another time, if there was going to be another time, although she didn't have any plans on becoming a regular.

She wasn't nervous, exactly, more terrified if the truth be told, but that wasn't going to get her anywhere, so rather than give in to it, she'd decided to worry about Jeff instead. They'd only found something else wrong with his car, so now it was going to cost a hundred quid more than they'd expected to get it back on the road, money they just didn't have. Even if they could raise it, how long was it going to be before they had to shell out for the bloody thing again? It was very definitely more trouble than it was worth, but what was he going to do for a job if he didn't have a car?

Poor bloke, he was really down on his uppers. The only thing keeping him going was the fact that her cousin, Steve, had rung to say he was staying in Spain an extra week so Jeff could keep the car, provided he picked him up from the airport when he got back. Of course Jeff would do that, gladly, he was even going to make sure the tank was full before he handed the keys over.

He was a kind bloke, Steve, though Josie had to admit she didn't always approve of his carryings-on. Not that he was the only one on their estate making claims for disabilities or dependants they didn't have. It sometimes seemed to her that everyone was up to it, especially the foreigners (not the lovely ones who'd lived here for years, but the new ones who hardly ever spoke to anyone apart from to find out what they could get from the state). In truth, she didn't blame half of them for trying it on, after all conditions were even tougher where they were from, it was the people she'd known most of her life and were fit enough to work that made her mad. Bunch of spongers, as Jeff would say. On the other hand, there were hardly any jobs about, and it was becoming downright impossible to make ends meet now all these cuts were starting to bite. They'd have to start claiming themselves if it went on like this, especially if Jeff didn't have a reliable car. And now there was this flipping bedroom tax to be finding. If they didn't, they'd have to move out of the house they'd lived in all their married life to make room for a family with kids. Never mind that her kids still needed a place to call home, and if she didn't have somewhere for Ryan when he came out, she didn't even want to think where he might end up.

Don't fret yourself about that now, Josie, worry about it when the time comes, and plenty could happen between now and then.

Fortunately, she'd got her bonuses before Christmas, and she'd been lucky at Aldi too, which meant they'd sat down to a lovely roast goose on Christmas Day (something they'd never had before), with roasters, spicy red cabbage and deliciously sweet garden peas. For afters they'd had a slice of the fruitcake she'd got for a pound, and a dollop each of brandy cream. She'd even managed to pick up a box of crackers for 99p, which they'd had fun pulling before the meal started so they could wear the paper hats while they ate and told each other the corny jokes.

It had all gone off pretty well, she thought, with everyone on their best behaviour, mainly thanks to Jasper, who both her mother and Jeff's father seemed to think of as something close to royalty. The fact that he'd brought wine had helped, of course, and the way he'd lavished drinks on them during their hilarious evening at Chanter Lysee hadn't done him any harm either. What had really impressed everyone, though, was when he'd performed 'Baby It's Cold Outside' with Lily, which might have won them top prize had Bob not decided to award it to Josie and Jeff for their rendition of 'Don't Go Breaking My Heart' (always fraught with more feeling on Josie's part than on Jeff's, she thought). So they'd gone home with a lovely box of Lindt chocolates and a bottle of Harvey's Bristol Cream, which her mother had managed to polish off on Christmas Eve.

'What are you like?' Josie had complained, when she'd come back from Aldi to find Eileen slumped in front of the telly with an empty bottle in one hand and a cigarette in the other. 'And you know we don't allow smoking in here, so put that out.'

'Oh for God's sake,' Eileen had groaned. 'You're always having a go about something. Loosen up a bit, will you?' Though Eileen was still a reasonably glamorous woman, in a mutton sort of way, with good legs, a generous bust and a beehive-type hairdo that, she claimed, kept her on trend, she rarely looked her best when drunk. In fact, considering how much she boozed and smoked, it was a bit of a miracle she was still alive, never mind able to look halfway decent. As for blokes, Josie didn't know of one that had lasted more than six months, and given the state of most of them she could only feel glad when they went.

'This is my house, Mother,' she'd declared, 'so if you want to stay here you have to live by my rules. No smoking, and definitely no more drink tonight. Look at you, you're an embarrassment to yourself. I can't believe you've drunk the lot. That sherry was supposed to be for tomorrow morning. I've invited some neighbours round for a glass and now we don't have anything to give them.'

'Bullshit,' Eileen slurred. 'I saw all the wine your son-in-law-to-be brought in with him.' After a rowdy hiccup followed by a cough, she wheezed, 'Can you lend me a tenner, kiddo? Just till I get paid.'

'No, I can't, I don't have it and even if I did you'd only go and spend it up the pub, so forget it. You've had enough. I'll get Jeff to see you home when he comes back.'

Eileen looked mutinous. 'What's wrong with me staying here for the night? Ryan's not going to be using his room, is he? So I can sleep there.'

'No you can't,' Josie shot back, furious that her mother could be so insensitive as to treat the one big heartache for her this Christmas as though it was a happy convenience for Nan.

'Rose Granger?' a nurse called out.

Coming back to the present, Josie's heart gave a jolt as she watched a stout elderly lady, helped by someone who might have been her daughter, heave herself out of a chair and make her way across the waiting area to where the nurse was smiling a greeting.

'Come on through,' the nurse said kindly, ushering them both towards a side room. 'How are you today, Rose?'

Josie didn't hear the reply, but she wasn't much of an eavesdropper, or certainly not where people's health matters were concerned.

She looked around at her companions. There were about ten of them, all told, all in pairs and talking quietly to each other. It had said on the leaflet the doctor gave her that it was a good idea to have someone come with you, but there wasn't anyone she'd felt right about asking. It was too much to ask of Lily, she had enough to be worrying about with her finals looming. Dawnie would have come if she was still here, but Dawnie was long gone, so she might as well put that out of her mind. She wondered when she might be called through, and though she was dreading it, at the same time she hoped it wouldn't be too much longer, or she'd be late home and if Jeff was there he'd want to know what had kept her.

Counting up the number of people she was sure had already been here when she'd arrived, she reckoned she should be about third in line now, though that didn't tell her much since she had no idea how long each appointment took. There might even be more than one specialist, in fact she was pretty sure there must be. There were definitely quite a few nurses because she'd been smiling at them as they came and went, as though being nice to them might give her a better result at the end of the day.

They were lucky to have this unit at Kesterly, the doctor had told her when she'd rung to make sure Josie could keep her appointment. If it had been this time last year she'd have had to go up to Bristol for the One Stop Clinic at Southmead, and for any follow-up treatment, if it proved necessary. Now, however, most of it could be taken care of at the infirmary in town.

Lucky, that, Josie supposed, if there could be anything at all lucky about having to be here.

Glancing up as a young woman came in wearing an expensive-looking camel coat and cream-coloured scarf, she watched her stop in front of a noticeboard next to the reception. On it was all sorts of info about fund-raisers, support groups, home care and even bereavement counselling, which Josie had found a bit startling. Actually, she hadn't given any of it much of a lookover, preferring to study the fish flicking about the aquarium, or to try to make out the titles of the second-hand books for sale on a shelf by the water cooler.

This woman seemed pretty engrossed in it, though. Perhaps it was her way of distracting herself before admitting to the receptionist she was actually here. It seemed a funny way of taking your mind off things, but each to their own, Josie always said, and anyway, she might not have been here for an appointment. She could have come to collect someone, or to assess the unit in some official capacity. Actually, she didn't seem like an NHS busybody, or a medical rep, or even a local-government type. She struck Josie more as someone who threw fancy dinner parties and drove about in a convertible Merc. An executive wife sort of person. She was quite tall, probably about five nine, and her short blonde hair made Josie wonder if it had just grown back after treatment. Whatever, it looked lovely.

'Bel,' someone said, and as the young woman turned to see who it was she broke into a smile.

Josie couldn't hear what she said, but she knew the man

looking pleased to see her was one of the consultants, because the receptionist called him by name as she passed him a file.

'Mr Beck, can I give you this?'

Josie didn't listen to any more, merely watched as the doctor ushered the young woman into the Visitors' Information Room and closed the door. He was who Josie was here to see. Mr Harry Beck. She couldn't remember how she knew they stopped using the title of doctor when they became surgeons, probably from *Casualty* or *Holby City*. Given his name she hadn't expected him to be Indian, or Asian anyway. Not that she minded, it just hadn't occurred to her, that was all. She hadn't imagined him to be about her age either, more in his late fifties or sixties, and the last thing she'd given any thought to was how good-looking he might be. Very, was what that quick glimpse of him had told her.

She didn't think any of it was making a difference, in fact she knew it wasn't, she was simply having to readjust her way of thinking, which might have been easier if she'd even known what it was.

Feeling her mobile vibrating, she pulled it out of her pocket and found a text from Lily. *Had letter from Ryan today, did you? He got his presents and says thanks. Wants to know when we're going to see him again. XXX PS Saw great hat in John Lewis for you yesterday.*

It pleased Josie to think there might be a letter from Ryan waiting when she got home. If Jeff saw it first he'd put it in front of the clock over the mantelpiece and probably not mention it, even when she sat reading it. He never asked what Ryan had to say, claimed he wasn't interested, but she knew he was really, which was why she usually left the letter hanging about so he could have a crafty look when she wasn't around.

Luckily her last visiting order was going to be honoured for her next visit, but she'd been too late to get in this coming Saturday, so she was aiming to go up there again the Saturday after. Apparently a couple of inmates had managed to escape when she and Lily were there before Christmas, but had been hauled back before they'd gone very far. It was a relief to know that Ryan hadn't been one of them.

'Mrs Josie Clark?'

Josie's heart somersaulted as she looked up to see Mr Beck smiling at her from reception, his white shirtsleeves rolled to the elbow, his blue tie slightly askew. He was wearing glasses now, which she wasn't sure she'd noticed before. There was no sign of the young blonde woman he'd taken into the Visitors' Information Room.

For a fleeting moment Josie wondered if she was still here somewhere, but then everything went out of her mind as she began following Mr Beck down the corridor that had various doors either side of it, some with names on, others with signs such as Radiology or Quiet Room or Ladies, and others with nothing at all.

'Here we are,' Mr Beck declared, stopping at the fourth one down on the left (why was she counting?).

Following him into the room, she tried not to look around. If she didn't it might be like she wasn't really there. *Pull yourself together.*

'Take a seat, Mrs Clark,' he said, waving her to one next to the desk. 'May I call you Josie?'

Josie nodded as she did as she was told, pulling the strap of her bag from her shoulder, and clutching it on her knees. She liked the sound of his voice, it was soft, but strong, if that made sense, and a little bit posh, but not to a point that made her feel lowly. She just felt very vulnerable in his hands, which was all right, since he was the one who knew all about everything while she knew nothing at all.

She waited quietly as he read the file he'd brought in with him, and let her eyes wander cautiously to the examination couch, half hidden by a modesty screen, and on to a couple of windows masked by white blinds. Next to the couch was a machine of some sort, a worktop with tidy piles of boxes and other equipment and a sink with a tap. There were lightboxes on the walls for him to hang up X-rays, and various charts that obviously meant something to him, but were a total mystery to her. She found herself thinking of the dozens, maybe hundreds of women who'd been in this room before her, and wondered how many of them had ended up hearing the news they most dreaded.

She was so tense now she was starting to hurt.

'OK,' he said, turning to look at her with a smile that she might have warmed to if she'd felt capable of warming to anything. She liked him though, he had kind eyes and a way of looking at her that was making her feel safe, even though she wasn't – yet! 'So you have a problem with your right breast,' he said, his tone not seeming to make it much of a big deal. 'Can you tell me how long you've had it, and whether it's causing you any discomfort?'

'Um, well,' she began, and had to clear her throat. 'I first noticed it about a month ago.' Would he be able to tell when he saw it that she wasn't being completely truthful? The trouble was, if she confessed she'd been aware of the swelling and redness since before last summer he might get impatient with her and call her a fool for not coming sooner.

'Does it hurt?' he prompted.

She shook her head. 'Not really. I mean, it feels a bit sore sometimes, and my skin goes a bit red,' but that was probably because she kept prodding the lump to try and make it go down.

'Do you know if there's a history of breast cancer in your family?' he asked.

Flinching at the dreaded word, she replied, 'I don't think so. My mum's never had it, and my gran didn't either. She died of a heart attack. My gran, I mean, not my mum. My mum's still alive, and smokes like a chimney, which I keep telling her she shouldn't.' *Stop talking, Josie. He doesn't want to know all this and you're making yourself look stupid.*

'OK, shall we have a little look?' he suggested. 'If you take off your coat and top, and make yourself comfortable on the couch, I'll be right back.'

As the door closed behind him Josie put her bag on the floor and walked over to the couch. It made her feel queasy to look at it, so turning around she unzipped her parka, hung it on a hook next to the screen, then pulled her red polo neck over her head. It seemed daft not to take off her bra when she was here to have her boobs examined, so she unfastened the back and drew the straps down over her arms. There was a mirror on the wall behind the couch, but she didn't want to look at her reflection. She knew she had quite nice boobs for a woman her age, a normal 36B, not too big, or droopy, just a few stretch marks left over from feeding, and dark rosy nipples puckered now from sudden exposure to the air.

And a lump you couldn't really see that was probably a cyst.

Hearing Mr Beck's voice outside, she crossed her arms over her breasts and watched him come in. A nurse was with him, a woman in her thirties, by the look of her, with a luscious sort of face and twinkly eyes. 'This is Yvonne Hubert,' he told her. 'She's our senior breast-care nurse, so you're in very good hands today.'

Josie whispered a hello, as Yvonne smiled and stood to one side while Mr Beck gently lowered Josie's arms to begin his examination. First he explored the lump itself, which Josie felt sure had suddenly swollen to twice the size it had been before. Then he had a good feel around the rest of the breast before doing the same to the other. None of it hurt until he began prodding under her arms, but even that wasn't too bad.

'Mm,' he said in a way that seemed to threaten the bottom of her world. He brightened again as he asked, 'Have you ever had an ultrasound, Josie?'

She shook her head. 'I mean, yes, when I was pregnant.'

'Then you know they're wonderfully pain-free. We're going to do one now. Don't worry, it's all part of the procedure. You just have to lie back on the couch here while Yvonne squeezes some jelly on to your breasts. It'll feel quite cold at first, but that's normal. Then I'm going to run this little probe over the surface of your skin, which'll enable me to have a better look at what's going on here.'

Hardly able to breathe now, Josie watched Yvonne lay a paper sheet over the bed. Sitting on to it, she swung her legs up and lay back awkwardly. She wished there was a pillow, because being so flat was making her feel more vulnerable.

Mr Beck was right about the gel being cold, but the feel

of the probe, as he called it, was a bit like he was giving her some sort of massage. She stole a glance at the monitor beside her, but it only showed a lot of shadowy images and since he didn't explain what they were she was none the wiser.

'OK,' he said, replacing the probe and wheeling his chair away from the couch, 'time to go with Yvonne for a mammogram. I'm guessing, given your age, that you've never had one before?'

She shook her head. *And she didn't want one now.*

Yvonne was handing her a bunch of paper towels to wipe the gel off her breasts.

She almost blurted out something about her boobs not having received this much attention in years, but thankfully managed not to. It would be right off colour, and make her sound a proper saddo. Not that Jeff neglected them or anything, but he was a lot less thorough with his foreplay these days than he'd been when they were first together.

Putting on the gown Yvonne was passing her, she followed the nurse out into the corridor and along to the mammogram room. She'd heard about these X-rays, of course, but now she was about to find out for herself how painful it was to have your boobs squeezed between two square plates and a massive machine come down on them.

The only good thing about it was that it didn't take very long.

'There, hopefully not too bad,' the radiographer smiled as she ended the session. 'You can get dressed again now, then if you pop back to the waiting room the nurse will come and get you as soon as Mr Beck's ready.'

As the door closed behind her Josie found herself starting to shake, which made it really hard to get her bra done up. What was the matter with her? She'd been all right a minute ago, and now she seemed to be all over the place.

I need a cup of tea, she decided, and once she'd finished zipping up her parka she went in search of one. The drinks machine in the waiting room turned out to be on the blink, so she settled for a plastic mug of cool water and returned to the chair she'd been in before.

There were a few more people in here now, none she

recognised from earlier, but once again they were mostly in twos. Apart from one woman who had no hair, it wasn't possible to tell the patients from the companions. The bald woman had lovely big brown eyes, she noticed, and her skin was like porcelain. She was laughing at something the woman with her was saying.

Josie's eyes went down as tears welled up from nowhere and threatened to spill on to her cheeks.

Bel was parking her car next to the sea wall on Kesterly Promenade, half smiling to herself as she remembered how she and Talia used to tease each other over their crush on Harry Beck.

'We have to have some perks while we're going through this,' Talia used to say. 'I swear, if I weren't married, and down to one boob, I'd be making a play for him by now.'

'I don't think he'd mind about the one boob,' Bel would reply, 'but I bet his wife gets fed up with all his fans.'

'Do you think everyone fancies him, not just us?'

'Are you kidding? Anyway, speak for yourself. He's not my type.'

It was true, he wasn't, though not because she wasn't attracted to him, despite how good-looking he was, and charismatic and heroic (for those who survived, and even those who didn't, given how hard he fought for them), but because he was married. In her book that made him strictly off limits, and anyway he'd never once given her, or Talia, the impression that he had anything but a professional interest in them. He was friendly, of course, but she was certain he was like that with all his patients, and his ability to make a person feel as though they mattered more than anything was almost certainly a gift any surgeon would want.

'How lovely to see you,' he'd said, capturing her with those velvety brown eyes of his as he'd taken her into the Visitors' Room earlier. 'But what are you doing here? Please don't tell me . . .'

'No, no, I haven't had a referral,' she quickly assured him. 'And my latest check told me I'm still in the clear.' She had yearly mammograms now, and would continue to for the rest of her life, or until they found something in her. If they did, it wouldn't be the same cancer that Talia had suffered from, because she wasn't carrying the gene. How could Talia have had it and not her? 'I'm still doing the occasional volunteer work for Breast Cancer Care,' she explained, 'so I brought these along.'

'Excellent,' he responded, taking the leaflets from her. 'A great organisation. I've given a couple of talks for them in the past.'

She knew, since she and Talia had attended one of them.

'So how are you?' he asked. 'You're looking great.'

'Thank you,' she smiled. He'd remember, of course, how she'd shaved her head when Talia had lost her hair so Talia wouldn't feel so alone, or keep being reminded of how she'd been before the chemo had done some of its worst. 'Life feels a little different to when I last saw you.'

'I'm sure it does.' He was still regarding her intently, maybe even seeing through the mask she put on for the world. 'You and Talia were very close,' he stated, telling her with those few words that he understood how the loss, much like the cancer, didn't just go away, and maybe for a twin it stayed even longer. 'How're Nick and the children?'

Touched that he'd ask, she told him about Kristina and how pleased she was for her brother-in-law that he'd found someone else already.

'It's often the case,' he responded, 'that someone who was happily married is keen to repeat the experience after their partner dies, so I hope it works out for him and his new wife.' He glanced at his watch.

'You have appointments,' she said.

'I'm afraid so, but it was good to see you.'

It had been good to see him too, in spite of all the painful memories it had evoked, memories that continued to swirl around her as she left. He'd played such a vital role in trying to save Talia that a part of Bel would always feel attached to him just for that.

Still feeling the poignancy of the short encounter, she pushed open the door of the Seafront Cafe and went to one of the window booths. She and Talia had fallen into a habit of coming here before chemo sessions. Though Talia wouldn't eat one of the full English breakfasts herself, she loved to pick at Bel's, always stealing the sausage and usually managing a mushroom or two.

Bel hadn't driven down to the Promenade with the intention of coming to the café. She was only here because she was early for her meeting at the town hall to discuss plans for renovating the summer house at the end of her garden. Ordinarily she'd have left the car in the underground park on Victoria Square, but for some reason she'd driven on to the front and ended up here.

It couldn't be that Talia was guiding her moves, that was just nonsense. However, since no one had ever been able to prove or disprove that there was life hereafter, maybe she shouldn't dismiss it. Why not imagine what she'd say were she able to talk to Talia now? Maybe she'd try to find out what it was like where Talia was, if Talia really was waiting for the other part of herself, her twin, to come and join her. She wanted to ask so many questions, like did Talia mind that Nick had married again? What did she think of Kristina? Was it tearing her apart to be able to see the children and not be able to touch them? Was she with their mother now; had their mother forgiven Bel for what she'd done?

'Can I get you something?'

Bel looked up at the waitress whose name badge said Fliss, and whose creased complexion told of too much stress, lots of cigarettes and probably more than her share of sleepless nights.

'It's mostly self-service,' Fliss told her, 'but we're not exactly run off our feet today.'

Bel smiled as she glanced around the empty café. 'I'll have a peppermint tea,' she said.

The waitress cocked her head to one side. 'Don't I recognise you?' she asked curiously. 'I know, you used to come in here with your sister. Funny, I didn't recognise you at first, I suppose I got so used to seeing double where you two were concerned.' She laughed at her little joke. 'It was the peppermint tea that tipped me off. You're the only one who ever had it, and your sister used to order cappuccino with a full English.'

Realising Fliss thought she was Talia, Bel was about to correct her when she decided there was no point. 'You have a very good memory,' she told her. 'Do you remember all your customers' orders?'

Fliss's smile was wry. 'We don't have that extensive a menu to make it difficult to remember orders,' she replied, 'but no, course I don't remember them all. We get too many tourists coming in for that. It was just that you and your sister, well, if you don't mind me saying, you stood out from the crowd, you being twins and so striking and all.'

Realising it was probably the headscarves she and Talia had worn that had made them stand out, Bel simply smiled.

'Where's she today then?' Fliss ran on. 'No, don't answer that, I'm just being nosy and I expect you get fed up with people asking when it's not like you have to be welded at the hip, just because you look the same. I'll go and get your tea. Let's hope we've still got some, because it's been a while since we saw you in here.'

Feeling faintly odd about being served tea that had been sitting here as though waiting for Talia's return, Bel turned to the window and let her eyes travel along the stretch of wind-torn beach opposite to where a small group of children from the Pumpkin playgroup, over by the station, were climbing on to a carousel. Oscar and Nell adored riding that thing, choosing something different every time, a horse, a bus, a police car, a golden carriage. She must bring them here at the weekend, while Nick and Kristina went to a party in London. She was looking forward to having them again. She might treat them to the cinema too, depending on what was showing, and maybe a pizza after.

Taking out the condolence card she'd brought with her, she rummaged for a pen and tried to think what to write to a couple she'd never met, who possibly didn't even speak English, about the death of their daughter. Their names were Beryx and Jenica Bojin, the police had told her, they lived in a town called Slatina and Anca was the youngest of their three children.

Dear Mr and Mrs Bojin, my name is Isabella Monkton. I'm writing because my sister's name and address was found on your daughter at the time of her death.

She stopped, wondering if it was too brutal to use that word. Nothing could be as brutal as what they must already be going through, and she couldn't just ignore it even though they had no idea who she was.

I'm sad to say that my sister, Natalia, has passed on since she and Anca met at the Wayfarer Centre, here in Kesterly, but I know she'd have wanted me to write to you at this time to express her – and my – sadness at your loss. I only wish Anca had called before things got so bad, as I'm sure one of us could have helped her. At the very least we'd have been able to give her shelter and food and take her to a doctor.

Much good that was going to do them, or Anca now.

If there is anything I can do for you at this time, please let me know. My address is on the back of the card.

Respectfully yours,

Isabella

'There you go, my old love,' Fliss said, putting a cup and saucer and teapot in front of her. 'I brought you a couple of biscuits too. Nothing fancy, but they're on the house.'

Touched, Bel said, 'That's lovely, thank you.'

As Fliss walked away, her large hips sashaying under her crisp nylon overall, Bel wondered what her life was like, out of here. Was she married? Did she have children? What kind of tragedies might she have suffered over the years? Almost everyone had been through something, a death, an accident, an illness, a miscarriage of justice, divorce, rape, the loss of a daughter under a viaduct, it could be anything and no one would ever know from looking at them. They simply went about their days the way they had to, putting on a front, doing their best to overcome the challenges life had thrown their way. Some were subjected to more than their fair share, while others got off more lightly.

What was the point of it all, she kept wondering. She could never find a good reason for the world's cruelties, and these days she no longer wanted to try. Almost nothing seemed to make sense, and apart from Oscar and Nell almost nothing seemed to matter any more.

*

Josie could hardly believe she was still waiting. Not that hours and hours had gone by, only a couple, in fact, but she'd really expected to be out of here by now and already home. Instead, she was still watching the comings and goings of the unit and had even got into a little chat a while ago with another woman who'd come on her own. It turned out she was having a check-up following a lumpectomy.

'Lucky they caught it when they did,' she'd commented. 'I'm hoping they're going to say I only need a few sessions of radiotherapy now. No chemo, please God, because you don't want that if you can avoid it.'

'No, of course not,' Josie had agreed. Though she wasn't particularly knowledgeable about the disease, or its treatment, she'd heard enough about chemo to be sure it wasn't a route anyone would want to take.

She knew other things now, thanks to sitting here for so long and paying a bit more attention to stuff on the noticeboard. For instance, women of her age were only supposed to have a one in fifty chance of getting breast cancer, which seemed all right as long as you were amongst the forty-nine. If you turned out to be the one, you'd feel really hard done by, wouldn't you? And then there was the lifetime risk, apparently one in eight, which didn't sound very good at all.

Still, according to one of the leaflets survival rates were getting better all the time, and, most important of all, her lump could easily turn out to be benign. She wasn't sure what they'd do if it was, maybe they'd still want to remove it; she guessed she'd find out when they got round to calling her back in.

Eventually, just after four, the nurse Yvonne, who seemed to be run off her feet, came to get her.

'Sorry this has taken so long,' Yvonne apologised. 'We've had quite a few referrals to get through today, and we're all behind with ourselves. Anyway, here we are. Go on in and sit down, Mr Beck'll be right with you.'

'I'm already here,' he called out, drying his hands as he appeared round the screen. 'Hello again, Josie. Sorry to have kept you.'

'That's OK,' she assured him, pleased that he'd remembered her name, 'as long as you're going to give me some good news,' she added chirpily.

His smile told her nothing as he sat down in front of his two-screen computer and waited for her to sit down too.

Finding herself on the edge of the seat, she tried to slide back, but couldn't.

'Well,' he began, his lovely brown eyes coming to hers, 'I'm sorry to tell you that your lump is showing all the signs of being cancer . . .'

She started to sway.

'Of course we're going to run a lot of tests to find out more about it, starting with a core biopsy . . .'

Josie was losing track of his words. They were coming at her too fast. Had he really just told her she had cancer? He'd said something about tests, so maybe he still wasn't sure.

'. . . which I'd like to carry out now,' he was saying. 'It's very quick. We'll give you a local anaesthetic to make sure you don't feel anything. Are you aware of what a biopsy is?'

She nodded, then shook her head.

'It means I'm going to remove some tissue from the lump so we can send it off to the lab for analysis. This'll confirm it's cancer and tell us the type and grade you have, and from there we can decide how we're going to treat it.'

'So . . .' Josie cleared her throat. 'So, I will have to have treatment?'

His smile was gentle. 'Yes, you will,' he confirmed. His eyes didn't waver from hers. 'The tenderness of your breast and the puckering of the skin tells me that you almost certainly have what we call an inflammatory cancer.'

Her mind switched off again; she didn't want to hear any more. The trouble was, his words just kept getting through.

'. . . so are you ready to get undressed again now?'

She swallowed drily. She wasn't sure any of this was sinking in, yet at the same time it was so terrifyingly real it was making it impossible to move.

She had cancer.

She was that *one in fifty*.

What was she going to do? She couldn't afford to have cancer. She had to work. Jeff would go mad. The children needed her . . .

Mr Beck was on his feet, directing her towards the couch.

Standing up, she began taking off her coat, jumper and bra. Yvonne was here now. She couldn't remember seeing her come in.

The injection for the anaesthetic didn't hurt, or not very much.

Don't cry, Josie. That would just make everyone embarrassed.

A few minutes later, Mr Beck made sure she was numb and said, 'OK, this is going to sound a little bit like a staple gun going off. You won't feel anything, but the noise might make you jump.'

Her eyes were closed. She didn't want to watch.

He was right about how it sounded, but she didn't jump, probably because he'd prepared her.

'OK, all over,' he announced, straightening up again.

She opened her eyes and wanted to beg him to make her all right.

She should have come sooner.

This was all her fault; she only had herself to blame.

After applying a dressing, Yvonne said, 'Is there anyone you'd like to call? Perhaps someone could come and pick you up?'

'No, no, I'm fine,' Josie assured her. 'The bus stop's right outside.'

'It shouldn't be long before we hear back from the labs,' Mr Beck told her. 'They tend to be pretty quick these days.'

She could wait for ever.

'If you experience any discomfort from the wound,' Yvonne said, as Mr Beck excused himself, 'don't be afraid to take painkillers.'

Josie nodded absently. She wondered how many other women had been in here today, and of them how many had heard the same sort of news she just had.

'It can't be all that easy doing your job,' she commented, buttoning her coat.

'It's lovely when we make someone well again,' Yvonne assured her.

Josie wanted to ask if they were going to make her well, but being afraid of the answer, all she said was, 'Yes, I can imagine that part is what it's all about really.' Hearing her mobile vibrating she pulled it out of her pocket and saw there was a text from Mr Crover-Keene.

Got your message about changing days this week, that's fine. I was hoping to have a little chat with you before Saturday if possible, so could you call when you have time. Thanks.

Guessing he wanted to make sure she was done and gone before his guests arrived, she put the phone back in her pocket. 'Is it OK to go home now?' she asked Yvonne. 'My husband'll be wanting his tea on the table and if the traffic's bad I'll end up being late.'

'You've had a bit of a shock,' Yvonne reminded her, 'so it might be a good idea to sit quietly for a minute or two. And if there's anything you want to ask, you just go right ahead. It's what I'm here for.'

Josie looked away awkwardly. She could tell Yvonne thought she might not have taken everything in, and maybe Yvonne was right, but she'd heard enough for today. She tried to inhale, but found her chest was too heavy to take in any air.

'Are you sure you don't want to call someone?' Yvonne pressed kindly. 'A friend, maybe?'

Josie shook her head. She was thinking about Dawnie again, but that was just daft when Dawnie was history.

'You shouldn't keep this to yourself,' Yvonne cautioned. 'The support of loved ones . . .'

'It'll be OK,' Josie cut in, more harshly than she'd intended. 'I'm sorry,' she mumbled, and as though to make up for it, she said, 'Mr Beck seems a very nice man.'

'Yes, he's one of our more popular surgeons. You're with one of the best.'

That was good to know, except she didn't want to be with him at all. 'So, what – what he's saying,' she stammered, 'is that it's definitely cancer?'

'What he's saying is that your test results should be back within a couple of weeks . . .'

'Is there – is there anything I should do during those weeks?' Josie interrupted, already wondering how she was going to get through them with this hanging over her. 'I mean, is there a particular food I should give up, or an exercise I should do? I've got one of them Pilates balance boards: my husband gave me it for Christmas. The doctor said I should use it to try and strengthen my core. I was getting these backaches, you see. My husband gets them too. I'm sure it's our mattress. We've had it since we got married, which is over twenty years, so time we looked into getting a new one.'

Fat chance of affording one. They had to sort out the car first.

The nurse was speaking. 'What sort of backaches?' she asked.

Josie frowned. She didn't know there was more than one sort.

Yvonne smiled. 'I'll be back in two shakes, just wait here.'

Left alone, Josie stared down at the blank computer screen and tried to think what to do. Part of her wanted to scarper before the nurse reappeared, but suddenly she was afraid to leave. Once she was out of here it was going to be just her and the cancer, and everywhere she went it would come too. It was hard trying to make herself accept that her body was being invaded by something so awful and destructive.

Inflammatory cancer. It sounded so bad, but maybe it was something that flared up and then just calmed down again. It probably wasn't quite as simple as that, but it could be something along those lines.

You're going to have to be brave, Josie. It's not the end of the world, people have been through a lot worse, so you can get through this.

'Sorry,' the nurse smiled as she came back, 'I needed to catch Mr Beck before he left for the day, and I grabbed some literature for you to take home with you. It'll answer a lot of questions you probably haven't even thought of yet.'

'Thank you,' Josie mumbled, taking the leaflets. 'I really should be going now.' She attempted a smile. 'You've been very kind.'

Twenty minutes later she was on the bus, sitting squashed between the window and a woman who was so large that she really needed the entire seat to herself. Josie was barely aware of her as she stared out at the passing streets, vaguely dazzled by headlights and neon shopfronts as they passed in a surreal sort of blur. She was thinking about Jeff and Lily and Ryan and what this was going to mean to them. It was sure to scare them half out their minds, especially Lily and Ryan. She couldn't do it to them, she just couldn't. Lily had her finals and wedding to be thinking about, and Ryan depended on her visits . . .

She felt so choked up all of a sudden that it was hard to stop herself crying.

Feeling sorry for yourself's not going to make it any better, is it? she scolded herself.

Anyway, people were getting breast cancer all the time, and most of them survived. Or she thought most of them did.

'Your GP will be kept informed of everything,' Yvonne had said as she'd walked her out, 'and you'll find details of local support groups in the brochures I gave you. I've written my number on one of them, in case you have any further questions.'

Panic suddenly welled up inside her. *I don't want support groups or brochures, or anything else. Please, please, please, don't let me have cancer.*

Remembering the woman she'd spoken to earlier, she felt a shaky calm returning. A lumpectomy and radiotherapy didn't sound too bad, and the woman had been there on her own so she obviously wasn't being a burden to anyone else, dragging them along to go through it all with her. If she, Josie, could have something like that woman had, it would be over and done with in no time at all and she could get on with her life. She might not even have to take any time off work, which would be a blessed relief, because no way in the world could they manage without the little bit she brought in.

Realising her phone was vibrating, she turned it over to see a text from Lily.

Hey Mum. Any chance you can come to Bristol this w/e? I

know we can't see Ryan, but have an appt with dress designer.
Would be brill if you were there too.

Though gripped in the horror of what was happening, Josie managed to text back.

Working in morning, but could be there by two thirty. Is that OK?

Totally cool. Will meet you at station.

Minutes later another text came through, this one from Jeff.

Where the heck are you? I'm starving.

Be home in about ten minutes, she messaged back. *Some crisps in cupboard to be going on with. Make a start on potatoes.*

He texted back: *Already peeled. Boiled or chips?*

Boiled. We'll have some mash with sausage and beans. As far as she could remember there was one tin left, so if they shared half of it they could have the other half tomorrow.

A few minutes later she sent him another text saying, *Why don't we open a bottle of that wine Jasper brought and have an early night?*

By the time she was ready to get off the bus he still hadn't responded, which could have been because he'd left his phone in the lounge while he was in the kitchen. Or the telly was up too loud; or maybe he just wasn't in the mood. She didn't blame him when his car was causing so much hassle.

It was lovely that he was going to be there when she got in with their tea already under way, and the gas fire on for some warmth. It was a lot more than some women could hope for, those whose husbands were forever in the pub, or down the dog track, or in some other woman's bed. Jeff had never been much of a drinker, or a gambler, and as far as she knew the only time he'd ever been unfaithful was that once with Dawnie.

Tonight it was bothering her more than it had for a long time to think of how two people she loved so much had betrayed her. She'd never forget the day she'd caught them in Dawnie's front room with the curtains pulled. She'd assumed Dawnie had one of her headaches so was having a lie-down. She'd been lying down all right, and she'd probably had a terrible headache after, the way she'd cracked her skull on the table as she'd shot to her feet. What she'd been doing down there with Jeff hadn't left anything to the imagination.

One of the worst parts of it had been finding out just how serious they were about each other. They'd never have done it, they'd assured her, if it hadn't meant something; it was like they just couldn't help themselves.

A quick fling would have been easier to bear.

A lot of cruel things had been said afterwards, plenty of them by her, but Dawnie hadn't held back either. It had been a terrible time, trying to keep it from the children while everyone wondered why she and Dawnie weren't speaking, jumping to their own conclusions and finding out soon enough that they were right. In the end Dawnie had rung Josie to say,

'We can't go on living around one another, not after this. I've got really strong feelings for Jeff, and they won't go away if I carry on seeing him.'

Jeff had never actually said what his feelings were for Dawnie, but Josie had felt sure that if it weren't for the children he'd have upped and gone with Dawnie and she'd never have seen them again. If that had happened it would have broken her heart so badly it might never have mended. Thankfully it hadn't. Jeff was still here, and though the first couple of years after the affair had been rough on their marriage, they were more or less back to normal now. Or that was what she liked to tell herself, but if she was being honest, Jeff had never been the same since Dawnie had gone. He didn't light up inside the way he used to when something made him laugh, nor was he the man everyone had to have at their party. Sometimes she told herself it was shame that had changed him; after all, he wouldn't feel proud of hurting her, whether he still loved her or not. Other times she felt sure he was wondering when might be the right time to go.

Hopping off the bus, she hunched more cosily into her coat as she headed towards home.

'At last,' Jeff declared, as she let herself in the front door. 'I've had a call-out so you'll have to put my dinner in the oven. Potatoes are already on the boil, and sausages under the grill. There's a letter on the shelf from your son. Should be back in about an hour,' and brushing past her as she hung up her coat, he hurried out to the car.

Your son, as though Ryan wasn't his any more.

Going to the kitchen, Josie checked nothing was about to burn before opening the food cupboard and taking out a bottle of wine. It was only after staring at it for several minutes, with the words *your son* going round in her mind, that she put it back again. She'd heard on the news how alcohol could cause cancer, so it was a daft idea to open a bottle anyway. She'd finish making the tea, try to eat some herself, then put her feet up in front of *Corrie* with Ryan's letter.

They didn't have any proper results yet, so there was every chance Mr Beck had got it wrong. He was human, after all, and humans were always making mistakes, even people like him.

Chapter Six

'Is this seat taken? Would you mind . . . ?' Harry Beck laughed in surprise. 'Bel! The second time in as many weeks. How lucky am I? Are you waiting for someone?'

'No, no,' Bel replied quickly, delighted to see him. 'Please, sit down.'

Putting his coffee on the table, he shrugged off his coat and sank into the chair opposite hers. As usual, the garden centre's café was full, though mainly with OAPs today, since Mondays and Wednesdays were special discount days for the over sixties. 'Are you OK for a drink?' he asked. 'Can I get you another?'

'Thanks,' she smiled, 'but I've only just started this one.' She raised her cup. 'Cheers. You're certainly not someone I expected to run into here, but I guess even surgeons have gardens. And days off.'

'We do,' he confirmed, 'though I confess I'm not on a mission for plants. They do great cards in the gift shop, and it's my mother's birthday next week, my aunt's the week after, and my son's the week after that.'

'And how old will he be?' she asked with a smile.

'Eleven,' he replied, sipping his coffee. 'And you? Are you blessed with green fingers, or are you also on the hunt for cards?'

'Advice,' she informed him. 'My niece and nephew want to create a vegetable garden, so I'm here seeking guidance.'

His eyes twinkled as he said, 'I take it we're talking about Natalia's children?'

'They're the only niece and nephew I have.'

Sitting back, he said, 'It must be lovely for them, having you so close by.'

'It's certainly lovely for me. It makes everything feel so much more alive when they're around. When they leave . . .' She pulled a face, not wanting to go any further with that.

Raising an eyebrow, he replied, 'I know what you mean. You get so used to children filling up the house with toys and noise and God only knows what else. When they're suddenly not there, the place seems so empty it could drive you nuts.'

If only you knew, she was thinking, profoundly relieved that he had no idea what kind of thoughts went round in her head during those horribly silent hours. 'How many children do you have?' she enquired, sipping her coffee.

'Two. Both boys. Josh, the soon-to-be eleven-year-old, and Neelmani, who was nine just before Christmas.'

'Neelmani? An unusual name.'

'It was my father's. He died the year before Neel was born, so my wife agreed to make my mother happy by naming our son after his grandfather.'

'You sound a close family.'

His eyes shone with irony. 'Don't get me wrong,' he said, 'I adore my mother, but it's always a little bit of a relief when she goes off to the old country to stay with her sister, which is where she is now.'

'Do you have a lot of family in India?'

Affecting an Indian accent, he said, 'Very many cousins and uncles and aunties, but most of them I am not seeing for very many years.' Reverting to his normal voice, he went on, 'We used to go regularly when my sister and I were children, until my father developed a desire to see other parts of the world. So his country of birth was given the heave-ho, at least as far as we children were concerned. He and my mother continued to spend several weeks a year there, working at hospitals in deprived areas. In case you're wondering, they were both surgeons. He was a neurologist, she was a paediatrician until she retired about ten years ago. My father passed on just before that.'

'I'm sorry.'

He waved a dismissive hand. 'It was a long time ago.'

'Were you born in India?'

'No, but my sister was. I didn't come along until seven years later, by which time my parents were settled in London. Have you ever been to India?'

Bel nodded, and felt memories stirring their warmth into her heart. 'Talia and I spent about four months there during our gap year,' she replied, wishing she could relive every moment, even if only in the telling. 'We absolutely loved it, and always said we'd go back.' Though her smile remained in place, an inevitable sadness clouded her eyes.

'Maybe you should,' he suggested gently. 'India's known for its healing powers.'

Swallowing, she said, 'I've promised to take the children when they're older. They say they want to go to all the places I visited with their mummy, but even if Nick agrees, they'll probably have different ideas of where they'd like to go by the time it comes around.'

'Wouldn't that be just like children?' he commented wryly. 'Am I allowed to ask how they're getting along with their new stepmother?'

Hoping her ambivalence towards Kristina didn't show, she said, 'Pretty well. She's definitely not of the wicked variety, though not a natural Mother Earth type either. Actually, I don't suppose I'd have put Talia or me in that category. As for you, I'm guessing you love being a father.'

Breaking into a laugh, he took out his mobile as it rang. 'More than anything else,' he assured her. 'Excuse me, I ought to take this,' and clicking on he answered with his name.

Though he said almost nothing Bel couldn't help noticing how his expression darkened, and by the time he rang off he wasn't looking at all happy.

'Is everything all right?' she ventured, when he didn't get up to go. 'Not a patient who's . . .'

'No, no, no,' he interrupted. 'It's nothing to do with that, thank goodness. It was someone from the hospital Trust who's been . . . Well, we don't need to go into that. All part of the job, I'm afraid.' He put on a smile. 'Where were we? Ah, someone else to hijack my attention. One second,' and clicking on his mobile again he said, 'Hey Ben, tell me some good news.' His eyes brightened with laughter as he looked at Bel. 'That's terrific,' he declared. 'When did they confirm? Sure I can make it. It's already in my diary. OK, email me the details . . . Course I know where it is. We've played there before. I'm just amazed they're having us back . . .' With a shout of laughter, he said, 'I'll hold you to that,' and after ringing off he sat back in his chair with a very satisfied look on his face.

'Am I allowed to ask?' Bel prompted.

'You most certainly are. What are you doing next Saturday night?'

Startled, she said, 'I'm not sure. Why?'

'How would you like to come and watch my band? We're playing at the White Hart out on the Moorstart road. Do you know it?'

Yes, she knew it. 'Your band?' she echoed. 'You mean, as in rock and roll?'

'More swing jazz, or that's what we like to call it. We're on at nine, apparently. If you're interested I'll put some tickets aside for you. Not that I'm anticipating a sell-out, you understand, but we do have our followers.'

Enjoying his irony, she said, 'Which instrument do you play, or are you the singer?'

'Good God no. I'm on trumpet. Jim Sayer from Paediatrics does vocals and drums; Ray Ullman from Orthopaedics is our keyboard chap, and Ben Weaver, the pathologist who just rang, plays a mean guitar.'

'And does your band have a name?'

'Are you going to cringe if I tell you it's The Medics?'

'I'm trying not to,' she promised.

Laughing, he said, 'Do you care for swing jazz?'

'What's not to like about it?'

'You haven't heard us yet . . . How many tickets would you like?'

Not wanting to admit that she had no one to take, she said, 'Can I call or text you about that? I . . . Well, to be honest, I haven't been out much lately, so I'm not sure who to invite.'

'Understood. Tell me your number, if I ring it now you'll have mine and I'll also have yours.'

After entering his details into her contacts, she asked, 'Will your wife be there? It would be nice to meet her.'

He pulled a face. 'I wouldn't bank on it. She's never been our biggest fan, but that might be because she has a musical ear.'

Smiling, Bel said, 'What does she do?'

'She runs a school for children with special needs. Her younger brother has Down's, which is what got her into it. Just like my sister having breast cancer got me into what I do.'

Her eyes widened. 'Your sister . . . I had no idea. Where is she? I mean . . .'

'She didn't make it,' he said sadly. 'She was seven years older than me, so I was still in my teens when she went. We were very close, in spite of the gap in our ages. It hit me hard, which is why I understand, to some degree, how it's been for you, losing Natalia. My fear is,' he went on gently, 'that you're in danger of losing yourself now, which can happen after the death of someone you love. Please don't let it be the case for you. I promise, it's not what she'd want.'

Bel lowered her eyes. How could he possibly know what Talia wanted, when she couldn't even be sure of it herself?

'I'm sorry,' he said. 'I'm speaking out of turn . . .'

'No, no, it's fine,' she assured him. 'You're probably right, I am dwelling on it too much, or not doing enough to get over it.' She looked up and smiled. 'But I will come to your gig next Saturday night, provided I don't have the children.'

'Great,' he beamed. 'I'll look forward to it. Now, I guess I should be on my way, or I'll be late for this afternoon's clinic.'

As he wound a path through the tables Bel watched him go and couldn't help feeling slightly relieved to be alone again, given how out of practice she was at being witty or erudite. She had far too little in the way of adult conversation these days, which wasn't good; she just hoped he'd enjoyed their little chat as much as she had. On the other hand he was, and would always be, one of the most painful reminders of Talia, and because of that she couldn't be sure now if going to see his band next Saturday night would be such a great idea after all.

*

Karaoke nights were nearly always a laugh, and tonight's had turned into one of the best for ages. Though Josie and Jeff wouldn't normally have gone out boozing on a week-night, seeing it was a mate's birthday they'd made an exception and Josie was sure Jeff had enjoyed it even more than she had. He'd sung his daft old heart out up there on the stage, getting everyone up dancing and singing along to all the old faves. Even his father, who could be a miser-able sod at times, had been spotted tapping his foot and mumbling the words to 'Waterloo', before he'd managed to drop off in spite of the noise.

Jeff had driven him home now, dispensing Eileen on the way, while Josie, feeling lovely and tipsy thanks to four rum and Cokes, was weaving her way along the high street on Carly's arm.

'I don't know about you,' Carly declared, wobbling on her high heels as she brought them to an abrupt halt, 'but I'm bloody starving.' She was a large woman with short silvery hair (when it wasn't plugged with extensions and backbrushed beyond gravity), pale blue eyes and what Jeff called a happy gappy grin on account of the space between her front teeth. 'Let's go over the road and get some fish and chips.'

Finding she was hungry too, Josie tripped along after her, still singing 'I Should Be So Lucky', while managing a little dance. She and Jeff really ought to come out more often in the week, it broke things up a bit, even if the weather was bloody freezing and it meant him missing out on a couple of fares. Life was too short to be working all the time; they needed to have more fun.

'Just a couple of bags of chips for me,' she told Chen the Chippie when it was her turn to order, 'and some curry sauce. Jeff's very partial to curry sauce.'

'Spring rolls?' Chen suggested, making ready to tong some into a wrapper.

'No, no, I don't want to get fat,' she laughed.

'Listen to her,' Carly chided. 'You never got enough meat on those bones, my girl. You want to be a bit more like me, all T and A and plenty in between.'

'Whatever that's supposed to mean,' Josie giggled. *Please*

don't let her start flirting with Chen. It was beyond embarrassing when Carly teased the poor bloke, even though he barely knew enough English to understand the words. Or maybe he did and pretended not to.

'A cod lot with double chips for me,' Carly told him, 'and you can throw in a nice big sausage if you've got one.' As she nudged Josie, Josie cringed behind her smile as the little chap's glasses caught a cloud of steam from the fryer.

'Wonder what sort of action he gets from his stick of a Mrs,' Carly commented, as they carried their greasy parcels out into the night.

'What do you care?' Josie replied, pulling her collar up higher to keep out the wind. 'It's not like you fancy him, or is it?'

'Give me a break,' Carly laughed. 'I'd squash the poor bugger to death if I as much as sat on him. No, six foot six, beefy and bagloads of cash is how I like 'em, so if you know of anyone, be sure to send him round my place, won't you?'

'It's a promise,' Josie assured her. 'What happened to the bloke you met at Bar 4 One last week? The one who said he'd ring when he was back in Kesterly. Have you heard anything yet?'

'Have I heck. He was only after one thing, same as the rest, but at least he was polite and gave us a kiss before he left in the morning.' Hooking Josie's arm, she drew her in closer as she said, 'I swore I wouldn't tell anyone this, so keep it to yourself, right?'

'Of course,' Josie promised, already knowing she was probably the only one who would keep the secret.

'Don't laugh now,' Carly warned, 'but remember I told you Esme Spark went home with some bloke when we went out on Saturday night? A right good-looker he was too, wouldn't have minded him for meself, but she got in first so you have to respect that. Anyway, wait for this, you're going to piss yourself when I tell you. She only wakes up on Sunday morning to find he's gone and left a couple of twenties on the bedside table.'

Josie's eyes widened. 'You don't mean . . .'

'I do.'

'No way!'

'I swear. The bastard only thought she was a prozzie. I could hardly keep a straight face when she told me. She was that mad I thought she was going to smash something, or do me some sort of injury. But like I said to her, at least it was a couple of twenties, think how she'd have felt if it had been a couple of tens!'

As Carly hooted with laughter, Josie dutifully laughed too and felt thankful all over again that her friends had long since given up trying to talk her into joining them for girls' nights out. It wasn't that she never enjoyed the odd binge on the town, sometimes they could be a good laugh, but she always hated it when the others started getting off with blokes. She never knew where to put herself, and if anyone tried to chat her up she just about wanted to die.

'You're definitely not your mother's daughter,' Carly would often tell her.

'Nothing like,' Eileen would confirm in disgust. 'She's a right bloody prude if you ask me.'

'No I'm not,' Josie would protest. 'I just happen to be married and it's how I want to stay.'

Fortunately no one ever mentioned the business with Dawnie Hopkins, or not these days anyway. They used to though, quite regularly, telling her to get her own back so Jeff would know what it felt like; or that she deserved to have a bit of fun after what she'd been through, 'so get on with it, girl'.

The trouble was, her idea of fun had never been to meet another bloke. All she'd ever wanted was for her marriage to mend.

'Hey, you heard about what's happening with Trev and Nina, haven't you?' Carly prompted.

Josie hadn't, but was sure she was about to.

'It turns out he's definitely got something wrong with his waterworks, so he still can't get it up, and everyone knows how desperate she is to have another kid. If you ask me, I reckon it's why he's having a problem, all the pressure is making him impotent. And who can blame him? The three they've already got would be enough to turn me celibate for life. It's just that she wants a girl, and I suppose we can understand that, you and me, when we've been so blessed with ours. Which reminds me, my Amy tells me your Lily's thinking of moving nearer to Jasper's parents after they get married. Is that right?'

Feeling suddenly sober, Josie said, 'I don't think she's got any particular plans yet. It'll depend on what jobs they manage to get when they graduate. Maybe they'll stand more chance of one if they live over that way. We'll see.'

'It would be really hard for you though, wouldn't it, if she wasn't just up the road any more. And let's face it, Bristol's not a million miles away. I know I'd hate it if my Amy moved to London, or somewhere over that way. It's bad enough that she's in Kesterly with her mates, but at least she's got a good job in Topshop and if she needs her mum she can be here in twenty minutes on the bus. If you ask me, that's the trouble with kids having an education. It makes them leave home, and though I know that's not always a bad thing, there doesn't seem any need for it if you all get along. Amy's always saying to me, "Mum, I could never manage without you," and I've got to tell you, I don't think she could.'

Though Josie would have loved Lily to be closer, she wasn't going to admit that to Carly in case it made her seem critical of Lily, or weak, or clingy. 'Wouldn't you rather she was able to stand on her own two feet?' she asked. 'I know Amy earns her own money now, but if anything was to happen to you, what would she do, with her being so dependent?'

Carly's sigh formed a white cloud around her face. 'I must admit, I do worry about that sometimes,' she confessed, 'but I expect once she's met the right bloke and they settle down together, it'll all sort itself out. I just hope he's from around here, that's all, because I'd hate it if she was somewhere I couldn't see her very often. I don't know how you stand it with your Ryan. I'd be worried out of my tiny mind if I had a kid in nick, that's for sure. Well, I know you are, and I hope he realises what stress he's putting you under. Boys! They never think about anyone but themselves, do they? When are you seeing him again?'

'Saturday,' Josie replied. 'Did I tell you Lily and I went

to the dress designer's last weekend?' she went on, changing the subject.

'Yeah, you did. Sounds bloody lovely it does, ivory lace and a fishtail bottom. She'll look like a movie star, so she will. You'll have to be finding yourself an outfit soon. Are you going to look in Bristol, while you're up there? I don't mind coming with you if Lily's busy.'

'That's kind of you. I'll let you know how it goes.' As they'd reached Carly's front gate by now, Josie gave her a quick peck on the cheek and after saying goodnight she skirted round the bins and hurried along the path to home. She was fond of Carly, she really was, but she couldn't deny a part of her was often glad to get away from her.

After putting the chips in the microwave to reheat, she was just lighting the gas fire when Jeff came stomping in through the front door, scraping his feet on the mat and banging his hands together.

'It's bloody warmer in the car,' he grumbled, keeping his coat on as he came into the lounge.

'I expect it is,' she sympathised, turning the fire up high. 'Why don't you pop up and put the electric blanket on so it'll be all nice and snug for when we get into bed.'

With some muttering under his breath he took himself off upstairs, and by the time he came down again Josie was laying out plates of curry sauce and chips in front of the fire.

'Thought we'd have a little picnic,' she told him as he came into the room.

'Did you win the lottery?' he asked. 'I thought you were skint till Friday.'

'I was, but you lent me a fiver, remember, and we've only got chips, no fish.'

'That fiver was for your bus fare tomorrow,' he reminded her. 'How are you going to manage to get home again if you've already spent half of it?'

'I might pick up some tips at the caff. If I don't I'll ask Fliss for an advance. She's usually quite good about that. So, are you going to come and eat?'

Stripping off his gloves, he sank down next to her, and

picked up his plate. 'Bloody good idea,' he told her after the first mouthful. 'This is really hitting the spot.'

She smiled. 'I thought it might. So, you got your dad home all right?'

'Just about. Stupid bugger tripped on the front step, but I managed to catch him before he hit the deck. Swore at me blind, he did, as if it was my fault, but at least he never minds going home. Your mother, being your mother, tried to persuade me to take her into town for a bit more action.'

Josie shook her head. 'Why aren't I surprised by that? I hope she doesn't start playing her music and upsetting the neighbours again. One of them threatened to call the police last week, and she never helps matters the way she screams at them to shut up, like they're the ones making the noise.'

'She's always been the same, and I can't see her changing any time soon.'

'Chance would be a fine thing. Anyway, you haven't told me yet how much Trev wants for a down payment on a new car.' She wondered if he and Trev ever discussed Trev's waterworks problem, but somehow doubted it. Nor would she tell him, since he was no fonder of gossip than she was.

'He said he'd be happy to take the old one off our hands as a deposit, but we'd have to find a hundred and fifty a month after that, and I don't reckon, once I've paid me insurance, and road tax and petrol and everything, that we'd be able to pull that much together. Not if business goes on the way it is.'

'It's always slow at this time of year,' she reminded him. 'It'll change come the spring, and we'll manage somehow till then.' She wasn't sure how, they just would.

'I wish I had your optimism,' he grunted, and helped himself to more chips.

'You do,' she teased, 'you just feel you have to hide it, but I know it's there somewhere.'

Cocking an eyebrow, he ate some more, and watched her as she ate too.

'What?' she asked when she realised he was still staring at her.

He shook his head. 'Nothing.'

'Yes there is. I can tell.'

'I was only wondering,' he finally confessed, 'if Bob plies all the women with free cocktails, or if it's just you.'

She laughed in surprise. 'Two rum and Cokes is what he gave me, so not cocktails, and if you count his buy one, get one free offer tonight, he didn't give me anything.'

'So who paid for the two, because I know I didn't?'

She blinked. 'I thought you did.'

He shook his head. 'I'm telling you, that bloke's got the hots for you, always has had.'

Josie started to grin. 'You wouldn't be jealous, would you?' she teased, dipping her head to peer up into his face.

'Give me a break,' he growled. 'I'm just saying, that's all, but you ought to go careful, you don't want people talking about you like there's something going on.'

Josie waved a hand. 'Even if they did they'd be wrong, so what's there to worry about?'

'He was your boyfriend once.'

'Yeah, when we were twelve. Anyway, you should be thankful you didn't have to pay, given how tight things are this week. Have you got any fares booked for tomorrow?'

'Not yet, but I'll give the cab office in town a ring tomorrow, see if they've got anything going over there. If they have, and it works out, I might be able to give you a lift in.'

'That'd be nice,' she said, reaching over to turn down the fire. 'I was going to ask Fliss if she might need me for an extra couple of days now Mr Crover-Keene's given me the heave-ho.' Bloody nice that was, letting her clean his place top to bottom before telling her he'd decided to hire a Filipino couple to take care of the house and garden from now on. Still, at least he'd had the decency to give her a hundred-quid pay-off, which had gone straight into financing the car repair.

Realising he was watching her again, she put her head to one side and regarded him steadily. 'What's going on?' she prompted. 'Why do you keep looking at me?'

Finishing his chips, he said, 'I had to go and pick up Debbie Prince from Eastbrook today.'

Josie's insides started to knot. Debbie Prince was

renowned on the estate for being as aggressive and potentially lethal as her husband and brothers, all of whom were serving time for murder. She was also the mother of Shane Prince, the boy who'd got Ryan into trouble. Eastbrook was the nearest women's prison.

'She's a right piece of work,' Jeff went on sourly. 'Cussing and screaming into her phone at someone the whole way back.'

'So, has she been inside?' she asked.

'From the sound of it she'd been visiting one of her daughters. They're a bad lot, those Princes.'

'You didn't tell her who you were, I suppose.'

'What kind of fool do you take me for? It was bad enough having to be in the same car as her, I definitely didn't want to get into how we're connected.'

Flinching at the mere thought of being connected to a woman like that, Josie said, 'So where did you drop her?'

'At home, if that's what she calls it. Looks a right dump to me with plastic sheeting in half the windows and a smashed-up old telly in the garden. It's streets like hers, and families like hers, that give this estate such a bad name.'

'You have to wonder how she can afford a taxi,' Josie commented.

He snorted his derision. 'They're never short of cash, that lot. It's how they come by it you shouldn't ask about. It's just a shame they don't use a few bob of it to buy a bar of soap once in a while, because I'm not lying when I tell you she stank. I felt like going to fumigate the car after she got out.'

Shuddering, Josie collected up their plates and carried them out to the kitchen. 'Did she say anything about Shane?' she asked as he came to put the kettle on.

'Not that I heard,' he replied.

'I wonder if she even cares about him,' she said, squirting a short stream of washing-up liquid into the bowl, and running the hot tap. 'I never see her at the prison.' Thinking of Ryan was making her feel sad, and needful of being able to put her arms around him. She guessed he was probably in bed by now, maybe even asleep, alone in his cell. It was how she wanted to think of him, how she *must* think of him at night or she'd never have a minute's peace. During the day she'd learned to tell herself he was busy working in the kitchen, or the library, or learning how to weld, which he'd recently got into. She couldn't allow herself to think of what hell the Prince boy and his gang might be putting him through, or any of the other inmates. She just hoped to God they weren't doing their worst, or he wasn't self-harming or starving himself half to death.

What good was going to come of him being in that place?

None she could even begin to imagine.

'The best times of all,' he'd written in his last letter, 'are when you come to see me, Mum. It makes me feel better to see your face, and after you've gone I look at your photo and remember all the things you said.'

What on earth was he going to do if she had to tell him she had cancer? Though she'd made up her mind not to think too much about it until she got the results, she had to accept that the surgeon might have got it right. If he had she'd still go to see Ryan, obviously, but it might not be so often if she had to have treatment.

Feeling suddenly afraid, she slid her arms round Jeff's waist and rested her head on his back. Though she was aware of the dressing on her boob, she was sure he wouldn't be able to feel it too, not through her bra.

'What's all this about?' he asked in surprise.

'Just feeling like a bit of a cuddle,' she said, keeping hold of him. She'd had a letter yesterday, telling her to go for a bone scan next Monday and a CT scan the day after. She'd rung her GP in a bit of a panic, but Dr Moore had assured her the scans were simply a precaution to make sure nothing had spread.

It didn't feel as comforting now as it had after she'd spoken to Dr Moore. Did everyone have these scans? And what if it had spread? What was she going to do then?

'Do you have to squeeze so tight?' Jeff grumbled.

Easing her grip a little, she said, 'I wish you'd come with me to see Ryan.'

Breaking away from her, he said, 'I've never set foot in a prison in my life, and I don't intend to start now, not for anyone.'

'But he's your son! How can you just turn your back on him?'

'I'm not going over this again, Josie. You know my position on it, and it's not going to change. Now, I'm going up to bed. I'll set the alarm for six,' and leaving her to finish the washing up alone, he took himself off upstairs.

'Have you ever been here before?' Kristina was asking Bel as their taxi pulled into the White Hart car park. It was a pitch-dark night, rainy and cold, making the brightly lit pub seem as welcoming as a lighthouse in a storm.

'Actually, a few times,' Bel admitted. Should she add that it had always been with Talia, Nick and the children? Deciding not to, she said, 'The food's usually very good, and there's a reasonable selection of wine. Now we just have to hope that the music is up to scratch.'

'I looked them up online,' Kristina confessed as Bel paid the driver, 'and they've had some pretty good write-ups.'

Having done the same, Bel said, 'I can imagine Harry telling us they've all been posted by his mother, especially the one that singled him out as a "top trumpeter".' Smiling as Kristina came to link her arm, she said, 'Thanks for coming.'

'I'm looking forward to it,' Kristina assured her. 'It's not often I get a night out, or that we manage to spend some time together.'

Knowing that they'd never been anywhere or done anything just the two of them, Bel tried hard to continue feeling friendly towards her as they hurried over to the main doors. Actually, it wasn't that difficult given how grateful she was to Kristina for offering to come tonight, since she'd never have braved it alone and she really hadn't wanted to miss it. She couldn't remember the last time she'd been out in the evening – without Nick and the children – and though she'd hoped Nick would offer to accompany her, she'd accepted that it was perhaps more appropriate for it to be Kristina.

'Don't forget to send Harry my best,' Nick had said as he'd walked her and Kristina out to the taxi. 'I'm sorry to be missing the show, tell him, but someone has to babysit.'

As he'd hugged her Bel had wondered what he was really thinking about her being in touch with the surgeon who'd played such a huge part in their lives over the past few years. Was he confused, or upset by it? Did he feel it was time they moved on and tried to forget the pain and sadness that had filled the time they'd known him? To a degree Nick had already managed that, given the fact he was married again. As for her, it wasn't as though she'd gone out of her way to see Harry Beck, it had simply happened when she'd dropped into the clinic, and in truth a large part of the reason she'd felt compelled to come tonight wasn't so much to see the band, as to avoid seeming rude if she didn't.

Which is just plain nonsense, she was telling herself as they waited inside the door for the receptionist to find their tickets. *He's almost certainly forgotten he's invited you, and even if he hasn't why would he care whether you're here or not?*

'Got them,' the receptionist declared, and handed over a small white envelope. 'Two tickets for Isabella Monkton.'

'How much is that?' Kristina asked, reaching for her purse.

'No, let me,' Bel insisted. 'Tonight's my treat.'

'They're complimentary,' the receptionist informed them.

Kristina turned to Bel with interested eyes.

Since Harry wasn't there to thank, Bel could only shrug. 'Which way do we go?' she asked the receptionist.

'Straight through to the main bar. We're expecting a bit of a crowd in tonight.'

'So they're quite popular?' Kristina enquired.

'I'd say so, especially with the oldies.'

Somehow knowing Harry would find that amusing, Bel enjoyed the moment and followed Kristina along a shadowy hallway into a large, heavy-beamed bar. Fires were crackling in the hearths each end and the crowd seemed to be made up from all generations.

Since there were no free tables, they squeezed their way through to the counter, ducking to avoid dripping pints as they passed overhead, and doing their best to avoid being trodden on.

110

'I had no idea it was going to be like this,' Bel shouted above the noise. 'Are you OK? Do you want to leave?'

'No way,' Kristina cried. 'We'll be fine once we find somewhere safe to stand.'

Bel quickly slipped into a small space as it opened up and after finally managing to order two glasses of Sauvignon Blanc, she followed Kristina to a pillar with a narrow shelf attached.

'They're not due on for another twenty minutes,' Kristina shouted as they clinked glasses. 'Why don't we see if there's somewhere to sit in one of the other bars?'

Agreeing that might be a good idea, Bel led the way to a small lounge next to the restaurant with a sluggish fire in the hearth, and an empty booth in a corner where they made themselves cosy.

'That's better,' Kristina sighed, unwinding her scarf and shaking out her glorious dark hair. She really was lovely, Bel was thinking. She could see why Nick was so smitten; any red-blooded man would be when confronted with so much alluring femininity.

'So, come on,' Kristina whispered, her eyes sparkling with mischief, 'what's he like?'

Bel regarded her in surprise. 'Do you mean Harry?' she asked. Of course she did. 'Actually, he's very good-looking, and charming and generous,' she added, holding up the tickets. 'And he's also very much married, so if you're thinking what I think you are . . .'

Kristina's face fell. 'I was,' she admitted. 'Honestly, why is it all the best ones are taken?'

It was on the tip of Bel's tongue to say something about Nick, but realising it might sound bitter, or worse, jealous, she managed a simple shrug as she replied, ''Twas ever thus. Anyway, I'm sorry if you feel it's a waste of time being here now . . .'

'Oh no, no, no.' Kristina jumped in at once. 'I was just teasing, though I have to confess, I'd be so happy for you if you were to meet someone special, and I know Nick would be too.'

Bel's smile was faint as she took a sip of wine.

Apparently sensing she'd caused some sort of offence,

Kristina went on, 'I never seem to get it quite right with you, do I? I keep trying, but nothing I say . . .' She shook her head helplessly.

Bel started to speak, but Kristina hadn't finished.

'I know you resent me for taking Talia's place,' she said frankly, 'and I understand . . .'

'I don't resent you,' Bel interrupted, wishing they'd stayed in the bar where the noise would have prevented any kind of heart-to-heart.

'Yes you do,' Kristina informed her, 'and in your shoes I'm sure I'd feel the same. It hasn't been long since your sister . . .'

'Please, let's not talk about this,' Bel cut in quickly. 'There's nothing to be gained . . .'

'But I think there is,' Kristina insisted. 'Whether you like it or not we're part of the same family now, and I want to be your friend, Bel. I really do.'

'You are,' Bel assured her. 'OK, I realise I might seem a little standoffish at times, but that's just the way I am, so please don't read anything into it, or think that I feel anything negative towards you, because I truly don't.' How convincing she sounded; she might even have believed it herself.

Kristina was regarding her sceptically. 'I know how close you were to Talia,' she said carefully, 'so I get that you're not happy about Nick marrying again . . .'

'Nick has his own life to lead, and if being married to you is what he wants I'm happy for him.'

Though Kristina didn't contradict her, disbelief seemed to hang in the air anyway. 'You also have your own life to lead,' she said gently, 'and I worry that we take up too much of it, always relying on you to have the children when we go away, expecting you . . .'

'They're my niece and nephew, I've been in their lives since they were born, so it makes sense for them to come to me. I don't think you'd find that they'd want to go anywhere else.'

'Of course they wouldn't. They adore you, anyone can see that, but it concerns me – Nick too – that they've become such an enormous part of your life.'

Bel would have liked to walk out now, or at the very least to argue with that, but how could she when Kristina was right? She was absorbing herself in Talia's children as though they were all that mattered, which actually they were. She could also see how difficult she must be making it for Kristina to bond with them when she was holding them so close to her. The trouble was, she didn't want Kristina to be the one to watch them grow, to be there for them when times were hard, to share their laughter and tears, failures and triumphs, when all those precious moments should belong to Talia. And if not to Talia, then to her.

'I'm not quite sure how to say this,' Kristina began awkwardly, 'but I want to ask you . . . I mean, it's probably none of my business, except it is actually. I'm sorry, I'm not making much sense, am I? What I'm trying to say is I understand if you have feelings for Nick . . .'

'For God's sake,' Bel cried angrily. 'He's my sister's husband . . .'

'But your sister isn't here any more, and I know you and Nick have always been close.'

'Like brother and sister.'

'Yes, but maybe it goes deeper than that – for you.'

'And maybe it doesn't,' Bel snapped. 'Frankly, Kristina, you're speaking way out of line now, and all I can say is I hope you haven't been discussing this with Nick, planting your suspicions in his mind . . .'

'I didn't have to. He's the one who brought it up. He's really worried about you and how . . .' she grimaced, 'well, how dependent you've become on your relationship with him and the children. Not that he doesn't want to be there for you, that truly isn't the case, because he cares about you deeply. He's just concerned that you're feeling you have to step into Talia's shoes . . .'

Bel's eyes flashed furiously.

'I'm sorry, I'm sorry, that didn't come out right. What I'm saying is, if you do have romantic feelings towards Nick . . .'

'I don't, so can we spare ourselves any more embarrassment and end this conversation now?'

113

Kristina's eyes fell to her drink.

'Did it ever occur to you,' Bel suddenly heard herself saying, 'that Nick married you on the rebound? You met so soon after Talia died, at a time when he needed to escape just how awful everything had been so he could pretend, at least for a while, that none of it was real. You provided him with that, you were wonderful to him, warm, understanding, supportive in ways that it wasn't possible for the rest of us to be when we were trying to deal with our own grief. You were great for him then, a real godsend, but frankly . . .' Suddenly realising what she was about to say, she reeled back in horror. *I don't think he loves you at all.* No matter if she believed it to be true, and she didn't even know that she did, to hurt Kristina that way would be utterly unforgivable.

'Go on,' Kristina prompted.

Bel shook her head. 'I'm sorry, I'm not really thinking straight,' she mumbled. Realising she needed to say more, she added, 'You're right, I am still struggling with Talia's death, and perhaps I'm too close to the children. You're so good with them, and they're clearly very fond of you . . .' She took a breath. 'Maybe we shouldn't spoil the evening by getting any deeper into this tonight.' It could be that the evening was ruined anyway, but they couldn't leave now she'd collected the tickets or Harry might end up thinking they'd walked out of the performance.

Did it matter what Harry thought?

Actually, yes it did.

It mattered too that she wasn't trying hard enough with Kristina, and that Kristina thought she was in love with Nick, and maybe a part of her was – and always would be, because that part was Talia. They couldn't be separated, they'd shared too many of each other's genes for that, which was why so much of her had died that day and so much of Talia continued to live.

For the next few minutes Kristina grew considerably in Bel's estimation as she took it upon herself to try lightening the mood in spite of how forthright, even cruel Bel had been to her. She chatted on merrily about various concerts she'd been to over the years, the type of music she preferred, and the way Nick's passion for Irish folk music was starting to appeal to her. In return Bel made her own effort by recalling some of the live shows she'd helped design sets for during her time at uni, and how she'd once had a brief fling with a musician who'd gone on to great fame. When she confessed who it was Kristina's eyes rounded in awe.

'Are you ever in touch with him now?' she asked.

'No way,' Bel replied. 'He was completely self-obsessed and coked out of his mind half the time. From what I read in the press he hasn't changed.'

'Mm, I've read much the same,' Katrina commented, glancing at her watch. 'Maybe we should think about going back now?'

Getting to her feet, Bel made to pick up her drink, but instead she impulsively caught hold of Kristina's hand. 'Thanks for coming,' was all she could manage, in spite of there being a lot more she wanted to say, in regret, friendship, perhaps even in anger.

Kristina smiled and closed her other hand around Bel's.

A few minutes later they were at the back of the main bar again, with a reasonable view through to the stage where The Medics were already tuning up their instruments and exchanging some light-hearted banter with the crowd.

'Which one's Harry?' Kristina asked, leaning in to Bel.

'The trumpeter,' Bel reminded her.

Kristina slid her a look. 'Are you sure he's married?'

'Totally sure.'

'Wife here?'

'I don't think so. Apparently she's not a fan of his type of music.'

Appearing both surprised and unimpressed, Kristina turned back to the front, and as the band launched into the opening bars of 'All the Things You Are' the audience fell away from their conversations to listen and sway with the beat.

Though Bel could not claim to be an expert judge in these matters, to her mind Harry was sensational on the trumpet, it truly seemed to breathe and sing as he played, and when his first solo ended it seemed everyone else thought so too, from the resounding applause. Next came

'Bumpin' on Sunset', which got several people dancing, and when 'Stompin' at the Savoy' began even more people swung into motion. By the time the fifth or sixth number was under way just about everyone was on their feet, and many were singing along. Bel had to admit she didn't know all the words, or indeed the tunes, but it didn't matter, the beat and atmosphere were irresistible. As was the comedy the band injected into proceedings, either squabbling about what to play next, or encouraging members of the audience to come up and join them, or hitting a sudden pause in the middle of a song to try and catch people out.

It was no wonder they were so popular, Bel was reflecting to herself an hour or more later as they played a fourth encore. They weren't only good musicians, they were born entertainers.

'And they're all surgeons?' Kristina asked above the cheers.

'Apart from the guitarist, apparently. In his other life he's a pathologist.'

'Amazing. If they didn't all have such fantastically important jobs I'd say they were a great loss to the jazz world. As it is, I guess we'd rather have them doing what they're doing. I wonder how many people here are colleagues, or patients?'

Having no idea, Bel only smiled and raised a hand as Harry caught her eye and tipped his bowler. It gave her quite a thrill to be recognised and even sort of singled out.

'Fancy another drink?' Kristina said in her ear.

'Why not?' Bel replied. 'Neither of us is driving.'

'Great. Two more Sauvignons coming up, if I can get to the bar.'

As she braved the crush a table in front of Bel started to empty, so quickly plonking herself down she grabbed another stool for Kristina and took out her phone. Not that she expected there to be any messages, it was simply habit – and the fact that she didn't want to sit there with nothing to do.

To her amazement there was a text from Harry sent only a minute ago. *Great to see you. Stay for a drink if you don't have to rush off?? H.*

Unsure whether or not to respond, she glanced towards the stage and with a small rush of pleasure she spotted him coming towards her.

'Hey,' he smiled, helping himself to Kristina's stool. 'Did you come alone?'

'No, Nick's wife is with me. She's at the bar. Can we get you a drink?'

'Ben's already on the case.' His eyes narrowed slightly as he regarded her.

Feeling herself flush, she said, 'The show was fantastic. I think I'm a fan.'

'Only think?'

Laughing, she watched with mounting amusement as he teased a bunch of older women who fluttered around him claiming to be groupies. Though no one said so she guessed at least one was a patient, the silk scarf around her head being the giveaway. Another was so skeletal it was highly probable she was part of his caseload too, though she might simply have been naturally thin. As the women moved on a young couple descended upon him, tousling his hair and embracing him warmly.

'My cousin, Semeena, and her husband Joel,' he explained. 'You two, this is Bel Monkton, kind of an old friend, and a new one too.'

The stunning Semeena quickly broke into a smile. 'Hey, Bel, lovely to meet you,' she said, grasping Bel's hand. 'Is this the first time you've seen the band?'

'It is,' Bel confessed, 'but I hope it won't be the last.'

'Hold back on the flattery,' Joel warned, 'or it'll go to his head. Are you here alone, Bel? Can we get you a drink?'

'I'm fine, thanks,' Bel assured him. 'My friend's at the bar, but please join us if you're not rushing off.'

Before Joel could answer Ben Weaver, the guitarist-cum-pathologist, was setting a tray of beers on the table while Jim Sayer, the vocalist-drummer-paediatrician, followed up with bags of crisps, nuts and pork scratchings.

'Glad to see the medics sticking to a healthy diet,' Semeena commented, helping herself to a beer. 'Joel, grab those stools over there so we can all sit down.'

Quickly scooping up four, Joel passed them round, and

by the time Kristina returned the entire band plus several more friends were gathered around the table with Bel.

'This is Kristina,' Bel informed Harry, as a surprised-looking Kristina handed her a drink. 'Kristina, meet Harry Beck and The Medics . . .'

'Hey, I like that,' Harry cried.

'Yeah, don't get used to it,' Jim Sayer told him. 'Good to meet you, Kristina. Here, take this seat. I'll get another.'

For the next half an hour, as everyone talked over each other, teasing, baiting, competing with jokes and criticising their performance, Bel was reminded of the old days when she'd had dozens of friends. It felt good to be with people again, uplifting, almost intoxicating, yet at the same time she was aware of being slightly anxious, as though this wasn't where she ought to have been.

'Are you OK?' Harry asked, apparently noticing she'd gone quiet.

Immediately she brightened. 'Yes, I'm great,' she assured him. 'Just a bit overwhelmed, I suppose. It's the first time I've been with so many people for a while.'

'Then I'm doubly glad you came. You need to get out. Someone as attractive as you shouldn't be hiding themselves away.'

Her eyes sparkled as she looked at him. 'Doctorly advice I can take,' she responded. 'Compliments I have a bit more trouble with.'

He scowled. 'I should have thought you'd be used to them by now. Maybe that's what it is, you've heard them all before and really don't want to hear them again.'

'Oh, I think I can manage it,' she laughed. 'Do you always pull such a crowd when you play?'

He waggled a hand from side to side. 'Often depends who we're doing it for. Tonight's beneficiary is the children's hospice where Jim's one of the trustees. We almost always get a good crowd for them. Actually, we don't usually do too badly for your lot either.'

'My lot?' Bel asked, making a mental note to send a donation to the hospice.

'Breast Cancer Care,' he stated. 'Don't you belong?'

'Yes, of course, well kind of.'

118

'And what do you do the rest of the time, if I'm allowed to ask?'

'Of course you are. Normally I'm buying and renovating houses, but that came to a halt when Talia got sick. I'm kind of getting back into it now . . .'

'Harry, is that your phone?' Semeena shouted, glancing at it on the table.

Realising it was, he scooped it up and cried in mock horror, 'Oh my God, it's the wife!' and getting to his feet he clicked on.

Leaning towards Bel, Kristina said, 'I'm not sure I'd let him out on his own if he was mine.'

Not rising to it, Bel said, 'What time's our taxi supposed to be coming?'

'Eleven.'

'Where do you have to get to?' Jim Sayer enquired. 'Maybe one of us can give you a lift.'

Kristina grimaced. 'I'm all the way out in Senway, so I couldn't . . .'

'That's where Ben lives,' Jim informed her. 'I'm sure he won't mind dropping you off. How about you, Bel? Are you Senway too?'

'No, I'm Kesterly, so . . .' She broke off as Harry returned saying, 'Apparently the Beck boys are refusing to go to bed, so I've been summoned to lay down the law.'

'Oh, they must be so scared,' Semeena mocked.

'Terrified,' he agreed, picking up his beer to down it. 'Bel, it was lovely to see you. Thanks a million for coming. Actually, how are you getting home? Can I drop you somewhere?'

'No, I'm fine,' she assured him. 'I have a taxi booked.'

'OK, if you're sure. Great to meet you, Kristina. Please give my regards to Nick.'

'Of course,' she smiled. 'And thanks for a great evening. We're definitely going to follow you on Facebook and Twitter.'

Harry chuckled. 'Good luck with that. We're hopeless at keeping it up. Anyway, sorry to rush off. See you guys whenever. Take care of yourself, Bel, and keep in touch.'

A moment later he was gone, and Bel couldn't help feeling glad that her taxi was due.

'Are you sure you're OK about going back on your own?' Kristina asked as they walked outside together.

'Of course,' Bel insisted. 'It makes much more sense for you to go with Ben. I'll give you a call in the morning.'

'Are you coming over for lunch? The children have made your favourite dessert.'

Bel's eyebrows arched. 'And that would be?'

'White chocolate cheesecake?'

She laughed. 'I thought that was last week.'

'It was, but they wanted to make it again. Shall we say twelve, as usual, and go to the pub for a drink before we eat?'

'Sounds lovely. Thanks for coming this evening. I hope you've enjoyed it.'

'I really did. The music was wonderful, so was Harry. I expect half his patients fall in love with him.'

'Probably more than half,' Bel agreed wryly.

'And the other half think he's better than God.'

'Yes,' Bel smiled, 'I imagine they do.'

Chapter Seven

'Josie, there you are. Do come in,' Harry Beck invited as a nurse brought Josie to his door. 'How are you? No trouble getting here this morning, I hope?'

'No, the bus was on time,' she assured him. 'I got the right one this time. It brings me straight to Blackberry Hill.'

'That's good, and you don't have to worry about parking if you use public transport. Would you like to sit down?'

Feeling as jittery as the wrens she'd put crumbs out for that morning, Josie perched on the same chair she'd sat on before and clutched her bag to her chest. It was a bit milder out today, so she was wearing her dusky pink wool coat and smartest brown leather boots. She'd put some make-up on too, though she wasn't quite sure why. Maybe she'd thought it would bolster her confidence if she made an effort, or it could have been because Jeff had said she was looking peaky.

'Are you all right?' he'd asked, as she'd come down the stairs at seven o'clock this morning. 'You didn't see a ghost up there, did you? You've got no colour in you.'

'I'm fine,' she'd insisted. 'Just didn't sleep all that well. Unlike some,' she'd added with a twinkle. 'Snoring for flipping England, you were. I had to stick my earplugs in or you might have burst my eardrums.'

'Very funny, given you're the snorer in the family. Are you going to the jobcentre today, or did Fliss give you an extra shift at the caff?'

'Both. Jobcentre this morning, caff this afternoon.' It was only half a lie since she was working later, and anyway, she might manage to get to the jobcentre after her appointment with Mr Beck, in which case there would be no lie at all. Not that she didn't tell little fibs where she had to, especially if it was going to spare someone's feelings; she just didn't like hiding things from Jeff, in spite of all he'd hidden from her in the past.

She was sure that didn't happen any more though; in fact they'd seemed quite close lately, ever since the night they'd had a chip picnic in front of the fire. They'd ended up having a lovely cuddle when they'd gone to bed, all snug and warm with the electric blanket on and duvet wrapped around them, and Jeff hadn't seemed to mind, or even particularly notice, that she'd kept her bra on. The next day he'd only brought home some flowers. He hadn't done that in ages . . . Actually she couldn't remember him ever doing it, and she didn't care a bit that they'd been reduced to a pound in Asda because they were about to go over, it was the thought that counted. Two cuddles in as many days was almost unheard of for them, and though they hadn't been that intimate again since, she felt sure they would have been if she hadn't been afraid of him insisting she take off her bra. She didn't want him finding the dressing and start asking questions, especially when she had no proper answers to give.

Of course, the flowers had made her worry that he'd found himself another woman, because that was what men did when they were cheating on their wives. Flowers, chocolates, lacy undies. He hadn't done that when he was seeing Dawnie. Maybe if he had she'd have cottoned on sooner.

Harry Beck was fixing her with those magnetic eyes of his and she could feel herself starting to shrink inside. He was going to confirm what he'd said before, then she'd have to face what it would mean, and she didn't think she could.

Yes you can, Josie. You're not a coward, and remember it might not be as bad as you fear.

'So, Josie,' he began gently, 'how did you get on having the scans? They weren't too bad, were they?'

'No, they were fine,' she assured him, because actually they hadn't been any trouble at all. Quite straightforward, was how one of the nurses had put it, and she was so matter-of-fact that Josie had more or less felt the same way. *Please don't let them have found anything else. Please. Please.*

'That's good,' Mr Beck was saying. 'Any more backaches?'

Surprised by the question, since she was sure it was the nurse, Yvonne, she'd mentioned them to, not him, she said, 'No, not really.' They weren't significant, were they? He was probably just being thorough, or polite.

He turned to have a read through his notes. She gazed at his profile, very dark and Roman, and his hands, which were elegant for a man, and probably perfect for a surgeon. Was he going to be cutting her open? She recoiled from the thought of it.

'So, the results of your biopsy are back,' he stated, turning to look at her.

Her heart began thudding so hard he could surely hear it. The news was bad. She could see it in his eyes.

'I'm afraid they're confirming what I suspected, that you have a grade three inflammatory breast cancer,' he told her gently.

Even though she should have expected it, she still felt as though she'd been punched. Grade three? Out of how many? What did it mean?

'It's also spread to the lymph glands,' he added.

Oh God, was that as serious as it sounded?

'It's all treatable,' he assured her, as though reading her mind. 'Have you looked up this type of cancer on the Internet since you were last here?'

She shook her head. 'I didn't want to scare myself,' she confessed, 'and I hoped you were going to be wrong. If you were I wouldn't need to know what it was.'

Smiling his understanding, he said, 'The pathology shows that your cancer is HER2 positive. HER2 is a protein which promotes the growth of the cells, but we can treat it with a specific targeted drug . . .'

Promotes the growth. Josie was too stunned even to react any more.

'It's the aggressive nature of this type of cancer,' he was saying, 'that made the scans particularly important. We needed to find out if it has spread to any other part of your body, and from what we can see it's still not clear whether it has.'

Josie was barely breathing. A strange noise was buzzing in her ears, making it hard for her to hear. She wanted to pass out, or wake up and find she was dreaming. *Please God don't let any of this be real.* An aggressive cancer, spread to the lymph nodes and they couldn't even tell her if it had gone any further. *It's all treatable,* he'd said. *Hang on to that Josie, just hang on to that.*

'I realise how upsetting this is for you,' he said, seeming upset himself, 'but I promise we're going to be doing everything we can to beat this into remission, starting with a course of chemotherapy in order to shrink the tumour.'

Josie's mouth went dry. *Chemotherapy. Tumour.* She hated those words, didn't want to accept that they were being applied to her.

'. . . the end of the treatment,' he was telling her, 'is when I'll operate. In your case I'm afraid this is likely to mean a mastectomy. I want to warn you of that now to give you some time to come to terms with it before it happens.'

Josie tried to speak, but could find no words. This was so much worse than she'd allowed herself to imagine. Chemotherapy; mastectomy; scans with no proper results.

'Yvonne, the senior breast-care nurse,' he continued, 'is going to talk to you in a minute about what happens from here, but basically we've already made an appointment for you to see the oncologist so she can go through everything with you. If I'm right,' he checked his computer, 'you're booked in for next Monday at eleven.' His eyes returned to hers. 'The sooner we start the treatment, the sooner we'll be back in control, and that's where we want to be. In control.'

Josie's voice was hoarse as she said, 'My daughter – my daughter's getting married in August.'

The darkness of his eyes seemed to deepen. 'Then I promise to schedule the operation so it won't clash with the wedding.'

As though caught in his magnetism, Josie continued to regard him. She wondered how hard it was for him to break this sort of news, how many times he did it in a day or a week, how many women went to pieces when they heard the worst. It was where she was now, in pieces, shattered to her very core, but he was a busy man. He had lots of other people to see, so she mustn't take up any more of his time.

Holding her handbag close, she rose to her feet. 'Thank – thank you very much for seeing me,' she stammered. 'I should probably . . .' As she swayed, he caught her and sat her down again.

'Did you come alone?' he asked gently.

She nodded.

'Then sit here for a while. There's no need to rush.'

'I have to go to work,' she told him.

'And where's that?'

'At the Seafront Cafe, down on the Promenade.'

'I know it. I take my boys in there from time to time.'

'That's nice. I've got a son too.' As the words were swallowed by a sob, she pushed a hand to her mouth. 'I'm sorry,' she whispered. 'I'm making a fool of myself. It's just a bit of a shock. I'll be right as rain in a minute.'

'As I said, there's no rush. I'm sure your employer will understand if you're a little late. Would you like to call him?'

'Her. It's a woman. She's ever so nice, but she gets a bit stressed when she's rushed off her feet and there's no one to help her. Her little boy was killed in an accident a few years ago and her husband blamed her because she was driving the car. It was terrible. The things some people have to go through. If she can survive that, then I can definitely survive this. I mean, it's not as though it's happening to my daughter. I wouldn't be able to stand that, I really wouldn't. Or if it was my son.' The mention of Ryan brought more tears flooding to her eyes. 'I don't know how I'm going to tell them,' she choked.

'All in good time,' he said soothingly. 'You need to assimilate the information for yourself first, and feel free to ask as many questions as you need to . . .'

'Are you absolutely sure?' she broke in helplessly. 'You don't think you might have got my results mixed up with someone else's?'

He shook his head sadly.

She looked at him and found herself wanting to ask where he was from, if he'd been born here, if he'd ever ridden on an elephant, because they had them in India. If that was where he was from. She'd like to go there herself and have her picture taken in front of the Taj Mahal, like Princess Diana. Someone else whose husband had gone off with another woman.

At least Jeff had stayed.

What was he going to say when she told him about this?

Hearing the door open, she glanced up to see Yvonne putting her head round. 'OK to come in?' she asked.

Josie stood up again. 'I have to go,' she told them. 'You've got lots of other people to see, and I've already taken up enough of your time. My next appointment's on Monday at eleven, you said?' She must have blanked for a moment then, because the next thing she knew Mr Beck was telling her that she must call Yvonne at any time if she had a question, or if she simply needed to talk.

Then Yvonne was steering her back along the corridor to a small waiting room and encouraging her to sit down. 'Would you like a drink?' she offered.

Josie shook her head. 'Where do I have to go for my appointment on Monday?' she asked, still clutching her bag.

'You can come here to the unit for that,' Yvonne replied. 'The treatment itself will be at the oncology centre, over on Pixashe Drive, so not far away. I'll write it all down for you.'

'How often will I have to have it?'

'Dr Pattullo will go over all that with you when you see her, but it's likely to be every three weeks for six months.'

Six months!

'And what about the side effects?' she managed. 'We can't afford for me to be out of work. I'm supposed to be going to the jobcentre today, because I lost my cleaning job a couple of weeks ago. It wasn't my fault; my employer wanted someone to live in. We've been skint ever since, and my husband's getting fed up with it. So am I. I have to bring in some money or we'll fall behind with everything and . . . Sorry,' she said, putting a hand to her head as she realised she was ranting on. 'I was asking about the side effects.'

With a comforting hand on her arm, Yvonne told her, 'They can vary according to the individual, some suffer more than others, and you may find you'll be able to work at least some of the time.'

'But what if I can't?'

'Then you'll be given other drugs to help you combat whatever the chemotherapy is doing to you.' Waiting for Josie to absorb that, she said, 'One of the really big issues for most women is the loss of their hair. Again, it may not happen to you, but if it does you'll receive plenty of information about wigs and scarves, where to get them, how to dress them, even how to help pay for them.'

Josie stared towards the door. She wasn't taking this well; she needed to get a grip and make herself understand that Yvonne was trying to be helpful. But Yvonne didn't have to face breaking this to her husband and children, or deal with what it would be like to lose her hair, or her breast, because it wasn't happening to her.

What did I do wrong to make it happen to me?

'How much time off will I have to take for the chemo itself?' she asked, bringing her head up.

'For the actual treatment, you'll be at the oncology centre for a couple of hours,' Yvonne replied. 'If they can schedule you in on a Friday, it could be that you'll be ready for work again by Monday. Obviously, no one can guarantee that, but . . .'

Josie wasn't listening. She couldn't think beyond being too sick at the weekends to go and see Ryan, and if she didn't go no one would, apart from Lily. It was already breaking Josie's heart to think of her babies in that miserable visitors' room without her, worrying about her and not knowing what to do to help.

'I have to get the bus now,' she said, rising to her feet. 'You've been very kind giving me so much time. Thank you. I'll come back on Monday. What did you say the doctor's name was?'

'Pattullo,' Yvonne answered. 'Emma Pattullo.'

'What about Mr Beck? Will I see him again?'

'Of course. When you're getting ready for surgery, and he'll be kept informed of your progress throughout the chemotherapy.'

Wishing he was the only doctor she had to see, Josie attempted a smile and was just starting for the door when she heard someone screaming,

'No! No! Please, no!'

Tears immediately stung her eyes. The poor woman, whoever she was, had obviously just been given her own bad news. Josie longed to be able to comfort her, but what on earth could she do when she was in the same state?

Unless the woman had just been told she was terminal.

Dear God, please don't let that be the case, Josie prayed inwardly as she hurried out of the unit. *Please help her, whoever she is. Please God, please, help her.*

She was feeling like she'd got off a train, and no one had noticed. Life was rushing on by, impervious to the fact that everything had changed for her. Except that wasn't true, nothing had changed really, and she was still going along as normal, looking no different to what she had before and actually feeling quite glad to be at the caff. It was like stepping into comfortable old shoes after someone had tried to force her into something that didn't fit. They were still trying, but she was having none of it for now.

'Make that three,' Rod Grimshaw, one of the caff's regulars, instructed as Josie cracked two eggs into the frying pan. 'I've got a sizeable appetite on me today.'

'Tell me a day when you haven't,' she retorted wryly. 'How many rashers?'

'Four,' he replied, rubbing a hand over his giant belly, 'and a couple of bangers. Got any black pudding and hash browns?'

'Would we ever let you down?'

Treating her to a playful wink he went to join his truck-driver mates, who were already enjoying their own lunchtime breakfasts in a corner booth next to the steamy windows.

'Do you want toast, Rod?' Josie called after him. *See, it*

was easy. All she had to do was be herself and everything was fine.

'No, fried bread for me,' he called back. 'Fliss, over here with the coffee when you're ready.'

After topping up a table full of hikers, Fliss collected an extra mug and took it to Rod with a long-suffering sigh. 'I don't know what your last slave died of,' she grumbled, 'but I bet it was something to do with coffee.'

'Bet it wasn't,' he guffawed in a way that got the others snickering too.

'Hey Jose,' Pete Little called out, between bites of his bacon buttie, 'just remembered, saw your old man this morning. He said you were looking for another cleaning job. Our Cath's about to finish up at the brewery down Flintock Lane if you're interested.'

'What are the hours?' Fliss demanded. 'I don't want it interfering with what she does here.'

'Monday to Friday, eight till midnight,' he replied. 'Hard graft, and hard on the old social life, but the pay's good. You ought to give them a call, Jose. Get in before anyone else does.'

'I will,' Josie promised, sliding Rod's eggs on to an oval china plate. *How on earth was she going to take on more work now?* The brewery wasn't an option. She didn't know what was any more. 'What's your Cath going to do, then?' she asked.

'Oh, she's got herself fixed up with some delivery company. She has to use her own car, and she only gets paid on the amount of parcels she delivers, but the hours are good and one of her mates is doing quite well with it.'

Wondering if that might be a better job for Jeff than cabbing, Josie was about to ask more when Pete's mobile grabbed his attention. 'There you go,' she said, delivering Rod's meal. 'OK for ketchup and everything?'

'Looks like it,' he replied, checking the bottles.

'So when are you going to divorce that miserable old git of yours and marry me?' Steve Vickers – Carly's ex – wanted to know. He was a good-looking bloke in a weighty, Alex Ferguson sort of way, but he'd never held any more appeal for Josie than she was sure she did for him.

'I'm working on it,' she promised, 'but there's a long line in front of you, I hope you know that.'

'You're breaking my heart,' he groaned, clasping his hands to his chest. 'Fliss, don't you turn me down too.'

Fliss wasn't listening; she was busy seating an elderly couple who'd just come in from the rain with a pushchair containing a small dog and several bags of shopping.

'Hi, Joy and Fred,' Josie called to them. 'I'll bring your usual egg on toast and will it be a sausage for Scruffy today, or a slice of streaky?'

'I think we'll have the bacon,' Fred replied, patting his dog. Though they weren't really supposed to allow pets inside the caff, Fliss always turned a blind eye to Scruffy, as long as he stayed in his pram.

'You realise I could have you up in front of the law for that,' Josie warned Steve as he gave her bottom a playful slap on his way to the Gents. 'It's called sexual harassment in the workplace.'

'I'm even better at it in the bedroom,' he assured her, and laughing along with his mates he disappeared through the swing doors.

Shaking her head, Josie set about Joy and Fred's all-day-breakfast of choice, whisking up the eggs, slotting bread into the toaster and heating up more butter ready for the scramble. The usual midday rush was only just starting, and as far as she was concerned the more customers she had to cook for today the better. Left to herself she'd probably be getting into a terrible state by now, and that wasn't going to get her anywhere, was it? No, far better to have this chance to practise hiding everything away, which was definitely what she wanted to do, at least for now, anyway.

She'd worked it all out on the bus coming back down the hill. The fact that she had cancer wasn't anyone else's business, and even if she told them they'd only end up feeling embarrassed, or start telling her about someone they knew who'd had it, or getting themselves in a pickle not knowing what to say, or how to treat her from now on. So best all round that she kept it to herself and if it turned out she had to let on at some point, well she'd deal with that when, if, the time came. And it might not, at least not for a while, because if she could persuade them to let her have chemo on Mondays, she could be sick on Tuesdays and Wednesdays, work for Fliss on Thursdays and Fridays and still go to see Ryan on Saturdays.

The only problem with that was not working for three days out of five, and given how tight everything was already . . . One answer was to try and claim benefits, but until she looked into it further she had no idea if she was entitled to any. She'd go on the computer as soon as she got home, see what she could find out – that was provided Jeff wasn't around, because he'd do his nut if he thought she was aiming to live off the state rather than get herself a job, even if she did have a good reason. She wasn't going to tell him about the cancer. Why give him the worry when he was having a difficult enough time of it already, what with his car, his lack of fares, not being able to pay for Lily's wedding, not to mention the strain of his son being in prison.

No, this was her problem to deal with, which meant it was her responsibility to make as little fuss as possible while she got it sorted, and with any luck, by the time it was all over no one, except her and Jeff, would even notice that she only had one boob.

Dear Miss Monkton,
I hope this letter finds you well.
Your recent payment has been received, for which I thank you.
There is nothing to report at this time.
Yours sincerely

There was no name at the bottom of the page, but there was no need of one since Bel knew very well who it was from.

Throwing it into the fire she watched it curl and burn, only wishing she could do the same with her memories.

Returning to her desk she picked up her mobile as it rang, and seeing it was Harry Beck she felt a ray of light breaking through the gloom.

'Hi, am I interrupting anything?' he asked.

'No, not at all,' she assured him. 'What can I do for you?'

'Actually, I'm after a favour, and I've been trying to think of a way to broach it . . .'

Curious, she said, 'Maybe just asking would help?'

'Yes, that would definitely be one way of doing it,' he responded drily. 'But I'm wondering if you might be free for an hour. I should be leaving the hospital around four. I could either come there, or we could meet somewhere in town if you'd prefer.'

Since she was waiting for a delivery, she said, 'I'm happy for you to come here. Do you remember where I live?'

'West Bay Road. Remind me of the number.'

'Two three six. The house is called Stillwater. Before you ring off, are you going to give me a clue what it's about?'

He hesitated. 'I think I'll leave it till I get there.'

Clicking off the line she sat staring at the screen for a moment, trying to puzzle out what it could be. Though a few random suspicions were happy to flaunt their temptations, she had no idea if any of them were true, so attempting to dismiss them she set about straightening the place up.

After putting another log on the fire to add more cheer to the room, she hurried upstairs to change from her running gear into a decent pair of jeans and soft wool sweater. Inspecting her reflection in the mirror, she decided on a quick coat of mascara and blusher. Not too much, or it would look obvious, just enough to liven up her complexion and brighten her eyes.

What was it about that man, she smiled wryly to herself as she started back down the stairs, that made women want to present themselves to him in the best possible light, when not only was he unavailable, but most of them were too? Of course, the fact that he was so drop-dead had to play a part in it, but for her, she guessed the main reason was pride. She wouldn't want him, or indeed any man, coming into her home to find it in a mess and her in scruffy old trackies and a sweatband. That dubious privilege belonged solely to Nick, who'd caught her in some pretty awful states during the time she'd known him, particularly over this past year. There again, she'd managed to catch

132

him at plenty of low points too, and it had never made a difference to their relationship.

Fortunately, when she'd gone over to Senway the day after her and Kristina's night out, no mention had been made of the awkward conversation of the night before. In many ways it might never have happened, though Bel hadn't forgotten it, and she didn't imagine that Kristina had either. She'd half expected Nick to bring it up when he'd walked her out to the car at the end of the day, but he'd either had too much to drink to remember, or he simply hadn't wanted to go there.

That had been almost ten days ago, and though she'd seen, or spoken to him several times since, and hadn't failed to notice how much more he was drinking these days, there had still been no mention of how close she was to the children, or what her feelings might be for him. So maybe Kristina had been testing her, trying to find out just how serious a rival she might be. If that was the case Kristina must be feeling a lot more insecure than she was letting on, which actually Bel didn't blame her for. In Kristina's shoes she probably wouldn't want the ex-sister-in-law playing such a big part in her life either.

Hearing the bell chime in the hall she checked the video-phone, saw Harry standing next to a black BMW and pressed the button to let him in. He'd only been here once before, during Talia's final days, not as her doctor, surgeons didn't make house calls, but as someone who'd got to know the family and wanted to show them that in spite of there being no more he could do, he still cared. Though he'd attended the funeral too, albeit briefly, Bel had little recollection of that day now; she wasn't even sure if she'd ever thanked him for coming.

Watching him mounting the front steps she felt ludicrously pleased to see him, and couldn't help matching his grin that was as infectious as the merriment in his eyes.

'I'd forgotten,' he declared, as she led the way into the living room, 'just how amazing this place is with that view.' He walked to the window, taking in the sluggish estuary and purpling sky where a small blade of sunlight was streaking through a distant cloud, lending an Excalibur sort of dash to the horizon.

'Would you like a drink of some kind?' she offered, as he turned back to her. 'Tea, coffee, beer, wine?'

'I'd love a beer,' he confessed. 'It's been one of those days, I'm afraid, trying to deal with the Trust, getting more funding, fighting over issues that shouldn't even be issues . . .' He sighed and shook his head. 'Don't get me started. Cheers,' he smiled as she handed him a chilled bottle of Peroni.

'Cheers,' she echoed, raising her own bottle before taking a mouthful. As she watched him drink she wondered if he'd operated this morning; he always used to on Thursdays, but maybe the schedule had changed since Talia was his patient. 'So, I'm madly intrigued,' she told him, gesturing for him to sit down at the table. 'What sort of favour do you have in mind?'

He was about to answer when his mobile rang. Checking who it was, he said, 'Sorry, I'd better take this. Won't be long.'

As he listened he took a sip of beer and glanced briefly at Bel.

'No, I'm not still at the hospital,' he declared. 'I left about twenty minutes ago.' His eyebrows shot up. 'What does it matter where I am now? No, I don't have any reason . . . Carla, will you hold up a minute?' His eyes closed as he continued to listen. 'You're kidding me,' he said in the end. 'What time?' He checked his watch. 'Why the heck didn't you give me more notice? OK, OK, I'll do it. I have to go now. See you later.' Ringing off, he took a deep breath and shook his head in clear exasperation. 'Sorry about that,' he said. 'It was my wife. Apparently I have to go and collect Neel from his football training, which means I should be leaving here in the next two minutes.'

Feeling disappointed that he couldn't stay longer, she said, 'I guess that's what happens when you have kids.'

'Tell me about it. Anyway, what I want to ask you . . . I'm probably taking liberties here, in fact I know I am, but your father's Edwin Monkton, right? The artist?'

Bel stiffened and tried to hold on to her smile. How did he know that?

'Well, I was wondering if you might be able to help me with tickets for his show next month,' he said. 'I've been reading about it, so I know tickets are only being made available to a select number of guests, but I'm totally mad about his work . . . Obviously I've tried getting some myself, but by the time I rang up they were all sold out.' He regarded her doubtfully. 'This is a real cheek, isn't it? You must be getting these requests all the time . . .'

'No, really I don't,' she assured him, thanking God that he'd have no way of knowing why, 'and if there was anything I could do, I promise I would, but I'm afraid my father and I have nothing to do with one another.'

'Oh God,' he groaned, putting a hand to his head, 'please forget I said anything. I was completely unaware of that . . .'

'Of course you were, and it doesn't matter. It's just that I'd rather not be in touch with him, so if . . .'

'It's OK, I understand. I'm sorry for bringing it up.'

'Please don't be. I'm glad you felt able to.' She'd reacted too quickly; she shouldn't just dismiss him as though there really was nothing she could do, when all it needed was a call to the organiser. She wouldn't even have to speak to her father. 'Which gallery is it?' she asked. 'If I can get hold of the owner I'm sure he or she will be able to work something out, once I tell them who I am.'

'No, please, I'm feeling bad enough . . .'

'Harry,' she laughed, 'let me do it. I'd have offered right away, but I'm afraid it threw me a little . . . When is the show on, and when would you like to go?'

After giving her the dates and the venue, he said, 'If you change your mind and decide you don't want . . .'

'It won't be a problem,' she assured him. 'How many tickets should I ask for?'

'Two?' He regarded her sheepishly. 'I guess there's no point asking if you might be free to come with me?'

Startled, she wasn't sure what to say.

'No, of course not,' he answered for her. He glanced at his watch. 'I really should be going. Sorry to have landed this on you. If I'd had any idea . . .'

'Please put it out of your mind. It's the least I can do after Kristina and I had such a lovely evening at the White Hart.'

He laughed. 'Hardly in the same league, but I'm glad you enjoyed it.'

'If you're playing again, let us know,' she insisted as she walked him to the door. 'We're happy to pay for our tickets next time.'

'Speaking of which,' he responded hastily, 'please don't think I'm asking for freebies to your father's show. I'm more than happy to pay . . .'

'Let's deal with that when we know if I can get them. I have your number, so I'll give you a call when I have some news.'

As they reached the front door he turned to her, and she felt disturbed by how close they suddenly were.

'Out of interest,' she said, taking a careful step back, 'was it Natalia who told you Edwin Monkton was our father?'

He frowned as he thought. 'Actually, I think it was Nick who mentioned it. I can't remember how it came up, but I should have realised there was a problem or presumably your father would have been around more.'

'I'm sure he would have been if we'd allowed it,' Bel admitted.

His eyes were intently on hers, seeming to probe the thoughts behind them, though she knew he'd never ask. 'It was good to see you,' he said softly.

'You too,' she replied.

'I'll wait to hear from you,' and opening the door he ran down the steps to his car.

After the gates had closed behind him Bel returned to her computer to look up the gallery, still thrown by his invitation to go with him. Since he had no way of knowing that she'd rather pluck out her own eyes than look at her father's art, she could allow herself to feel flattered, even pleased, unless, of course, he'd meant it as some sort of date . . . That was never going to happen, no matter how attracted she might be to him, and not only because he had a wife.

Having found the gallery's details, she phoned and asked

to be put through to Veronika Boykov, the owner. The name sounded Russian. Was that who her father was mixing with these days, the Russians with their endless millions in need of laundering? Another good reason not to be in touch with him, as if she needed one.

'I'm afraid Ms Boykov isn't available at this time,' she was told by a snooty-sounding female. 'Can I take a message?'

Not wanting to risk her father calling back, Bel asked, 'When would be the best time to get hold of her?'

'She's usually here on Mondays, but if you can tell me what it's about . . .'

'I'll call next Monday, thank you,' and she abruptly rang off.

Moments later her phone rang, and seeing it was Nick she clicked on right away. 'Hi, just the person,' she told him, 'but aren't you supposed to be lecturing today?'

'I am, and I was. Now I'm on my way home and I thought I'd call to find out how things are with you.'

Was he sober? Surely he wouldn't be driving if he weren't. 'I guess they're OK,' she replied. 'Harry Beck was just here. He wants me to try and get him some tickets to one of my father's shows.'

A beat of surprised silence passed before Nick said, 'Well I guess you didn't see that coming.'

'Not for a minute. He said it was you who told him that Edwin's my father.'

'I did? Yeah, I guess I probably did when he was asking about Talia's family. Should I apologise? Is it a problem?'

'I don't think so. I'd just rather forget there's any association at all.'

'Of course. So what are you going to do?'

'I just tried to get hold of the gallery owner, but she's not there until next week. I'm sure she'll come through once I tell her who I am. I just hope, if my father hears about it, he doesn't presume the tickets are for me and try to get in touch.'

'Would you like me to make the call for you?'

Loving him for thinking of it, she said, 'Maybe. I'll let you know, thanks. So now, are the children coming to me this weekend?'

'It would be wonderful if they could. We're off to London again, just for Saturday, back in time for lunch on Sunday, if that works for you?'

'No problem. Just let me know what time you'll be bringing them, or I can pick them up if you prefer. What are you doing in London?'

'Um, you know, I've forgotten. Some conference, I think, and a party after. Kristina has the details.'

Was he really sounding cagey, or was it her imagination? 'OK, well I guess I'd better let you go,' she said. 'I'll see you at the weekend, if not before.'

After ringing off she wandered to the window and stood staring into the darkening estuary. Though the unwelcome reminder of her father was dominating her mind, she wouldn't, couldn't, revisit her memories of him. She would only go so far as to regret with all her heart that he was still alive while her mother and Talia had gone.

Chapter Eight

'Oh Ryan, what's happened to your eye?' Josie cried, as he came to sit with her and Lily in the cavernous visitors' room. Other families were gathering to spend an hour with their own offenders, and as usual the noise was deafening, echoing around the steel pipes in the ceiling, and punching off the brutal stone walls, while the smell of old cooking and sweat curdled the air.

Glancing anxiously around to make sure no one had heard, Ryan muttered, 'Keep it down, Mum. Don't make a fuss.'

'But it's all bruised,' she protested, the mere sight of it causing flurries of horror inside her. 'Did someone attack you?'

'No!' he said through his teeth. 'I knew you'd think that, but it was an accident, all right?'

Josie and Lily exchanged glances, neither of them believing it for a minute.

'I swear,' he insisted, his pale complexion flushing with colour.

He looked so thin, Josie was thinking as she regarded him with her careful mother's eye, and so vulnerable with his tufty ginger hair and baby-smooth cheeks, marred only by the bruise, which was so livid it made her wince all over again. She wanted to sweep him into her arms and hug him like she used to when he was small. He was her little guinea pig, she used to tell him, on account of his wayward, wiry hair.

'So what happened?' Lily wanted to know, her lovely face seeming to glow with health in comparison to her brother's.

'Nothing, it doesn't matter,' he mumbled.

'Someone did that to you,' Josie insisted. 'You have to report them, Ryan . . .'

'Don't be stupid, Mum. This isn't a school, it's a nick where stuff happens. Anyway, no one did it. I dropped one of the weights when I was working out in the gym.'

'On to your eye?' If only she hadn't watched that flipping documentary. Ever since, she'd found it impossible not to think of all those terrible things being inflicted on him.

'Can we just leave it now?' he retorted. 'Tell me what you've been up to.'

Letting Lily answer first, Josie watched him absorbing every one of his sister's words as though it was something magic to take away with him for later. Different as they were they'd always been close, usually with Lily looking out for her little brother, since he'd never been all that good at taking care of himself. He was too kind-hearted for one thing, and downright gullible for another. Ever since Josie could remember he'd given away his sweets before having any himself, or he'd let someone have the first ride on his new bike, anything to make people like him, and no one ever really did. He'd been better off indoors with her and Jeff watching the old cowboy films he loved, or helping his dad in the garden, or putting model forts together. Of course, he'd been a blinking handful at times, especially as he'd grown older, cheeking her back when she got on to him about tidying his room, or coming home with his best clothes covered in mud when she'd told him not to go over the park in them.

Of course she knew he'd probably been pushed in the stream, or deliberately splashed in puddles; it wasn't easy being a boy with ginger hair, and living on their kind of estate made it harder still. There were so many ruffians about, older, bigger lads, yobs, who got a real kick out of picking on someone younger and smaller than them. It could break her heart to think of how hard he'd tried to be friends with them.

And now here he was, serving time for a crime they'd committed when all he'd actually done was provide a key for the real offenders to break into a house and rob it. That repulsive bunch of lowlife ought to be looking out for him while he was in here, not punching him in the face, or knocking weights out of his hands. And if they weren't responsible for his injury they should be sorting out those who were; after all, they owed him big time for taking the rap for them. Most of them were going to be out in less than a year, but not Ryan. Or Shane Prince, come to that, who'd been facing at least a fifteen-year stretch if he'd been found guilty of that dreadful assault – the assault that *he'd* committed. As it was, with it being his second time in front of a judge for robbery with aggravating factors he'd got seven years, two more than Ryan.

'What are you doing, Mum?' Ryan whispered angrily.

Confused, she said, 'What do you mean?'

'Why are you looking around at everyone?'

'I was just wondering . . . Is Shane Prince still in here, or have they moved him?'

'No, he's here,' Ryan answered miserably.

Josie glanced around the hall again, but there was no sign of the cocky little scumbag whose neck she'd like to wring. 'Doesn't he get any visitors?' she asked.

Ryan shook his head. 'Not very often.'

'Half his family's in clink,' Lily reminded them.

'Ssh,' Ryan seethed.

'Well they are.'

'Yeah, but you don't have to shout it.'

Quickly changing the subject, Josie said, 'We brought you some chocolate and a malt loaf and a couple of football magazines.'

'What about cigarettes?' he asked.

Knowing they were a vital form of currency in this place, she said, 'There's only one packet, I'm afraid, and a fiver in cash. I'm sorry, but I couldn't spare any more this week. Dad's still not getting much work, and now I've lost my cleaning job . . .'

'I thought you were going to get another,' Lily cut in.

'I'm looking,' Josie assured her, 'but they go so fast these days.'

'I'll check online for you. I bet I'll come up with something a bit better than cleaning.'

Josie's eyebrows rose. 'I hope you're not looking down your nose at me.'

'As if,' Lily soothed. 'I just want you to earn more so you can treat yourself now and again. When was the last time you bought any new clothes? And you never go out anywhere, apart from the karaoke bar about once a month. I know you love the cinema, and you used to be really good at tap. Remember the class we went to in town? Oh God, do you remember that, Ry? We used to tease her something rotten, but she had the last laugh when she only *won an award*.'

Breaking into a grin, Ryan said, 'Yeah, and she got really tipsy after so Dad had to practically carry her to the car.'

'Actually, it was Nan who got tipsy,' Josie protested.

'Blotto, more like,' he corrected. 'Oh my God, then she went over the park when we got back and only chucked up on the kiddies' roundabout after whizzing round on it too fast. Do you remember that?'

Josie grimaced as Lily laughed. 'I'd rather not,' Josie replied. 'At least I'm not quite such an embarrassment for you two.'

'No, you're just lovely,' Lily said, putting an arm around her. 'And we love you to bits, don't we Ry?'

Glancing at the inmates either side of him to check if any were listening, he said, 'Definitely. Best mum in the world.'

'Best boy,' Josie whispered. 'And best girl,' she added, taking Lily's hand.

'Best tapper,' Lily smiled. 'Oh God,' she suddenly exclaimed, charging back down memory lane, 'do you remember that barbecue when Dad set fire to the hedge and we had the council round on the Monday trying to find out who'd done it? That was hilarious. Dad hid in the shed while they were there, leaving Mum to do all the talking.'

'And I was the lookout to tell him when the coast was clear,' Ryan added.

'And Dawnie nearly gave the game away when she

turned up in a fireman's hat to make us all laugh,' Lily giggled.

And if I'd known about him and Dawnie then, I'd have shopped him, Josie was thinking, but she hadn't found out until the following week, which effectively made that little episode with Dawnie the last of their happy memories with her.

As the hour ticked on and they tripped even further back in time to when they'd never seemed short of money and she'd always been sure of Jeff, Josie could only feel glad that they hadn't known then what the future held. It would have spoiled things if they had, which just went to show that living in the present was the very best way to carry on, or they'd never enjoy a bit of happiness again.

'Who are you looking at?' she asked, glancing over her shoulder to follow the direction of Ryan's straying attention.

'No one,' Ryan replied, a crimson flush spreading up from his collar.

'It's that bloke over by the window,' Lily whispered in Josie's ear. 'The one in the blue polo neck.'

Catching the young man's eye, Josie found herself being treated to a sunny smile. 'Who is he?' she asked, turning back to Ryan.

'His name's Paul,' he replied. 'He's the chaplain here.'

Josie's eyes widened.

'He's a good bloke,' Ryan stated. 'I mean, not just in a God sort of way, he's like really easy-going and into all sorts of stuff.'

Pleased to think he was relating to someone with good moral fibre, Josie was about to tell him so when Ryan said quickly, 'He's coming over. Be nice to him, won't you?'

'Like as if we wouldn't,' Lily protested.

'Hello Ryan,' the young man said warmly. 'I hope I'm not interrupting?'

'No, not at all,' Josie assured him, guessing he must be in his late twenties, possibly thirty – and she really liked the clean-cut, educated sort of look to him. 'Ryan was just telling us you're the chaplain here,' she smiled.

'For my sins,' he replied with an ironic laugh. 'Ryan's

told me a lot about you. It's good that he has such a close and supportive family.'

Wondering what Ryan might have confided about Jeff, Josie said, 'Well, we do our best, because we love him very much and we . . .'

'*Muu-uum!*' Ryan muttered through his teeth.

'. . . do worry about him in here, don't we Lily?'

'All the time,' Lily confirmed. 'I'm Lily, Ryan's sister,' she explained, holding out a hand to shake the chaplain's. 'He shouldn't be here really, because he didn't clobber that bloke. He only said he did because . . .'

'He knows,' Ryan broke in harshly. 'And you can't talk about that stuff here. You don't know who's listening.'

'I don't care who's listening . . .'

'Leave it,' Josie said to Lily. 'We don't want to make things even harder for him than they already are. So how often are you here?' she asked the chaplain.

'Three or four times a week,' he replied, his gaze moving from her to Ryan. 'I try to get the lads interested in various projects, and I have to say Ryan is very receptive to new ideas and he's doing extremely well with his reading.'

Baffled, Josie said, 'Well, it's not like he couldn't read before he came in here.'

Paul smiled. 'I was meaning in his choice of literature. He seems to have quite a fondness for Robert Louis Stevenson, who happens to be a big favourite of mine.'

Realising Ryan was probably trying to impress again, Josie was about to announce that she'd read *Kidnapped* at school when a child let rip with a piercing scream. The next instant a fight had broken out between two women in the play area.

'*Scrap, scrap, scrap,*' a bunch of inmates chanted as three officers rushed in to pull the women apart.

Josie turned back, and seeing the way Paul's hand was resting protectively on Ryan's shoulder she felt a surge of relief rise from the knotted angst inside her. He had a friend, someone who was looking out for him, and though they'd never really been a church family, she couldn't have wished for someone more worthy, or more sensitive, to help her boy through this time.

'I'll be back in a fortnight,' she told Ryan when she had to hug him cheerio. 'You take care of yourself in the meantime, and don't forget to write. I love reading your letters.'

'Don't you forget either,' he said, his voice choked with tears. 'Love you, Mum, more than anything.'

'Love you too,' she whispered, smoothing his face.

'Keep your chin up,' Lily told him, as he turned to embrace her. 'You're the best.'

'So are you. Say hi to Jasper for me.'

'Will do. He says hi too. See you in a fortnight.'

As they reached the door Josie and Lily turned back to find Ryan still watching them, clearly struggling to hold on to his tears. The chaplain was next to him, lending comfort and friendship. They looked like brothers, Josie thought as she gave them a wave, both redheads, both slight, though Paul was taller and a little larger in build.

'Do you reckon he's gay?' Lily asked as soon as they were free of the crowd.

Startled, Josie glanced at her as she raised her umbrella. 'You mean the chaplain? What makes you say that?' she said, the thought never having crossed her mind.

Lily shrugged and tucked an arm through her mother's to huddle under the brolly. 'He just struck me that way, that's all,' she replied. 'Not that there's anything wrong with it. In fact, it could be a good thing if he is.'

'Why?' Josie asked, bewildered.

'Well, for one thing it'll make him a lot more human than those gorillas Ry's locked up with, and for another, I've often wondered if Ry's not more that way himself.'

Shocked into silence, Josie could only blink.

'Haven't you?' Lily prompted.

'No, never.'

'Oh come on, Mum. It's got to have crossed your mind. He's really feminine in his ways, and he's always preferred hanging out with girls than with boys.'

'I wish he had hung out with more girls,' Josie retorted crossly. 'He might not be where he is now if he had.'

'He's where he is now because he was trying to prove he was one of the lads, when he's never been that.'

They walked on in silence.

'You wouldn't have a problem with it, would you?' Lily pressed.

Josie didn't have to think for long. After all, Ryan was her son, so nothing he did would ever make her stop loving him. 'No, I wouldn't,' she replied, 'but I dread to think how your father would take it.'

Lily sighed. 'Yeah, well I don't suppose he'd be thrilled, but I bet it wouldn't be that much of a surprise.'

'Oh, I think it would,' Josie corrected. 'He's never said anything like that to me, so I don't think it's ever even occurred to him.' Suddenly she felt her heartbeat slowing with dread. 'If you're right,' she said, glancing at Lily, 'isn't that going to make it even worse for him where he is?'

Resting her head against her mother's as they stopped at a crossing, Lily said, 'I don't know, but if he's got the chaplain as a friend, that's surely no bad thing.'

Unable to make her mind up about that, Josie walked with it for a while, and finally said, 'To be honest, I really don't mind whether he's gay, straight, transvestite or something I've never even heard of, just as long as he's happy. The same goes for you.'

Smiling, Lily hugged her arm. 'I'm definitely happy,' she assured her. 'I've got so much to look forward to this year, what with graduating and the wedding, how could I not be?'

Realising she couldn't even begin to answer that with the truth, Josie lowered her brolly as they reached the bus shelter, and to keep her mind off everything else she encouraged Lily to chat about guest lists, hats and whether to go vintage with the car, or see if Dad knew someone who could cut them a deal for a Roller.

There would be plenty of time to worry about her appointment with the oncologist when she was there on Monday. No need to do it now.

'Shall I tell you what I love most about you, Auntie Bel?' Nell whispered sleepily.

Bel's eyes twinkled as she knelt next to the bed and rested her arms beside her niece. 'Go on then,' she whispered back.

Gazing up from her pillow, her sweet little face flushed

from her bath, Nell said, 'It's that you're just like Mummy, only better because you're still here.'

Bel's heart twisted as she smoothed Nell's hair. 'But you understand why Mummy isn't here, don't you?' she asked.

Nell nodded. 'I know she died, but I don't know why she had to. Oscar says people have to go when their number is up, but I don't think Mummy had a number.'

'Oscar's just using a phrase some people do when they talk about people who've died. Mummy had to go because she got sick and there wasn't any way the doctors could make her well again. They tried, but in the end she was in a lot of pain so it was for the best that she went.'

Nell's eyes were troubled. 'Where did she go?'

'I'm not sure, my darling. No one's ever been able to find out where we go when we die, but they do say it's a much better place than here, with no pain and lots of happiness.'

'My teacher says she went to heaven.'

Glad to think the teacher had said that, even if she didn't believe in such a place herself, Bel said, 'I think she probably did.'

Nell frowned. 'She wouldn't go to hell, would she?'

'Oh no, not Mummy. She was much too lovely a person for that.'

Nell's eyes gazed trustingly into hers. 'You're a lovely person too,' she said, starting to smile. 'You're my favourite person in the whole wide world,' and throwing her arms round Bel's neck she treated her to a mighty hug.

'And you and Oscar are mine,' Bel told her. 'And I think Daddy's your favourite person too, isn't he?'

'Oh yes,' Nell gasped, realising she'd forgotten. 'He's definitely my favourite too.'

'And Kristina.' She deliberately didn't make it a question.

Nell's bottom lip jutted forward. 'Yes, I like Kristina too,' she conceded. 'Oscar says she might have babies with Daddy. Do you think she will?'

Feeling herself resisting the very thought, Bel said, 'It's certainly possible. Wouldn't you like a little brother or sister?'

Nell's face puckered. 'I'm not sure. If it was a sister I might like it. Are you going to have any babies?'

'I don't think so,' Bel whispered. 'Now it's time you were asleep.'

'Can I have a story?'

'You've already had one. Close your eyes and think happy thoughts and when you get up in the morning we'll finish digging our vegetable patch.'

After tucking her in and pressing a kiss to her cheek, Bel turned out the light and went to check on Oscar. Finding him already lost to the world, she switched off his light too and leaving both their bedroom doors ajar, she returned to the chaos they'd left downstairs.

It didn't take long to tidy up, or to pour herself a large glass of wine; what took a little more time was making herself sit down at the computer to start sending emails to her old friends. It had to be done, she kept telling herself, or she was going to moulder away here in Kesterly with no adult company apart from Nick and Kristina, who were too kind to tell her it was time to move on. It would cramp their style somewhat if she was no longer on hand to babysit, of course; it was also going to tear her apart not to see the children as often as she did now.

However, she simply couldn't go on the way she was.

'Have you considered one of the online dating agencies?' Mrs Fairclough, her cleaner, had asked when she'd come in on Friday and found Bel in a state of utter despair. 'I know it's none of my business, but I reckon you're lonely, that's what you are, and it's not right, a smashing young girl like you. You should be out there enjoying yourself, making the most of all the lovely things God has given you.'

Like money and looks and perfect health, she hadn't added, but Bel had known she was thinking it, and who could blame her when she was right? Bel had been blessed in ways plenty of people could only dream about, and it wasn't that she didn't appreciate what she had, she simply couldn't find the will, or the confidence, to pick herself up and start rebuilding her world. She thought about it a lot, and kept telling herself to get on with it, but even now as she sat gazing at the screen she could feel herself shrinking inside.

148

'So what do you want?' she asked herself aloud, as if she had the power to make anything happen. Some might say she did if she put her mind to it, but even they would have to concede she'd have a problem trying to bring back the dead.

If her mother were still alive, maybe Talia would be too. She knew it was crazy to think Talia had been taken to punish Bel for what she'd done to their mother, but it was how it felt and she could never make it go away.

You have to try, she could hear Talia saying. *What happened to me had nothing to do with Mummy.*

She had to think of something to do with her life. There were any number of properties out there she could breathe new life into, and more charities she could become involved with, but no matter what she did for either, at the end of each day when she returned home there would still only be her and these four walls. She needed someone to talk to, a friend she could confide in, a lover, even, who'd take her out of herself for a while.

No, not a lover. She could never have one of those again.

She'd made too many disastrous attempts at relationships in the past to run the risk of another when she was feeling so vulnerable and unable to cope. Perhaps, if it could be someone like Harry, it might be different, but Harry was married and even if that didn't mean anything to him, it certainly did to her. She was sure it did mean something to him though, and his suggestion of her accompanying him to the gallery no doubt had a lot more to do with her being the artist's daughter than with some clandestine sort of date.

How perverse fate was, using him to bring her father back into her life. Or into her mind, anyway.

Deciding that she simply wasn't in the right mood to start making contact with her old friends tonight, she got up from the computer and went to flick through the TV. Finding nothing she felt like watching, she poured herself another glass of wine and went to run a bath. *Where are you going to run it?* she could hear Talia teasing. *Make sure you catch it if it goes too fast,* she'd cry. *Will they fit in the linen cupboard?* she'd ask when someone folded their arms.

149

Make sure you don't drop it, she'd say if Bel tossed her head. It was a silly little pastime that had kept them entertained when they were young, made even funnier by the fact that no one else knew what they were talking about. They'd explained their jokes to their mother, of course, they'd shared most things with her, but not with their father. It had been to forget the times spent with him that they'd started the game.

Covering her face with her hands as though to block out the past was about as effective as using them to empty a bath. It would always be there, as irrefutable and unchangeable as the fact that she hated him as much as ever, probably even more.

Now that Mummy's dead and we're about to start college, she and Talia had written in a letter only days after their sixteenth birthday, *we have no need of you in our lives any more. Nor do we have any reason to stay silent about the things you did when we were too young to understand or defend ourselves. Out of love and respect for Mummy we are trying to put it behind us, but if you ever attempt to be in touch with us again you have our solemn promise that we will go to the police.*

So what was he going to think when he found out she wanted tickets to his show? Being as arrogant as he was, and as blame-free as he clearly considered himself, he'd probably assume she was ready to let bygones be bygones so they could take up being father and daughter again. She might have laughed at that if it hadn't made her feel sick to her very soul.

She was sorry she couldn't get the tickets for Harry herself, but it would be best all round if Nick made the call. Though Nick had never actually met her father, Edwin was sure to know his son-in-law's name and was no more likely to refuse him than he was to refuse her. She'd talk to Nick when he came for the children tomorrow. It would be a relief to share this with him, since harbouring secrets about her father was reminding her far too much of the way she'd been forced to keep silent when she was young.

Time to move on, Bel, she could hear Talia saying. *It really is time to move on.*

Chapter Nine

'Why don't we have a look into fostering?' Jeff suggested, glancing up from the morning news as Josie came down the stairs. 'They're saying social services are crying out for people to take on kids in this area.'

Josie stopped in disbelief, the undrunk glasses of water she'd brought down with her spilling over her hands. 'You've always been against it,' she reminded him, wondering why, today of all days, when it could hardly be less possible, it should suddenly come up. Of course he didn't know she was seeing the oncologist, but even so, why couldn't he have opened his mind to it years ago when she'd practically begged him to consider it?

'Yeah, well, when needs must and all that,' he responded, taking a bite of his toast. 'It'll bring in a bit of extra cash, and at the same time it'll stop us getting stung for that bedroom tax.'

'You can't foster children based on financial needs,' she retorted irritably, moving on to the kitchen. 'We have to do it because we care.'

'We do. Well, you more than me, I have to admit, but I expect I could get used to it, provided they're properly house-trained and don't cause any trouble.'

'Some of them are bound to be troublemakers,' she told him. 'You would be too if you came from the kind of backgrounds they do. Anyway, I don't think it's a good idea.'

Surprised, he said, 'Well you've changed your tune. You used to be all for it . . .'

'Yes, and for the right reasons, but now's not the time.'

Seeming mystified by that, he asked, 'So when is?'

'I don't know. After Lily gets married, I suppose. We'll need her room till then.'

'We've got another . . .'

'That's Ryan's, and I don't want to talk about it any more so let's change the subject.'

Glowering in her direction, though unable to see her as she flitted about the kitchen, he said, 'All right, let's discuss you getting yourself down the jobcentre, shall we, because we can't go on the way we are.'

'Why don't *you* go down the jobcentre?' she snapped angrily. 'It's your car that's in the shop again . . .'

'It's where I'm going this morning,' he growled over her, 'and there's no need to get worked up about it. I was just trying to come up with a way of bringing in some money, and seeing that on the telly reminded me of how you used to go on about fostering. I thought you'd welcome the idea.'

'Well I've changed my mind.'

'Why?'

'I don't know, I just have. Do you want another cup of tea?'

Glancing into his cup and finding it empty, he said, 'Yeah, why not? And some more toast if you're making it. Oh bloody hell, look at that, they've only gone and put Frankie Baldwin on the transfer list. What are they thinking? He's one of our best players.'

Tuning out of his grumbling, she slotted another slice of bread into the toaster and poured more boiling water into the teapot. She didn't want any food herself, which was just as well since there was barely enough spread for one piece of toast, let alone two. If she could persuade Andy at the Spar to wait till Friday for paying, she could pick up a packet on her way home later. If he was feeling especially generous she might even be able to add a box of fish fingers to make some sandwiches for tea. Not very nutritious, but it was either that or eggs, since money was tighter than ever this week, and now Jeff's car was out of action again their situation wasn't going to get any better.

Feeling fussed and worried, she reached for the milk, dropped the carton and swore as it spilled all over her boots.

'What are you in such a bad mood about this morning?' Jeff wanted to know as she brought in his cuppa.

'Nothing. I'm fine, just a bit hassled about how we're going to get through the week. We might have to go to one of those loan shops . . .'

'Don't even think about it,' he cut in darkly. 'A bunch of charlatans if ever there was one, and once you're in hock to them you're never out of it. Remember what happened to your mother.'

She did, only too well, since Eileen's runaway debt had ended her up in court, and then hospital, she'd got herself into such a state over it.

'There are better places these days than the one she went to,' she told him. 'It's all regulated now . . .'

'That's what they want you to think, but take it from me, they'll bleed us as dry as a witch's tit and still they'll come back for more.'

Afraid he was right, she said, 'So what are we going to do? I'm not sure we can put food on the table after today, unless you've got a couple of fivers stashed away.' He did that sometimes, and produced them just when she thought they were about to go under.

'Get jobs, that's what we're going to do.'

Not arguing, since there was no point, she headed back into the kitchen, washed up the few dishes soaking in the bowl and felt her insides clench with nerves as she checked the time.

If she was like this about meeting the oncologist, what the heck kind of state was she going to be in when it came time for the treatment?

'Where are you going?' Jeff asked as she went to put on her coat.

'Into town,' she replied. 'I saw a job advertised in one of the bucket and spade shops when I was passing on Friday.'

'So why didn't you go in then?'

'Because it was six o'clock and they'd already closed.'

'You should have gone on Saturday,' he grunted, knowing full well that she hadn't because she'd been visiting Ryan. 'You've got to act fast these days.'

'I know, I know. Good luck at the jobcentre. Give me a ring if there's any news.'

'Have you got enough for your bus fare?'

Digging out her purse to make sure, she counted four pounds forty-three, enough to leave her with almost a pound by the time she got home again, and giving him a quick kiss she let herself out of the door.

No lunch for me, she was thinking, as she pulled up her hood to hurry through the rain, but as she was unlikely to have much of an appetite anyway, she wasn't too worried. What was bothering her more was the start of the lies; there was no vacancy in a bucket and spade shop, she only wished there was. Except, given what she was facing, she wouldn't be able to go for it, any more than she could consider taking needy children into their home.

To her surprise, when she got to the clinic, in spite of the crowd in the waiting room it was only a few minutes before she was being called in to see the oncologist. As she was led down the stark white corridor with all its medical bits and pieces and noticeboards she spotted Mr Beck coming out of his office, but before he noticed her he disappeared inside again. He probably wouldn't have recognised her anyway, considering how many people he saw in a day. She didn't blame him for not knowing all his patients, it was only to be expected when there were so many, and maybe there was some comfort in anonymity. If someone stood out it would be because things were pretty bad, or they weren't coping very well, so she didn't want to be one of those who stood out.

'Here we are,' the nurse announced as they reached an open door. 'Dr Pattullo, this is Mrs Clark.'

A smartly dressed woman with girlishly dainty features and a neat blonde bob looked up from her desk and smiled. 'Hello Mrs Clark,' she said warmly, getting to her feet. 'Do come in. I hope you didn't get too wet on your way here. The rain's dreadful this morning, isn't it?'

'They're saying it's going to last all month,' Josie told her as the nurse closed the door behind her. The room wasn't unlike Mr Beck's with its desk, examination couch, workstation and sink, but no computer here, and only one window.

Once she was settled in the visitor's chair, Dr Pattullo sat back in her own and regarded her with friendly eyes. 'Before we start, is there anything you'd like to ask me?' she invited.

Unprepared for the question, Josie simply shook her head.

'You understand the results of your biopsy, and that Mr Beck and I have decided you should have chemotherapy to shrink the tumour before he operates?'

This time Josie was able to nod. 'He said he'd schedule things so I can go to my daughter's wedding,' she told her, thinking it was better to get that in now in case it ended up forgotten. 'It's in August, so still a way off yet.'

Dr Pattullo smiled. 'I'm sure that won't be a problem,' she assured her, and opening up the file with Josie's name on the front she made a note before continuing.

There was either something strangely hypnotic about her voice, or Josie's near-sleepless night started to catch up with her, because for the next few minutes she seemed to drift in and out of what she was being told. It was mainly about where the oncology centre was located, and how important it was to be on time for her appointments. It was when they got on to her possible hair loss, and other side effects, that Josie wished with all her heart she could stand up and say she'd changed her mind, she didn't want to go through with it after all.

Don't think about your hair now, just don't, she told herself fiercely, but how could she not when it was the only truly lovely thing about her? She wasn't vain or anything, she just knew that without her hair she'd be ugly, and what woman wanted to be that? What man wanted to be married to it? Imagine how it was going to be for Jeff, having to look at her. She wasn't sure how much he fancied her these days as it was, and he'd never been able to cope with illness of any sort. He hadn't even come to see her when she'd been so poorly after giving birth to Ryan.

He was going to hate having a bald wife.

She'd have to make sure she got a good wig, but they cost a lot and how was she going to afford it?

After examining her Dr Pattullo told her to get dressed

again, and began talking about receptors and oestrogen and things she'd have to look up later, because nothing seemed to be going in properly this morning.

Pull yourself together, Josie. Listen, and you might learn something.

'. . . we'll start the FEC treatment next Monday,' Dr Pattullo was telling her, 'and bring you back every three weeks for two more doses. I'll give you a fact sheet explaining what'll happen before and during the session, along with details of the drugs we'll be using. I can tell you now, if you like, but fluorouracil, epirubicin and cyclophosphamide aren't easy to say, never mind take in.' She gave a smile.

Josie tried to do the same. 'What happens after that?' she asked, her voice sounding strangely hollow inside her head.

'That's when we'll switch you over to another drug called Docetaxel. Again you'll have three doses at three-weekly intervals. Don't worry, we've prepared a package for you to take home containing all the information you'll need about the drugs, how they're administered, their possible side effects and other changes that might take place over the period. And Yvonne, the senior breast-care nurse, will have a chat with you before you leave.'

'Am I . . . Am I going to be very ill?' Josie wanted to know.

Dr Pattullo glanced down at her notes. 'I'm not going to pretend that chemotherapy is easy to go through,' she replied, looking up again. 'What it's doing essentially is trying to destroy any cancer cells in your body, but in so doing it'll also harm many normal cells, for example in the bone marrow, digestive tract and hair follicles. This is what causes side effects such as reduced numbers of blood cells, nausea and hair loss. So to answer your question, everyone's different in the way they react. Some are more able to cope with it than others. On the whole though, I'd say that at first you're likely to make quite a quick recovery from the treatment. But over time it'll become harder to bounce back quite so swiftly.'

Josie swallowed. 'Is there any chance I won't have any

side effects at all?' she ventured, feeling ludicrously naïve even to hope for it.

'As I said, everyone's different, but I think you should prepare yourself for there being some. You'll be given anti-sickness drugs during your treatments to help prevent nausea; if you find it happening anyway there are several alternatives, so they can always be changed. Yvonne will go through everything with you before you leave, and the chemotherapy nurses will be able to advise you on any concerns you might have during the treatment. There are also a number of extremely helpful and well-informed charitable organisations such as Macmillan and Breast Cancer Care who provide help and support from experienced professionals, free of charge. You'll find their information sheets in your package, including websites and helpline numbers. You don't have to be on your own through this, Mrs Clark, no one does, and reaching out to those who've already been through it, or who are currently undergoing treatment themselves, can take a lot of the fear out of things. So I recommend you get in touch with at least one of the charities and/or a local support group.'

Though Josie nodded, she wasn't sure that she would. After all, it was hardly a club she wanted to belong to. Best to get started, was her feeling, have it over and done with as quickly as possible so she could put it behind her and get on with her life.

For the next hour or so Josie sat in the waiting room watching dozens of women coming and going, none of whom probably wanted to belong to this club any more than she did. Even so, most of them seemed far more accepting of it than she'd noticed before, which was making her feel pathetic and ashamed and as though she wasn't made of strong enough stuff and would never fit in. It might have helped if she'd had a friend or relative to lean on, the way most of them did. She'd been OK about coming on her own before, but for some reason it was feeling different today. She'd have really liked someone to hold her hand right now, the way a couple of blokes were doing for their wives or girlfriends. One even kept kissing his partner's head, which was resting on his shoulder. How lovely of him to do that. Jeff had never been one for public displays of affection; she always joked she was lucky she'd got him to kiss her on their wedding day.

How was he going to take this? It was going to come as a horrible shock. Somehow she'd have to work out how and when to tell him.

Feeling her phone vibrating she pulled it from her bag, and finding a text from him she suddenly wanted to cry.

Kev Allsop's broken his arm so taking over his taxi for couple of weeks. How's it going in town? Job still vacant?

Having no choice but to continue the lie, after all she could hardly break this to him by text, she sent a message back saying *Job gone, but looking round in case something else crops up. Good news about taxi, but not for Kev.*

What would he say if he knew where she really was?

Your wife has cancer.

'Josie?'

She looked up to find the nurse, Yvonne, smiling down at her.

'Would you like to come with me?' Yvonne encouraged.

As she followed her to the Visitors' Information Room, Josie wondered why she hadn't already just got up and left. There had been plenty of time to, and it wasn't as if this was where she wanted to be. She had her chemo appointment, and a bunch of brochures, so what was she still doing here?

'So how did it go with Emma – Dr Pattullo?' Yvonne asked, closing the door and waving Josie to one of the easy chairs that lined the walls.

'OK I think,' Josie replied, skirting the large coffee table that dominated the centre of the room. She couldn't help noticing the boxes of tissues and wondering how many they went through in a week.

'I expect you've a lot of questions now,' Yvonne said, sitting down too, 'so feel free to fire away, it's what I'm here for.'

Josie glanced at her hands. What she really wanted to ask was how to break it to her husband, or how to make it easier for her children, but what she said was, 'How long before I start losing my hair? I mean, please don't think I'm shallow and all I care about is my looks . . .'

'It's OK,' Yvonne came in gently, 'it's the biggest concern for most women.'

'You mean bigger than losing a breast? You'd think that's what I'd be most worried about, wouldn't you, because Mr Beck said it's probably going to happen.' Tears were strangling her voice; suddenly she couldn't bear it, any of it.

Passing her a tissue, Yvonne said, 'It's a horrible shock, I know, and it never seems to sink in all at once.'

'I'm fine,' Josie sobbed, dabbing her eyes. 'Honest. I just . . . Oh, look at me, making a fool of myself. There's no point getting in a state, is there? It's not going to change anything.'

'The way you're feeling is completely understandable, so don't be too hard on yourself. We're here to support you in any way we can.'

'Thank you. It's really kind of you. I just wish I could think of something sensible to ask, but the nicer you are to me the worse I seem to get.'

As they laughed together, Yvonne reached for the folder she'd brought in with her. 'This is for you to take home,' she explained. 'Read it at your leisure. You'll probably find it has most of the answers you're looking for, but anything else you need to ask, just give me a call. My number's on the front.'

'Actually, there is something,' Josie told her. 'I remember reading once about a kind of hat or helmet that's supposed to stop you losing your hair. Does it exist?'

Yvonne nodded. 'It's called the cold cap, but I'm afraid we don't have one here at the KRI. Even if we did, it doesn't offer a guarantee of no loss, because some women end up losing their hair anyway, while others find the coldness difficult to cope with.'

Unable to imagine it could be any worse than being bald, Josie asked, 'What about wigs? The trouble is, I can't afford one.'

'I'm sure we can get you one on the NHS.' Yvonne rummaged in the folder and came out with a booklet entitled *Breast Cancer and Hair Loss*. 'There, this will tell you everything you need to know. Are you on Income Support of any kind?'

Josie shook her head. 'I might have to be now, because I'm going to have a problem finding a job while I'm going through this. I mean, I've got one at the caff, but that's only Thursdays and Fridays. It's why I asked Dr Pattullo if I could have my treatment on Mondays, to give me time to get over it so I'd be ready for work by Thursday.'

Yvonne smiled. 'You should probably explain to your employer that you might have difficulty turning up some weeks.'

Realising she hadn't spared a thought for how this was going to affect Fliss, Josie said, 'I have to make it, no matter how bad I feel. I wouldn't want to let my boss down, and anyway we need the money.'

'I understand, but if you fall into financial hardship there are benefits you can claim.'

Josie's eyes went down. She could imagine what Jeff would have to say about living off the state.

Whatever he said, it would be better than living on the streets.

'What other side effects are there?' she asked. 'I know about the sickness, but is there anything else?'

'Well, it's different for everyone, of course, but you might suffer from constipation, or fatigue which is common. Do you have any ongoing dental problems?'

Josie shook her head.

'Good, but do try to get a check-up with your dentist in the next couple of weeks to let him know you're going to be having chemotherapy.'

'Oh my God, don't tell me my teeth are going to fall out,' Josie cried, half laughing, half horrified.

'Don't worry, it hasn't happened to anyone yet,' Yvonne assured her, 'but you might suffer from a sore mouth, or bleeding gums. Your dentist will advise you on how to deal with it, but essentially you should make sure you clean your teeth after every meal, always with a soft tooth-brush; use an alcohol-free mouthwash; drink plenty of water to keep your mouth moist, and chew sugar-free gum to stimulate the production of saliva. You'll find all this information in the Breast Cancer Care chemotherapy booklet, which is in your package.'

Glad of that, since she was sure she wouldn't retain it all, Josie tried to think what else she needed to know. 'What about sex?' she suddenly remembered. 'Is it possible while I'm having treatment?'

'It is, but you should use a condom during the first few days to avoid your husband becoming exposed to the drugs. Actually, you should be prepared for finding yourself less interested in sex during this time, either because you're anxious, or nauseous or even menopausal, which is something we ought to discuss, because your ovaries are going to be affected by the treatment.'

'You mean,' Josie cleared her throat, 'you mean I'm going to end up infertile?' It wasn't that she wanted any more children, they couldn't afford them, but going through the change at forty-two . . .

'It's possible, considering your age and the type of drugs you'll be given. Do you already have children?'

'Yes, two.'

'How old are they?'

'Twenty-one and eighteen.' More tears suddenly flooded her eyes. 'I have to be there for them,' she told the nurse brokenly. 'I know they're older, but they still need me.'

'Of course. They never stop needing their mother.'

Josie tried to smile, but she was falling apart. 'I have to beat this,' she gulped. 'I don't care what the side effects are, well I do, but what's really important is that I get through it and come out the other side.'

'Indeed it is,' Yvonne agreed, 'and believe me, we're going to be doing everything in our power to make sure you do.'

Bel was frowning to herself as she sorted through the dozens of brochures she'd just received from Breast Cancer Care. It seemed Holly, her contact at the charity, had appointed her official delivery person for the Kesterly area. Not that she minded, she was happy to help in any way she could, she just felt sad that it took so little time for supplies to run low. It wasn't only the clinic she needed to stock up again, but a couple of health centres, several doctors' surgeries and two local support groups.

Setting them aside to go through the rest of the mail, she found an envelope with a Romanian postmark and immediately opened it.

Dear Mrs Isabella, thank you letter you send for Anca. I very sad her go to God. Maybe she see your sister there. I am sorry for this loss. You are kind writing. Fii binecuvantat, Jenica Bojin.

Feeling the sadness weighting those few words, Bel turned to the window and gazed out at the horizon. She couldn't imagine ever meeting Jenica Bojin, but this small contact between them seemed to matter in a way that was both perplexing and moving. It felt as though an invisible distance was closing, proving how small the world could be and how important it was to connect to people in pain. This wouldn't have happened were it not for Talia, and her attempt to be there for a girl in distress.

'Thanks for contacting her mother, Bel,' she could hear Talia saying. *'I'd have done it myself if we had pens over here.'*

No pens, no computers, no telephones, no way of contacting their loved ones at all, and yet somehow Talia always seemed to be in touch. *Just because you can't see me doesn't mean I'm not there.*

As the memory of those words closed around her she quickly pulled free of them. She couldn't think about her own mother now. *Just think about Talia.*

'See this?' Talia cried, holding up a sheet. 'It's the fabric of time and we're going to tear right through it to find out what happens when there are holes we can step in and out of. Maybe we can hide in a different dimension.'

'Why are you doing that?' Talia asked when Bel kept blowing out imaginary candles.

'I'm creating the winds of change,' Bel explained. 'If we can make them strong enough they might blow him away.'

They'd hardly ever referred to him as Daddy, he was just *him*, or *the artist*, or *that man.*

That man had left a message on Nick's mobile saying how thrilled he was to hear his son-in-law wanted to come to the show. 'I hope you're going to bring Bel,' he'd added. 'It's been too long since I saw her and it's time to let bygones be bygones.'

So that was how he summed up the past these days, as bygones.

Reaching for her mobile as it rang, she saw it was Nick and clicked on. 'Hi, how're things?' she asked, using a cheery tone to bring herself back to the present.

'OK,' he replied. 'What about you?'

'Fine. Nothing new. What can I do for you?'

'Are you going to be there this evening? I thought I'd come over.'

Surprised, and pleased, she said, 'Do you mean we're going to have an evening just the two of us?' They used to have them all the time, before Kristina.

'If that's OK with you.'

'Of course. I'd love it. Shall I make supper?'

'I'll come after, if that's OK. Kristina needs help putting the children to bed, and they're sure to want a story. Shall we say eight thirty?'

'Sounds good. I'll look forward to it, just don't think you're going to talk me into going to that show.'

'I know I could never do that, nor would I try, and the tickets aren't for me, remember? Have you contacted Harry Beck yet to let him know his wish has come true?'

'I sent a text earlier.'

'Great. The tickets arrived this morning. I'll bring them with me later.'

After ringing off, she carried on sifting through the mail, binning half of it and taking the rest to her computer. She'd barely sat down when the phone rang again. This time it was Harry.

'Hi, did you get my text?' she asked, feeling in a better mood since speaking to Nick.

'It's why I'm ringing,' Harry replied. 'I'm deeply in your debt now, I hope you realise that.'

'As far as I know the tickets are complimentary,' she teased.

'You know what I'm saying, and I'm going to find a way of showing my gratitude – I just have to come up with it.'

'You honestly don't need to. It was Nick who made the call. He's bringing them later so I'll pop them into the clinic tomorrow or Thursday to save you coming out of your way.'

'No, no, I insist on picking them up. It's the least I can do.'

'It's OK, I have to drop some brochures off anyway, so it won't be any trouble.'

'Hang on.' He went off the line for a moment and though she was able to hear him speaking she couldn't make out what he was saying. 'Sorry about that,' he said, coming back. 'I'm afraid I have to go.'

'No problem. Sounds like a busy day.'

'Every day is that, and this one's turning into a particularly difficult one. If you let me know when you're coming I'll do my best to pop out and say hi. If you time it right, I might even treat you to a sandwich at the infirmary caff.'

'Sounds irresistible,' she laughed, and after promising to text when she was on her way, she rang off, preparing once again to tackle the mountain of paperwork in front of her that never seemed to get any smaller.

Just after lunch Barry Burgess, the builder she'd used to renovate Stillwater, rang to tip her off about an old barn in the village of Dodderton that was about to come on the market.

'If you're interested,' he said excitedly, 'I know the farmer, so I can probably get you in ahead of the game.'

Since it had long been her ambition to convert a barn she decided to waste no time, jumped in the car and drove straight there. Barry was waiting with the farmer, who turned out to have no teeth and a decidedly off-colour sense of humour. However, his old hay barn with two acres of land and a milking shed was, for her, an absolute dream of a project.

She offered him a hundred thousand less than he was asking, he pushed her up by forty grand and the deal was sealed with a handshake.

By the end of the day solicitors were already involved, and not for a single moment did she regret such an impulsive buy. She hadn't felt this excited in way too long, and the fact that it was going to tie her to Kesterly for at least the next year or two was hardly a problem when Nick and the children were here.

'Wow, that's fantastic,' Nick laughed, as she poured two glasses of champagne. 'Where is it?'

'Dodderton, so only a couple of miles from Senway. I won't be living there when it's done, it's far too big, but I should make a fabulous profit once I've pulled it all together. Barry Burgess is going to do the work. You probably remember him from when he did this house.'

'Of course. Great choice. If I remember rightly he came in on time, and more or less on budget.'

'Give or take fifty grand,' she added wryly, 'but that was mostly me adding things and changing my mind as we went through. I've already left messages for the surveyor and architect I used last time around, so I'm hoping we can meet at the barn sometime later this week.'

'You really don't hang about, do you?' he grinned as she clinked her glass to his.

With a wry grimace, she said, 'We've got the planning nightmare to get through yet, but you wait till you see it. The position is amazing, countryside views that go on for miles, and it has *two* cart doors, front and back.'

'No,' he gasped. '*Two*. You've really landed on your feet with this one.'

Laughing, she led the way to the sofas and sat down with a contented sigh. 'Honestly, I haven't felt this positive about anything in way too long,' she told him. As the words left her she felt suddenly weighted by guilt. She didn't want to move on without her sister, but how could she stop it?

'She'd be thrilled for you,' Nick said softly, clearly reading her mind.

Bel had to agree. 'She was always far more generous-spirited than I can manage,' she confessed, 'but I'm doing my best to be more like her.'

'You're a lot kinder than you give yourself credit for, and I have two children who'd definitely back me up on that.'

Smiling, she said, 'Talia was always so proud of them.'

'Yes, she was,' he agreed sadly, 'and I am too. They've coped really well since she went, and it's largely thanks to you.'

'You too,' she insisted. 'You're a great father. They really couldn't wish for a better one.'

His eyes went down and she was about to reach for his hand when he said, 'Speaking of fathers, Edwin rang when I was on my way here.'

Feeling the joy drain out of her, she put her glass down and pushed her hands through her hair. 'Do I need to know that?' she asked.

He shook his head. 'Maybe not, but I thought I should tell you anyway.'

They sat quietly for a moment, the spectre of her father seeming to grow more stifling by the second.

'Did you tell him the tickets aren't for you?' she prompted in the end.

'I did. He was very disappointed, he said, and he wants to know if there's anything he can do to change our minds.'

'He could die, then he wouldn't have to bother doing anything,' she retorted angrily.

Nick nodded, apparently having guessed that would be her response.

She regarded him carefully. 'Nick, please tell me you're not about to ask me to reconsider,' she begged.

'No, not at all,' he assured her.

Not as convinced as she'd have liked to be, she said, 'So what did you say to him?'

He looked away.

'Oh my God, Nick, you did tell him you'd try to persuade me, didn't you? How could you? You know what he did . . .'

'Bel, stop. What I told him was that nothing was ever going to change your mind, and if he thought he could talk me into trying he should save his breath.'

More satisfied with that, she continued to regard him. 'So why am I getting the impression there's more?' she said.

He seemed surprised, but then his expression changed again and she almost felt his mood sinking. 'There isn't, or not about him,' he replied, 'but I do have some news I need to share with you.'

Chapter Ten

'I have some news,' Josie announced, closing down the computer as Jeff came in the door. It was Wednesday afternoon now and she'd told him she was going for an interview at a sandwich kiosk on the trading estate, so he'd be wondering what she was doing here.

Lies, more lies.

'I hope it's good,' he retorted, throwing down his keys, 'because mine is.'

Surprised and intrigued, she said, 'OK, you first.'

'No, no, go on, let's hear what yours is. Did you get the job?'

Feeling anxious, since she could already guess how he was going to react to what she was about to tell him, she said, 'Well, I've been checking online with the Department of Work and Pensions and it turns out I'd get more on benefits than I do working if I . . .'

His expression darkened. 'You should have known that already,' he growled, 'but it's not who we are. We work for a living, not like all them scroungers out there.'

'You keep saying that, Jeff, but most of them are finding it as difficult to get a job as we are . . .'

'But we're still managing to keep the wolf from the door without going looking for handouts. No, Josie, you're not signing up for benefits and that's that. We'll get through this difficult patch, same as we always do, and that's where my news comes in. I've only got a fare to Heathrow tomorrow *and* wait for this, one back again. That'll net me over six hundred quid, plus tip if I get one.'

Josie's eyes rounded in amazement. '*Six hundred quid,*' she echoed incredulously.

He was grinning in a way that got her laughing. 'What did I tell you?' he chuckled, as she came to hug him, 'we'll get through this difficult patch, and if you ask me I reckon our luck's already changing, because with that sort of money I'll be able to get my car back on the road, or make the first couple of payments on a new one.'

'Tell you what, I'll make something special tonight to celebrate,' she declared rashly. 'Or shall we go out somewhere? It's been ages since we last went into town for a night out.'

'Steady on there,' he cautioned, 'I haven't got the cash in my hand yet, but we'll do something when I have. Now, I only came home to pick up one of those air-freshener things our Lily gave me for Christmas. I thought they could start doing their stuff in time for the Heathrow run tomorrow.'

'You mean the ones you hang from the rear-view mirror? If you haven't already used them I expect they're in the drawer on your side of the bed.'

Making sure her folder of brochures and factsheets was out of sight, Josie went to put on the kettle. He might welcome a cuppa before going out again.

'Don't have time,' he told her, snatching up his keys as he came back downstairs. 'And you ought to be out there looking for a job, not sat here working out how much you could get if you signed on.'

Josie flinched as the door slammed behind him. She didn't blame him for getting on at her, she felt like getting on at herself the way she was sitting around here doing nothing all day. Well, not nothing, exactly, because she always had plenty of housework to keep her busy, and for months now she'd been meaning to sort out Lily's and Ryan's old clothes and toys for the charity shop. She'd make a start on it just as soon as she'd drunk her tea, and if the bags weren't too heavy by the time she'd finished she could take them up to the high street today. She might even have a browse around the shop while she was there to see if there was something suitable to wear for a night out in town.

Or for when she was having chemo. She'd found websites

that recommended wearing tracksuits for this (or 'snazzy pyjamas', someone had suggested), and hers were a bit tatty now.

Feeling the dread of what was to come hardening like a stone in her chest, she took a deep breath and tried to carry on as though it wasn't happening. *Drink your tea, rinse the cup, wipe down the worktop and empty the bin.*

She'd found another website earlier called Cancer be Glammed, but it turned out to be American and anyway, she'd never have been able to afford the silk scarves or handy bags or clever-zip sweatshirts they were promoting.

What the heck was she doing, worrying about what to wear when it could hardly matter less? It was like pretending to be deaf when someone was screaming for help, or blind as a truck came speeding towards her. What she needed to do was stop being so bloody cowardly and get back on the computer to read up about her treatment and the type of cancer she had. She might not be able to do anything about it herself, but learning about it had to be better than tiptoeing around like she was afraid of waking it up. If she was a bit better informed she might be able to work out how to break it to Jeff.

Several hours later she was still sitting in front of the computer, aching and stiff and wishing with all her heart that she'd gone out, or got on with the cleaning, or done anything except this. That was the trouble with plucking up the courage to do something you really didn't want to; once you had there was no going back.

Getting to her feet she went into the kitchen to make some tea. She hadn't felt this afraid, or alone, since she'd thought Jeff was going to leave her for Dawnie; or when she'd waited to hear if Ryan was going to be sent down, only in its way this felt worse. Apparently there was nothing about the type of cancer cells she had dividing and growing inside her that was temporary or unthreatening. From what she'd just read hers were aggressive, fast-moving, a rampant living force intent on taking her over.

Until this minute she hadn't allowed herself to think about dying; now she could think of nothing else. She was teetering on the edge of panic. Even as she stood there, trying to take it all in, the cancer was at work spreading through her lymph channels, breast tissue and even threatening her skin.

Feeling suddenly sick she bent over the sink and retched.

Nothing came up, but it was several minutes before she could stand straight again. She was still shaking; her eyes were watering, her head felt as though she'd banged it against the wall.

She took a breath and heard it waver and sob into her lungs.

She had to find a way of coping with this. If she didn't no one else would be able to, and she couldn't let her family fall apart. It was her job as wife and mother to be strong for them and make sure they always knew she was there to keep them together. If she was going to cry the way she was now, stupidly, loudly, self-pityingly, she'd have to do it in private; if she needed to shout and rant and swear at God, she'd wait until no one was around. She might even go to the church and give him a piece of her mind – except if she did that he might pay her back by doing something bad to Lily or Ryan.

He wasn't a merciful God; he was cruel, vindictive, had no time for people who already had enough problems on their plates, thank you very much. Well let him stew in his meddling, because it was going to be all right, she'd make sure of it. She just needed to stay in control of her emotions, and go back in there and read everything through again to make sure she understood it properly. It could be that fear had made her blow it out of proportion, or shock had blinded her to something vital that would put a more positive picture on it all.

Half an hour later, certain now that it was as bad as she feared, she forced herself to pick up the phone. Mr Beck had said she could call any time, so she was going to ring and ask if it was possible to have her breast off straight away. Better that than spend the next however many months feeling like hell thanks to the chemo, while this vile cancer, that had got the wrong person, tried to take over her body. Why not cut it out now and be done with it?

*

170

'You look hassled,' Bel commented, as Harry joined her at a table in one of the hospital's coffee shops. Being early afternoon, their only companions were the lady serving and an elderly man snoozing over a sandwich at a table just inside the door.

'I've just spent the past twenty minutes,' he replied, removing his coat, 'trying to explain to a patient why she should have chemotherapy before a mastectomy, rather than going for the mastectomy straight away.'

'And were you successful?'

He sighed and nodded. 'I think so.'

'But you're still troubled?'

'Yeah, I guess so, but only because it's a hell of a thing for anyone to go through, as you know only too well.'

'Is she young?'

'Early forties; two grown-up children. Usually it's the ones with very young kids that get to me, like your sister, but there's something about this one . . . To be honest, she seems more concerned about her family than she is about herself, though I guess that's not so unusual.' He sighed and dashed a hand through his already dishevelled hair, then apparently making an effort to let the matter go, he brightened as he said, 'It's good to see you.'

'The feeling's mutual,' she replied, 'and I'm sorry I didn't make it before today. I hope you got my messages.'

'Of course. Something about buying an old barn?'

'Indeed, and I need to move swiftly in case the farmer decides to double-cross me and sell to somebody else.'

Sitting back as the server brought his coffee, he said, 'So where is the barn?'

'Just outside Dodderton. There's a massive amount to do before I can even begin the conversion, but I'm in need of a massive project so it couldn't have come at a better time. Anyway, don't get me started or I'll bore you to death with it. I have the tickets and I see from the date that they're for next Thursday, which could be a problem? Isn't that your day for surgery?'

'It'll be fine,' he assured her. 'I should be through by three, four at the latest, so if I drive like the clappers I could make it for seven, is it?'

'That's right. It's the opening, so you'll be treated to champagne and speeches and no doubt the artist himself will be there.'

Though clearly impressed, his eyes narrowed slightly as he asked, 'Will he know I've got my tickets through you?'

'Through Nick,' she corrected, 'and yes, he will. So, if he tries to engage you in conversation . . . Well, I'm sure you'll be happy to talk about his art, but if he should ask about how you know Nick, I'd be grateful if you left me out of it.'

'Of course,' he agreed.

She smiled. 'So, who have you decided to take with you?' she enquired, moving them on to safer ground.

'A cousin who lives in Chiswick. He's also a big fan, so I've shot way up in his estimation since I rang to say I had tickets. I'll probably stay over at his place rather than attempt to drive back that night. Do you want to get that?' he prompted, as her phone started to ring.

Seeing it was Nick she said, 'It's OK, I'll ring him later,' and letting the call go to messages, she changed the subject again. 'So how are bookings going for The Medics? Any more gigs coming up?'

Laughing, he said, 'Not for the next couple of weeks, but would you believe we've been asked to play at a bat mitzvah at the end of March? Actually, it might be slightly more impressive if the bat-ee, or whatever you call her, wasn't our drummer's niece, but hey, if they're up for it, who are we to let them down?'

Amused by his modesty, she said, 'If the way you got everyone dancing at the White Hart is anything to go by, it should be a great party.'

'Let's hope so. Actually, we've had an enquiry from your guys to play at the beginning and end of a walk at Blenheim Palace.'

Realising he must be referring to Breast Cancer Care's annual Pink Ribbonwalk, she said, 'Well that should get things off to a rousing start.' Last year she and Nick had walked in memory of Talia; this year, if she made it, she'd do the same, but probably alone.

I have some news, Nick had said, *I've been offered a position at the University of Sydney and I'm probably going to take it.*

'Are you OK?' Harry asked.

'Of course,' she replied, releasing her breath. 'So will you be joining the walk, or limiting yourself to the musical accompaniment?'

'Probably the latter if we need to play everyone out and back again. I expect my wife and Semeena, my cousin who you met, will represent the Becks.' He took another sip of his coffee and glanced at his watch.

'You have to go,' she said for him.

'I'm afraid so. It's one of those days, same as all the others.'

'Well, far be it from me to keep you from those whose need is far greater.'

Though his expression was droll, all he said as he stood up was, 'It's been great seeing you, albeit brief, and thanks for bringing the tickets. I haven't forgotten I owe you big time, and I'm determined to pay the debt.'

'You really don't have to,' she assured him, allowing him to help her into her raincoat.

As they reached the door, he asked, 'Will you be interested to know what I think of the show?'

She couldn't help but smile. 'If you want to tell me, I'll be happy to listen,' she replied, but only because it was him. Were it anyone else she wouldn't want the subject raised.

Seeming pleased with that, he said, 'Good, then I'll ring when I get back and hopefully you'll let me buy you dinner to say thanks,' and before she could object he pushed the door open for her to go ahead of him.

'Ah, rain,' he declared, as if it hadn't been pouring down for most of the month. 'Where's your car?'

As she started to answer an ambulance sped into A&E, siren blaring. 'In the pay and display over by Blackberry Hill,' she replied when she could.

'Then I'll walk part of the way with you,' and taking her umbrella, he held it over them both as they started along one of the hospital's main artery roads.

Trying not to feel so conscious of how close they were, she said, 'Are you up to anything special for the weekend?'

'Well, depends what you term special,' he replied. 'I'll have the boys all to myself while their mother's out of town at some conference. How about you? Are your niece and nephew going to be with you?'

'No, not this weekend.' Her words seemed to fall into the emptiness that lay ahead. 'They're going away with their father and stepmother.'

'Oh? Somewhere nice?'

'To see Kristina's parents.' She wondered how they were going to take the happy news of their daughter starting a new life down under. 'It'll give me the chance to get some preliminary plans together for the architect,' she ran on. 'I'm meeting him at the barn on Tuesday to start playing around with ideas.'

Handing her the umbrella as they reached the entrance to the clinic, he said, 'Well good luck with that. When it comes to interior design I'm in a category all of my own, that being completely useless.'

Laughing, she said, 'I don't think I'd be any better at what you do, so why don't we make a pact and stick with what we're good at?'

'Done,' he agreed, holding out a hand to shake.

Taking it, she was about to wish him a lovely weekend when he pulled her forward and kissed her cheek.

'Thanks again for the tickets,' he said, 'and for bringing them,' and letting go of her hand he answered his mobile as he turned in through the blue swing doors. 'Yes, I'm coming, I'm coming,' he told the caller.

Still startled by the kiss, Bel walked on to her car, not sure what to make of it, if anything, but the moment was soon gone as the bombshell Nick had dropped the other night hit her again.

She understood now why there had been so many trips to London of late: he'd presumably been meeting people from Sydney. It would also account for why he hadn't seemed himself since his honeymoon. He knew a major change was coming up, and he'd presumably been having as big a struggle with that as he was with breaking the news to her.

'Kristina – and I,' he'd said, 'think it'll be a great opportunity for her to start bonding with the children in a way that hasn't really been possible up to now.'

So they were going as far as they possibly could from her.

Feeling more wretched than she could bear, she got into the car and sat with her hands on the wheel, watching raindrops staggering down the windscreen.

He'd tried to make it sound as though the final decision hadn't yet been made, but she wasn't stupid. She could tell it had and he was simply trying to lessen the blow by not confirming it.

She kept wondering how the children were going to take it when they found out. She could see their little faces, confused and afraid as they clung to her the way they had when she'd told them their mother wouldn't be coming home again.

'Do you realise it could feel like another death for them?' she'd said to Nick. 'For the past two years they've been as close to me as they were to Talia . . .'

'Which is why we have to give Kristina a chance,' he'd cut in raggedly, 'because *she* is their mother now, Bel.'

Not you. He hadn't said those words, he'd never have been so cruel, but they'd been there anyway, stark and uncompromising in their truth.

'Let's not discuss it any more tonight,' he'd said. 'I can see you're upset, and I think it would be good for you to have some time to think it over before we speak again.'

So here she was, thinking it over, and over and over, and nothing, *absolutely nothing* was making it any easier to bear. The wrench, the loss, already felt as physical as it had when Talia had gone, and she could only see it getting worse. The children were going to be as devastated as she was when they found out. They wouldn't want to go, she just knew it, and nothing she, or anyone else, could say would make them understand why they had to. *For heaven's sake Nick, they're only five and seven, they shouldn't have to be coping with all this loss.*

'Nor should you,' Talia said.

'Nor should I what?' Bel replied.

'You know.' They both knew.

'But I'm the eldest.'

'By twenty minutes, so it doesn't count.'

175

'Do you think Mummy knows?' Bel asked.

Talia didn't reply and Bel felt her heart closing like a fist in her chest.

Just because you can't see me doesn't mean I'm not there.

Bel looked to the sky as though she might catch a glimpse of someone watching her.

'What will you do with the glimpse when you catch it?' Talia whispered.

'Keep it, like a butterfly, then we can use its wings to fly away.'

In the end it wasn't them who'd flown. It was their mother.

Taking out her phone as it rang, she saw it was Nick again.

'Hi, how are you?' he asked when she clicked on.

'Fine. How are you?'

'Worried about you.'

'There's no need to be. When will you go?'

'They'd like me to start at the beginning of the second semester.'

'Which is when?'

'The end of July.'

A few short months away. 'And you're sure it's what you want?'

'What I want to do is the best for us all.'

'Of course.' How could she argue with that without sounding desperate and possessive? The children weren't hers, his future was with Kristina, so perhaps it would be for the best if she wasn't in their lives any more. 'I have to go,' she said, tears of self-pity stinging her eyes.

'Bel?'

'Yes.'

'Let me come over this evening.'

She didn't want to end up begging him, or even breaking down in front of him. 'I don't think that's a good idea.'

'Why?'

'I just don't.'

'What are you doing now?'

'Does it matter?'

'It does to me.'

'I've just brought the tickets to Harry. I'm sorry, but I

176

really do have to go,' and before he could say any more she clicked off the line.

'Talk to him, Bel,' Talia said.

'There's no point. I have no rights here.'

'The children need you. They're more yours than Kristina's.'

Knowing she couldn't allow herself to listen to that, she started the engine and drove out of the hospital grounds, heading in the direction of Dodderton. Though she had no meetings at the barn, and it would be dark by the time she got there, she didn't want to go home yet in case Nick decided to turn up.

Stop it, she sobbed angrily, he's not your husband, or your partner, so you have no claim on him.

'He is your best friend,' Talia reminded her. 'Your only friend.'

'Thanks for reminding me.'

'You need someone of your own.'

'You think I don't know that?'

'Then do something about it, or the only person you'll have left is that man.'

Chapter Eleven

'Mum, what are you doing?'

Josie glanced across the waiting room to where a short plump woman with a pierced lower lip and no hair was slumped in one of the comfy chairs.

'Just finding something to read,' an older woman replied, carrying a magazine back to her place.

'You can go if you like,' her daughter told her irritably. 'I'll be all right on my own.'

Her mother sighed and sat down.

They were Josie's only companions in the waiting room. When she'd arrived it had been full, but the others had already been taken through to begin their treatment.

The plump woman with no hair shot a look in her direction, but when Josie smiled she didn't smile back.

No one wanted to be here; no one wanted to be friends with her, it seemed. Although from the things Josie had read online it wasn't usually like that, and some of the other patients who'd been here earlier had greeted each other like old friends. What a way to build up your Christmas card list; definitely not one they'd have chosen, she felt sure about that.

Sitting here in this dismal room with no windows and only one door, she was doing her best not to be downcast or nervous, though she had to admit she wasn't making a very good fist of it so far. It just didn't seem right, walking in here, feeling like a perfectly healthy person, to have all sorts of chemicals pumped into her system that were likely to make her feel worse than she ever had in her life.

'There are a couple of reasons for giving you chemo-therapy before we operate,' Mr Beck had explained when she'd rung at the end of last week. 'The first is to shrink the tumour to make it easier to remove. The second is to destroy any cancer cells that might have spread elsewhere in your body.'

Spread elsewhere! She wasn't even going to think about that.

The wait now was for the pharmacist to prepare her drugs. Apparently they were so toxic that he had to wear protective clothing while he worked with them. *And then they were going to send them into her veins!*

'Mum, your phone's vibrating,' the plump woman snapped crossly.

Realising it was probably fear making the younger woman edgy, Josie felt a bolt of it shudder through her.

She tried to imagine having her mother here, and could only feel glad that she wasn't. Eileen had never been big on patience, so all this sitting around would get right on her nerves. No doubt she would have had to keep popping outside for a smoke, completely oblivious to the fact that she was in a cancer unit.

How would she react when Josie finally broke the news? Being so concerned about Jeff, Lily and Ryan she hadn't given much thought to her mother, and decided she probably wouldn't start now.

Jeff thought she was covering a cleaning job for a mate today. Luckily he hadn't asked which mate, or she'd have had to make someone up in case he ran into whoever she chose. He'd been in quite a good mood since doing the Heathrow run last week, although they hadn't had a night out in town yet. It was too extravagant to be thinking of anything like that, anyway, especially when he needed to get his car back on the road. Less of a rush for that while he had Kev's taxi to drive, thank goodness.

'Josie? Are you ready to come through?'

It was Jenny Eastment, the pretty, tousle-haired nurse who'd checked her blood pressure earlier and taken some blood.

What would happen if she said no?

As she got to her feet the thoughts in her head seemed to swim off somewhere else, out past Kesterly lighthouse, around the rocks, all the way out to sea. Who was sailing up and down the estuary today? How many birds were diving into the waves plucking up fish?

'Are you OK?' Jenny asked, taking her arm. 'Bit nervous?'

Josie managed a smile. 'Just a bit,' she responded drolly.

'You'll be fine,' Jenny assured her. 'The first time's always more of a challenge, but we're going to make you nice and comfy, and if you want a cup of tea, or anything to eat, you just let us know.'

Unable to imagine being hungry ever again, Josie followed her into the unit, where a dozen or so people were already settled in large, mock-leather chairs with translucent tubes and cannulae attaching them to the apparatus behind them. She remembered seeing a chemo unit on the news once being opened by Terry Wogan or Graham Norton, or someone like that. It was so plush it could have been a five-star hotel. This one was nothing like that. The room was a cavernous old hall with tall, arch-top windows, peeling paint and a vaulted ceiling. Each place had a curtain next to it, with a track looped out over the chair like a wonky halo, and in front was a bed table similar to those in the care home she used to clean.

Feeling it was rude to look at anyone, she kept her eyes straight ahead as Jenny took her to one of only two empty chairs and gestured for her to sit down.

'Are you expecting anyone to come and keep you company?' Jenny asked, fiddling with the drip bag that had already been attached to a steel pole to one side of the chair. Also on the pole was some kind of computer with a large keypad and screen. Josie presumed all these things had proper names, but she had no idea what they were, and anyway, what did it matter? Knowing what they were called wasn't going to change what they did.

No, she wasn't expecting anyone to come and keep her company.

It wasn't long before Jenny had attached a tube to the cannula she'd planted in the back of Josie's left hand. Good job Jeff wasn't having to go through this, he'd never have survived the whacking great needle. By God it had hurt going in.

'We're giving you what's called a flush-out first,' Jenny explained. 'Basically, it's to clear the veins so the drugs can run through more smoothly. It'll take about fifteen minutes. Would you like a couple of magazines to look at while it's going on?'

'That would be lovely, thank you,' Josie replied, sounding slightly breathless. 'Is it – is it OK to leave my phone on?'

'Yes, of course, but we ask everyone to switch to vibrate only. Cup of tea? Coffee? Juice?'

'Tea, thank you. No milk or sugar.'

Jenny was at the nurses' station now, filling in some forms, while Josie flipped through a copy of *Closer* magazine and sipped her cuppa. It was quite nice having waitress service, she decided. Best to enjoy it while she could, because once this jolly little flush-out was over there wasn't going to be much to feel good about, not if all the stuff she'd read during the last few days was anything to go by.

The side effects are a thousand times worse than anyone prepares you for, someone had written in a blog.

The chemo damaged my heart, another had posted.

I had to give up work for over six months, was another. *I ended up losing my job, and my husband left me. Not the best time of my life.*

Josie had stopped reading at that point.

'What's yours?' a woman in the next chair asked.

Josie turned to her.

'Mine's bowel,' the woman told her.

'Oh, breast,' Josie said. 'Is this your first time too?'

'No. Fourth. It's bloody awful, don't let them tell you anything else.'

Josie didn't know what to say, but it appeared nothing was required, as the woman closed her eyes and let go of a wavery sigh.

Further along the room a nurse was closing a curtain to give a young man some privacy, while another nurse typed information into his computer.

All the things they had to know, these nurses. It was making Josie's head spin to try and think of it.

Hearing her phone buzz, she lifted it out of her lap and found a text from Lily. *Dad doing my head in. He won't come to*

Bristol this weekend even though J and I are offering to treat you out to lunch for his birthday. I told him he doesn't have to come to the prison after, but he's still saying no. Please speak to him.

Knowing only too well how stubborn Jeff could be, Josie sent a text back saying *Why don't you and J come to Kesterly on Saturday night? Dad would probably prefer that. We can go to Chanter Lysee.*

She just hoped she was going to be all right by then, because if she couldn't make it out on Jeff's birthday, the last present she wanted to give him was the reason why she wasn't up to it.

Was he going to end up leaving her?

OK. Will talk to J, Lily texted back. *What are you getting him?*

DVD of 'Wild Weather'.

Having always been fascinated by earthquakes, hurricanes and the like, Jeff hadn't missed an episode of this series when it was on BBC, so she felt sure he'd enjoy watching it all over again.

Brilliant idea. Wish I'd thought of it. Any suggestions for me?

Will think about it. How many on wedding guest list now?

Eighty-eight. Invitations due at end of week. So excited. Where are you?

The question hit Josie's heart. Where was she? She looked around and tried to think what to say, but all that kept going through her mind was that she shouldn't be here. This was a place other people came, not her.

Having a sit-down with a cup of tea, she texted back, knowing Lily would presume from that that she was at home.

Sorry. Got to go. Love you.

Love you too.

As the messaging ended Josie found herself being engulfed by a horrible sense of doom. She couldn't allow it to stay, mustn't listen to the voices in her head telling her she'd never make the wedding, or see Ryan this side of a prison wall again. It was all nonsense. Mr Beck had already told her he'd schedule the op to make sure she could go to the wedding, so he obviously thought she was still going to be around in the summer.

Would she still be here when Ryan came out? He wasn't due for release for another two years.

People with cancer lasted that long. A lot longer, actually, so she had to stop scaring herself like this.

'Are you feeling OK?' Jenny asked, coming to inspect progress. She reached up to hang another bag on the pole. This one had Josie's name on the front – her very own Molotov cocktail.

'Fine,' Josie assured her, as Jenny carefully detached the tube from the cannula in her hand. 'Didn't feel a thing.'

Jenny smiled. 'Excellent. So, we're going to start your first cycle now,' she explained, pulling up a chair. 'You've probably already been told which drugs we're giving you, but I'm going to run through them again. OK?'

Josie nodded, but though she heard what Jenny went on to say, she knew she'd never be able to remember it if anyone asked. Who would? *Fluorouracil, epirubicin, something else and something else. Five milligrams, or was it a hundred and five? One would make her hair fall out, another might push her into menopause, maybe it was the same one.*

'It's all written down for you,' Jenny assured her, 'and I'm here to answer any questions you might have.'

Josie found herself in another struggle with doom as she asked hoarsely, 'Will I – will I be able to do ballet after?'

Jenny looked impressed. 'Absolutely, if you're feeling up to it.'

'That's good,' Josie replied, 'because I couldn't do it before.'

An old joke that Jenny must have heard a hundred times, but her laugh was so merry that Josie was able to laugh too.

Lighten up, Jose, it's going to be all right.

After entering information into the computer, and making sure the slow drip feed had begun, Jenny sat down again and held her free hand. 'It'll be fine,' she whispered gently. 'You just let me know if you feel unwell, or experience any kind of pain . . .'

'I didn't realise it might be painful,' Josie interrupted, staring at the clear liquid as it passed through the syringe and on into her vein. *The destruction begins.*

'It shouldn't be,' Jenny told her.

'Will it burn?'

'You shouldn't feel anything at all.'

'Apart from nauseous after?'

'Metoclopramide is an anti-sickness drug.'

Presuming this was one of the names that had passed her by, Josie looked at the young nurse and smiled. 'It's a marvellous job that you do,' she told her. 'No wonder people call you angels.'

Jenny laughed. 'That's definitely not what my boyfriend calls me,' she admitted, 'but I'm going to tell him what you said.'

Josie was still watching her. 'I've got a daughter about your age,' she said, knowing that Lily was probably five or six years younger. 'She's getting married in the summer.'

Jenny's eyes lit up. 'Oh, how lovely. I bet you're really looking forward to that.'

Josie nodded. 'Very much. I've got a picture of her on my phone, if you'd like to see it.' As she scrolled to it she realised how tedious this must be for Jenny, and stopped. 'You've got better things to do than look at my family snaps,' she declared.

'No, no, I really want to see it,' Jenny insisted.

Finding one of Lily and Jasper at Christmas, Josie passed it over.

'Oh wow, she's really pretty.' Jenny sounded as though she meant it, and why wouldn't she when Lily *was* pretty, even if Josie said so herself? 'And he's dead cute,' Jenny added with a wink. 'What're their names?'

'Lily and Jasper. My son's name is Ryan, and my husband's called Jeff. So there, now you know us all. What's your boyfriend's name?'

'Alistair. He's a vet in Taunton, so I don't get to see him as often as I'd like, but he's hoping to join a practice here in Kesterly later this year. Is that your phone?'

Checking to see who it was, Josie started to say it was her husband, but for some reason the word wouldn't come. She looked at Jenny who was seeming hazy and distant, as though she was floating away.

'Are you OK?' Jenny asked.

Josie still couldn't make herself speak. Everything was going dark, then lighting up again. Sounds were dragging and slurred.

'Bronia,' Jenny called over her shoulder.

Josie turned her head, and saw nothing but swirling darkness . . .

The next thing Josie knew, cold towels were being pressed to her face while someone fanned her with a clipboard.

'Ah, you're back,' Jenny chuckled. 'We lost you there for a moment.'

Josie blinked, and looked up at the other nurse. 'Sorry,' she mumbled, still feeling light-headed, but less giddy now.

'There's nothing to be sorry for,' Jenny chided. 'It happens sometimes, but you should be all right now. Tell me if you're not.'

Josie tried to assess how she was feeling, and decided it was only slightly groggy.

'Am I going to make it through to the end of this?' she asked, not sure whether she meant the session, or entire course of treatment.

'Absolutely,' Jenny said firmly. 'We'll give it another half-hour or so, and if you're still not handling it we'll call Dr Pattullo to alter your prescription.'

Amazingly, at least to Josie, by the time she was finally released from the chair, two hours later, all she felt, physically, was slightly stiff from having sat for so long, and ready for the loo after so many cups of tea. No more dizziness (perhaps a little, because she'd got up too fast), or weird sense of everything floating around her; she wasn't really feeling very much different to when she'd come in here.

'Keep this on for the next few hours,' Jenny advised, as she bound a compress to the puncture in Josie's hand. 'The bleeding should have stopped by then.'

Covering the dressing with her sleeve, Josie said, 'Thank you. You've been very kind today.'

Jenny smiled. 'How are you getting home?'

Josie stifled a yawn. 'By bus. Let's hope I don't fall asleep on the way back and go sailing past my stop.'

'Why don't you set your phone?' Jenny suggested, handing her a small white bag, stapled at the top. 'Anti-sickness pills with instructions,' she explained, 'some painkillers, just in case you need them, and the emergency number, which hopefully you won't need.'

Taking the bag, Josie thanked her again, and after helping to clear the dishes from her table, and being told she really didn't need to wash up, she walked out of the unit into a wet and windy day.

One down, she was thinking as she headed for the bus stop, five more to go.

Josie was still feeling fine. She kept waiting for a blanket of tiredness to wrap her up in some sort of fog, or the urge to throw up to overwhelm her, but so far neither was happening. Her hair was still rooted to her scalp (not that she'd expected it to drop out just yet), and the reason she couldn't wait to get in the front door was because it was so cold and blustery, not because she had anything bad going on.

So why, she had to ask herself as she peeled off her coat, was she feeling so bloody depressed? Having no side effects was something to feel pleased about, not glum, *so pull yourself together woman, and get on with the ironing.*

After taking off her boots and putting on the kettle, she wondered if she should run upstairs to have a look at her boob. As if it was going to look any different already! *Get a grip, for heaven's sake. There's plenty to be getting on with, and the world doesn't come to a stop just because you've had a shot of chemo.*

What was it going to be like when she got undressed tonight? With all those chemicals inside her she might glow in the dark.

At least she could still make herself laugh.

Having heaved the laundry basket out of the linen cupboard, she settled it on the sofa and reached for her mobile as it rang.

'There you are,' her mother stated testily. 'Are you at home?'

'Just got in,' Josie replied, going into the kitchen for the ironing board. 'Is everything all right?'

'No, it bloody isn't. Karine's got the flu so I need you to help me with my roots.'

'I'm not a hairdresser,' Josie reminded her.

'I know that. I'll tell you what to do. I've got all the stuff . . .'

'Mum, I can't do it . . .'

'Yes you can, I'm coming over there now,' and the line went dead.

Putting the ironing board down, Josie rang her back. 'Why can't you wait till Karine's better, or go to Mimi's on the high street?' she demanded.

'I took the day off specially to have this done,' her mother retorted, 'and I haven't been speaking to that stupid cow Mimi since she invited everyone to her fiftieth and left me out. I'll see you in twenty minutes,' and down went the phone again.

Tempted to go out rather than have to deal with her mother and her roots, Josie plugged in the iron and went to find out what had just dropped through the letter box. The local paper. As she put it on the arm of Jeff's chair, ready for when he got home, she remembered he'd rung earlier, so she dialled his number and almost wished she hadn't got through when he answered.

'You'll never guess what's bloody happened,' he growled angrily. 'Kev's only gone and taken his car back. Not because he can drive it, but because his brother-in-law, that waste of space Frankie Root, thought he'd have a go at cabbing.'

'Oh no,' Josie groaned. 'So where are you now?'

'On my way to Houseman's Storage. Apparently they're looking for a security guard.'

'How are you getting there?'

'By bus, how do you think? Have you got yourself another job yet, because it's high time you did? Kev's Mrs says they're looking for people at the ice-cream factory over by Mulgrove.'

'It'd take me two hours to get there,' she pointed out, as if it were even possible for her to apply.

'Yeah, well, beggars can't be choosers, and if they're paying well . . . Go on their website, see what you can find out, and if it's full-time, all the better. I know it'll mean letting Fliss down at the caff, but she can always find someone to fill your place. OK, I'm there now, so I'm going to ring off. I'll let you know how it goes.'

By the time her mother bustled in through the door with a bulging plastic sack in one hand and a vanity case in the other, Josie had drunk a nice cup of tea and managed to press a few shirts and sheets.

'Effing washing machine's on the blink again,' Eileen grumbled, kicking the large bag across the floor, 'so I thought I'd bung this lot in yours while I was here. Got the kettle on?'

'No, and I'm not doing your roots, so you can forget it.'

'Well someone has to,' Eileen snapped. 'I never ask you for nothing and the only time I do it's too much trouble. Bloody typical!'

'Mother . . .'

'No, it's all right, I know where I'm not wanted,' and bundling on through to the kitchen she began jamming her laundry into the machine. 'That's a nice way to treat your own mother,' she grumbled, turfing out a stray white thong that had found its way into the coloureds and stuffing it in her pocket.

'Why don't you go and see if Carly's in?' Josie suggested. 'She does her own roots all the time so she'll know what to do.'

'Actually, that's not a bad idea,' Eileen agreed. 'Why didn't I think of it? Got any detergent?'

'Didn't you bring any?'

'Oh, begrudge me that and all, would you?'

Sighing, Josie said, 'There's some under the sink, but don't leave me short.'

After starting the machine, Eileen came back into the room. 'What's up?' she demanded, her pale blue eyes peering from pools of black liner. 'And don't say nothing, because I can tell something is.'

'I'm fine,' Josie insisted. 'Just got a lot on my mind.'

'Anything you want to talk about?'

'Not really, thanks.'

'You need to loosen up a bit, have some fun and stop looking on the black side all the time,' Eileen advised.

'I don't look on the black side,' Josie protested, 'although it's hard not to, the way things are. And it's all right for you, you've got a job and regular income . . .'

'Yeah, I'm a millionaire me,' Eileen muttered.

'Compared to us you are.'

'Oh don't give me that. If you got yourself off that back-side of yours and went out to find a proper job you'd get one just like that.' She clicked her bony fingers, rattling her bracelets. 'Or why don't you ask Fliss for more hours? I bet she'd jump at it.'

Knowing Fliss probably would, Josie said, 'I might,' and answering her mobile as it rang she didn't get a chance to speak before Jeff said, 'Job's already gone. Wasted my bloody time coming over here, never mind the fare. Now I've got to get back again. I'm going to stop at Trev's to find out what's going on with the car. There's a couple of hundred left from that fare last week, with any luck it'll be enough to get me back on the road.'

Knowing better than to argue, in spite of needing to pay the council tax and water bills, Josie said, 'OK. Give me a ring when you're on your way home. I'll make sure your tea's on the table.' *There was a jar of tomato sauce in the cupboard, she could pour that over some spaghetti to save her going out again.*

'I'll make sure your tea's on the table,' Eileen mimicked, as Josie rang off. 'What are you, his bloody slave?'

'Why don't you mind your own business and go and bug Carly,' Josie snapped irritably.

'Don't worry, I'm on my way.'

As the door closed behind her Josie pulled a pair of Jeff's jeans from the basket and laid them out on the ironing board. She still wasn't feeling tired, or sick, only glummer than ever and angry, she realised, with her family for being so wrapped up in themselves.

They might not be if you told them what was going on with you, she reminded herself.

Question is, would they care?

Don't be ridiculous, of course they would.

They wouldn't be able to do anything about it though, and Jeff was already frustrated enough, the way things were. He didn't need her problems piling on top of him like a bloody avalanche.

As for her mother . . .

Sighing, Josie ran the iron up and down Jeff's jeans. It seemed horribly disloyal to feel the way she did about her mother, but she couldn't help wishing Eileen was a bit more like other mothers. The ones who went to chemo with their daughters, for example. Eileen wouldn't have to sit there the entire time, or even get up early to catch the bus with her, but it would be lovely to have someone to meet when it was over so she could talk about how it had gone.

Who are you kidding? You don't want to talk to anyone about it, so quit putting a downer on Eileen. If you gave her half a chance you might discover she's just the shoulder you need.

Having had long experience of Eileen's shoulder, Josie almost shuddered. 'It's your bloody fault,' she'd shouted when Josie had told her about Ryan being bullied at school. 'You baby him too much. What you have to do is tell him to get back to that school and thump the fucking daylights out of the little bastards who're picking on him.'

'I don't want you round here giving them to me,' she'd cried, when Josie had admitted the children had come home with nits. 'Get some stuff from the chemist and let me know when the coast is clear.'

'What are you getting so upset about?' she'd snorted after Josie's dad's funeral. 'Meself, I feel like dancing on the old bugger's grave.' Not understanding, it seemed, that Josie had lost her father, she'd even turned up drunk at the end of the wake and started telling anyone who'd listen how lousy the old sod had been in bed.

Not her finest hour, that was for sure, but she wasn't all bad, Josie had to remind herself. For one thing she was a devoted nana, even if she said so herself. She'd even offered to go and take on Debbie Prince when Ryan had been sent down (though what having a go at Debbie Prince would have achieved, apart from hospitalisation for one or other, possibly both, presumably only Eileen knew). And there was no doubt she adored Lily. 'I'd do anything for that girl,' Eileen often declared. 'She's special, she is, a real one-off. Mind you, she's a lot like me when I was her age, all that lovely hair and big blue eyes.' As far as Josie was aware her mother had never been a redhead in her life, not even out of a bottle, and Josie wasn't entirely sure which shade of blue brown was, but presumably Eileen knew.

This isn't a good time to start thinking about Dawnie, Josie told herself as her ex-best friend popped into her mind. *She's long gone, and good riddance after what she did. It doesn't matter that she'd come with you to chemo if she was here, or run the house, help Lily sort out her wedding, even visit Ryan if you weren't up to it. She'd also sleep with your husband and end up running off with him when it's all over, that's what she'd do and where would you be then?*

Sighing sadly, Josie folded the jeans and shook out a pair of boxers. Her husband might have cheated on her once, and was definitely grumpier than he used to be, but he was still her husband and she'd never want to be with anyone else.

You have to tell him what's going on, Josie, he'll only keep on about you getting a job if you don't.

She would, she just needed to find the right words, a way of breaking it to him so that it didn't sound too serious, but nevertheless he would understand why she couldn't apply for any vacancies while all this was going on.

On the other hand, if she turned out to be one of the lucky ones who didn't suffer much from the side effects, maybe she'd manage to bluff her way through it without telling anyone at all.

And exactly how, she asked herself as she started up the stairs, *would you explain a missing boob in a few months' time?*

It still might not come to that. OK, Mr Beck seemed convinced that it would, but all sorts of things happened where people's bodies were concerned, and if one woman could will away her cancer, the way Josie had read online, then who was to say she couldn't?

*

'What the bloody hell's the matter with you?' Jeff grumbled, as Josie climbed back into bed and snuggled under the covers. 'Up and down, up and down like a bloody yo-yo. I'm trying to get some sleep here.'

'Sorry,' she whispered raggedly. She was shivering like she'd been dunked in a barrel of cold water, her throat was burning from all the bile she'd brought up, and the pain-killers weren't helping her head. It was throbbing like someone was chucking a jackhammer at her skull.

She closed her eyes. *Please no more,* she begged silently as another wave of nausea caught her.

She lifted a hand to put it to her head and caught the dressing on the duvet.

'What's that?' Jeff had demanded when they were getting ready for bed. She hadn't felt sick then, or not like she did now. 'I hope you haven't been trying anything daft, things aren't that bad, you know – or not yet.'

A lame joke that hadn't made either of them laugh.

'Oh, I burnt it with the iron,' she'd lied dismissively.

'Must be some burn, a plaster that size.'

The need to get up suddenly seized her again, and staggering back to the bathroom she slumped to her knees, only just making it in time. The wrench on her insides was so brutal she'd have cried out with the pain if she'd had the breath. Quickly transferring her head to the sink, she sank down on the loo as the rejection of the drugs began flooding from both ends. It was like passing fire while someone drilled nails into her brain. Her eyes stung with acid tears, her skin felt like it was crawling off her bones.

Please God, please, please, she was crying inside. *Make it stop. Please make it stop.*

It went on and on, pausing for brief moments before coming back like a blowtorch.

'Here,' Jeff said, coming to wrap a blanket around her. 'I don't know what you ate, but I'm glad I didn't have any of it.'

'Thanks,' she managed to mumble, feeling the blanket's warmth sinking into her.

'Best sleep in Lily's room,' he told her, 'or I'll end up missing the alarm.'

Though she wanted him to put his arms round her and tell her it'd be all right, she knew if he did she'd end up spewing all over him. Besides, he didn't go in for hugging as much as patting, and she didn't think she could stand to have anyone do that.

As he closed their bedroom door she began retching again, and again, the pull on her stomach, the strain on her chest so bad she felt she was turning inside out. She wondered if she should call the emergency number, or if what was happening to her was normal.

It was over an hour later before, depleted and exhausted, she was able to splash her face with cold water and drag herself into Lily's room, where she slumped on the bed, heart pounding, breath tearing raggedly at her lungs. Her hair was matted with sweat; her skin flamed as she shivered and shook. She was as weak as a kitten, and beyond parched. She needed water. Why hadn't she drunk some while she was washing her face?

'Jeff,' she whispered, knowing he wouldn't hear. 'I'm sorry, I left a mess in the bathroom.'

She must have passed out then, because the next thing she knew Jeff was shouting, 'What the bloody hell? You could have cleaned up after yourself.'

He appeared in the doorway and she struggled to sit up. 'I'll do it now,' she said, trying to move her legs off the bed.

'Don't bother, I'll do it,' he growled. 'You look terrible, best stay where you are.'

Sighing with relief, she sank back into the pillow.

'If you're not any better by lunchtime,' he said, from the bathroom, 'get yourself up the doctor's.'

She lay quietly, staring into the early-morning darkness, waiting for her system to revolt again. Her head still ached, her skin felt prickly, but for the moment her insides seemed calm.

She closed her eyes. She was so tired she wanted to sink right into the bed and never get up again. She hoped Jeff wouldn't mind seeing to his own breakfast. It would only be this once; by tomorrow she'd be up and about, and even if she didn't feel too special she was sure she'd manage to get through the day.

Chapter Twelve

'Bel? It's Yvonne Hubert here, from the breast clinic. Is this a bad time?'

Panting as she slowed her run to a stop, Bel managed to say, 'Hi Yvonne, how are you? Just give me a moment to catch my breath.'

'No rush,' Yvonne responded.

After bending at the waist to stretch out her legs, Bel rotated her neck and shoulders and turned in the shale to face the sea. There was a time when she'd dreaded calls from Yvonne, but these days she had no reason to be afraid, only surprised and curious. 'OK, I'm with you,' she said, still slightly breathless, 'but it's difficult to hear you in this wind, so I'll head home and call you back. Ten minutes?'

'That's fine. I'll be here.'

After ringing off, Bel jogged back along the beach, round a pile of windsurfers' gear, over a narrow ravine and up the steps in the rocks to the meadow that sloped up to her garden. Today was the first time in over a month that the rain had held off long enough to allow her to go for a run, and though she guessed she'd ache later, she was already feeling a high from being out in the fresh air. *Just don't think about Nick taking the children to Sydney.*

After tearing off her sweatband and grabbing an apple from the fruit bowl she rang Yvonne back. 'OK, what can I do for you?' she asked, biting into the apple as Yvonne picked up.

Coming straight to the point, Yvonne said, 'We have a lady who's recently been diagnosed and began chemotherapy a week ago. The reason I'm calling you is because she's finding it hard to tell her family about what she's going through, and I was hoping you might agree to see her.'

Though Bel had undergone some volunteer training with Breast Cancer Care a while ago, this was the first time she'd actually been called upon to provide support, and as the request wasn't coming directly from the charity itself she wasn't entirely sure what to say. But what difference did it make who the request came from?

'What this lady says she wants,' Yvonne continued, 'is to talk to the relative of someone who's been diagnosed. In other words, someone who can give her some insight into what it's like from the perspective of a family member.'

Bel's apple stopped mid-air. She'd never imagined being asked to share her grief with a stranger, least of all someone whose own loved ones were about to go through the same. What on earth could she tell the woman that would make her feel any better? Nothing, was the answer, because there was nothing about cancer that allowed anyone to feel better, unless it was cured, or at least beaten into remission, and this woman wasn't at that stage – yet.

'What do you think?' Yvonne prompted gently.

Bel put the apple down and turned to the window. 'To be honest, I'm not sure I'm the right person,' she said, gazing out at the surfers. 'Remember, Talia didn't make it. I can't imagine that's what this woman would want to hear.'

'No, I don't suppose it is, but if you do agree to talk to her we'll be sure to tell her what happened to your sister, and then let her make up her mind if she wants to go through with making contact.'

Still thrown by the request, Bel tried to think what to say. She really didn't want to do it, everything inside her was resisting it, but how was she going to feel if she said an outright no?

'Of course we can always put her in direct touch with Breast Cancer Care,' Yvonne continued, 'but I know you're affiliated with them, and as you're in the Kesterly area . . . A face-to-face meeting with someone like you would prob-ably help her a lot.'

Like me? 'Can you tell me any more about her?' Bel asked.

'If she has small children, I honestly don't think I could handle it . . .'

'Her children are young adults,' Yvonne came in quickly. 'She's married, living with her husband, and has a part-time job in a café. She's very sweet and unassuming, still a bit shell-shocked by it all, but the one thing she's insisting on is being able to talk to someone who's been through what she has to inflict on her family, as she puts it.'

Feeling for the woman, Bel said, 'She should be more worried about herself. That's what'll matter to them, that she's getting all the support she can to help *her* deal with it, never mind them.'

'Of course, and you can say that to her, but as you know very well mothers tend to put their spouses and children first.'

Yes, Bel did know that. Sighing softly, she tried running the probable ramifications through in her mind. In the end she said, 'I'm not saying no, but can I have some time to think about it?'

'By all means. There's no obligation, naturally. No one's going to pressure you if you don't feel comfortable with it. The woman concerned won't know who you are, or even that you exist.'

The assurance turned out to be small comfort over the next hour or so, as Bel simply couldn't stop thinking about the woman, whoever she was. And knowing that she could be sitting somewhere in Kesterly right now, waiting to hear if someone would help her, was making it worse. It seemed so cruel and unnecessary to keep her hanging on, when all it would take was an hour of Bel's time to explain how she'd felt when she'd found out that her beloved sister's tumour was malignant.

Devastated, angry with the world, terrified, helpless.

Was that really what this woman wanted to hear?

She didn't have to be too blunt about it. She could always focus more on how relieved she was for Talia that she'd had someone to lean on.

'Hi, it's Bel,' she said when she got through to Yvonne again, 'I've decided I'll talk to her.'

'Really?' Yvonne cried, sounding thrilled. 'That's marvellous. I'll get on to her now and give her your details.'

'OK. What's her name, so I'm prepared?'

'Josie Clark. I can't say when she'll be in touch, or even that she will be for certain. It'll be up to her, of course, and as we're going into the weekend I don't imagine you'll hear right away. The important thing is she'll have someone to call when she feels ready to pick up the phone again.'

It was Saturday afternoon now, and Bel was so engrossed in drawing up initial plans for the barn's conversion that she'd all but forgotten her promise to speak to Josie Clark. More prominent in her thoughts at the moment, aside from what she was doing, was the fact that Nick and Kristina hadn't been in touch, so she wasn't sure whether she'd see the children this weekend or not.

Each time she thought about them leaving she could feel herself becoming swamped in as much agitation as despair. It wasn't that she didn't understand the need for them to bond with Kristina, and she could accept that she was standing in the way of that, but to take them to the other side of the world, where she'd only ever be able to communicate with them through Skype and email, was nothing short of intolerable.

They wouldn't want to go, she was sure of it, but there was no way in the world Nick would ever be persuaded to leave them with her while he took up his new post. Besides, the last thing she wanted was to set up a contest between her and their father. That was in no one's best interests, least of all theirs.

She just couldn't help wondering if Nick had given enough consideration to what being separated from her was going to mean for the children. Losing both their mother, and her, in such a short space of time could have disastrous consequences later in their lives. All kinds of problems were likely to start raising their ugly heads: abandonment issues, separation anxiety, an inability to trust, fear of rejection. He really needed to give these matters some thought. It wasn't that she presumed herself indispensable; she simply wanted to make sure they felt safe and loved, and able to trust someone when they said they were there to stay. There was no doubt in her mind that they trusted her every bit as much as they loved her.

'And let's face it,' she cried when Nick came over later that day, 'even you haven't been there for them throughout everything. OK, I'm not blaming you, but someone had to take care of them, explain what was happening and why you went away after their mummy died.'

Nick flushed with guilt. 'I wasn't thinking straight at the time,' he retorted defensively.

'None of us were, but you put yourself first, Nick, and you're doing it again. You don't have to take the job in Australia; you could stay here in a place they know, where they have friends, an aunt who loves them and who you can rely on to take care of them when you and Kristina go off on a dig. Who's going to do that for you in Sydney?'

Having no answer for that, he shot back with, 'You accuse me of putting myself first, but it's *you* who's being selfish, Bel. You're behaving as though they're yours, and that I have no right to start a new life with them . . .'

'*Of course you do*, you're their father so you have all the rights, but I don't think you're exercising them well. I know this is because Kristina feels insecure . . .'

'Oh come on, I can hardly manufacture a job offer to make her feel better.'

'But when it came I expect she jumped at it, and to keep her happy you're doing the same. She's not the one who matters, Nick, it's the children. They depend on you to make the right decisions, with *their* interests at heart as well as your own.'

'No! What you're asking is for me to put your interests first, but I can't do that, Bel. I care about you, and I always will, but you're not their mother, or my wife.'

'I'm well aware of that, but do you really think this is what Talia would want, for you to take them away . . .'

'It can't be about what she wants,' he cried. 'She's not here any more, and no one regrets that more than I do, but we can't live our lives based on what she might or might not have wanted.'

'Why not? She's their mother!'

'*Was* their mother.'

'OK, was, but no one will ever take her place. If you think that, you've got no understanding of what a mother is.'

'I know that if Talia had had her way *we'd* be married and *you* would be their mother now,' he raged, 'but I'm not going to let her rule me from the grave. I loved her, I truly did, still do, but we have to move on and seeing you, being with you . . .' He broke off, silenced by the shock on her face.

'Are you saying Talia wanted you to marry me?' she demanded, feeling suddenly light-headed.

'You know she did.'

Bel shook her head.

Dashing a hand through his hair, he said, 'I'm sorry, I thought . . . I assumed . . . I shouldn't have blurted it out like that . . .'

'What did she say?' Bel wanted to know.

'She wasn't thinking straight at the end, you know that better than anyone, but she kept telling herself, *me*, that you'd take care of us, and that we must take care of you. She wanted us all to be together, but you have to see how . . . *incestuous* that feels.'

'Incestuous?' Bel echoed incredulously.

'OK, maybe that's the wrong word, but for God's sake, Bel, you don't need me to tell you, you look just like her. Every time you speak, laugh, turn your head, make any sort of move, you remind me of her. It's the same for the children, though obviously they associate it all with you now, and you've got to see how difficult that is for Kristina. She deserves a chance and you're not giving her one. You don't even try to be friends with her.'

Bel could only stare at him.

'Try to imagine how it is for her,' he ran on, 'knowing that every time I look at you I'm seeing my dead wife. She can't compete with that, and even if she tried she'd never win, not where the children are concerned.'

'Tell me,' Bel said carefully, 'did you marry Kristina to stop me thinking there could ever be anything between us? Is that why you rushed into it, to convince me that you really didn't intend to marry me, no matter what Talia wanted?'

The way his colour deepened showed that she might not be so very far from the truth.

'That's crazy,' she exclaimed. 'I've never wanted to be your wife, and if you married Kristina to prove to me that the feeling's mutual, then for God's sake, it's *you* who's not being fair to her, not me. Do you love her?'

'Of course I do.'

'Are you sure about that?'

He threw out his hands. 'That's not what we're discussing.'

'Yes we are.'

His face was tight with anger as he said, 'OK, at the beginning . . . Everything was so mixed up . . . I don't think I knew what I wanted, or even what I was doing. I just didn't want you thinking . . . I was sure Talia had made her wishes known to you . . .'

'Don't you think I'd have told you if she had?'

'I don't know. All I know is that when you never said anything I assumed you were waiting, expecting me to . . .' He broke off, clearly not wanting to put his mistake into any more words.

'Kristina and I have talked about it,' he continued, 'and she understands that it wasn't the same for me as it was for her when we met, but it is now. And that's what's important. I *want* to spend my life with her, and she wants to be every bit as much of a mother to Oscar and Nell as she will be to the children we might have together. As long as they're as attached to you as they are, that's not going to be possible.'

Bel's heart was aching with the pain of his words.

'I'm sorry,' he said raggedly, 'I realise how hard this is for you; it is for me too, but when this job came up, it was as though something out there was offering me the answers I'd been looking for.'

'You mean a way of escaping me?'

'Please don't see it like that. You'll always be a very special part of our lives, and I don't want that to change . . .'

'How can it not when you're going to be over ten thousand miles away?'

Since he couldn't answer that, he didn't try.

Realising how close she was to breaking down, she forced herself to say, 'I think you should go now. Kristina and the children will be wondering where you are.'

'Bel . . .'

Her hand came up. 'We've said enough for today.'

He continued to watch her as she turned away. 'Will you come for lunch tomorrow, as usual?' he asked.

'I'm not sure.'

'The children will want to see you.'

'Of course they will,' she cried, spinning round angrily, 'but do you really think prolonging our old habits is going to help when it comes time for them to go? We have to start making the break now so it's gradual, doesn't come as too much of a shock or feel as devastating as . . .' She couldn't hold on any more. Tears were streaming down her face as sobs shook her body.

'Oh Bel,' he murmured, coming to take her in his arms. 'I wish things could be different, I swear I do . . .'

'Just go,' she choked, pushing him away. 'Please. I need to be on my own.'

He watched helplessly as she went to the window. All the years of knowing and loving one another, the happiness and grief they'd shared, the secrets, the pride and the shame, seemed to hang in the air between them.

In the end, he picked up his keys and turned to the door. 'Call if you want to,' he told her, 'any time, and if you change your mind about tomorrow . . .' He stopped as she put her hands to her head, and murmuring sorry again, he left.

Bel was still standing at the window trying to stem her grief when her mobile rang. Suspecting it was him calling to check on her, she let it go through to messages and continued to stare out at the darkening sky. How many eyes were watching her now, how many ghostly ears had heard what had been said? Only one heart would feel her anguish. In her own, misguided way, Talia had tried to make sure everyone was all right when she'd gone, and this was the result. It wouldn't have been what she'd intended, or even imagined, that Nick would rush into marriage with someone else and take the children to the other side of the world.

'You can't live other people's lives for them,' she whispered. 'And I can't live yours for you.'

'It's what you've been doing,' Talia whispered back. 'More or less.'

'I know, but the children needed me. So did Nick, and I needed them. I still do, but somehow I'll have to make myself let go. It's going to be like losing you all over again.'

'Just because you can't see me doesn't mean I'm not here.'

More tears blinded her as their mother's words closed around her heart. The sense of loss, the shame, the guilt was too heavy to bear, and dropping to her knees she clutched her head in her hands as the terrible grief tore through her. It was never-ending, was always with her and nothing she did would ever make it go away.

'Mummy,' she sobbed desperately, 'I'm sorry. I'm so, so sorry.'

'Stop, Bel,' Talia whispered. 'It wasn't your fault.'

'You know it was.'

'I'm with Mummy now and she doesn't blame you.'

How fervently Bel wanted that to be true. How urgently she longed for it.

'Answer the phone,' Talia said. 'It might not be Nick.'

Getting to her feet, Bel rubbed the back of her hand over her eyes as she picked up her mobile. It was a number she didn't recognise. Though tempted to ignore it, she found herself clicking on.

'Hello? Is that Bel Monkton?' a tentative voice enquired.

'Speaking,' she replied, aware of how nasal she sounded.

'It's Josie Clark here. Yvonne, at the breast clinic, gave me your number.'

'Oh, yes, that's right,' Bel said, managing to pull herself together. 'I'm glad you rang. Would you like to meet?' Was she saying this too quickly? Should she have asked how she was first?

'If it's not too much trouble,' Josie was saying. 'I'll try to fit in with you, but I work on Thursdays and Fridays.'

'That's fine, my time is pretty much my own.' She was meeting the architect and builder on Monday. 'Would Tuesday work for you? Say three o'clock?'

'That would be lovely. Thank you.'

'Where should we make it? I can come to you, if you like. Or you're welcome to come here.'

'If you don't mind, I'd rather come to you.'

Of course, she'd be worried about her family being around. After giving her address and establishing that Mrs Clark would be arriving by bus, Bel said, 'I can always pick you up in town, if you prefer.'

'Oh no, no,' Josie protested. 'I wouldn't dream of putting you out. You're being kind enough already.'

'It's no trouble,' Bel assured her. 'I just hope I'll be able to help.'

There was a moment before Josie said, 'I'm – I'm sorry about your sister.'

'Thank you,' Bel murmured, her heart fracturing again. 'I'll see you on Tuesday. If there's any change, or if you need to talk before that, you have my number.'

Chapter Thirteen

Josie was standing outside the gates of the house called Stillwater, feeling anxious about taking her problems into such a grand-looking place. It seemed a bit like bringing chips to a wine and cheese party, or a football programme to a literary evening. True, it wasn't the biggest property on the street, but it was still pretty posh, which meant the woman who owned it probably was too. She'd certainly sounded it on the phone, not in a snobby, better-than-she-ought-to-be kind of way, but like someone who pronounced all her words properly in spite of having a cold.

Are you feeling better now? Josie had texted this morning. *If you still have a cold I could come another day.* She was supposed to be avoiding infection while having chemo, though that was going to be a lot easier said than done.

I'm fine, the reply had come back. *Thank you for asking. See you at 3. Bel.*

Bel Monkton. It was a nice name, Josie had decided when she'd first heard it, though she'd assumed it was spelt with two 'l's and an 'e' until she'd received the text.

At the sound of a car slowing up she glanced along the road to where a silver Aston Martin was waiting to turn into the gates next door. There was plenty of money up around this way, that was for sure, a bit like on the other side of their hill where the properties all had full-on sea views. It was another world, nothing like the one she came from, which was why she couldn't get to grips with how presumptuous it felt being here, especially when she ought to have been able to sort out her problems for herself. Heaven knew other people did, so what was she thinking, asking for help from a woman she'd never met, would normally never have anything to do with, and who very probably had enough problems of her own.

If she did, it didn't look as though money was one of them.

She'd lost her sister, that couldn't have been easy, and for all Josie knew her husband might have cheated on her, or one of her children could be in a terrible rebellion. And who was to say this house wasn't about to be repossessed? It was happening all over these days, though less to the rich than to people like her.

Maybe she should turn around and go home. After all, what was she expecting Bel Monkton to do? Tell Jeff and the children for her? Actually, a part of her wouldn't mind that, though she'd never let anyone do it, any more than she'd expect them to offer.

Feeling the phone vibrating in her pocket she pulled it out and found a text from Jeff. *Just had a customer compliment me on my new gloves.*

She smiled at the message. She'd found the gloves in the Oxfam shop opposite the caff; brand new, still in the box and made out of real leather, so she'd snapped them up for Lily and Jasper to give him on his birthday. Pleased as Punch he'd been, had even kept them on in the karaoke bar until Lily had made him take them off.

Josie's first thought when she'd seen them had been to wrap them up and say they were from Ryan, but she'd been afraid of spoiling the evening if she did that. She'd given him the card Ryan had signed for him though, *Happy Birthday Dad, yours truly, Ryan.* Lily had laughed when she'd read it, and teased him for being so formal.

'I wouldn't send one at all if Mum hadn't brought this one,' he'd retorted stroppily. 'I'm only doing it for her.'

'And for Dad,' Josie had insisted. 'He'll be thrilled to bits even though he won't show it.'

'I wouldn't bank on that,' Ryan told her sulkily. 'Anyway, how is the old goat? Is his taxi back on the road yet?'

'It is, at least for the time being. He hasn't had any more fares like the one he had up to Heathrow a couple of weeks ago, but business seems to be picking up a bit lately.'

'At least that'll put him in a good mood for tonight,' Lily commented.

'He's always in a good mood with you,' Ryan reminded her. 'It's me he can't stand.'

'Don't talk nonsense,' Josie chided. 'You're his son, he loves you, but he's not very proud of the fact that you're in here. Now tell us what you've been up to. I enjoyed your letter about *Treasure Island*. If you'd written essays like that when you were at school I reckon you'd have been top of the class.'

Lighting up at the praise, he said, 'Paul reckons I ought to do an English GCSE while I'm in here. Not that it'll be much use when it comes to finding a job, like the welding, but he says it's good to have a qualification anyway.'

'And if you're enjoying reading,' Lily piped up, 'which you obviously are, it'll help the time to pass a bit faster.'

'That's what Paul says.'

'Where is he today?' Josie asked, looking around.

'He was here earlier, but he's gone to visit his gran up north until Monday.'

As prison visits went it had been one of the better ones, though her dear son, with his freckly face and wide-eyed stare, had still looked wretched when they'd left and had clung to her like he was afraid he might never see her again.

It was during the train journey back that she'd rung Bel Monkton, taking advantage of the hour on her own while Lily and Jasper drove to Kesterly in their two-seater car.

And now here she was, still not pressing the bell, which was just stupid when it was starting to rain. The woman obviously wouldn't mind talking to her, or she'd have said no when she was asked.

To her astonishment the gates started to open. A moment later a tall, lovely-looking woman with short blonde hair was coming out of the door. 'Mrs Clark? Josie?' she called out.

Realising she must have spotted her hovering, Josie headed along the drive, feeling foolish and slightly shabby in her pink wool coat.

'Sorry,' Bel Monkton said, 'I hope you weren't waiting long. I don't think the bell can be working.'

'Oh no, I'm sure it's fine,' Josie told her, feeling certain she'd seen this woman before. 'I just hadn't got round to ringing it yet.'

Bel smiled, and held out a hand in welcome. 'Come in before you get wet,' she urged.

Stepping into a large, hexagonal-shaped entrance hall with lots of photographs hanging on the walls, and several closed doors, Josie let her bag slide from her shoulder as she gazed up at the skylights. Wow, this was impressive.

'It's such a horribly grey day, isn't it,' Bel commented, shutting out the rain, 'and it's supposed to be spring next week. Who'd have guessed? Come on through, the fire's lit and I've already put the kettle on.'

'It's really kind of you to see me,' Josie said, following her into a room that was bigger than the entire downstairs of her house, and yet still managed to seem cosy in a fancy-magazine sort of way. 'Oh my, you've got a lovely view from here. I don't expect you ever get tired of it.'

'I think there would be something wrong with me if I did,' Bel smiled. 'Can I take your coat?'

Unfastening the buttons, Josie handed it over and hoped her best turquoise sweater and black cotton trousers didn't look too over the top for a Tuesday afternoon, especially when her hostess was wearing blue jeans and a black polo neck.

'What sort of tea do you like?' Bel asked, hanging the coat over the back of a chair and heading into the kitchen. 'I have most kinds: regular, Earl Grey, peppermint, jasmine . . .'

'Whatever you're having,' Josie told her, not wanting to be any trouble. 'No milk or sugar.' It seemed strange having this woman waiting on her, but she could hardly offer to take over, so she stayed where she was and had a quick look round. 'You have a lovely home,' she stated, wondering what Jeff would say if he knew she was here.

'What do you want to go bothering anyone else for?' he'd probably grumble, or something along those lines. 'They're not interested in what's happening to you, they're just doing their bit for charity the way they do, so they can boast about it to their mates.'

'I used to clean a house a bit like this,' she said to Bel, 'over on the north side of the bay, but they hadn't done it up nearly as nicely as you have. Did you do it yourselves?'

'There's only me,' Bel told her. 'I'm not married or with anyone, and renovating old properties is kind of what I do. I'm glad you like it.'

Surprised that her opinion would matter, and that someone so lovely was on her own, Josie asked, 'Have you been here long?'

'About five years. I keep meaning to move on, but I haven't quite got round to it yet. Shall we sit by the fire?'

As Josie perched on the edge of a sofa, she watched Bel setting a tray on a coffee table before sinking into a giant black beanbag. The teacups and saucers were colourfully decorated with oriental patterns and the matching teapot had a bamboo handle. It was one of the prettiest things Josie had ever seen.

'Thank you,' she smiled, as Bel passed one of the delicate cups.

'Jasmine,' Bel told her, 'one of my favourites.'

'Mine too,' Josie declared, though she'd only ever had it at the Chinese on North Walk, had never thought to buy any for home. The familiar, sweet scent of it made her feel slightly more relaxed, or maybe it was how easy this woman was to be with that was putting paid to her nerves.

'Cheers,' Bel said, raising her cup. 'It's lovely to meet you, though I'm sorry it's under these circumstances.'

Josie grimaced. 'It's kind of you to see me. I hope I don't end up wasting your time.'

'I can't imagine you will. Would you care for a biscuit?'

Taking one, more out of politeness than hunger, Josie nibbled the edge and put the rest in her saucer.

'In case you're wondering,' Bel said, 'the toys belong to my niece and nephew.'

Glancing to where they were stacked in a corner, Josie asked, 'Your sister's children?'

Bel nodded. 'They live with their father and stepmother over in Senway, but they're often here. I believe your children are more or less grown up now.'

'That's right. Lily's at uni in Bristol. And Ryan's . . . Well, he's not living with us for the moment.' She felt herself starting to flush. 'Actually, he's in prison,' she admitted. She had to be straight with this woman, or they were never going to get anywhere.

'Oh no, I'm sorry to hear that,' Bel responded with feeling. 'It must be quite a worry for you. Do you see him much?'

Touched by the genuine-sounding concern, Josie said, 'Thankfully he's only in Bristol, so I try to get up there every other Saturday. That's all the visits he's allowed. It's a horrible place, and he really shouldn't be there, because he didn't do what they charged him with. I know everyone says that when they go down, but Ryan only copped to the charge because the yobs he got involved with threatened to harm us, his family, if he didn't.'

Bel looked aghast. 'That's awful,' she declared. 'Isn't there anything you can do about that, someone you can talk to?'

Josie almost smiled. In Bel Monkton's world there was probably always someone to talk to, and something to be done. 'We used up all our savings on a lawyer,' she admitted, 'but when someone confesses to a crime there's not much anyone can do. Sorry, you don't want to hear about all that . . .'

'But I do, it's important.'

She really seemed to mean it. 'Thank you,' Josie said, 'it is to me, but as you know, it's not why I'm here so we ought not to get sidetracked. Well, I suppose it *is* why I'm here in a way, because at some point I'm going to have to make myself tell him what's going on with me. Before that, though, I've got to break it to my husband.' She took a breath. 'I don't know why I'm finding it so hard . . . Well, I do, I suppose . . . He's not been having very much luck lately, so to land this on him when we can barely make ends meet as it is . . .' She shrugged and almost spilled her tea. 'I keep telling myself he'll be all right about it, comforting and that, but he's never been good with illness and if he thinks I'm going to stop pulling my weight . . .' She glanced worriedly at Bel. 'I'm not painting a very nice picture of him, am I, but he's a good bloke really. I just . . .

Well . . . I keep thinking if I could understand what it feels like to be on his side of things I'd know better how to handle it all.'

Bel was regarding her closely, her blue eyes both gentle and concerned.

'Can I ask you,' Josie went on hesitantly, 'would you mind telling me what it was like when you found out your sister had cancer? I mean, did you feel as though it was your fault, that you'd let her down in some way; or angry because it was . . . well, inconvenient . . . No, I'm sure you didn't feel that, but I read online that sometimes families don't take it well, at least not at first . . .' As her words ran out she had to lower her eyes from the intensity of Bel's gaze.

'I was with my sister when the surgeon confirmed she had cancer,' Bel said, her voice quiet and steady. 'Like you, she didn't want her husband to know anything until she was sure there was something to know. Though I'd prepared myself for the worst, or thought I had, it still came as a terrible blow. I think the first thing I felt, apart from upset, of course, and afraid, *was* anger. Not because it was inconvenient, although it was, because how could it ever be convenient for anyone to have that dreaded disease, least of all a mother with two small children? No, I felt angry because she was the sweetest, kindest, most loving person I knew, who didn't deserve to be diagnosed with any kind of illness, never mind one that was threatening her life. I was furious about it, but I didn't know who to be furious with, the doctor, God, my father, I was ready to blame anyone and everyone. More than that, I desperately wanted to take it away from her and go through it myself, because *I* was the one who deserved it.'

Josie blinked in surprise, and the sudden fire seemed to dim in Bel's eyes.

'I won't get into why I deserved it,' Bel continued, 'but I thought I did. I didn't tell her that, or not at first, we talked about it later, but it was a long time later, and I think what you want to hear about is how it was when I first heard? How I coped with it myself, how we dealt with it as a family?'

Josie nodded and cleared her throat. 'Actually, I'd like

to hear anything you're willing to tell me,' she said. 'There's so much on the Internet about the cancer itself, forums you can join, helplines you can ring, all kinds of information which is fantastic, and I'm reading quite a bit of it, I just don't want to talk to anyone about what's happening to me. It's enough that I've got it, I'm having it treated and like it or not I have to get on with it. What's bothering me more is how it's going to affect my husband, Jeff, and our children. I need to know if there's anything I can do or say that will help them to deal with it in a way that won't be too hard for them.'

Bel's smile was tender. 'You're like my sister in that respect,' she told her. 'All Talia was interested in was caring for us and making sure we didn't worry too much. Of course we did, how could we not when we loved her so much? Needless to say her children were the biggest concern, for all of us, but being so young made it slightly easier in a way, because they didn't understand. For you, I can see why you're so anxious, since your children are older. They'll be afraid, of course they will, and so will your husband . . .' She took a breath. 'I'm sorry, that's probably not what you want to hear.'

'No, but I'm sure you're right, especially where the children are concerned. So do you think I should tell my husband first, then them, or should I tell them all together? Well, obviously we won't be able to with my son being where he is, but I could get my daughter to come home for the weekend . . .'

'I think you should break it to your husband first,' Bel said, 'then he can help you to tell the children. Apart from anything else, it'll give him some time to come to terms with it himself, and I think it'll mean a lot to your daughter to see him supporting you.'

Josie's eyes went down.

'Do you think he won't?' Bel prompted.

'I don't know. Like I said before, he's not good with doctors and hospitals and the like . . .'

'Maybe not for himself, but for you . . . Think how upset he'd be if he knew you were struggling with this on your own because you can't find a way to tell him.'

Accepting she had to come out with the truth now, or there would be no point to being there, Josie said, 'To be really honest, I'm afraid he might leave me.'

Bel blinked in shock. 'No, no,' she protested. 'He wouldn't, no one would . . . Why do you think that?'

Though Josie hadn't intended to spill everything, it was there now, needing to be said, and Bel was such a good listener. 'A few years back,' she said hoarsely, 'he had an affair, and I think he's always regretted not going off to be with her. The children were younger then, so he stayed, but now . . . Once he finds out about this . . . He might see it as time he went.'

Bel was shaking her head. 'I can't believe he'd do that. No one would, and if he stayed back then, it was probably for you as much as for the children.'

Josie's smile didn't quite reach her eyes.

Sitting forward, Bel said, 'Josie, you have to give him the chance to be there for you. I'm absolutely sure he'll want to be. How long have you been together?'

'Twenty-two years married, three before that when we were courting.'

'There's just no way he'd turn his back on you now,' Bel insisted.

Josie didn't argue; there was no point.

'Yvonne, the breast care nurse, mentioned that you've already had your first bout of chemotherapy,' Bel went on. 'Did you suffer any side effects?'

Josie rolled her eyes. 'Did I? They were awful. I've never felt so bad, but I was lucky, because I got over them in a couple of days, so I was able to go back to work, and to see my son on Saturday.'

'Did your husband realise you were unwell?'

Josie nodded. 'It was hard to miss. He thinks it was food poisoning, but obviously I won't be able to keep putting it down to that.'

'No, but how was he with you when you were unwell?'

Josie shrugged. 'A bit annoyed that I didn't have the strength to clean up after myself. He brought a blanket to keep me warm while I was in the bathroom, which was nice, and he didn't get on too much when he came home that night to find no food on the table.' She took a sip of her tea and found it had gone cold. 'If I'm being really honest,' she went on, looking down at the large leaves floating around randomly, rather like her thoughts, 'I think I'm still in denial about it all, which sounds mad, doesn't it, when I've already had chemo?'

Bel didn't agree. 'In my experience it takes a long time to accept it fully,' she said. 'You keep waking up in the morning and thinking it was a bad dream. Or you tell yourself the diagnosis was wrong.'

'It was like that for your sister?'

'For us all, actually.'

Josie said, 'I feel like, if I tell my family it'll make it more real.'

'It will,' Bel said honestly.

'I suppose thinking like that makes it a bit more about me than I was realising.'

'There's nothing wrong with that, because it is about you. It's about all of you, of course, but you're the one who matters, and believe me, that's what your family will think. You can worry about them as much as you like, but I can promise you, they'd far rather you worried about doing whatever it takes to get yourself well.'

'I wish there was something else I could do, apart from going through this chemo. Did your . . . Do you mind me asking, did your sister have chemo?'

'Yes, she did, and you're right, it's awful. That's not the case for everyone, but I think it is for most.'

'And how – how long was it before she lost her hair? Maybe she didn't.'

'Yes, she did. It started to fall out after the third or fourth session. She'd never been particularly vain, but it was devastating. Another confirmation of what was happening to her, one more reality check.'

'And how was it for you, being reminded every time you looked at her that she was sick?'

'I was more concerned about how it was for her, looking at me and seeing how she used to be. We were twins, you see. So I shaved off my hair to make us look the same again.'

Josie's eyes widened with surprise. 'You did that for her? You must have loved her very much.'

'Yes, I did, but she was furious when she first saw what I'd done. We had a terrible fight, but it was too late by then, and in the end I think it turned out to be important for us both. I understood a little more of how she felt to have lost such a crucial part of her femininity, and she understood why it mattered to me that she wasn't alone in the loss.'

Josie felt so moved by the closeness of the sisters that she almost couldn't bear the fact that they were no longer together. 'She was very lucky to have you,' she said. 'I don't know anyone else who'd do so much for their sister.'

'I don't think it's entirely unheard of, and the way I looked at it was, it's just hair. Some people donate kidneys or bone marrow, a part of themselves that truly makes a difference. I'd have done that too, of course, if it had been necessary. And I'd have gone through the chemo if it would have made hers any easier to bear, but obviously it doesn't work like that.'

'You went with her for treatments, though?'

'Yes, unless Nick, her husband wanted to go, but he had to work so usually it was me. Does someone go with you?'

Josie shook her head. 'I don't have any brothers or sisters, and my best friend, Dawnie . . . Well, she's the one my husband had an affair with.'

Bel's expression softened with sympathy. 'That must have been tough.'

Josie didn't deny it. 'She's moved away now. We never see her. She'd have come though, if she was still here and things were different.'

'What about your mother?'

Josie pulled a face. 'If you'd met her you'd understand why she wouldn't be the best person to take with me. No, I don't mind going on my own, the nurses are lovely and the time went by quite quickly. Speaking of which,' she said, glancing at her watch, 'oh my goodness, I can't believe how long I've been here. I hope I'm not holding you up.'

'Not at all. It's barely been an hour.'

'I didn't expect to take up even half of that. I ought to be going.' She was already on her feet.

'Please don't rush off,' Bel protested. 'Stay and have another cup of tea?'

'I'd love to,' Josie said truthfully, 'but the bus is due in five minutes and if I miss that one I'll have to wait another hour.'

'I can drive you home.'

'Oh no, no, I wouldn't hear of it. You've been kind enough as it is.'

'I don't feel as though I've helped in any way,' Bel confessed as she walked her to the door.

'Oh but you have. It's done me the power of good, talking to you.' It was the truth, it really had helped.

'Do you think you're any closer to telling your husband?' Bel asked.

Feeling the light dulling inside her, Josie said, 'I'm not sure. I'll know better when I see him.'

'You need to do it,' Bel urged gently, 'and sooner rather than later, you know that, don't you?'

Josie regarded her askance.

'Give him a chance, I'm sure he'll be every bit as supportive as you need him to be.'

Hoping she was right, Josie opened the door.

'Will you let me know how it goes?' Bel asked, stepping outside with her.

Surprised, Josie said, 'Of course, if you want me to.'

'I do. You have my mobile number. Give me a call, or send a text, and if you need to talk again, you know where I am.'

After watching Josie walk out through the gates and giving her a wave as she turned back, Bel closed the door and returned to the kitchen. She hadn't expected to be so affected by Josie, but there was something about her that had really got to her. It wasn't only the fact that she had cancer, which was enough on its own to make Bel care, it was that she was so sweet and natural and touchingly honest. She just hoped that husband of hers wasn't a bully, or worse, because Bel would hate him if he were and want to do everything she could to protect Josie from him.

'*The way you used to protect me,*' Talia said.

Bel looked across the room, half expecting to see her sister sitting there. Had she been listening while Josie was here? It had felt as though she was; talking about her often made her seem present.

'*You told me to hide under the stairs and then you pretended not to know where I was,*' Talia reminded her.

Their father hadn't appreciated that.

Taking a quick breath, Bel pressed the memory back into the darkness it had escaped from.

She couldn't help wondering if Josie was any closer to telling her husband than she'd been before coming here. Sadly, she didn't feel convinced. Surely to God he wouldn't leave her when he found out; Josie had to be wrong about that. If she wasn't, then maybe she'd be better off without him, though Bel was hardly in a position to make that judgement, and even if she were, she knew only too well how hard it was to persuade a woman to stop loving a man who was self-absorbed and abusive.

Not every man is like your father, she reminded herself. Jeff Clark could easily be as sweet-natured as his wife, albeit in a gruffer, more macho sort of way.

Then why was Josie afraid of him?

Perhaps it wasn't fear as much as a wretched insecurity, resulting from the time he'd cheated on her. *With her best friend.*

And the son was in prison.

Bel wondered what had put him there, and felt for Josie all over again at how devastated she'd seemed by it.

'*Don't get too involved,*' Talia cautioned. '*You've already been down this road once, you don't want to go there again.*'

It was true, Bel had no desire to support someone through that dreaded disease again, but since it wasn't what Josie was asking, it was hardly an issue. Josie did need to talk to someone though, whether she realised it or not.

'*I had you,*' Talia said, '*but I still lost.*'

'*Not everyone loses, we were unlucky.*'

'*And you're thinking Josie might be one of the lucky ones?*'

216

'Is there any reason why she shouldn't be?'

'No, of course not.'

Reaching for her mobile as it rang, she saw it was Harry and her heart gave a skip of surprise. As she clicked on she found herself wondering if he was Josie's surgeon. She wouldn't ask, it wasn't any of her business, and anyway, it would be wholly inappropriate.

'Hi,' she said warmly. 'How did you enjoy the show?'

'To quote my sons,' he replied, 'it was awesome. Some really great new works, I only wish I could have afforded one. What I can afford, however, is a slap-up dinner at a restaurant of your choice to say thank you.'

Laughing, Bel said, 'Honestly, you really don't have to. Remember, it was Nick who got the tickets, not me.'

'Don't worry, I was intending to invite him too. And his wife, since it would seem rude to leave her out. I just need you to decide when would work best for you and where you'd like to go. Personally, I can do this weekend on Friday or Saturday, or next week on Thursday.'

Deciding now wasn't the time to tell him that relations between her and Nick were strained, she replied, 'I'm sure one of those days will work, but it'll probably only be two of us as someone will have to babysit.'

'Of course, just as long as you're one of the two. Is that selfish? I guess it is, but I don't think I'll take it back. Now, before you go, how're things progressing with the barn?'

Surprised and pleased he'd asked, she said, 'Well, I'm getting ready to hand over a deposit just as soon as the surveyors have come back with their report, which should be sometime this week or next. Provided there's nothing too drastic to worry about there, we'll start wading in for the real headaches which begin when we get involved with the town planners, though I'm glad to say they're not as bad in this area as some I've dealt with.'

'Is the place listed?'

'Grade II, which happily isn't anywhere near as difficult as Grade I. Not that it's a picnic, but it shouldn't throw up quite as much lunacy. You'll have to come and see it sometime.' Had she really meant that? Why on earth would he want to?

'I'd love to,' he assured her. 'Just let me know when. And get back to me about dinner as soon as, so I can book a table.'

Clicking off the line, she frowned deeply as she tried to catch her thoughts. They seemed to be going off in all directions, random fragments of warning, hope, common sense, relief that he hadn't got into talking about her father.

In the end she let it all go, and went back to thinking about Josie.

Chapter Fourteen

'What the heck's this when it's at home?' Jeff demanded, peering suspiciously into his mug.

'It's jasmine tea,' Josie informed him. 'I thought we'd try some for a change.'

He gawped at her incredulously. 'What, did we win the lottery or something? How much did it cost?'

'Not much more than our usual,' she lied, since it was almost double the price for half the amount, 'and I thought it would be nice to try something different for once. You always like it when we go to the Chinese.'

'Yeah, but that's there, where they don't serve a proper cuppa. I don't want it in my own home.'

Josie took a sip of hers and felt sorry it didn't taste quite as good as when Bel Monkton had made it. Most likely Bel had had a better-quality brand, and maybe the size of the cups helped. Serving it in mugs wasn't quite the same. 'I bet you'd be loving it if Lily had made it,' she declared, deciding she wouldn't mind if he did.

'Well, it's the sort of crack-brained thing I'd expect from her, not from you.'

'So you're not going to drink it?'

'I didn't say that. There's no point wasting it. I'm just saying, I like my normal brew, with milk.'

Josie twinkled. 'You're turning into a bit of an old stick in the mud,' she teased, 'but it's part of why I love you.'

Rolling his eyes, he took a sip of the tea and put the mug down next to his phone. 'Anything good on telly tonight?' he asked, opening the paper.

This is your moment, Josie, come on, girl, get on with it. 'I haven't looked yet,' she replied, managing to sound like her normal, unflapped self. It was nearly a week since she'd had the chat with Bel Monkton, and she still wasn't any closer to finding the right words, if they even existed, and she wasn't sure that they did. She could hardly just blurt it out, and beating around the bush would only end up confusing them both.

Actually, she'd almost got there yesterday, but the first time he'd been called out on a job, and the second time her mother had turned up unannounced wanting to celebrate her lottery win.

'Come on, I'm treating you down the pub,' Eileen had insisted, turfing Jeff out of his chair. 'It's only two hundred and forty quid, but it's better than a slap round the face with a wet fish.'

'You could put it towards a new washing machine,' Josie reminded her.

'Oh God, will you listen to her?' Eileen groaned. 'How did someone like me end up with a daughter as boring as her, that's what I want to know.'

And how did that boring daughter end up with cancer when she'd never smoked a cigarette in her life, and hardly ever had a drink, that was what Josie would like to know. It didn't seem very fair, did it, when she did her best to play by the rules and people like her mother never did? Not that she'd wish cancer on any one of them, no way would she ever do that, she just felt the question needed asking, that was all.

'Who's that now?' Jeff grumbled, as someone knocked on the door, and taking his mug with him he went to find out.

Smiling to herself, since he clearly liked the tea more than he was letting on, Josie took a sip of her own and thought it was a shame that it wasn't making her feel as relaxed as she had been at Bel Monkton's. Maybe relaxed was putting it a bit strongly, but she certainly hadn't felt as uptight or self-conscious as she'd expected she would.

She was a really lovely young woman, Bel Monkton, not only beautiful on the outside, but inside too. She'd remembered now where she'd seen her before; it was at the clinic. She'd gone into the Visitors' Information Room with Mr Beck, which probably meant he'd been her sister's surgeon until it all went wrong. Josie wondered how many people Mr Beck saw it go wrong for. It couldn't be easy, doing his job.

Fancy cutting off all her hair to make her sister feel better. Josie couldn't imagine doing that for anyone, apart from Lily, of course, but it was different between mother and daughter (unless the mother was Eileen). Whatever, Bel obviously still really missed her sister, and Josie could see how much harder it was likely to be losing a twin. There hadn't been any mention of a mother, so presumably she wasn't around either.

The remark Bel had made about her father was interesting, that he'd been in the line-up of people she'd wanted to blame for her sister's illness. Though Josie was no expert in these things, she'd come away with the feeling that Bel Monkton was hiding a lot more pain than she'd want to admit to, or some kind of guilty conscience, considering what she'd said about deserving to have cancer.

How could anyone deserve that, especially someone like her?

Josie would have liked to ring her again, but knew she probably wouldn't. She'd texted, a couple of days after her visit, to say thank you again for the chat.

Have you told him yet? Bel had messaged back.

Getting there, Josie had replied.

'All right, doll?' Carly demanded, bustling in through the door. 'Can't stop, on my way out, but Mandy Berry's having one of those Ann Summers parties the Monday after next. All the girls are going. Remember what a scream we had at the last one? Tickets are only a quid so she can cover the cost of a glass of wine and some nuts. I can give her yours in the morning, if you've got it, save you traipsing over there.'

Since it was the day of her next chemo, Josie had to say, 'I'm not sure I can make it.'

Carly looked up from her mobile, shocked.

'I might have an extra shift at the caff that night,' Josie improvised.

'Oh no,' Carly groaned, 'everyone wants you to be there. It makes us all laugh even more when you laugh.'

Knowing that was true, probably because of how much more naïve she was than most of them, Josie said, 'I'll check and let you know. Who's Jeff talking to out there?'

'Oh, Jack Moss,' Carly replied, glancing over her shoulder. 'He's trying to drum up support for something or other. Anyway, got to rush, hot date. Let me know when you can about the party.'

As she left, Jeff came back into the room, still holding his mug.

'So what was Jack going on about?' Josie prompted. 'Did you tell him about our dodgy boiler while you were out there?'

'I fixed it,' Jeff responded indignantly. 'At least for now. Anyway, he wasn't here as a plumber, he wants to know if we'll vote for him when he runs for the council.'

'I hope you said yes. He's one of the few people around here who's prepared to do something about our bins not being emptied often enough and those bloody rats in the park. The rest of us are too blinking lazy to stand up for ourselves, that's our trouble.'

'Speak for yourself,' Jeff retorted. 'I'm dead beat after a full day's work, that's why I don't get involved. Whereas you, with the way you've been going on lately, you'll be able to run for Prime Minister come the next election, you got so much time on your hands.'

'Well I couldn't make any bigger a mess of it than the halfwit we've got there now,' Josie responded, feeling the discomfort of his words creeping over her, 'but since we're on the subject of me and my two-day week, I've been meaning to talk to you about that.'

'Good. I hope you're going to tell me you've found something else, because it wouldn't be before time.'

With her insides fluttering badly, Josie took a sip of her tea and said, 'It's not that I don't want to find something, you know me, I'm not a shirker. It's just that at the moment it's a bit difficult.'

He looked up from his paper. 'Difficult? In what way?' he demanded.

'Well, it's just . . .' Where were the words? They had to come now. She took a breath and tried again. 'Well, you remember I was a bit off colour last week?'

'Yes,' he replied, his eyes starting to narrow. 'What are you trying to say?'

'Well, just that, it wasn't food poisoning I had, it was . . . it was side effects from having chemo.'

It took only a moment for shock to turn his face white. 'What do you mean, chemo?' he said. 'You only have that when you've got . . .'

Their eyes were locked on each other's as Josie nodded.

She could see, almost feel, his confusion. 'Are you saying what I think you're saying?' he asked.

'I've got breast cancer,' she stated, and found, to her surprise, that it was almost a relief to say the words. 'It's not a big deal, or anything,' she went on hastily. 'They've caught it early, and now they're giving me treatment to shrink it.' It didn't matter that it wasn't the entire truth, and she didn't have tell him yet about the mastectomy, either. That could come later.

'How long have you known?' he asked darkly.

'Only a couple of weeks. I didn't want to bother you with it until I knew for certain, and like I said, it's not a big deal. It just means I won't be able to hold down another job for a while, till the treatment's over.'

'What about the one you've got?'

'Oh, that should be fine. They're treating me on Mondays, so I should be OK for work by Thursday.'

'I meant, should you be doing it?'

'Yes, definitely. I was right as rain by Thursday last week. A bit tired, I suppose, but that could be said about most of us these days. Anyway, we don't have to talk about it any more. It's all under control . . .'

'Have you told the kids?'

She flushed. 'No, not yet. To be honest, I'm not sure I even need to. I mean, what's the point in worrying them if I can get through it without them knowing?'

He continued to look at her, seeming lost for words.

Reaching into her bag, she said, 'I got this for you.'

He watched her put a booklet on the coffee table, and turn it round so he could see its title. *In it together: for partners of people with breast cancer.*

'Right,' he grunted, making no attempt to pick it up.

It didn't matter, at least she'd given it to him, and because she'd read it herself she knew that his reaction, or lack of one, wasn't all that unusual. She just had to hope that he did end up reading it, since it was very informative and she was sure he'd find it helpful. 'So,' she said, snuggling deeper into her chair, 'what are we going to watch?'

Passing her the paper, he replied, 'Here, you look. I'm going up to have a shower.'

Harry was already waiting when Bel arrived at the Crustacean Brasserie, the only restaurant in Kesterly able to boast a Michelin star plus a sweeping view of the bay. Not that there was much to see from the wall of windows on this inky-black night, just a few disembodied lights on the horizon as vessels passed from the estuary into the Bristol Channel, and the glistening spume of waves as it washed on to the nearby rocks.

With Harry was a man Bel had never seen before, though it came as little surprise when Harry introduced him as his cousin, Ozzie.

'He's staying with us for the weekend,' Harry explained, as she shook Ozzie's hand, 'and he didn't want to miss out on being able to thank you for the tickets.'

'Which I do, wholeheartedly,' Ozzie assured her, clasping both his hands round hers. He was several inches shorter, and rounder, than Harry, but was almost as good-looking and appeared to be equally charming. 'It's a great honour to meet you,' he declared, as Harry held out a chair for her to sit down. 'I've heard much about you, all good, I hasten to add.'

Bel smiled as she said, 'I'm relieved to hear that.'

Laughing, Harry asked, 'Isn't Nick joining us?'

'He's supposed to be,' she assured him. 'He should be here any minute.'

'Would you care for an aperitif?' Ozzie offered as a waiter approached with the vodka tonics he and Harry had ordered.

'A glass of wine would be lovely,' Bel told the waiter. 'A Macon-Villages, or something along those lines?'

'Medium or large?'

'Medium, thanks. Ah, here's Nick,' she declared, spotting him coming in the door. She waved out as Harry and Ozzie got to their feet, ready to greet him.

To her surprise he seemed to take an inordinate amount of time checking in his coat, then he stumbled on the steps up to their table.

'I'm fine, I'm fine,' he chuckled as Harry and Ozzie sprang forward to help him, and using the banister to haul himself back to his feet he said, 'Harry, my old friend, how are you? It's been a long time.'

Realising, to her horror, that he was drunk, Bel could only watch as he shook hands with Harry, then Ozzie, only just managing to hold his balance.

'Bel,' he declared, coming to embrace her, 'and was a woman ever more *belle*, I ask myself. You look ravishing, my darling.'

Stunned, and almost recoiling from the sour stench of whisky on his breath, Bel hissed, 'What's going on? Where have you been to get like this?'

Ignoring the question, he slumped down next to her and raised a hand to summon a waiter. After ordering a double Scotch, he folded his hands on the table and broke into a smile. 'So, this is nice, isn't it?' he remarked. 'All friends together. Thanks for inviting us, Harry. It's a great pleasure to meet you, Ozzie.'

Since he'd already said that when greeting them, Bel attempted to deflect attention away from him. 'I was wondering,' she said to Ozzie, 'what you do in London?'

Ozzie grimaced. 'I'm sorry to say, I'm in banking,' he confessed.

'Which is how come,' Harry chipped in, 'he was able to go back to the art show and put a red sticker on one of the paintings. A birthday present for his wife.'

Nick was blinking wildly. 'You bought one of Edwin's paintings?' he cried. 'That's not going to earn you any points with Bel, I hope you know that.'

'Nick,' she whispered harshly.

Shrugging, he sat back in his chair and seemed to drift in and out of awareness as Harry returned the conversation to safer ground by enquiring about Bel's new project.

'Have you seen the barn yet?' he asked Nick, as a waiter turned up with the double Scotch.

'No ice, thanks,' Nick said, waving it away. 'I haven't been invited yet,' he told Harry.

'But you will be,' Bel assured him, 'when you have time.'

Raising his glass to everyone, he took a sip and said, 'Never enough of that, is there? Time, I mean.'

'Tell me about it,' Harry responded wryly. 'Are you still lecturing at Exeter?'

'Sure am,' Nick replied, loosening his tie. 'For now, anyway.'

'Nick's been offered a job at Sydney University,' Bel informed them. 'It's a great opportunity, so he's intending to take it.'

'Really?' Harry said, his eyes moving worriedly between her and Nick. 'Sounds . . . interesting, Nick. Same subject, I guess?'

Seeming not to have heard the question, Nick said, 'Of course, Bel doesn't want me to go. She's worried about not seeing the children, and I can understand that . . .'

'Nick, we don't need to discuss this now,' Bel interposed, putting a hand on his arm.

Turning to her, he said, 'You're the one who brought it up.'

'About the job, yes . . .'

'I don't want to leave her behind,' Nick confided to Harry. 'It tears me up just to think of it, but what choice do I have? The children treat her like she's their mother . . .'

'Ah, the menus,' Harry declared as a waiter began handing them out. 'I must admit, I'm liking the look of that lobster floating about in the tank over there, but if anyone else has an eye on it . . .'

'Oh no, how could you?' Bel laughed as she shuddered. 'The poor thing's never done anything to you.'

Harry appeared puzzled. 'You know, I don't think he has, so how about we buy him and set him free?'

Bel's eyes widened. 'You don't mean that?' she challenged.

'Yes I do.'

'Can we do that?' she asked the waiter.

He shrugged. 'I am afraid another customer has already ordered him,' he replied, in heavily accented English. 'So can I propose to you the specials of today?'

'Yes, please do,' Ozzie encouraged, rubbing his hands together. 'It's the only reason I come to Kesterly, to dine at this place.'

As the waiter began running through the various delicacies the chef was offering, Bel kept a cautious eye on Nick, half afraid he might topple off his chair, or erupt into some sort of drunken diatribe that would end up embarrassing them all, as if they weren't already embarrassed enough. She'd never known him this drunk before, at least not in public, and since it was wholly unlike him to be rude, or unkind, she couldn't imagine what had triggered it.

'So how are the children, Nick?' Harry asked, after they'd ordered.

'Oh, they're fine,' Nick replied, attempting to pick up the wine list.

'Let me,' Ozzie insisted, discreetly taking it from him. 'Red or white?' he asked Bel.

'I'm happy with either,' she replied.

'Did you notice,' Nick said to Harry, 'she objected to you having the lobster, but she's ordered the sole for herself.'

'The sole isn't in the tank,' Bel reminded him, 'so I'm presuming it's already dead.'

'Ah, I see, so it's all right if someone else killed it, but not if you're involved in the murder?'

He was the only one who laughed.

'I'm sorry, Nick,' Harry suddenly piped up, 'I haven't congratulated you yet on your marriage. I've met your new wife, of course. She came to one of our gigs at the White Hart.'

'Mm, I seem to remember,' Nick mumbled.

'How old are your children?' Ozzie asked him.

'Seven and five. Do you have kids?'

'Just the one, a girl, who rules the house and she's only three.'

'Girls are like that,' Nick informed him. 'Nell always thinks she's the boss at ours.'

'Because she is,' Bel smiled fondly.

He didn't argue, mainly because his focus seemed to have slipped again.

'What about your boys?' Bel said to Harry. 'Do they rule the roost in your house?'

'Oh no, I'm definitely the boss,' he declared manfully.

Ozzie laughed. 'Yeah right.'

'At least let me pretend,' Harry scowled.

'I have to go to Sydney,' Nick broke in, 'because it's not fair on my wife if I don't.' He turned to Harry. 'You see that, don't you? You, of all people, will understand why it's so difficult being around Bel when she looks so much like Talia . . . It's like Talia's still with us and Kristina can't handle it.'

Bel's cheeks were hot with discomfort as she asked, 'How did you get here, Nick? Please don't tell me you drove.'

Appearing confused, he said, 'I came by taxi.'

'Then I'm going to order another to take you home.'

'What?'

'You're spoiling the evening,' she told him bluntly.

'How? Why?' he protested. 'I'm just making conversation.'

'You're too drunk to realise what you're saying.'

'Have I caused offence?' he demanded worriedly, looking to Harry and Ozzie. 'If I have, I apologise, because I certainly didn't mean to.'

'It's me you're offending,' Bel told him, 'and embarrassing.'

Seeming chastened, he lowered his head and dashed a hand through his hair. 'Maybe I should go home,' he muttered miserably. He turned to Bel. 'Will you come with me?'

Astonished, she said, 'We've just ordered our food, and we're Harry's and Ozzie's guests.'

'Of course. Sorry, I don't seem to be thinking straight this evening.'

'Have some water,' she said, 'and best not to have any wine when it comes.'

Nick looked at Harry. 'Would you think me terribly rude if I left? Not in the best shape this evening.'

'I'm happy for you to do whatever suits you,' Harry answered tactfully.

Nick tried to focus on Ozzie. 'It was good to meet you, and I'm sorry about . . .' He waved a hand rather than speak the words.

'No problem,' Ozzie assured him. 'Thanks for the tickets, by the way.'

'What tickets? Oh, those. Did you see the old boy? Was he there?'

The way Ozzie glanced at Harry told Bel that he'd been warned not to get on to the subject of her father. 'Yes, he was,' he said awkwardly.

'Did you speak to him?'

'Not for long.'

Bel was growing tenser by the second. *Please don't let him start blurting out things no one wants to hear.*

'Did he ask about Bel?' Nick wanted to know.

'No, he didn't,' Harry replied. 'As Ozzie said, it was only a brief chat. I don't think he realised we were the people you'd got tickets for.'

Nick nodded. 'Have you ever told Harry?' he asked, turning to Bel.

Bel got to her feet. 'Come on, I'll get you that taxi.' Forcing him up she dragged him to reception, where an obliging hostess summoned a cab from the rank outside.

'Come with me,' Nick said, clinging to her hand.

'Don't be ridiculous,' she protested. 'I can't.'

'Why?'

'You know why,' and making sure the driver had his address, she hurried back to the table to find the first course had arrived.

'Is he OK?' Harry asked, seeming genuinely concerned.

'I guess he will be, when he sobers up,' she replied. 'I'm really sorry. I don't know what got into him, he's never normally like that.'

'Please don't apologise,' Ozzie insisted. 'He's obviously got some issues, and sometimes the only answer seems to be at the bottom of a bottle. I know, because I used to go there looking myself.'

Bel glanced at him gratefully.

'Maybe we should start again,' Harry suggested, reaching for his glass. 'Here's to you, Ozzie, congratulations on a new painting; to me, just because I like being toasted, and to you, Bel, for being so bloody marvellous.'

She gave a laugh of surprise. 'That would be me,' she agreed, feeling modesty would dampen the mood. 'Here's to all of us, and a lovely rest of the evening.'

By the time coffees were served, with a tray of mouth-watering handmade chocolates, they were enjoying each other's company so much that the disastrous episode with Nick was all but forgotten. Bel was even tempted to suggest a nightcap somewhere, possibly back at her place, but remembering Harry had a wife to go home to who probably wouldn't be best pleased if her husband and his cousin rolled in after midnight, she simply walked outside with them and thanked them both again before getting into a taxi.

As it pulled away, she was aware of how happily she was smiling. It had been a long time since she'd enjoyed an evening so much, laughing at the cousins' banter, entering into a lively debate on the ethics of bankers' bonuses, and an even more spirited discussion on whether Kesterly deserved its new accolade as Britain's most boring seaside town. They'd touched on so many subjects she couldn't even remember them all now, but it hardly mattered. It had simply been a wonderfully stimulating few hours that, mercifully, hadn't been affected at all by the disastrous beginning.

Thinking of Nick, she switched on her phone to see if there were any messages, but he'd neither rung nor texted. Since it was too late to check if he'd got home safely, she decided to ring first thing and give him a piece of her mind, if he was up to hearing it. She might even, she decided, ask if she could have the children for the day; after all, he surely couldn't be intending to keep them from her until he left for Sydney.

'Am I on the right road?' the driver asked, glancing at her in the rear-view mirror.

'Yes, another hundred yards along on the right,' she instructed, fishing out her keys. 'It's called Stillwater.'

As he put up a thumb, she found herself wondering if by some amazing coincidence he might be Josie Clark's husband. One glance at the ID badge dangling from the mirror told her that this driver's name was Gibbons, not Clark, but even if it had been Clark there was no way she could have asked if he knew Josie. Their meeting had been confidential, and as far as she was concerned it would stay that way.

She'd thought about Josie a lot these past two weeks, and had hoped to hear more from her than the short reply she'd received to a text she'd sent only this morning.

Just wondering how you are, she'd said.

All fine, thank you, Josie had messaged back. So whether she had got round to telling her husband yet, Bel still had no idea. Maybe she had and didn't feel the need to talk any more.

Whichever, Bel hoped she was all right and felt able to call if she needed to.

'You didn't have to get up,' Jeff said, as Josie padded into the kitchen in her dressing gown and slippers. 'It's not even six o'clock yet.'

'I know,' she yawned, 'but I thought you might want some breakfast before you left. What time's your pickup?' He had a good fare this morning, taking a couple of punters all the way to Wincanton.

'Quarter past,' he replied, 'I should be going in a minute. Tea's made, if you want a cup. I was going to bring one up.'

Touched by the thought, she rubbed her hands up and down her arms to warm them as she reached for a mug. 'You should've set the heating to come on earlier,' she told him. 'It's cold enough in here to freeze the whatsits off monkeys.'

'Brass,' he said, sipping his tea.

She glanced at him curiously.

'Brass monkeys,' he explained.

She nodded and filled her mug. To her surprise it was jasmine tea. She turned to him with a smile.

Scowling, he said, 'Well, I thought, now you've bought it, we can't let it go to waste, be bloody stupid that,' and grabbing a slice of bread as it popped out of the toaster he turned his back to butter it. 'Do you want a piece?' he offered.

'No thanks, I'll have something later. I'll cut you some sandwiches though . . .'

'You don't have to worry. I've already done it. I used up the rest of the cheese.'

Taking a sip of her tea she stood watching him, his dark head bent over his task, his stubby male hands seeming awkward as he handled the small knife. If she hadn't known better than to fuss him she'd have asked what he was thinking, but he'd never liked that sort of question, and would probably like it even less now. It would be good to know though, just to have an idea of how worried or upset he might be. Probably not very, since she hadn't made a big deal of her news, and he wasn't one to get himself worked up about something unless he thought he needed to.

'What time do you reckon you'll be back?' she asked, as he bit into his toast.

Waiting until he'd swallowed, he said, 'Not sure yet. I'll call later and let you know. What are you doing today?'

'You know what I'm doing.' It was Saturday; she was going to see Ryan.

He said nothing, simply carried on eating as he walked into the living room. 'If you need picking up from the station later,' he said, 'let me know.'

'I'll be fine on the bus,' she assured him. 'Save you coming out of your way. Don't want to be wasting petrol, do we?'

Finishing up his toast and tea, he put the mug on the mantelpiece and picked up his keys. 'Right, I'll see you when I see you,' he said. 'Give our Lily my love. Tell her I'm still wearing the gloves.'

'She'll be pleased to hear that,' she replied, following him to the door. 'I'll give Ryan your love too, shall I?'

He paused in putting on his coat, then continued. 'Do what you want,' he retorted, and before opening the door, he said, 'get out of the draught now, or you'll end up catching cold.'

Doing as she was told, she stepped back into the living room, and went to the window to watch him scraping the ice off the windscreen. The weather was all over the place these days, one minute sunny, the next rain, but it never seemed to get any warmer, and now they were waking up most mornings to these terrible frosts.

She was still at the window, trying to smile past her tears, when he got into the car and started the engine. She wondered if he could sense her watching and was deliberately ignoring her, or maybe he had no idea she was there. It didn't matter, she still gave him a wave as he started down the road, and she'd send Ryan his love later, because she was sure he wanted her to really, he just couldn't make himself say it.

'Auntie Bel, it's us,' Oscar and Nell cried into the entryphone.

Surprised and delighted, Bel quickly released the gates and tugged open the front door. She hadn't been expecting them this morning, hadn't even received a call saying they were on their way, yet here they were hurtling along the drive, clearly as thrilled to see her as she was to see them.

'Ooof,' she gasped as Oscar ran into her full force, and sweeping him up she spun him round and round as Nell cried, 'Me, me, me.'

'Yes, you too,' Bel laughed, setting Oscar down and doing the same for Nell. 'Come on, let's go inside, it's freezing out here.'

As she hurried them up the steps Nick's BMW came to a halt behind them, but it wasn't Nick who got out. It was Kristina, looking pale, harassed and as though she hadn't had much sleep.

'Go on through,' Bel said to the children. 'I was about to make pancakes, so you can sort out what we need.'

As they charged across the hall, Bel turned to Kristina. 'What's happening?' she asked worriedly, closing the door on the bitter wind. 'Where's Nick?'

'At home,' Kristina replied shakily. 'I'm sorry about this, I should have rung first, but is it OK to leave them with you?'

'Of course, it goes without saying, but what's going on? Did Nick get home all right last night?'

Kristina nodded as she pushed a hand through her hair. 'Just about, but we need to talk and I thought, with Oscar and Nell around . . .' She looked at Bel, her eyes seeming as helpless as a child's.

'It's OK,' Bel assured her, though it clearly wasn't. 'You did the right thing bringing them here. Just tell me before you go, how come he got so drunk last night?'

Kristina shook her head. 'It's been getting worse lately,' she confided, 'and it's becoming increasingly difficult hiding it from the children.'

Alarmed to hear that, Bel said, 'You should have told me sooner. If there's anything I can do . . .'

Kristina slanted her a look. 'Thanks,' she muttered, and turning away she pulled open the door. 'I'll call you later, let you know what's happening,' and without as much as a goodbye she ran back to the car.

Bel stood in the icy cold, watching her drive out through the gates, the wheels skidding on the gravel as she turned on to the street. Part of her was tempted to call Nick before Kristina got back to ask what the heck was going on. However, it was hardly her place to interfere, and given the size of the hangover he probably had it wasn't likely she'd get much sense out of him anyway. What she would acquire, however, was frostbite if she stayed here a moment longer.

In the kitchen coats and boots were littering the floor, and Oscar was on top of some steps. 'How are those pancakes coming along? Oscar, you're not supposed to use those unless I'm in the room,' Bel reminded him.

'That's what I said,' Nell informed her.

'Here you are,' Oscar urged, spilling the flour over Nell as he handed it down.

Taking it, Bel said, 'What am I going to do with you two?'

'You're going to eat us all up,' Nell giggled, throwing her arms round Bel's legs.

'She'll have a really bad tummy if she eats you,' Oscar snorted.

'No, if she eats you,' Nell insisted.

'I'd rather eat pancakes,' Bel declared.

'Me too,' Oscar cried, and launched himself at her.

Catching him just in time, Bel swept him over to a bar stool and plonked him on it.

She was doing the same with Nell when her phone rang.

'It's Daddy,' Oscar announced, seeing his father's name come up, and handing her the mobile he began twisting back and forth on the stool.

Mindful of the children's big ears, Bel said, 'Nick, are you OK?'

'Yes, I'm fine,' he answered, sounding far from it. 'Is Kristina still there?'

'No, she's on her way back.'

He sighed wearily and she could easily imagine how he looked, unshaven, bleary-eyed and hair all over the place.

'What's going on?' she asked.

'Nothing. It's fine. Did she leave the kids with you?'

'Yes, they're here.'

'We're here, Daddy!' they shouted.

'We're making pancakes,' Nell added.

'That's good,' he replied, as if they could hear.

Bel waited for him to say more.

'I'm sorry about last night,' he finally managed. 'I hope . . . Well, I hope I didn't ruin the evening.'

'As it happens, you didn't, but I think you owe Harry an apology.'

'Yes, of course. I'll do it on Monday.'

'And we should talk.'

Apparently he had nothing to say to that, because after a brief silence the line went dead.

Putting her mobile down, Bel looked up to find Nell regarding her curiously. 'Is Daddy all right?' she asked.

'Yes, of course,' Bel replied, lightening her expression.

Apparently satisfied with that, Nell set about out-twisting her brother, while Bel fetched some eggs for the pancakes. Though something clearly *wasn't* right with Daddy she was hardly going to say so, especially when she had an uncomfortable feeling she knew what it was.

Chapter Fifteen

Josie was having a good look through old photos, something she hadn't done in years, and the memories they brought back were making her smile and laugh, and occasionally filled her eyes with tears. Life had seemed so much simpler when the children were small, and if these photos were anything to go by the sun had always shone too. That could be because she was looking at a lovely holiday they'd had one summer in a caravan, just outside Dawlish. There was Ryan on the go-karts, with Jeff, looking so pleased with himself he might burst; and another of Ryan burying his dad in the sand. There were plenty of six-year-old Lily, pretty as a primrose in her sun hat, jelly sandals and little else to cover her modesty. Proper exhibitionist she'd been as a toddler, could hardly keep the clothes on her. Jeff used to laugh a lot more then, probably because there was more to laugh about when he had a regular job where he earned good money and never had to worry about how he could afford to repair his car, or put food on the table, or new clothes on the kids' backs.

She wasn't sure if it was a good idea to bring old albums to a chemo session, especially seeing how nostalgic it was making her feel, but there again, why not? She treasured these memories more than any jewels; they showed how happy they'd been back before life had started taking a few turns for the worse. Of course they all still loved each other, it was just different now, especially where Jeff and Ryan were concerned, maybe her and Jeff too. That could be a bit more one-sided than she'd have liked it to be, and now, with all this, he probably really was wishing he'd gone off with Dawnie.

Glancing up as a nurse brought a new patient to the chair next to hers, she felt her heart dissolving. The dear, sweet-faced girl couldn't be much older than Lily, and here she was about to be plugged into a bag full of lethal drugs that had already made her hair fall out.

Not wanting to stare, she put her album aside and picked up the tatty old copy of *David Copperfield* she'd kept since school. This was the book Ryan was reading now, at Chaplain Paul's suggestion, so Josie had decided to keep him company. She wondered if Ryan remembered watching it on telly when he was young. How he'd cried when he'd realised young David's mummy was dead! In the end they'd had to abandon the series, it was just too upsetting for him. Silly old sausage, he hadn't been able to distinguish between fact and fiction, and she sometimes wondered if he was any better at it now.

Putting her head back she closed her eyes, not sure if she was feeling woozy all of a sudden, or just a bit tired. Fortunately she hadn't passed out yet, and she'd been attached for over an hour, so with any luck it wouldn't happen again. They'd given her a different anti-sickness drug this time, in the hope this one might be more effective.

'Hello, my name's Kelly.'

Opening her eyes, Josie turned to the young girl next to her and smiled. 'I'm Josie,' she said, 'nice to meet you.'

'Is this your first time?' Kelly asked.

'No, second. What about you?'

'I'm on my second regimen, so this is my fifth. Mine's breast, what's yours?'

'The same,' Josie replied, thinking how wrong it seemed for someone half her age to have the same disease. 'Have they operated on you yet?'

'Yes, I had a lumpectomy three months ago. The chemo is to make sure they've got it all. My husband didn't want me to go through it, he says it's evil, but the surgeon persuaded me it was for the best. Who are you with?'

Realising she meant which surgeon, Josie said, 'Mr Beck.'

'Oh, they say he's really good. I'm with Daniel Skawinski. He's good too. My husband has a problem with doctors, he's never trusted them since someone left some forceps inside his dad.' She gave a little laugh, and as she tried to stifle it Josie found herself laughing too. The next instant they were giggling like a pair of schoolgirls.

'It's not funny really,' Josie told the nurse when she came to find out what all the hilarity was. 'We're just having one of those moments.'

'Well, we're all for them,' Jenny encouraged her, laughing too. 'Can I get you anything, ladies? Tea, coffee, a sandwich?'

'Nothing for me,' Kelly answered. 'Everything tastes so awful these days I've practically given up eating.'

'Not good,' Jenny said sternly. 'Have you spoken to your GP about it?'

'I have, and I'm doing my best. Has that happened to you yet, Josie, where everything tastes like metal in your mouth?'

Josie shook her head.

'It might not,' Jenny reassured her, checking the drip. 'Everyone's different. Not much longer, Josie. You're doing very well today.'

'I promise, this was never something I wanted to excel at,' Josie told her, 'but now I'm going through it, I'm dead set on coming top of the class.'

Smiling, Jenny moved round to inspect Kelly's medication and almost collided with a smartly dressed young man. 'Oh, Darren, sorry,' she said, moving aside for him to get past.

'Hi love,' Kelly said, as Darren stooped to kiss her. 'Thanks for coming. Were they all right about you taking time off?'

'Kind of,' he replied, pulling up a stool. 'I can only stay half an hour, but I'll be back to take you home. I just popped into your mum's to see Chels. Playing good as gold, she was.'

Kelly's eyes softened. 'Don't you just love her? She's hardly ever any trouble,' she told Josie. 'She was four last week, that's why I'm here today. They changed my treatments so I didn't have to miss her party. You should have seen it, kids everywhere, having the time of their lives. Do you have any?'

'Two, but they're more or less grown up now,' Josie replied.

'This is Josie,' Kelly told her husband. 'She's got the same as me.'

Darren glanced awkwardly in Josie's direction, his fresh face flushing as he mumbled a hello. 'I have to go over this stuff with you, Kel,' he said, taking some forms out of an envelope. 'If we can finish it today I can give it to the broker.'

Turning away to allow them what privacy she could, Josie opened her book, but was no more than a paragraph in when she felt the need to close her eyes again. She could hear Kelly and Darren murmuring next to her, and thought how lovely it was that he'd come to be with her for a while, and would be back later to take her home. Being as young as she was it would matter a lot to Kelly to have her husband's support, her mother's too, who was taking care of the toddler. What a frightening time this must be for their little family, and how brave Kelly seemed.

'Josie? Are you asleep?'

Opening her eyes, Josie found Bel Monkton standing next to her chair. 'Heavens,' she exclaimed, struggling to sit straighter. 'What a surprise. What are you doing here?'

Holding up a handful of brochures, Bel said, 'I was dropping these off when I remembered that you were due to have your chemo today, so I thought I'd pop in to see if you were here.'

Delighted, Josie glanced down at the cannula in her wrist. 'As you can see, I am,' she smiled. 'Gosh, it's really kind of you to come. How are you?'

Bel's eyes twinkled. 'I'm fine,' she replied, pulling up a chair. 'Question is, how are you?'

Still thrilled by this surprise visit, Josie said, 'Well, the nurse tells me I'm doing very well today, and I'm happy to take her word for it.'

'She should know,' Bel responded, digging into her bag. 'I brought some peppermint tea on the off chance you might be here. They recommend it while you're having chemo. My sister used to drink it all the time.'

Taking the box, Josie tried to think how to thank her

without gushing. 'It's lovely to see you,' she said in the end. 'I really enjoyed our little chat the other week, it was very helpful.'

Looking doubtful, Bel said, 'I don't think I did much, but if you've told your husband now, that would be good.'

Josie continued to smile. 'I have and it went all right – I think. He hasn't left me yet, anyway,' she added with a laugh.

Narrowing her eyes, Bel said, 'If he did then I'd have to say he wouldn't be a husband worth having.'

'Oh, he's definitely worth it,' Josie chuckled, 'or he is to me. I don't suppose he'd be your cup of tea, but that's all right, we wouldn't both want to be after him.'

Smiling, Bel asked, 'What about your children? Have you broken it to them yet?'

At that Josie grimaced. 'There hasn't really been the opportunity,' she confessed. 'I mean, I was with them both on Saturday, when me and Lily went to see Ryan, but it feels so mean to tell him and then leave. And I don't want this spoiling the build-up to Lily's wedding, so I thought if I can get through the chemo without too much trouble, it can all be over and done without having to worry them.'

Bel wasn't looking convinced. 'Does your husband agree with that?' she asked.

'Yes, I think so. It's difficult to tell with him, sometimes, but don't worry, if he didn't he'd be sure to say. Anyway, tell me about you. Did you have a nice weekend?'

With a smile, Bel said, 'I had my niece and nephew for both days, which was hectic, but wonderful.'

'I expect they love being with you. It's probably a bit like being with their mother.'

Bel's eyes went down.

'Sorry, I shouldn't have said that,' Josie came in hurriedly.

'No, no, it's fine,' Bel assured her. 'You're probably right, on one level, because they do associate me with their mother, but unfortunately our closeness is causing a few issues between my brother-in-law and his new wife.'

Josie's eyebrows rose. 'He's married again, already?' she said. 'How long has your sister been gone?'

'Seventeen months. He met Kristina soon after. They have similar interests and I think he saw in her a way to escape his grief.'

Josie blinked. As far as she was concerned it was way too early to be hooking up with another wife, but she could hardly say so when it wasn't any of her business. 'What's she like?' she asked. 'The new wife. Is she good with the children?'

Bel's head tilted to one side. 'She's not unkind to them, that's for sure, but to be honest I don't think she really knows what to do with them. She's never had any of her own, and I get the impression she hasn't spent much time around kids either.'

'So your niece and nephew are happier when they're with you?'

'Possibly, which obviously isn't very helpful where Kristina's concerned.' She took a breath as she glanced down at her hands. 'My brother-in-law's been offered a job in Sydney,' she said. 'He wants to make a fresh start, to give Kristina a chance with the children without me being around.'

Josie was appalled. 'But he can't just take them away from you! That would be cruel.'

Bel's smile was small. 'Actually, I've got a feeling Kristina might be trying to persuade him to leave them with me,' she confided.

Josie frowned. 'Do you think he would?' she asked. 'Would you want him to?'

'Of course I'd have them, but I don't want them to lose their daddy. They adore him, and he adores them . . .'

'They have to come first,' Josie insisted. 'They've only just lost their mum, it would be terrible if they lost him too. There again, it would be just as bad if they lost you. Oh dear, what a dilemma. Have you talked it over with him?'

'Not yet, but I intend to. He's in a dreadful state, feeling so torn he doesn't know what to do with himself, so he's started drinking, which obviously isn't any help at all.'

'No, it certainly isn't,' Josie agreed. 'My dad had problems in that department and I wouldn't wish it on anyone, least of all your dear little niece and nephew. When's he supposed to be going to Sydney?'

241

'Not until July, so at least it's not imminent, but arrangements have to be made.' Her eyes suddenly narrowed again, but this time they were shining. 'This isn't right,' she declared. 'I'm supposed to be here cheering you up, or lending moral support, and what do I do but start loading you up with all my problems?'

'And what's wrong with that? You were kind enough to listen to mine, so the least I can do is return the favour.'

'But now isn't the time for you to be burdened with other people's issues,' Bel pointed out.

'It gives me something else to think about.' Josie looked up as Jenny returned to check on her progress.

'I think you're about done for today, Josie,' she decided, pushing buttons on the computer to end the session. She cast a quick smile at Bel, then her eyes widened with surprise. 'Hello,' she said warmly. 'It's been a while since we saw you here.'

'Nothing personal,' Bel responded, 'but I wasn't intending to come again, apart from to deliver brochures for BCC. I'll wait outside,' she said to Josie, 'and I can drive you home if you like.'

'Oh no, you don't need to do that,' Josie protested. 'I can get the bus. It stops right outside . . .'

Bel didn't seem to be listening.

Ten minutes later, having signed off on the drugs she'd been given, and taking her package of anti-sickness pills and the emergency number, Josie found Bel in the waiting room – *with Jeff.*

'What are you doing here?' she cried, certain she was seeing things.

'I was up around this way,' he replied, fiddling with the gloves in his hand, 'so I thought I'd see if you needed a lift.'

Stunned, and delighted, Josie said proudly to Bel, 'This is my husband, Jeff. Jeff, this is Bel Monkton. She's . . . Well she's . . .'

'A friend,' Bel provided, holding out a hand to shake. 'It's good to meet you, Jeff. I just stopped by to say hello to Josie, and now I guess I should be going.'

*

'So how do you know someone like her?' Jeff wanted to know, as he and Josie started the drive home. 'She's a bit posh, isn't she?'

Josie rested her head on the seatback. 'You say that as though it's some sort of crime,' she replied, closing her eyes. She wasn't feeling all that special, if the truth were told, a bit heady and tired, as though someone was slowly pumping lead into her veins.

'I'm just saying, that's all.' He glanced over at her. 'You're not going to throw up, are you?'

'Not right at this moment.'

He was still eyeing her suspiciously as he indicated to turn out of the hospital complex.

'So, how do you know her?' he repeated.

'Through the nurse at the breast clinic. She put me in touch with her when I needed someone to talk to.'

He frowned. 'So what, she's like some sort of counsellor?'

'I don't think so, not really. We just had a chat, and I suppose I felt a bit better about things after.'

He seemed surprised. 'Why, what did she say?'

She sighed, and wished she could stop her head from spinning. 'It wasn't so much what she said, it was just having someone to talk to who wasn't family. Sometimes it's easier with strangers.'

Apparently having nothing to say about that, he continued to drive, only breaking the silence when he took a call from the dispatcher for a pickup in half an hour.

Feeling relieved about that, since all she wanted when she got in was to go upstairs and lie down, Josie absorbed herself in the quiet and how pleased she was that he'd come to get her. Her thoughts soon drifted to Bel, and from there to Kelly, who she sincerely hoped was going to end up with an all-clear after her treatment; it was too horrible, too difficult to think of it happening any other way. She guessed Bel had never wanted to think negatively about her sister either, with her having two small children. At least Josie's two were grown ups, though she wasn't sure that made it any easier. Maybe it was harder to lose someone who'd been there for you throughout the first twenty years of your life. You knew them so much better.

'Do you want me to come in with you?' Jeff asked, as they pulled up outside the house.

'No, you go on, you don't want to be late for your fare. I can manage.'

As she gathered her things, he said, 'I was thinking about going to watch the match over the Cross Hands later.'

'All right,' she replied.

'I thought you might want to be left in peace.'

She did, and didn't.

'You'll get through this, you know that, don't you?' he stated, making it sound more like an order than a question.

'Course I do,' she said with a smile. 'You're not going to get rid of me that easily,' and forcing the door open she got out of the car.

'You come out with the stupidest things sometimes,' he told her irritably, and pulling the door closed he turned the car around and drove back down the street.

Taking herself inside, Josie shrugged off her coat and went into the living room to turn on the fire. She noticed straight away that the booklet to help partners cope with a breast-cancer diagnosis was gone from the coffee table, and her heart gave a beat of hope – until she spotted it tucked into the paper rack and remembered she'd hidden it there when someone had come round the other day.

Too exhausted to think any more of it, she turned back into the hall and climbed the stairs. All she wanted now was to snuggle down under a duvet and let the next few hours, or however long it might be, pass without too much nausea or discomfort. The trouble was, she already felt like hell, shivering and burning as though someone was throwing iced water over her flaming body, and her head was thumping like it was trying to explode. She hadn't been this bad so early the last time, but maybe the sooner it came on, the sooner it would be over.

'Josie! Josie! Are you in there?' her mother shouted through the letter box as she rapped on the door. 'I know you are, I was in Carly's and saw you go in.'

Go away, Mum, please, please go away.

'Come on, open up. I want to have a talk with you.'

Josie carried on to the bedroom. A talk where her mother was concerned meant Eileen wanted to borrow something, probably money.

'What's the matter with you?' Eileen shouted. 'Why was Jeff bringing you home in the middle of the day? Where have you been?'

Fearing she wouldn't go away until she got some answers, Josie pushed open the bedroom window and looked down at her mother. 'It's none of your business where we've been,' she told her, 'but if you must know, he drove me into town for a job interview.'

'Don't give me all your bloody nonsense,' Eileen retorted tartly. 'I heard you was up the hospital. Penny Watts said she saw you coming out. So what's going on?'

Sinking inside, Josie said, 'Nothing's *going on*. I went to see a friend and Jeff came to pick me up. Satisfied?'

'What friend?'

'No one you know. I'm shutting the window now, before I turn my bedroom into a fridge.'

'Aren't you going to let me in?'

'No, because I'm getting ready to go out again. I'll see you later,' and pulling the window closed she collapsed on to the bed and just about managed to pull the duvet around her. Sleep wouldn't come though, nothing so kind, there was only wave after wave of nausea that turned to nothing, and the wretched feeling of being consumed from within.

Her mobile rang, but she couldn't answer.

It rang again and she still didn't reach for it.

When it rang for a third time she forced herself to dig into her pocket. *Please God don't let anything be wrong with either of the children, or Jeff, she didn't have the energy to sort it out.*

'Mum,' Ryan cried when she answered. 'Where were you? I've been trying to get you.'

Instantly worried, she tried to sit up. 'I'm sorry, love,' she managed. 'Are you all right?'

'They're moving me to a prison up north,' he sobbed.

Stunned, Josie said, 'They can't do that,' but she knew they could. 'When did you hear?'

'Just now. What am I going to do, Mum? I'll never see you, or Lily or Paul . . .'

'Have you talked to Paul? Maybe there's something he can do.'

'He's not here today. Mum, I'm scared. I don't want to go up north.'

She was trying to think, but right now she didn't have the energy to make a call, if she even knew who to ring. 'Listen,' she said weakly, 'I'm going to try and . . .' She broke off at the sound of jeering and laughter coming down the line. She heard Ryan grunt, as though he'd been punched, or shoved against a wall. 'Ry? Are you there?'

'Yeah,' he whimpered.

'What's happening?'

'Nothing, I got to go,' and to her dismay the line went dead.

Feeling more dreadful than she ever had in her life, she clicked off her end and tried to breathe steadily as she closed her eyes. She had to think who to call, who might be able to help, but there was only Jeff and Lily, and what was the point of worrying them when they'd have no more idea what to do than she did?

'Oh Ryan, Ryan, Ryan,' she sobbed inside, imagining all kinds of horrors being rained down on him even as she lay here, 'my baby, my boy. I don't want to let you down, but I don't know what to do.'

Chapter Sixteen

Two weeks had now passed since Bel had popped into the oncology centre to see Josie. During that time they'd been in touch regularly on the phone, and Bel had called round to Josie's home to check on progress a few days after the treatment. Though Josie had suffered quite badly again, and for longer than the first time, thankfully, by the second week, she was back on her feet, good as new, as she liked to tell Bel, though it was clear from the changed pallor of her skin that the chemotherapy was starting to take its toll.

It was surprising them both to find how comfortable they were in each other's company, particularly given how different their worlds were, or maybe it was because they were so different that the friendship worked. Who could say? What mattered was the way they each seemed to be filling a space in the other's life with no pressure involved, only support and plenty of laughter, something neither of them had had nearly enough of in recent times.

It was Wednesday afternoon now, five days before Josie's next treatment, and they were both at the barn, standing a short way back from the front entrance amongst years of accumulated farmyard debris and a great many puddles, some as deep as their knees. In spite of the gloomy day Bel was having no problem seeing past the tattered roof, dilapidated stone walls and mud-packed floor to the building's true magnificence. By the time it was converted to a dwelling both vast cart doors, with their crumbling stone archways, would be returned to their original splendour, with glass doors inserted. The dovecotes built into the fascia and the old oak lintels would be carefully restored, while the cavernous space inside, criss-crossed with centuries-old beams, would, eventually, become a home with five en-suite bedrooms, two staircases, three separate living areas and a huge family kitchen. The milking shed across the courtyard could serve either as a garage, stables, a guest cottage or perhaps a gym and a pool.

So far everything was going to plan. Bel's deposit was firmly in the farmer's bank, the surveyor's report hadn't delivered any knockout blows, and the architect and builder were almost as enthusiastic about the project as she was. All they needed now was to complete the deal, get approval from the planners and they could begin.

Just like that. If only things were so easy.

'So what do you think?' she asked, turning to Josie who was stoically braving the mizzling rain.

Josie's eyes were incredulous. 'Well, I don't have your imagination,' she admitted, tucking a windswept golden curl behind one ear, 'but I reckon even I can see it's going to be impressive when it's finished. Will you live here?'

'No,' Bel laughed, linking her arm and starting towards the barn. She needed to get Josie out of this weather before the damp seeped into her coat and she ended up catching cold. 'It's far too big for one person. By the time everything's done we could end up with as many as seven or eight bedrooms. Who knows, it might suit someone as a small hotel, or B & B. Do you know anything about the architecture of barns?' she asked, as they entered the shadowy interior.

Josie's expression was wry. 'Well, now, I can't say I do. In fact, I'm sure this is the first time I've ever set foot in one.'

'Me too, of this type,' Bel informed her. 'It's what's called a traditional hay barn, built on the cross. Do you see what I mean? Front to back is the spine of the cross, with huge doors either end for the carts to bring in their loads and exit without having to reverse. And the arms of the cross, so to speak, are the spaces where they used to toss the hay. Because it's late nineteenth century and Grade II listed, all of this has to remain intact, but we can probably put ceilings into the arms of the cross to create a dining room on ground level, with a staircase leading up to a galleried bedroom and bathroom. The same the other side, but with a sitting room on this floor.'

Josie was gazing around, trying to take it all in. 'What about windows?' she asked, seeing none in the arms of the cross.

'The cart doors will be all the windows we're allowed,' Bel replied, 'which is why it's fantastic to have two – usually there's only one at the front. They'll let in masses of light. The narrow slits you can see in most of the walls will also have to stay as they are – they were there for the hay to breathe – but obviously we'll have to glass them over to stop the wind howling through.'

'And the kitchen?' Josie prompted. 'Where are you going to put that?'

'Good question,' Bel smiled, and steering her to a ragged hole in the stonework, she led the way out into a decrepit lean-to littered with buckets, old hoses, tin cans and various rusting tools she wouldn't have been able to identify if she'd tried. 'This is most likely where we'll put the kitchen,' she declared. 'We'll source the same stone as everywhere else, put up five or six pillars where the wooden struts are now with French windows in between, and top it off with a conical roof. The architect's saying we could probably make it into a hexagon, which would be amazing, but we'll have to see what the planners have to say about that.'

'This whole space,' Josie laughed, looking up at the holes in the corrugated iron above, 'is going to be a *kitchen*! I wouldn't know where to put everything if it was mine, and I reckon you'd walk a mile every time you cooked a meal.'

Laughing too, Bel was about to carry on describing her plans when Josie's mobile rang.

'Lily,' Josie announced. 'I'd better take it.'

'Car,' Bel instructed, pointing to her Mercedes estate. 'It's warmer. I'll come and start the engine.'

After leaving Josie all wrapped up in a woolly hat and scarf with the heater turned high as she talked to her daughter, Bel picked her way across the yard to the milking shed.

There were so many possibilities for this structure, most fraught with the kind of problems that were going to cause endless nightmares, but nothing could make her back out of it now. She was wholly committed, not only because of the creative challenge, but because if Nick did end up taking the children to Sydney, she was going to need it to help fill the emptiness when they'd gone.

It was still unsettling her terribly even to think of losing them, though nothing more had been said on the subject since the morning Kristina had brought the children to her. So exactly what their plans were, when they were intending to leave, whether they were meaning to break it to the children sooner rather than later, she was having to wait to find out, since she didn't feel inclined to cause a scene by asking.

Sitting snugly in the car, Josie was assuring Lily she'd be happy to help write the invitations, and yes, she'd have a list of addresses ready for when Lily came at the weekend. 'And I'll go to the church to count up how many flower arrangements we're going to need,' she promised, 'but I thought you'd want to come with me for that.'

'I don't think I'll have time,' Lily groaned. 'We've got so much on this weekend, you wouldn't believe it. Anyway, what I want to know is if you're feeling better now?'

'Yes, I'm fine,' Josie told her, watching a plastic bag skittering across the yard in the wind. 'It was just a bit of a tummy bug that I couldn't seem to shake. I'm back to work tomorrow, so right as rain. Have you heard from Ryan this week?'

'Yeah, he rang the night before last for a little chat.'

'Was he OK?'

'Yeah, he was good.'

Having now established that the threatened move to another prison had been no more than a wind-up on the part of some fellow inmates, Josie was breathing a little easier. 'I wonder if he's got the copy of *David Copperfield* I sent?' she said, struggling past the listlessness that was spreading through her. Apparently someone had either stolen or destroyed the one he'd been reading, so he'd texted her to ask for another.

'He didn't say,' Lily replied, 'but if it doesn't turn up I'm sure he'll let us know. Anyway, I'd better go, loads to do. Glad you're better. Love you, see you at the weekend,' and hardly giving Josie the chance to say much else, she was gone.

Sliding the phone back in her pocket, Josie continued to sit where she was, enjoying the comfort of the car as the wind and rain chased round the barn and whipped up a frenzy across the surrounding fields. If she was being honest, it was all a bit beyond her, trying to work out how this place was going to look by the time Bel had finished, but not having the vision, or all that much energy, was in no way dampening the pleasure of being here. She'd been thrilled to bits when Bel had called to ask if she'd like to come, and she could still raise a little chuckle to think of Carly's face when she'd peered out of her nets and spotted Josie Clark getting into a Merc.

Josie had noticed that Bel never talked about any friends, so it would seem that now her sister had gone she was much more on her own than Josie would ever have imagined for someone like her. Which was such a shame, Josie reflected, because she had to be one of the kindest people she'd ever met. Fancy her ringing up the day after Josie's last treatment to find out how she was. Terrible, had been the answer, so sore and constipated that she'd felt as though her body was tearing in half. She hadn't told Bel that, but what she had ended up blurting out was how worried she was about Ryan. So Bel, cool as you like, had rung up the prison to find out what was going on. It was how they'd discovered that he'd been the butt of some other prisoner's joke, which wasn't a good thing to hear, it distressed Josie a lot to think of him being bullied, but it was far more welcome news than finding out he really was going to be shipped off up north.

The day after that Bel had insisted on coming to the house to see for herself how Josie was doing. She'd wanted to make sure, she'd said, that Josie wasn't suffering in silence when she really ought to be asking for help. By then the searing knife through Josie's nether regions every time she went to the loo had blunted a little and the throbbing in her head was starting to ease. Nevertheless, she'd missed her shifts at the caff that week.

'It's time to tell your employer what's going on,' Bel had advised. 'I'm sure she'll be very understanding once she knows what the problem is.'

'She will,' Josie agreed, 'but she'll also know that she has to find someone else, because she won't be able to cope with me constantly letting her down. And if I lose this job I won't be bringing in any money at all.'

'There are allowances, benefits, you can claim to help you through this time,' Bel insisted. 'I don't know the details, but we can easily find out. I'll call someone at Breast Cancer Care, they'll know exactly what we're supposed to do.'

We. She'd said 'we', just like it was her problem too, and it had made Josie want to cry.

True to her word Bel had got the information and had even offered to come to the jobcentre with her to go through the formalities, but Josie had drawn the line at that. She really wouldn't have felt comfortable about taking Bel Monkton to such a place, especially as it was in the Zone; she wouldn't have had any wheels left on her car by the time they came out again. Besides, it had made more sense for Jeff to go with her, which he had, bless him; he'd even taken her for a cup of coffee after to celebrate their windfall, as he was calling it. They were going to be nearly twenty quid a week better off as soon as she finished up at the caff, and he didn't seem to mind too much about the fact they were getting it from the state. Or he hadn't said that he did anyway, and she couldn't imagine he would when he obviously understood why it wasn't possible for her to hold down a job for a while. Once this chemo was over, and she'd got through the op, they'd be able to go back to normal, and work themselves to a standstill for less money again.

There was something to look forward to.

Meantime, five days to go until her next treatment, so best to make the most of them, and she had to admit she was happy as Larry, being here with Bel, wherever the heck Bel had disappeared to.

In the milking shed Bel was so engrossed in measurements, sketches and notes for the architect that it wasn't until she began packing her clipboard away that she realised a good twenty minutes had passed since she'd left Josie in the car. Hoping she had dropped off, and not found herself caught up in some problem with her daughter, Bel began picking her way around piles of hay and old cow dung back to the car. She'd done about as much as she could here today, and with the weather turning uglier by the second it was time to start heading home.

Opening the boot as carefully as she could, she put her attaché case inside and went to slide quietly into the driver's seat. It wasn't until she'd closed the door that she realised Josie wasn't asleep. She was staring at something in her hand, and when Bel saw what it was her heart burned with pity.

The clump of hair Josie was holding was large enough to confirm that the loss had begun, and remembering how traumatic it had been for Talia, Bel took Josie's free hand in hers.

Josie's face was stricken as she turned to her. It was as though, Bel thought, the shock of what was happening was setting in all over again.

'Let's go back to my place and decide what's best to be done,' she said softly. 'It'll be all right, so don't worry. I'll help you to choose a wig, or scarves if you prefer. I have several very nice ones that I'm more than happy to pass on, if you like them.'

Josie didn't answer, simply turned her gaze back to the shining golden curls in her hand. She combed her fingers through her hair again, and added more to what she was holding. 'I think I should cut it all off,' she said, her voice cracked with misery. 'I don't want to end up with bald spots, that'll look even worse.'

'Wearing it a bit shorter for a while is a good idea,' Bel advised. 'It puts less pressure on your scalp when you brush it, and it might not feel quite so traumatic to go from short hair to losing it altogether.'

Josie nodded vaguely. 'There won't be any hiding it from

the kids now,' she whispered, turning to look out of the window.

'It's best they know,' Bel responded. 'I understand why you want to protect them, but they can handle this, you just have to give them the chance.'

Josie continued to stare at nothing. 'Seems all wrong, me leaning on them,' she said. 'I'm their mother, it's not how it's supposed to be.'

Feeling for how difficult each step of this journey was, and knowing it was likely to get worse before it got better, Bel touched a comforting hand to her arm.

Turning to her, Josie gave her a grateful smile. 'Maybe we should go straight to a hairdresser and get it shaved off,' she said. 'I've got some money on me . . .'

'We can go tomorrow, if you still feel it's what you want to do.'

'I'm at the caff tomorrow.'

'We could go after you finish.'

Josie nodded. 'I suppose I ought to tell Fliss what's going on before I turn up looking like a boiled egg,' she said. There was a beat before her mouth twitched with a smile; a moment later she was laughing and Bel was joining in.

'A boiled egg,' Josie gasped, suddenly finding it hilarious.

'You won't look anything like that,' Bel protested.

Josie was dabbing the tears from her eyes. 'Actually,' she finally managed, 'I probably ought to wait till next week to tell Lily. She's coming on Saturday, and I don't want to end up spoiling her weekend.' She sighed quietly, and Bel could hear the anguish in her voice as she said, 'Jeff's always loved my hair. He says it's my best feature.'

'It is lovely,' Bel agreed, 'but so are your eyes, and your smile.'

Josie had to laugh. 'It's just hair,' she said. 'It's not like I'm losing a limb, so time to get over myself.'

Bel waited for a while. 'Ready to go?' she asked when she felt Josie might be.

'I think so.'

By the time they drove in through the gates of Stillwater they were laughing again, at something else that wasn't funny, but somehow that made it even funnier. They barely noticed the rain pounding the windscreen, or the way the sky appeared almost submerged in the sea, until they got out of the car.

'Remind me to install an integral garage, if I ever build a place of my own,' Bel told Josie, stripping off her hat and scarf as they ran in through the front door.

'Duly noted,' Josie promised, 'and could you remind me to put a helipad on the roof of mine?'

Laughing, Bel said, 'And where will you keep your yacht?'

'Oh, somewhere around the Med,' Josie replied flippantly, and copying Bel she kicked off her boots. 'Oh, feel this floor,' she swooned as the heat rose up through her socks. 'Forget everything else, I'll settle for one of these.'

'Come on,' Bel chuckled, 'it's throughout the house so you're not going to hit any cold spots. Shall we have some tea?'

'Can't think of anything better. Ginger?' Since Josie's last treatment Bel had introduced her to several different types of herbal infusions, all of which were supposed to help ease the side effects of chemo.

'How about liquorice?' Bel suggested, going to the cupboard. 'I'm sure there's some here.'

'Sounds good,' Josie replied, placing her hands in the small of her back.

'Aching?' Bel asked.

'Just a bit. I keep meaning to start again with the Pilates board, it was fine while I was doing that. I expect it's all the lying about in bed. I'll talk to Jeff about getting a new mattress, because he's been suffering again lately as well. Oh, my, is this your sister and her family?' she asked, spotting a framed photograph on the bookshelves. 'I don't think I noticed it before.'

'It was there,' Bel assured her, glancing up. 'I took it myself, about a year before she died.'

Josie was entranced. 'If I didn't know any better I'd think it was you,' she murmured softly. 'She looks lovely. So happy. And the children are cuter than cute.'

Bel smiled. 'I think so, but there again, I'm biased.'

After gazing at the photograph a while longer, Josie put it back and wandered over to the kitchen. 'So how are things with your brother-in-law?' she prompted.

Bel glanced at her mobile as it started to ring. 'Speak of the devil,' she muttered, reaching for it. 'Hi Nick, how are you?' she said, looking at Josie.

'Yes, I'm fine,' Nick replied, not quite sounding it. 'How about you?'

'I'm good, thanks. I've just been over to the barn with a friend.'

'Does that mean everything's going through?'

'It seems to be.'

'Good. So who was the friend? Don't tell me, Harry Beck.'

Taken aback, Bel said, 'No actually. Her name's Josie, and she's here now. We're about to have tea. Are you nearby? You're welcome to join us.'

'I'm still in Exeter,' he told her. 'I'm ringing because . . . Well, I felt I ought to in case you wanted to know . . .'

Bel's heart was twisting. He was about to tell her that they'd brought the departure date forward. 'Wanted to know what?' she asked.

There was an awkward silence before he said, 'Please remember, I'm the messenger here, it's not coming from me . . .'

Suddenly cottoning on, Bel's eyes turned cold. 'If this is about my father I don't want to know.'

'OK, fine. I just thought I should tell you that he wants to see you before he flies home.'

'Well you can tell him from me,' Bel seethed, 'if he tries to come anywhere near me I'll go straight to the police. There's no statute of limitations on what he did, and there'd be no holding the press . . .'

'It's OK, I get the picture,' Nick broke in. 'I just thought I should warn you that it's what he wants.'

'Then please warn him that he would be making a very big mistake if he tries,' and as though it were her father at the end of the line she cut it dead.

Several moments ticked by as Josie sat quietly watching her. Finally she slid down from her bar stool and went to carry on with the tea.

'Thanks,' Bel said shakily, as Josie put a cup in her hand. 'I'm sorry about all that . . .'

'You don't have to apologise to me. Just drink up, it's supposed to be helpful for stress.'

After taking a sip, Bel let go of a tremulous sigh and pushed a hand through her hair. 'I'm sorry,' she said. 'I wasn't expecting that call . . .'

'Please don't apologise,' Josie interrupted. 'Just drink up.'

Bel regarded her carefully. 'We were going to sort out something about your hair,' she said eventually. 'I've got . . .'

'Oh now, I don't expect the world to stand still because a silly old bit of my barnet came out. I'll cope with it.'

'And I'm going to help you,' Bel assured her. 'So let's pretend the last few minutes never happened.'

'If that's what you want,' Josie replied, and waving an invisible wand, she said, 'gone!'

'Bloody hell, Jose,' Jeff exclaimed as Josie got up from the bed.

Having thought he was still sleeping, Josie turned back in surprise. When she saw what he was looking at, her heartbeat slowed. She put a hand to her head, half expecting to find it all gone.

Their eyes locked on each other's in the semi-darkness.

'Sorry,' she mumbled, collecting up the fallen curls. 'I should have told you this was happening.'

He watched her pad across the room in her nightie. 'Are you going to lose it all?' he asked as she reached the door.

Keeping her back turned, she nodded.

'Bloody hell,' he repeated softly.

She wondered what he was thinking. Did he feel repulsed, shocked, sorry for her? She felt sorry for herself, but she didn't let it show as she turned round with a smile. 'I'm going to get it cut later,' she announced. 'That way it won't seem quite so drastic when it all goes.'

He was staring at the wall, clearly unable to look at her and not knowing what to say.

'It'll grow back,' she assured him. 'Once the treatment's over, it'll be like it never happened.'

He nodded. 'So are you going to go about with a bald head till then?' he wanted to know.

'No, I'll probably wear scarves, or a wig if I can find one. Once I'm on benefits the NHS will help to finance it. I've got all the forms.'

He inhaled shakily, seeming irritated, or maybe frustrated, she couldn't quite tell. 'Lily's coming today,' he reminded her.

'I know. I don't want to tell her yet though.'

'Well, she'll want to know why half your barnet's missing.'

Remembering she hadn't seen herself yet, she rushed to the bathroom mirror. To her horror a huge clump of hair had come away from the front of her parting, leaving the pale flesh beneath shyly exposed. There was no way she could hide it without a wig, or a scarf, and Lily would want to know why she was wearing either.

Fighting back the tears, she wrapped a towel round her head and went back to the bedroom. 'Will you tell her with me?' she asked, fearing a rebuff.

He swallowed and looked away as he nodded. 'If that's what you want.'

'Thanks,' she whispered.

A few moments ticked by.

'I'll go and make a cuppa, shall I?' she said.

'It's all right, I'll do it. You go and sort yourself out.'

Reminding herself that this was his way when he was worried or upset, to be withdrawn and unemotional, she returned to the bathroom and turned on the shower. Heaven only knew how much more hair was going to come out when she washed it, so maybe she'd better leave it for today and put on one of the lovely scarves Bel had given her yesterday.

She wanted to ring Bel now to tell her what was happening, but she couldn't keep turning to her every time she needed moral support, especially when Bel clearly had enough issues of her own to cope with. Heaven only knew what all that had been about on the phone with her brother-in-law. Obviously her father had done something terrible in the past, and Josie could only hope that her suspicions in that direction were way off target.

Half an hour later, having showered and tied a pretty pastel blue scarf around her head, she went downstairs and found Jeff watching the sports news. 'What do you think?' she asked, self-consciously.

Looking up from the telly, he regarded her briefly and nodded. 'It looks nice,' he told her. 'Where did you get it?'

'Bel gave it to me.'

'That was good of her,' he commented. 'I suppose she can afford to give stuff away.'

'Yes, but I don't think it's about affording it. She's just kind. A bit like you.'

His eyebrows rose.

'You can try hiding it from everyone else,' she teased, 'but I've known you a very long time, Jeff Clark. Kind is what you are, from the top of your daft old head to the bottom of your silly flat feet,' and before he could reply she sailed on into the kitchen, her smile acting like a sticking plaster over her tears. She didn't know if he was really thinking about Dawnie and wishing he was with her; that was just what she was telling herself, and she had to stop.

'What time're Lily and Jasper getting here?' he asked, coming to put his empty mug in the sink.

'She said about ten in her text, so I should have time to run up the shops for your paper and something for lunch.' Everyone would wonder about her scarf. She wasn't sure she was ready for it yet.

'I'll go,' he said, reading her mind, or maybe he needed to get out for a while. 'Write a list of what you want, and leave those dishes, I'll do them when I get back.'

She blinked in amazement. He never offered to do the washing up.

After he'd gone she went on rinsing the plates and mugs and tried to work out what might be going on in his mind. If she asked he probably wouldn't tell her, and even if he did how would she know if he was telling the truth? All she knew for certain was that he didn't like talking about things the way some people did, having to analyse every last detail of a problem, picking it apart and running

259

themselves round in circles until half the time they ended up making things ten times worse. She wasn't much up for flogging an issue to death, either. So maybe it was best if they just carried on as they were, not getting themselves worked up over something they could do nothing about, and putting it out of their minds as much as they could so their whole lives didn't become about it.

I am not cancer, she'd read in a forum on the Breast Cancer Care website; *I just have it in one small part of my body. The rest of me is the same happy-go-lucky, sporting, dedicated wife and mother I've always been. No cancer will ever change that.*

How she admired someone who could sound so positive and in control. She was trying to be like that, and there was no reason why she shouldn't succeed, because even during the times she felt like going to pieces no one needed to know. She wasn't going to be someone who spread misery and fear all over the place (or her hair, come to that, so she really must get it cut). She was someone who simply got on with things. Her treatment was going to be half over after the next session, and she was managing to cope with the side effects, just, and when she saw Mr Beck again in a couple of weeks she was absolutely certain he'd tell her that everything was going very well.

Josie's heart was aching as she watched Lily's smile disappear. Her lively honey curls were bunched randomly on the top of her head; her wide violet eyes were staring at her mother. Jeff had just told her to sit down, and Lily being Lily, had instantly guessed something was wrong. She reached for Jasper's hand as he sat down with her, and Josie noticed how worried he seemed too. There must be something in the air, she thought, or in her and Jeff's manner, or, more likely, it was the pale blue scarf that was giving the game away.

'Please don't let this be what I think it is,' Lily murmured, panic threading into her voice.

Josie glanced at Jasper and smiled. She wanted to keep things as calm and cheery as possible; there was no point spinning it out like a sentence of death when it certainly wasn't that, in spite of the dreaded C word hovering in the corner like the Grim Reaper himself. She had to say it and she would; she just hoped it wasn't going to be as hard to hear as she feared.

Jeff said, 'What your mother's trying to tell you, my love, is that she has breast cancer.'

Lily's face turned white, while shock had much the same effect on Josie. She hadn't expected him to blurt it out like that.

'Oh my God, Mum,' Lily cried, rushing to Josie. 'That's why you're wearing the scarf. Oh God, oh God, please don't let it be true.'

Tearing her eyes from Jeff, Josie patted Lily's back as she said, 'It's all right, sweetheart. It's going to be fine.'

'Of course it is,' Lily insisted. 'We'll make sure it is. Oh God, why didn't you tell me? How long have you known?'

'A couple of months, but it doesn't matter . . .'

'It matters to me. I knew something wasn't right, but you kept putting me off.'

'You've got enough to be thinking about.'

'Nothing's more important than you. Oh Mum, you shouldn't have to go through this. It's not fair.'

'Well, there we are,' Josie responded, 'it's here now, so we have to deal with it.'

'They've caught it early, right?' Lily wanted to know, trying to sound brave and capable in spite of the fear in her eyes.

Josie nodded. 'They're giving me some chemo now.'

'So you *are* losing your hair? That's what the scarf's about?'

'Yes, but it'll soon grow back.'

Lily was trying desperately to rally, but Josie could see what a struggle it was. 'It will,' she declared firmly, as if she knew about these things. 'It might even be lovelier than before.'

Josie looked at Jeff.

He was staring at nothing.

'That was your cue to say *not possible*,' she told him.

Looking both shaken and lost, he said, 'What?'

Josie rolled her eyes. 'Never mind.'

'Oh Dad,' Lily wailed, going to hug him. 'This must be horrible for you too, but she'll be all right, I promise.'

'Course she will,' he retorted. 'No one's ever said any different.'

'My aunt had it,' Jasper told them, 'and she's perfectly fine now.'

'There you are,' Lily announced to her mother. 'It's not as bad as it used to be. It's only people of your generation who are scared of it, because you remember how it was before, when your mothers were young.'

Though she had no memory of anyone suffering from breast cancer, Josie smiled her approval. 'Good, I'm glad we're all agreed,' she said, 'that it's not the monster it used to be.' She was prepared to accept Lily's reassurance, on the grounds that many more women survived breast cancer these days than ever before. And she would be one of them; there was no doubt about that.

The question they'd have to face sooner or later was whether Lily should be tested for the gene.

'So how long's the chemo going on for?' Lily wanted to know.

'Another three to four months,' Josie replied. 'So it should be over in plenty of time for the big day.'

'Yes, but what happens after?' Lily pressed.

'I'll probably have a little operation, but the surgeon's already promised it won't affect me coming to the wedding. I might have to find myself a nice wig for it though, but I expect you'll help me with that.'

'Of course I will,' Lily assured her, wrapping her up in her arms again. 'I'll do anything you need me to, you know that.'

'Same goes for me,' Jasper added. 'I might not be much good with wigs, but if there's anything else . . .'

'That's lovely of you,' Josie smiled. 'What matters to me is that you take care of our girl here.' To Lily, she said, 'I don't want you getting all maudlin about this, because there's nothing to be maudlin about.'

'She didn't say she was,' Jeff pointed out.

Josie glanced at him, and from the way he flushed she could tell he was sorry he'd just said that. It didn't matter, things were always coming out the wrong way at times like this, so she wasn't hurt.

'If you want us to postpone the wedding?' Lily offered.

'Don't be daft,' Josie scoffed. 'I just told you, there's no problem about me coming, and I'll still be able to help you organise it all.'

'You'll have to do your bit too, Dad,' Lily informed him.

'Did you hear me say I wouldn't?'

Lily regarded her mother anxiously. 'I don't want it to be too much for you . . .'

'Stop worrying about me, now . . .'

'I knew you'd say that, but you're my *mother* for goodness sake, of course I'm worried.'

'Well, it's not going to do anyone any good if you spend your time thinking the worst, so if you want to help, you should carry on as normal. That's what I'm doing. So's Dad, and we're coping just fine.'

Lily didn't look convinced. 'They say chemo's terrible . . .'

Josie rolled her eyes. 'It's not the best thing I've ever had, it's true, but others have a far worse time of it than me so I'm not complaining.'

'Yeah, well you wouldn't, would you?'

Josie threw up her hands. 'Speak to her,' she said to Jeff.

'What do you want me to say?' he protested. 'That she shouldn't care?'

Defeated by that, Josie turned to Jasper. 'Tell us about your aunt,' she encouraged.

Clearing his throat, he said, 'Well I don't actually know the details, only that she's doing really well now and she's not having any more treatment.'

'That's fantastic,' Josie smiled. 'She must be very pleased.'

'What about Ryan?' Lily broke in. 'He's going to take this really hard.'

At the mention of her son's name Josie collapsed inside. 'Not if we don't tell him,' she said.

Lily's jaw dropped. 'Don't you think he's going to guess something's wrong when you turn up with no hair?' she cried. 'You have to tell him. We can do it when we go next Saturday.'

'If she's well enough,' Jeff put in.

'What do you mean?' Lily demanded.

'She's got more chemo on Monday,' he explained, 'and the last time it wiped her out for over a week. She can't go gallivanting up to the prison if she's as weak as that.'

'I'll be all right,' Josie assured him.

'Would you like me to tell Ryan for you?' Lily suggested. 'I don't mind. I mean, I do, obviously, but Jaz'll come with me . . .'

'No, no, I need to be there,' Josie insisted. 'If I can't make it next Saturday, you're to promise me you won't say anything . . .' She broke off as someone knocked on the door.

'No peace for the wicked,' Jeff grumbled, going to see who it was.

'If it's Brenda Cartridge come to collect our stuff for the car boot sale tomorrow, tell her we'll bring it over later,' Josie called after him.

Wrapping her arms around her mother again, Lily wailed, 'I can't bear that you're having to go through this, but I'm going to be there for you every step of the way.'

'Me too,' Jasper added.

'What the heck's going on here?' Eileen demanded through a cough as she came in the door. 'You're a bit old to be sitting on your mother's lap, aren't you?'

'Not really,' Lily replied, getting up to embrace her. 'How are you, Nan?'

'Got a right bloody hangover, if you must know,' Eileen admitted, 'but it's me own fault for drinking too much last night.'

'Yeah, well one usually follows the other,' Lily told her wryly.

'All right, Jaz?' Eileen rasped, as he embraced her too. 'Reckon a spin in that car of yours might put the colour back in me cheeks, but I don't suppose you want to be seen with an old crock like me.'

'Any time you like,' he assured her.

Smiling as she coughed again, she said to Josie, 'What's that thing you got on your head? Makes you look like a bloody cancer victim.'

'Nan!' Lily said through her teeth.

'Eileen, you ought to watch your mouth,' Jeff told her sharply.

'What?' Eileen sniffed. 'I'm just saying, that's all. It's a nice enough scarf, it's just the kind of thing women wear when they're losing their hair.'

'Precisely,' Josie said.

Eileen's next cough died on her lips as she regarded her daughter. 'Are you saying . . . ?' She turned to Jeff. 'What's up?' she snapped, colour suffusing her cheeks.

'Josie's got breast cancer,' he informed her, 'that's why she's wearing the scarf.'

Eileen turned back to Josie in disbelief. 'You can't have,' she declared. 'I mean, it's not in our family . . .'

'It doesn't have to be, unless you're about to tell me I'm not yours after all.'

Eileen's eyes turned flinty. 'I know you'd like that very much,' she retorted, 'which just goes to show . . .'

'It was supposed to be a joke,' Josie sighed. 'You remember how I . . .'

'Always thought you were better than the rest of us, yes I remember. It was your bloody father who put those ideas in your head. Come to think of it, I'll bet you've got it from his side, because it's definitely not in mine.'

'It's all right, Mum, even if it was, I wouldn't be blaming you.'

'I should hope not. Is it serious?'

'Of course it is, Nan,' Lily piped up, 'it's *cancer*.'

Flinching, Eileen said, 'I meant, is it very far gone, because if it's not they can work miracles these days.'

'It's all under control,' Josie assured her.

Eileen's eyes suddenly narrowed. 'Hang on, that's what you were doing up the hospital a couple of weeks ago,' she stated.

Josie nodded. 'Jeff was picking me up after chemo.'

Glancing at her son-in-law, Eileen said, 'When do you have to go again, because if you want some company . . . You know I'll be there for you, provided I can get the time off.'

'It's OK, but thanks for the offer.'

Eileen sniffed again. 'Well, this is happy news, isn't it?'

she declared, seeming not to know what to do with herself. 'Not what I was expecting when I came over here, I can tell you that.'

'So what were you expecting?' Jeff snapped.

'Would you like a cup of tea, Nan?' Lily offered.

'I'll make it,' Jasper said, getting to his feet.

'I think I might need to sit down,' Eileen murmured, sinking into the place Jasper had left. 'You've taken the wind right out of me sails,' she told Josie. 'Fancy coming out with it just like that.'

'Oh stop going on,' Jeff objected, 'this isn't about you, hard as that might be for you to grasp.'

'How can you say that?' she cried. 'Of course it's about me, she's my daughter, for God's sake. Have you got any idea how much this is upsetting me?'

'Don't let's argue,' Josie interrupted. 'All that matters is that you know now, and if you can bear it, I'd like you to break it to Carly.' Between them they should have the entire estate covered by the end of the day, which would save her and Jeff the bother. Though Jeff was getting quite good at it, she reflected, with no small irony.

Failing to hide how ready she was to play messenger, Eileen said, 'She'll take it hard, I can tell you that. She's proper fond of you, is Carly. Everyone is round here. They all say she's a lovely woman, your Josie, the salt of the earth. I wish we could all be like her.'

'Well, I don't expect they'll be wishing that now,' Josie commented drily.

'That's a stupid thing to say,' Eileen retorted.

'Why?' Jeff demanded.

'Because it is.'

'You don't know what you're talking about,' he snapped, 'so why don't you just shut up?'

Eileen's nostrils flared. 'Don't speak to me like that!' she spat. 'I've just had a nasty shock, and now you're getting on at me . . .'

'It's all right, Nan, calm down,' Lily soothed. 'He doesn't mean anything. It's just that everyone's upset.'

'Yeah, and I'm getting the blame, when it's not my bloody fault.'

'No, but you could make a bit more of an effort to go with her for chemo,' Jeff growled. 'But not you, you can't take any time off . . .'

'I never said that . . .'

'You could change your bloody shifts around. She's your daughter, for God's sake, the only one you've got . . .'

'And she's your wife, so what are you doing, that's what I want to know?'

'Stop, just stop,' Josie cried.

'He started it,' Eileen raged, 'so don't shout at me.'

'You're the one who started it,' Jeff reminded her, 'coming round here, shooting your stupid mouth off . . .'

'Dad! You're not helping,' Lily protested.

Deciding to leave them to it, Josie took herself off to the kitchen and shut the door.

Jasper regarded her worriedly. 'Are you all right?' he asked, as she closed her eyes.

She could still hear them shouting over each other, Lily trying to calm things down, Jeff getting more and more worked up, her mother turning nastier than ever. She looked at Jasper and in spite of, or maybe because of, all the emotions building inside her, she found herself starting to laugh.

After a beat of surprise a grin spread across his face too.

'Do you think we should apply to go on Jeremy Kyle?' she asked, and finding the suggestion hilarious she bent double as he laughed too.

'You're amazing, do you know that?' he told her. 'I don't know anyone like you, apart from Lily, and you're where she gets it from.'

Josie turned round as the door opened and Lily burst in. 'I don't know what to do with them,' she cried.

'Let them sort it out for themselves,' Josie told her.

'But they're going to start throwing things . . . Hang on, are you two out here laughing?' she demanded incredulously. 'Yes, you are,' and as Josie went off into gales of mirth again Lily gaped at Jasper. A moment later she was bubbling up with laughter too, and throwing her arms round her mother, she said, 'It's not funny really, it's terrible, but there's no controlling them.'

'Best not to try,' Josie replied, dabbing her eyes. 'Everyone reacts differently, and I suppose this is how it happens for us.'

Standing back to cup Josie's face in her hands, Lily said, 'Did I ever tell you you're the best mum in the world?'

'Best girl,' Josie smiled, stroking Lily's cheek.

'We're going to be there for you,' Lily said, reaching for Jasper's hand. 'We're going to fight this together.'

Loving her more than ever, Josie said, 'All you have to do for me is get that degree and then turn up on your wedding day looking as pretty as a primrose and beautiful as any bride can ever be.'

Before Lily could reply the door crashed open again, and Eileen stormed in, puce in the face and ready to spit blood. 'I'm not staying out there to be insulted,' she raged. 'Where's my cup of tea?'

Though Josie drew breath to answer, all she could manage was another sob of laughter, which Eileen's shocked face only made worse.

'What the fuck?' Eileen snarled, as she realised Lily and Jasper were losing it too. 'You're all effing nuts in this house, that's what you are. People *die* of cancer, Josie, so I can't see what you're all finding so bloody funny.'

Sobering up, Josie put a hand on Eileen's shoulder. 'Thanks for pointing that out, Mum,' she said, 'we might not have realised it otherwise.'

Chapter Seventeen

'Yes, I'll be here all evening,' Bel was saying into her mobile as she let herself in the front door.

'I'll come about seven, if that's OK,' Nick responded.

'That's fine. Are you all right?' she asked. 'You sound a bit . . .' What did he sound? 'Tired?'

He cleared his throat and moved the phone closer to his mouth. 'Is that better?'

It wasn't, but she said, 'I guess so. I'll see you later then,' and ringing off she ran back to the car to start unloading her groceries. She wasn't going to allow herself to stress about the reason for his visit now; she had a busy afternoon ahead, and she didn't want to be distracted by lurking fears.

She'd spent the morning keeping Josie company at the oncology centre, and driving her home afterwards, as Jeff hadn't been able to make it.

'He had a really good fare, up to Bristol airport,' Josie had explained, 'so he couldn't pass it up.'

'Then it's lucky I rang to find out if you were on your own,' Bel had replied. 'You don't have to be, you know. I'm happy to be there for you.'

In typical Josie fashion, she'd insisted that Bel had plenty else to be worrying about, and that she was fine reading her magazines and getting the bus home when she was finished. 'Or the dispatcher at Jeff's taxi firm will send someone for me, free of charge,' she'd added. 'She called to tell us that yesterday. "Anything we can do," she said, which was really kind of her. "All the drivers want you to know they're happy to do their bit." Jeff was really touched by that, you could see it.'

Apparently most of Josie's family and neighbours now

knew about her condition, and Bel had found it quite moving, though not entirely surprising, to learn that so many had already been in touch with offers of support.

'Had no idea I had so many friends,' Josie had joked. 'The phone hardly stopped after my mother and Carly went out spreading the word, and people were in and out of our front door like it was a flipping railway station. Still, it was nice of them to say the things they did, although I could have done without some of the stories.'

Guessing they probably hadn't had happy endings, Bel had found herself smiling at one of Josie's endearingly wry looks.

It hadn't been an easy session for her today. At the outset they'd been worried about her white cell count, and had taken a while to decide that, in fact, it wasn't low enough to warrant a delay. So they'd gone ahead with her treatment, having to attach the cannula further up her arm, after being unable to raise the vein in her wrist. Before having a cannula inserted Talia had always dreaded the search for a vein, and from the way Josie had reacted she was probably going to start dreading it too.

Bel had left her at home an hour ago, all tucked up in bed with the curtains pulled and a good supply of anti-sickness drugs in easy reach, along with the emergency number and her mobile phone. She'd have stayed longer if Josie's mother hadn't arrived to sit with her. What a character she'd turned out to be. Bel was still thrown by the way she'd asked to be taken for a spin round the estate so everyone could see her in a Merc.

'Please ignore her,' Josie had begged. 'She can't help herself.'

'What?' Eileen had barked.

'I was asking for a cup of tea,' Josie told her.

'Bloody hell, what did your last slave die of,' Eileen grumbled, and it was only when she'd treated Bel to a wink that Bel had realised she was joking.

She'd call again later to find out how Josie was; with any luck Jeff would be back by then.

After unpacking the shopping, Bel picked up her keys and went straight out again. She was meeting the architect at the barn in an hour, and she wanted to be there ahead of time to assess the viability of further ideas for the conversion.

She was almost there when her phone rang, and seeing it was Josie she quickly clicked on. 'Hi, are you OK?' she asked.

'I think so,' Josie answered groggily. 'I just wanted to make sure you'd got home all right.'

Rolling her eyes, Bel said, 'What on earth are you doing worrying about me? You should be asleep, or at least getting some rest.'

'I am, I just wanted to check my mother didn't rope you into a joy ride.'

Bel laughed. 'Don't worry, I escaped while she was making the tea. Is she still there?'

'I don't think so. I can't hear anything downstairs, which is why I was afraid she'd managed to talk you into making her queen of the estate for the day.'

'Next time,' Bel promised.

'Please don't encourage her.' There was a pause before she said, 'I probably ought to go now.'

'Yes, you probably should,' Bel agreed. 'I'll call tomorrow to check up on you.'

Whether or not Josie heard wasn't possible to say, as there was no response from the other end.

Ringing off, Bel indicated to turn into the farm complex, and as she drew up in the yard she felt sorry that Josie wasn't with her to enjoy an hour or two of spring sunshine. After weeks of endless cold and rain, it was wonderfully uplifting to see daffodils starting to bud, and buttery-yellow primroses smiling from grassy banks. Swallows were soaring in and out of the barn as though they'd just been freed, while a handful of pigeons poked busily about the dovecote. She couldn't help thinking how happy Talia, the nature lover, would be here, but maybe, somewhere up there in the world of clouds and sea of sky, she was watching.

'*He didn't dare to get in touch,*' she could hear Talia saying. '*Good. He'll be gone by now, back to a world where his conscience isn't troubled by memory.*'

'*Is that how he lives, in denial?*' Bel asked.

'Where else would house him?'

'And when he's here? Where is his conscience then?'

'All around him, like the ribbons he used to make us wear in our hair, tying him up in knots, strangling him with guilt. He wants your forgiveness.'

'He'll never have it. Is Mummy with you?'

'You know she is.'

'Why doesn't she speak to me?'

'She does; you aren't listening.'

'Does she blame me?'

'It wasn't your fault.'

'You know it was.'

As the phone broke through the chatter in her mind, Bel looked at the screen and felt momentarily perplexed to see it was Harry. 'Hi, this is a nice surprise,' she said, this being the first time he'd been in touch since the night of the dinner.

'I'm glad you think so,' he responded, 'because I was afraid you might have written me off as a feckless friend by now. My only excuse is I was in Madrid for a week, at a medical conference, and then Istanbul lecturing on oncoplastic breast surgery. All pretty hectic, and my feet have hardly touched the ground since I got back, but I wasn't prepared to let another day go by without calling. So how are you?'

Slightly thrown by this need to be in touch, Bel said, 'I'm fine, thanks. I hope you got my text thanking you for dinner and apologising again for the way it started.'

'I did, and I'm sorry I didn't text back. So how's Nick? I trust he got home in one piece?'

'Fortunately, yes, and I think he's OK. I haven't seen much of him since, but he's coming over this evening, and I'm very much afraid it's to tell me that he's going to Sydney sooner rather than later.' Even saying the words was difficult. Imagining the reality was like tearing pages from a beloved book: it wouldn't make any sense without them, and there was nothing to fill the space.

Apart from the barn.

'Well, I hope you're wrong about that,' Harry declared, 'because I know you won't find it easy being so far from the children.'

The understatement almost made her smile. 'How are yours?' she asked. 'I expect they missed you while you were away.'

In his typically wry way, he replied, 'Oh, I doubt that, they're so busy all the time with their sport and music and countless after-school clubs. I've barely seen them since I got back, but I'm planning to reintroduce myself at the weekend when we all have some time off. I'll be interested to see how well they remember me.'

Laughing, she said, 'I'm sure they can hardly wait.'

'You don't know my sons, which could be a good thing. Anyway, I'd better come to the point. I was wondering if you might be free one evening this week? I have another big favour to ask, nothing to do with tickets this time, I promise. It's more of an opinion I'm after, but I'm aware it's using up more of your generosity, for which I'm very happy to pay with a drink, or dinner if you like. I'm hoping you'll opt for the dinner.'

Though she'd love nothing better than to spend another evening with him, she had to keep reminding herself that he was married, and even if it wasn't a date he was proposing, it still wasn't a good idea for their friendship to go any further.

On the other hand, what excuse could she give for not going?

'OK, you're hesitating. Does this mean you'd rather I rang off now?'

'No, no,' she said quickly. 'I'm just . . . It's kind of . . .' Oh to hell with it! 'Yes, of course I'm free, but maybe I ought to be asking what I'm supposed to be giving an opinion on.'

'Oh, that's easy. My mother's interested in buying an apartment on Kesterly seafront, and as you're the only property expert I know I was hoping you'd come and take a look at it with me.'

'Of course,' she replied. 'Will your mother be coming too?'

'No, she's still in India, but one of my uncles has told her it's time to expand her property portfolio, and in their dubious wisdom they've put yours truly in charge.'

'OK,' she said, drawing it out, 'so when do you want to do it?'

'The agent can make Thursday or Friday, so whichever suits you. It'll have to be after five for me, which is why I suggested a drink and dinner when we're done.'

It was still managing to sound like a date, but that was probably her overactive or suspicious imagination. If she turned out to be right, she could always explain at the time that she didn't play around with married men, no matter how attractive she might find them.

'You don't play around with anyone,' Talia reminded her.

This was true, so what was she worried about?

'Why don't we make it Friday,' she suggested. 'If you text me the address I can meet you there.'

'I'll do it right now,' he promised. 'Thanks for agreeing. I'll look forward to seeing you.'

Clicking off the line, Bel sat staring past the barn to the fields beyond. She was waiting for Talia to speak to her again, to come out with some little homily designed to inspire, or a memory to keep her in check, or even a tease, but it seemed she had nothing to say.

I know you're there, Bel told her. I can feel you.

There was still no response.

Josie was lying in bed, unable to move. She'd tried getting up a while ago, but it was like struggling with a tight band strapping her head to the pillow, and her bones were cracking with the effort. She didn't want to cry, but she was so close to it that tears kept burning her eyes. It was awful, feeling sorry for herself like this when there were people so much worse off than her, and they wouldn't be better in a couple of days. Or weeks, however long it took this time for her to get back on her feet.

She should have had her hair cut at the weekend when the second lot had come out, but she hadn't and now she looked like a broken, balding doll that ought to be stuffed in the attic, or better still, the bin. She had to keep a scarf on all the time, even when she slept, because it would have been horrible for Jeff to wake up and see the state she was in. Of course it slipped off when she turned over, but as far as she knew he hadn't yet seen the miserable curls still clinging to her head like seaweed to a rock. As soon as she was back on her feet she'd have to get it sorted, though the thought of going into the hairdressers on the high street and having them see her like this was making her want to cry again.

Everyone was being so kind, offering to do her shopping, or the housework, or anything else she might need. She was grateful, she really was, but she wished they'd stop calling. She wasn't up to speaking to them today, maybe by the end of the week, when she should be strong enough to tackle the chores anyway and to laugh off her balding head.

Was she ever going to find that funny? She couldn't imagine it, though she and Bel had managed a giggle when she'd likened herself to a boiled egg.

She and Dawnie used to be terrible gigglers.

Feeling her mobile vibrating, she checked who it was and seeing it was a woman she'd worked with years ago, she let the call go through to messages. Word was definitely getting around. She wondered if it had reached Dawnie yet.

She'd turn the phone off if she weren't hoping Jeff would ring to check on her.

He still hadn't looked at the booklet she'd given him for the partners of people with breast cancer. She wished he would, it might help them both if he had a better idea of how to cope, but she knew she couldn't force him to. He was probably frightened, a bit angry too, and feeling helpless wasn't something he'd ever taken to very well. It was part of the reason he wouldn't see Ryan; it reminded him that he was powerless to make things right for his son. She wished he'd come to the prison with her when she went to break the news, but she knew he wouldn't.

Lily would be there. Her dear, sweet Lily who was trying her best not to be scared, but Josie could see it in her eyes. That was what cancer did to people, it scared them witless before the doctors made it pack its bags and bugger off where it belonged.

Where was that, she wondered? Definitely not here.

Feeling the buzz of her mobile again, she lifted it up and seeing it was Bel she experienced a flicker of relief somewhere deep inside. Odd how a virtual stranger made her feel safe.

'Hi, how are you today?' Bel asked gently.

'Oh, not too bad,' Josie lied. 'A bit tired, you know.'

'Is anyone with you?'

'Not at the moment, but Lily's staying for the week. She's gone up the shops now, but she'll be back any minute.'

'That's good. Actually, I'd like to speak to her if I can.'

'Of course. Shall I give her your number?'

'Yes, please, and if I could have hers . . .'

Knowing she didn't have the strength to send a text, Josie said, 'If you've got a pen I can give it to you now.' As she reeled it off from memory, she closed her eyes. It was as though a lorry had mowed her down; every part of her ached, and her head continued to throb like her brain was trying to get out.

It's all right, she reminded herself weakly, *it'll pass.*

'Tell me again, when's your next appointment at the breast clinic?' Bel asked.

'I think it's the twenty-fourth. Just over two weeks.' She'd be halfway through by then; she wasn't sure she could take any more.

'Will Lily or Jeff go with you?'

'I don't know yet.' She couldn't think that far ahead.

'OK. I can tell I'm tiring you,' Bel said softly. 'I'll ring off now, but you know where I am if you need me.'

'Thank you,' Josie murmured, and without clicking off she let the phone slide from her hand.

She wanted to sleep so badly, but sleep wouldn't come.

A few minutes later she heard voices downstairs, and realised Jeff had come back with Lily. She was glad they were together; they'd keep each other's spirits up. As if to prove her right she heard Lily laughing as she came up the stairs.

'Are you awake?' Lily whispered, peering round the door.

Josie forced her eyes open. 'What were you laughing at?' she asked.

Lily smiled and came to sit on the bed next to her. 'I asked Dad if he wanted a cuppa and he said it was like a packet of fruit gums in the cupboard with all your different teas.'

Josie managed a smile in return.

Lily smoothed her cheek and gazed at her lovingly. 'Can I get you anything?' she asked.

'I'm all right.'

'You haven't eaten today.'

'I will, later.' She wouldn't tell her about the ulcers in her mouth, or the horrible taste, there was no need for her to know.

'I had a phone call just now,' Lily said, 'from someone called Bel Monkton.'

'Yes, she said she was going to ring you.'

'I've arranged to meet her on Friday. She says she wants to talk to me about you. Who is she?'

'She's someone I met through the breast unit at the hospital. She's a lovely person, you'll like her.'

'So do you think she wants to give me some advice on how to help you?'

'Possibly.'

Accepting that, Lily turned round as Jeff came into the room.

'Liquorice,' he announced, putting a mug down on Josie's nightstand. 'I forgot the biscuits. Do you want to pop down and get them?' he said to Lily.

After she'd gone he went on standing next to the bed, seeming unsure about sitting. 'I have to go out again in a minute,' he told her. 'I'm going to drive our Lily into Kesterly, then I've got a fare to pick up from the station.'

'OK,' she answered, closing her eyes.

'I don't expect Lily'll be much more than an hour or so.'

Bless him, he was worried, but she wanted to be alone.

'You'll be all right,' he stated, making it sound like more of an order than a question.

She managed a smile. 'Of course I will,' she said. 'Right as rain by tomorrow.'

Bel was staring at Nick aghast. 'What do you mean, Kristina's left you?' she cried, feeling horribly agitated by all the crowding implications. 'Where are the children, for heaven's sake? Please don't tell me she took them with her.'

'No, of course not,' he replied, his bloodshot eyes and unshaven chin lending a forlorn wretchedness to his despair. 'Suzie came down from Norwich. She's staying till the weekend.'

'Suzie? Your stepsister?' Bel exclaimed incredulously. 'I thought you two weren't speaking.'

'She contacted me a couple of weeks ago to apologise for the things she said when I married Kristina. Of course, I'm getting all the "I told you so's" now, but that's only to be expected.'

Bel almost slammed down his glass of beer. 'Let me get this straight,' she snapped. 'When Kristina went you turned to Suzie for help with the children, instead of to me?'

He regarded her helplessly. 'I understand why you'd feel hurt by that,' he responded, 'but, in the circumstances, it seemed the right thing to do.'

'What circumstances?'

He inhaled deeply, and as though retreating from her temper he turned his head away.

She found herself following his gaze, as if the answers he was seeking might be somewhere in the darkness outside. Angered and worried by how the children must be reacting to this, she was about to lay into him again when he said, 'You must know that the reason Kristina left . . .' His breath shook as he sighed and brought his eyes back to hers. 'She went because of you,' he told her.

Bel became very still, and as guilt rose up over her shock she felt her mind reeling.

'She thought – thinks,' he said, looking down at his hands, 'that I'm in love with you and can't admit it, even to myself.'

Bel could only stare at him. She had no idea what to say to that, or even what to think of it.

'I told her it's not true,' he pressed on, 'but she kept saying I was in denial. She wouldn't listen. I tried to explain, but she didn't want to hear the truth, and God knows I didn't want to tell her.'

'What truth?'

He sat back in his chair and pushed a hand through his already dishevelled hair. 'I shouldn't have married her,' he confessed. 'I thought I loved her, I mean, I do . . .' He shook his head as his words ran dry. 'Everyone was right,' he went on raggedly, 'it was too soon. I wasn't even close to getting over Talia . . . I didn't realise it then, or I suppose I wouldn't allow myself to think it. I wanted it all to go away, to be over, finished . . .' He flicked a glance her way, as though to gauge what she might be thinking. 'You know how it was, for both of us,' he said. 'How it still is, and Kristina's right, I can't look at you without thinking of Talia, and wishing we could go back to how things were when she was here.'

Feeling for his torment, Bel took his hands between her own. 'If it's any consolation,' she said, 'it's the same for me when I look at you. I realise I don't have to cope with you being her twin, and I understand how difficult that must be for you. Believe it or not, it is for me too.'

He regarded her curiously.

'There are times,' she explained, 'when I look in the mirror and allow myself to see her. It's like she's there, so close I could reach out and touch her, and I want it to be her so much that sometimes I pretend that it is her.'

His eyes remained on hers, as though connecting with her pain.

'I feel,' she said in a whisper, 'that when death came looking, it made a terrible mistake. It meant to take me, not her.'

'No, don't say that,' he protested.

'The children would still have their mother, and you would have your wife.'

'Yes, but we should have you too, and God knows we're glad that we do. You mean so much to us, Bel. Too much, is what Kristina says, and maybe she's right.' His head went down as the weight of his despair seemed to grow. 'I didn't want her to leave,' he said, 'but it's probably for the best that she did.'

'What have you told the children?' she asked.

'Just that she's gone to her parents for a while.'

Satisfied with that, she said, 'If you do still love her, you shouldn't let her go.'

'But it's not fair to do this to her. She tries with the children, and with me, but even when you're not there Talia's ghost is. We – *she* – can't escape it. And it's my fault, obviously. I'm in a terrible place. I hardly know what I'm doing from one minute to the next. The only time I can think straight is when I'm at work, but even there I'm not . . . I'm not the man I used to be. I don't have fun any more, I'm not engaging with my students, I'm finding it almost impossible to drum up the kind of enthusiasm I used to.' He picked up the beer he'd barely touched. 'I keep wanting to lose myself in this,' he told her. 'You saw me the night we met Harry, how I disgraced myself and embarrassed you. I was so angry with you, so bloody worked up over everything . . .' He stopped as more anguish engulfed him.

'Why were you angry with me?' she asked.

'For a hundred reasons,' he replied. 'If it weren't for you I wouldn't have a conscience about going to Sydney; my marriage wouldn't be in crisis; I wouldn't have to explain to my children why I was taking them away from you; I wouldn't be asking myself if I should have done as Talia asked and married you; I wouldn't be wishing that I had; I wouldn't be so damned jealous of your friendship with Harry. Do you see what a mess I am? I don't know what the truth of anything is any more. I only know that Kristina was right to leave, because I couldn't go on hurting her, and I can't take the job in Sydney, because I can't bear to leave you.'

Bel inhaled deeply as she tried to take it all in. She hardly knew what to say or do that would help him make sense of his confusion. Was he saying he had romantic feelings for her? She couldn't be sure, and guessed that he wasn't either. However, what did seem clear, at least to her, was that not dealing with his grief at the beginning was getting the better of him now, and unless he sought help it was going to drag him right under.

'I've thought of it,' he admitted, when she suggested counselling, 'but it'll mean having to talk about Talia and

I'm not sure how much good that would do. It's not going to bring her back, is it?'

'No, but you don't want to go on tearing yourself apart like this.'

'I suppose not.'

Several moments ticked by as they sought a way through the impasse. 'Maybe we could both go,' she said in the end. Did she want to? Maybe she needed it too.

His eyes came to hers, but instead of welcoming the idea, as she'd expected, he seemed uncertain. 'It might not be easy to talk freely if we're in the room together,' he said.

Accepting this was true, she didn't press it.

'Why would you want to go?' he asked. 'You're not screwing up your life the way I am.'

'Maybe not on the surface, but underneath I don't have anything like the kind of confidence I used to.'

'I should think being with Harry would do more to help that than counselling.'

'I'm not *with* Harry,' she retorted, almost crossly. 'I don't understand why you think I am when you know very well that he's married.'

'You're seeing quite a bit of him.'

'Once, when Kristina and I went to watch his band play, and again the night we met him for dinner.' Now wouldn't be the time to mention the day she'd run into him at the garden centre, or when he'd popped round to ask for tickets to her father's art show, or the apartment viewing later in the week, since it would only fuel Nick's suspicions.

'You have feelings for him,' he stated.

Trying not to be annoyed, she said, 'Yes, as a friend.'

'Are you sure about that?'

'Of course I'm sure.'

'Why are you being so defensive?'

'I'm not. I'm just trying to make you realise you're barking up the wrong tree.'

'Talia and I always used to say what a pity it was he was married, because you two seemed so well suited.'

Remembering how indeed it had been one of Talia's favourite refrains, Bel got up from the table to go and pour herself more wine. 'Whatever you think,' she said, 'the fact still remains that he has a wife and if he doesn't respect that, he'll never have any respect from me.'

'Respect and attraction aren't mutually exclusive.'

'Maybe not, but attraction and affairs with married men are, at least in my book, so shall we go back to talking about you and Kristina, because that's the real issue here? Not me, or Harry, or going to Sydney, or anything else you're trying to sidetrack yourself with.'

'I'm not sidetracking, I'm trying to work it out, and your relationship with Harry Beck is a part of it, because of how it makes me feel.'

Annoyed again, she said, 'As there is no relationship, you don't have to feel anything.'

Apparently deciding not to argue with that, he took a sip of his beer. After a while he said, 'Are you glad we're not going to Sydney?'

'Of course, but I can't feel glad about the reasons.'

'Really? I thought you'd be pleased that Kristina had given up on us.'

'How can you think I'd be pleased about something that's causing you so much heartache?'

'Ah, but Kristina's not doing that alone. You have to take some of the responsibility.'

'You don't know what you're saying.'

'Don't I?'

She shook her head.

'You don't think we should be together?'

'We are, as brother and sister. It can't be any more than that and in your heart you know it.'

He didn't argue, merely sat quietly contemplating her words. 'I've asked myself,' he said, 'if I can't leave you because of you, or because of Talia, and I don't know the answer.'

'Maybe it's a bit of both. And maybe it's still too soon.'

'The longer I wait, the more attached the children will become to you. Me too.'

She couldn't argue with that, because it was true.

'So what do I do?' he demanded.

'As I said, you should see someone, a professional, to help you straighten things out.'

'Do you know of anyone?'

'No, but I can always . . . I can ask around.' She'd been about to say she could ask Harry, but clearly that wouldn't have been a good idea.

He arched an eyebrow, letting her know that he'd followed her train of thought. 'Am I going to be welcome here after this?' he wanted to know.

She gave an incredulous laugh. 'You're always welcome here, you know that.'

'So you're not angry?'

'No, just concerned that you're going through so much. You should have told me sooner.'

'It wasn't this bad before. Kristina hadn't left me; I hadn't made a fool of myself in front of Harry . . . Please tell me I didn't accuse him of anything where Talia . . .'

'You didn't,' she assured him.

Seeming satisfied with that, he got to his feet. 'Suzie's going back at the weekend,' he said, 'would you like to spend some time with me and the children?'

'That would be lovely, but what are you going to do about Kristina?'

He shrugged. 'I'm not sure. Try to talk to her, I suppose.'

'Do you want her to come back?'

'The truth? I don't know. If I thought there was a chance with you . . .'

'Nick, please, it's not what you want. You might be telling yourself it is, but as much as I might look like her, I'm not Talia, and that's who you really want.'

He nodded sadly, and reached for his coat.

'It'll be all right,' she promised, as she walked him to the door. 'Grief is known to skew understanding and perception, but it can be worked through.'

Smiling, he pulled her into an embrace. 'I can't imagine why I thought I could go to Sydney,' he said into her hair.

'You had to consider it,' she responded, 'for the sake of your marriage, if nothing else.'

He didn't disagree. 'Just tell me one thing before I go,' he asked, 'are you keeping me at arm's length because you really don't feel anything, or because it's a habit you can't break?'

Chapter Eighteen

'So what do you think?' Harry asked eagerly as he and Bel took a second walk round the apartment, while the estate agent disappeared outside to wait.

'Well,' Bel replied slowly, casting a critical eye over the French waterleaf cornicing and arch-topped sash windows, 'it's obviously just undergone a major renovation, and from what I can tell they've done it very well.'

Clearly pleased with the approval, Harry said, 'The views would be amazing if it weren't dark out. The beach is right opposite, as you could see when we came in, and the station can't be more than a six- or seven-minute walk along the promenade.'

'So a great location,' Bel agreed. 'And provided your mother wants all this space . . . Three bedrooms, two bathrooms, and a really decent-sized kitchen,' she enthused, going through a set of open French doors to inspect the custom-built units and granite worktops. 'She could probably fit a table for four in here, though myself I'd be more inclined to install an island with a couple of bar stools, and use part of the enormous sitting room for dining.'

'Good idea,' he responded, noting it down, 'and the extra space through there, in the alcove, you said would make a good utility?'

'Absolutely. You could put up a few shelves, and build a tall cupboard into the corner for ironing board, vacuum cleaner et cetera. Is she going to live here alone?'

'Oh no, it's only an investment. The plan is to let it.'

Though surprised, Bel nodded approvingly. 'She should get a very good rent for a place like this. If you don't mind me asking, how much do they want for it?'

'Four hundred and twenty thou.'

'Mm, a bit over the odds perhaps, considering there's no lift and it's what, third floor?'

He nodded.

'On the other hand, there's a communal garden at the back which could be a real bonus for some.'

'So what would you offer, if you were buying it?' he wanted to know.

After going to check on the bedrooms and bathrooms again, she said, 'I'd start at four hundred and hope to land it at four ten.'

'Then that's what we'll do.'

She blinked. 'Just like that? Doesn't she want to see it first?'

'I'm sure she would if she was planning to live here, but I've told her about you and she's happy to trust your judgement.'

Bel opened her mouth, but no words came out.

He grinned. 'So, should I tell the agent tonight, or wait till morning?'

'If it were me,' she replied, 'I'd want to sleep on it.'

'OK, advice taken. Now, ready for a drink? I thought we could go to the Grape Escape on Castle Street in the old town. Do you know it?'

'I've heard of it, but I don't think I've ever been in.'

'Then allow me to introduce you to one of my favourite haunts. As you'd expect for a wine bar, it carries an excellent selection of vino, and I've taken the liberty of reserving a table in the restaurant upstairs in the hope I can persuade you to stay on for dinner.'

Not sure whether she was feeling railroaded, or swept off her feet, Bel followed him down a grandly sweeping staircase to where the estate agent was just coming in through the front door.

'We like it very much,' Harry informed him. 'I'll give you a ring in the morning to talk turkey.'

Bel choked back a laugh.

'Was that the wrong phrase?' he muttered as they stepped out on to the promenade.

'I don't think so,' she replied, 'it just sounded funny coming from you.'

Laughing, he put a hand on her elbow and steered her across the junction at North Road into the narrow cobbled streets of the old town.

A few minutes later they were perched on high stools either side of a bar table, with a glass of Sauvignon Blanc each and a dish of pretzels between them.

'Cheers,' he declared, touching his glass to hers.

'Cheers,' she echoed, 'to your mother's new apartment.'

'Indeed. She'll be delighted, I'm sure, but perhaps not as delighted as I'll be if it all goes through.'

Sipping her wine, she regarded him curiously.

'You are looking at Mrs Beck's first tenant,' he told her. 'I'm hoping to cut a good deal on the rent, given my connections, but she's known to drive a hard bargain so I'll have my work cut out.'

Baffled, Bel said, 'You're going to be living there? Well, I guess it's big enough for a family, I just thought . . .' What did she think? 'Don't you live in Sanford?' she asked.

'Correct. Opposite the common.'

And all those properties were large family homes. 'Surely it's a perfect spot for the children?'

'Indeed it is, and they'll be staying there, with their mother, while I move into town – and the great thing about the apartment is that they'll be able to have a bedroom each when they come to stay.'

Bel felt her mouth turning dry. She tried to think what to say, but for the moment nothing would come.

His eyes seemed to lose some of their humour. 'It's been coming for a while,' he confessed, 'but for the boys' sake we kept putting it off.'

His marriage was breaking up; he was about to become single. This wasn't what she'd expected.

'You're looking a little . . . stunned,' he told her.

'I'm sorry,' she said, trying to shake it off. 'I just assumed, I mean, I had no idea . . .' What was she struggling to say?

'Is it a problem?' he asked, seeming genuinely concerned.

'No, of course not.' But it was, because as long as he was married, or at least with his wife, he could expect nothing of her.

Maybe he didn't anyway. She could easily be jumping

to conclusions, and if she didn't take care she was going to end up making a fool of herself.

'I'm really sorry to hear things haven't worked out,' she sympathised, finally finding the right response. 'Perhaps you just need a little time apart?'

His tone was ironic as he said, 'I don't think any amount of time would be enough for my wife. She's had all she can take of me, she says.'

Surprised, since she hadn't imagined it to be that way round, Bel said, 'I can't believe that's true.'

He almost laughed, but something like sadness seemed to prevent it.

Oh my God, he has a broken heart and no one would ever know.

'She's met someone else,' he told her, looking down at his drink. 'I've known about it for a while. Actually, I blame myself . . .' This time he managed a laugh. 'She blames me, too. She says I'm married to my work and I can't deny it, because I am. Not that she has a problem with that per se, she just feels that I don't make enough time for her and the children.'

'Do you agree with that?'

'I guess, in part, but I have responsibilities in both areas. Obviously I'd put my children first in an emergency, and I do when I'm not at work, but we're so short-staffed at the hospital, and the women who come to the clinic . . . Well, at the risk of sounding corny, they put their lives in our hands. You can't just clock off from that, and sometimes it can really get to you, especially when you see how much belief they have in us and we know already that they're not going to make it.' He sat back and put up his hands. 'I'm sounding defensive now,' he said, 'like I'm arguing with my wife, so perhaps we should change the subject?'

'But what you're saying matters, because we need to know there are surgeons like you who care.'

He smiled. 'Luckily there are a few of us at Kesterly, and not just in my department. It's battling the system for our patients that makes life so hard, especially when you know full well that if someone lived elsewhere, in a different health authority, they'd have access to drugs they're being denied here.'

Unable to imagine how frustrating that must be, she said, 'I don't suppose any of us ever gives a thought to how much your dedication affects your personal life.'

'And why should you? It's not what you come to me for. In fact, if you're in my consulting room with a lump in your breast and a fear that's growing bigger and faster than any cancer, the last person you're thinking about, in a personal sense, is the man who's giving you the news you least want to hear.'

It was true, since she remembered only too well the day she'd gone to see him with Talia and he'd confirmed that her sister's lump was malignant. It was only later, once the shock had worn off and treatment was being dealt with, that they'd allowed themselves to become playful about his good looks, and have girlish fantasies about what if, and how could, and please let it be me.

'Bet you're glad you came out with me tonight,' he quipped.

In spite of everything, she had to smile.

'Now we really must change the subject,' he insisted. 'How are things progressing with the barn?'

Going with it, she said, 'Actually, not too badly. The architect should be ready to submit our initial plans by the end of the month, and my solicitor assures me the sale is going through.'

'You're submitting the plans even before you own it?' he asked.

'Oh yes, because if the council are going to cut up rough about something, or become intransigent over an issue that'll make it financially unviable, we need to know before we complete.'

'So you can pull out?'

'Precisely. But in this instance, the architect is pretty confident there won't be any problems. He knows the planners well, and he's done several barns in the past, so I feel I'm in good hands.'

He grinned. 'That's what we want to hear, that the best people are on the case and doing . . .' He broke off as a couple approached him, and getting to his feet he greeted them warmly.

'Bel, this is Felicity and Mike Tanslow,' he told her. 'Old acquaintances and . . .'

'. . . one very satisfied customer,' Felicity put in with a laugh. 'Nice to meet you, Bel.'

'Likewise,' Bel assured her, slightly thrown by the woman's frankness.

'Can I get you guys a drink?' Harry offered.

'Oh no, we don't want to interrupt,' Mike protested. 'We're on our way upstairs to meet my sister and her husband.'

Regarding Bel with interest, Felicity said, 'Are you . . . Mrs Beck, by any chance?'

'Oh no, no, Harry and I are just friends,' Bel replied, feeling herself blush.

Casting a knowing look at Harry, Felicity took her husband's arm ready to steer him away. 'Come on, we're already late,' she told him, 'but we'll see you at the Pink Ribbonwalk, Harry? Did I hear The Medics are playing us off?'

'We certainly are,' Harry assured her. 'Are you doing the ten or twenty miles?'

'Ten. We've got quite a big team together this year, so we're hoping to raise about two grand between us. I'll send you a link in case you want to sponsor me.'

Laughing as the Tanslows took themselves off to the restaurant, Harry said, 'If I sponsored everyone who sent me a link I'd be bankrupt by the end of the month.'

Bel smiled. 'Hint taken, I won't ask you to support me.'

'Are you up for it?'

'I'm hoping to be. Tell me, did you know the Tanslows before Felicity came to you for treatment?'

'Oh yes, she's on the hospital board and Mike was a neurosurgeon before he retired.' He nodded towards her glass. 'Can I get you another, or am I going to have the pleasure of your company for dinner? If so, we could go to the table.'

'Actually,' she replied, feeling a distant agitation starting to increase, 'I probably ought to be getting back.'

His face fell. 'OK, I understand,' he said, though she knew he didn't. 'Can I give you a lift? Or do you have your car?'

'I do, thanks.'

'Then I can walk you to it?'

'Of course, thank you.'

After paying for the drinks, he helped her into her coat and followed her out into the blustery night. 'I really appreciate you coming to view the flat,' he said, falling into step beside her. 'I'll call my mother, and the agent, in the morning to get things rolling.'

'You mean to talk turkey,' she teased.

He laughed, and moved aside to allow a rowdy hen party to pass.

As they crossed the promenade to where her car was parked, next to the sea wall, she was trying to think of something to say, but the only words she could find were in the form of an apology and she knew, if she got into that, she'd end up embarrassing them both.

'I was wondering,' he said, as they reached the car, 'if you and Nick and his family might like to come sailing one weekend with me and my boys.'

Trying not to stiffen, she said, 'That sounds lovely. I'll ask and let you know.' Now wasn't the time to tell him that Kristina had left, and there would probably never come a time when she'd admit that Nick was having issues over what kind of relationship she had with him, Harry.

Seeming pleased with her answer, he held out a hand to shake. When she took it, he pulled her forward to drop a kiss on her cheek. 'Thanks again for coming this evening,' he said, gazing directly into her eyes.

Feeling her cheeks starting to burn, she smiled and got into her car.

'Wow, that's some barrier you're putting up there,' Talia said. *'What do you expect?'* she replied.

There was no reply. Apparently Talia had released her conscience, leaving her to struggle with it alone. She had no reason to feel guilty, though. OK, she'd disappointed Harry, but to have had dinner with him, or to go sailing, or to see him at all on a friendly basis, would be leading him on in a way that wouldn't be fair at all when she was far too damaged by her past even to consider a relationship.

If she could have had one with anyone though, she'd dearly love it to be him.

The following morning Bel was already at the Seafront Cafe when the door opened and a pretty young girl with Josie's golden curls was blown in by the wind.

'Hi Fliss,' she called out, dumping her umbrella in the stand.

'Lily?' Fliss answered, looking up from the coffee machine. 'Are you here again? Twice in one week?' And coming round the counter she enveloped Lily in a maternal embrace. 'How's your lovely mum?' Bel heard her murmur.

'Still not great,' Lily replied, 'but at least she's up today.'

'Tell her she hasn't got to worry about how we're managing here. Terri's covering until I can find someone else, and once it's all over she can have her job back.'

'You're a star,' Lily told her. 'She'll be really happy to hear that.' She looked around the caff. 'I'm meeting someone . . .'

Bel was already getting up. 'Hi, you're obviously Lily,' she said, holding out her hand. 'I'm Bel. Thanks for coming.'

With eyebrows raised, Fliss asked, 'You two know each other?'

Lily glanced at Bel. 'We do now,' she said, and gave a laugh that was just like Josie's.

'I'll get you a cappuccino, Lil,' Fliss smiled. 'Anything else for you, love?' she asked Bel.

'No, I'm fine with the tea, thanks,' Bel replied.

As Lily shrugged off her coat her mobile rang. 'It's Mum,' she told Bel, slipping into the seat opposite her. 'Hi,' she said, clicking on. 'Everything OK?'

'Just wanted to make sure you got there all right,' Josie replied.

Rolling her eyes to Bel, Lily said, 'No terrorists on the way, or sudden earthquakes, or planes dropping from the sky. So yes, I'm here.'

'Have you met Bel yet?'

'Yes, just.'

'You'll like her. She's a lovely person.'

'You've already told me, and I don't doubt it.'

Able to hear, Bel smiled. 'Send her my love.'

'Tell her I send mine too,' Josie responded.

'Is Dad with you?' Lily asked.

'No, he just had a call-out, but Nan's coming over in a minute.'

'You'll enjoy that.'

'About as much as I did when she cut off the rest of my hair.'

'It saved you going to the hairdressers, which you didn't want to do.'

'I know. I'd better let you go now. Give me a call when you're on your way back.'

'Will do,' and ringing off Lily gave a protracted sigh. 'I don't know who worries about who the most,' she confessed, 'although that call was just her being nosy. She's trying to find out what you want to talk to me about.'

Smiling, Bel said, 'Well, you'll be able to tell her when you get back.' She looked up as Fliss brought the cappuccino and two chocolate muffins. 'You don't have to eat them,' she said, 'but they're on the house if you do.'

'I'll take mine home for Mum,' Lily told her.

'Oh, don't you worry about that,' Fliss responded, 'I've wrapped a couple up for her and Dad. How's your Ryan these days?'

'Oh, he's OK,' Lily replied, glancing awkwardly at Bel.

'Have you told him yet?' Fliss asked.

'No, Mum wants to do it, but if she can't make it tomorrow I'm going to tell him myself. He has to know, and if she misses another visit he'll just get panicked about what's going on. I mean, he will anyway, but it's best he knows the truth.'

Nodding her agreement, Fliss left them to it and went to wipe down the next table, where a couple of surfers had just plonked themselves.

'I don't know if Mum's told you,' Lily said to Bel, 'but my brother's . . .'

'Yes, she has,' Bel assured her, 'and I think you're right to tell him yourself. Breaking such news isn't easy for the person who's ill, and Josie would have worried all the way back from Bristol about how he was coping.'

Lily regarded her gratefully. 'Am I allowed to ask,' she said, shyly, 'have you had it too? Is that how come you're . . . helping Mum?'

'Not me, my sister,' Bel replied.

Lily watched her sip her tea. 'Where's your sister now?' she asked tentatively.

Taking a breath, Bel said, 'I'm afraid she didn't make it.'

Lily's face turned white.

'She had a different type of cancer to your mum's,' Bel told her hastily.

Clearly taking the straw, Lily said, 'Do you know what type Mum has? She says she didn't ask, but I'm afraid she did and doesn't want to tell me.'

'Actually, I don't know,' Bel lied. If Josie didn't want Lily to know the details yet, it wasn't her place to tell her. 'But I'm pretty certain it's not the same as my sister's, because that was Paget's disease, which is quite rare. Anyway, what really matters isn't so much the type, as how early they catch it. In my sister's case, because she was quite young, and the GP we had back then took over six months to send her for the tests she should have had straight away, the cancer had already spread to her lungs.'

'Oh God, I'm sorry,' Lily said, her eyes welling up. 'It must have been so hard for her.'

Touched by how personally she seemed to take it, Bel smiled and nodded towards the cappuccino. 'Drink up,' she encouraged, 'we're not here to talk about sad things.'

Lily's eyes lit with curiosity. 'So why are we here?' she wanted to know.

'Well, actually there are a couple of reasons, or I should say I've had a couple of ideas that I'd like to run past you. I wish they were going to provide an instant cure, or any kind of cure come to that, but what they might do is give a little boost to your mum's morale.'

Lily couldn't have looked more thrilled. 'That would be brilliant,' she declared, 'because I know she's feeling down. She'd never admit it, because she never does, but I can tell.'

'It's not unusual while someone's going through chemo,' Bel assured her. 'It takes an enormous toll on the body, which can be as hard to cope with mentally as it is physically. So, my first idea to try and cheer her up is to ask you if you'd like to be my partner for the Pink Ribbonwalk at Blenheim Palace in May.'

Lily's eyes rounded.

'It's to raise funds for Breast Cancer Care,' Bel explained, 'which is the charity that brought your mum and me together. If she's up to it, we can take her with us, though I doubt she'll have the strength to do the walk. She could join in some of the fun before and after though, and while we're out there covering our ten miles she can rest in the car, or have a chat with the BCC people who're organising it all.'

'Oh my God, that is such a fantastic idea,' Lily enthused. 'I'd love to be your partner. I'll be doing my finals then, but it's OK, I can take a day off. Do we have to get sponsors? I know nearly all our friends and neighbours will want to give if they think it's for Mum, and loads of my mates at uni.'

Loving her response, Bel said, 'That'll be wonderful. I'll get in touch with the events team to register us, then we'll set up a Just Giving page to take our donations.'

Lily looked about ready for the off.

'And my second idea,' Bel went on, using her voice to try and keep Lily in her seat, 'is much more radical, but I wondered if you thought your mum might like to take part in a fashion show?'

Lily's jaw dropped. 'What, you mean like on a catwalk?' she said.

Bel nodded. 'BCC holds one every year, usually at the Grosvenor House Hotel in London, and all the models are women who've been diagnosed with breast cancer.'

'Oh my God, that is totally awesome,' Lily gasped. 'When is it?'

'Not until October, which is breast cancer awareness month, but they're selecting the models now, and if you think Mum might be interested we can put her name forward.'

'Definitely,' Lily decided. 'I mean, she'll say no, because she'll feel shy about putting herself in the limelight, but she'd love to do it really. Oh wow, can you imagine her going up and down a catwalk? It'll be totally awesome. Where do the clothes come from?'

Loving this girl, Bel said, 'Well, the year before last, which was when Talia took part, they were from Topshop, Miss Selfridge, George at Asda, you name it, most of the high street stores were involved. And QVC, the shopping channel. They were amazing in how much they gave. It was styled by Hilary Alexander who used to be Fashion Director for the *Daily Telegraph*, and she made everyone look sensational. Even the men, because there were two brave souls who signed up for it – on the whole it's difficult to get men to show up, when everyone thinks breast cancer is a woman's disease.'

'So men get it too? I didn't know that.'

'It's much rarer in them, but there was one having treatment at the same time as Talia, so we talked him into taking part that year and he had the time of his life.'

Lily smiled. 'Where is he now?'

'As far as I know he's back in Spain with his wife.'

Clearly relieved to hear he'd survived, Lily said, 'We absolutely have to get Mum to do it.' She started to laugh. 'I can just imagine Dad's face when we tell him she's going to be a model. He'll be like, no way!'

'Well, we have to get her selected first,' Bel reminded her, 'but hopefully she'll be successful, and her chemotherapy will be well over by October. Actually, even long before August, which is when, I believe, you're getting married?'

Lily glowed. 'I can't wait,' she gushed. 'It's like totally amazing to think Jaz is going to be my husband. He's just the best. Mum and Dad love him, everyone does, and his family are fantastic. I haven't told Mum this yet, but his parents really want to meet her and Dad. They were planning to invite them over to their place in Kent for a weekend, which is totally amazing . . . You should see it, it's massive, in its own grounds, with a tennis court and woods and you name it. Anyway, now this has happened, Jaz's mum thinks it might be better if they came here so it wouldn't be too much for Mum. Do you reckon that's the right way to go?'

Touched to be asked, Bel said, 'Probably, given how far it is, and I don't expect Mum's eating all that much at the moment, is she?'

'Tell me about it,' Lily groaned. 'She's losing weight before my eyes, which she keeps saying she's happy about, but obviously she didn't want to lose it like this. Why do you reckon she's not eating? Is it the treatment making her feel sick?'

'That'll be part of it, but she might have mouth ulcers, and her sense of taste will probably be all over the place. If you get really worried you should persuade her to go and see your GP, or have a chat with one of the breast care nurses at the clinic. She'll have the number.'

'OK, I think I'll go online and get it too, just in case. Actually, Mum's due to go there in a couple of weeks to see the surgeon. It's her halfway check, apparently, and after that they change the chemo drugs. Let's just hope they're not as bad as the last lot.'

Knowing there wasn't much difference when it came to side effects, Bel said, 'She's with an excellent surgeon. He really cares about his patients.'

'That's good to know.' Lily shuddered suddenly. 'It's so horrible to think she has to go there, and that this vile thing is going on inside her. She so doesn't deserve it, but there again, I don't suppose anyone does.'

'No,' Bel answered quietly.

Lily's eyes came to hers. 'Thanks for caring about her,' she said, 'and for thinking of giving her these lovely treats.' She twinkled playfully. 'You're a bit like her fairy godmother: she *shall* go to the ball!'

Bel laughed. 'Or the fashion show, and she'll look a million dollars.'

Lily's humour suddenly died. 'If her hair's grown back by then,' she mumbled. 'It will, won't it, because I don't think she'll want to do it if it hasn't?'

'Provided she doesn't have to have another course of chemo, it'll be as lovely as ever, but even if she does, I can promise you she won't be the only one on stage in a wig.'

Chapter Nineteen

Josie would never in her life have imagined that one day she'd be sitting in the waiting room of the breast care clinic filling in an application form to be a catwalk model.

Whatever next!

The form had turned up in the post that morning, complete with a copy of last year's brochure that was so glossy and full of glamorous ads and articles that it looked a bit like *Vogue*. Imagine her photograph being in a magazine like that! Actually, she wouldn't be appearing in a professional model sense, only as someone who had taken part in the show. But first she had to be selected, and she couldn't imagine they'd want someone as ordinary as her.

'You're not ordinary,' Lily whispered crossly, as Mr Simmons, one of the surgeons, came to fetch a frightened-looking African woman who didn't seem to speak much English. Josie wished she could help in some way, though what she thought she was going to do when she couldn't speak a word of the woman's native tongue was totally beyond her. Still, at least she managed a friendly smile when the woman's nervous eyes glanced her way.

'OK,' Lily was saying quietly, 'we've got your date of birth, age and height, so now we need . . .'

When Lily didn't continue, Josie looked down at the form. The next requirement was bra size, and she felt a sobering despondency creeping over her as she realised she might only have one boob by the time the show was staged.

Her eyes went to Lily. 'I'm not sure how to answer that,' she said. 'They won't want someone who's had a mastectomy. I'll make the dresses look all lopsided.'

'Don't be daft,' Lily protested. 'That's what it's all about, to show everyone how women can still look lovely even if they have had mastectomies. Anyway, you might not have to have one yet, and if you do, you've got to ask if they'll give you a reconstruction at the same time.'

Feeling her energy draining as though to make room for more dread, Josie closed her eyes. The road ahead seemed so long, even endless, and she'd give almost anything never to have a moment's chemo again in her life.

'It'll be all right, Mum,' Lily said, taking her hand.

Josie smiled. 'Of course it will.'

Lily took out her phone as it beeped with a text. 'It's Bel,' she announced, as though certain this would lift Josie's spirits, 'she's coming to pick us up.'

As pleased as Lily could have hoped, Josie said, 'That's lovely of her. And then you're on the train back off to Bristol, young lady. I don't want all this getting in the way of your degree.'

'It won't,' Lily promised, 'but I had to come with you today. You need someone to hold your hand when you see the surgeon.'

'I want you to wait out here when I go in,' Josie told her. 'If you're there you'll only start asking questions and getting me confused. I'll tell you everything he says when I come out again.'

'As long as you do,' Lily insisted. 'Are you feeling OK? You're looking quite peaky.'

'I'm fine. Just a bit tired.' Actually she was more anxious than tired, but she certainly wasn't going to tell Lily that or it would be sure to upset her, and she'd done that enough times these past couple of weeks. And now her dear boy knew too, and the letter he'd sent after Lily told him was still tearing at Josie's heart.

Dear Mum, you haven't got to worry about me. I know you will, but don't, because all that matters is you getting better. I've talked to Paul about things and we're saying prayers for you three times a day (and I do some more in between). I'm sure God will listen and make you better. He does it for other people, and you're such a brilliant and lovely Mum I just know He'll do it for you.

I'm sorry Mum that I'm in here. You know I'd come home if

I could so I could do stuff for you. Come and see me when you can, but not if you're feeling bad. I'll manage all right, I promise. Lily and Jasper said they'll keep coming, and Paul's bringing me lots of books and talking things through with me so I don't have too much time to dwell on it all and don't have to feel too alone. That's really kind of him, isn't it?

I've been doing the same as Lily and using my computer time to search online for different kinds of cures and the right things to eat. Apparently beetroot's good, so are citrus fruits, mushrooms, herbs, free-range eggs and olive oil. Oh yes, brown rice and wholemeal bread are on the list too. They won't let me print anything out, or send you an email, but I'm going to see if I can find some recipes for you that include some of this and I'll send them in my next letter. I had to get off the computer before I could find some good alternative therapies, but I know Lily is on the case with that. She'll probably understand it better than I do anyway.

She told me about Bel who sounds really nice. I think it would be fantastic if you could be a model. You'll have to take loads of pictures so I can see you. I feel really bad that I'm missing everything, especially Lily's wedding. It really sucks, but I'm definitely learning my lesson and won't ever get in with the wrong crowd again.

I want you to know that you're the best Mum in the whole wide world, no contest. I love you masses and I know everything's going to be all right. Paul says we have to keep thinking positive because it really helps, and I think it does.

Your very loving and totally positive son, Ryan

How courageous he was being, her dear little guinea pig in there amongst all those thugs and druggies. She just hoped to God that fear of what was happening to her didn't drive him to do something stupid to himself.

'Bel also says,' Lily told her, 'that she's received our welcome packs for the Pink Ribbonwalk.'

Josie felt some of her tension ebbing. She was glad to know Bel was coming today. Funny how much better it could make her feel just having Bel there. It was a lovely quality that, being able to make a person feel secure and cared for the way Bel did. And it wasn't as though they saw each other often, though they spoke most days on the phone and sometimes they had really long chats about all sorts of things not to do with cancer or treatment or anything like that. For instance Josie knew now that Bel had grown up in Kingston upon Thames, just outside London, and that she'd gone to uni in Manchester, and travelled to places in the world Josie had barely even heard of. She'd been very close to her mother, by the sound of it, and if Josie wasn't greatly mistaken, she still missed her terribly. Her sister too. How awful for her to have lost them both – it just didn't seem fair. No wonder she was so relieved her brother-in-law had changed his mind about going to Sydney. It would have been heart-breaking for her to lose her niece and nephew on top of everything else.

She never mentioned her father, so Josie didn't either.

Josie had told her more about Dawnie, and how she missed her as a best friend, but couldn't forgive what she'd done. She'd even admitted being disappointed that Dawnie hadn't been in touch when someone was sure to have told her by now that Josie had cancer. She might even have heard it from Jeff.

'Mum?' Lily said, giving her a nudge.

Opening her eyes, Josie gave a start when she saw Mr Beck smiling down at her.

'Having a little snooze?' he asked as she hurried to get up.

'Miles away,' she confessed, feeling slightly dizzy. 'You'll be all right here,' she told Lily. 'I don't expect I'll be long.'

Happy that Mr Beck didn't contradict her, she followed him along to his consulting room, realising she was starting to shake, not with fear so much as cold. Maybe it was both.

'OK,' he said, once they were settled and he had her notes in front of him, 'you've seen Emma Pattullo, the oncologist . . .'

'Last week,' she confirmed.

He frowned slightly. 'Seems like you've had a bit of a rough time with side effects?'

'I've lost my hair,' she tried to laugh, patting the lemon and fuchsia scarf she was wearing, 'and I'm a good half a stone lighter than when it started.'

'Are you finding it difficult to eat?' he asked. 'Do you have mouth sores?'

She nodded.

'OK, we'll give you something to help with that. How are you sleeping?'

'Actually, not brilliantly,' she admitted. 'I'm tired most of the time, but I just can't seem to switch off.'

'And you haven't been to see your GP?'

She shook her head.

'Then we'll give you something to help with that too.' He read on for a while, before turning to face her. 'So how are the back pains?' he asked, seeming to give them more importance than she thought they were worth.

'Well, they come and go,' she said truthfully. 'It was definitely better when I was using my Pilates board, so I'm going to make more of an effort to use it again.' She twinkled playfully. 'I've got my husband on it now,' she confided. 'He looks a proper charlie and gives us all a good laugh, but he says it's helping his back no end, so it just goes to show that it works.'

Smiling, Harry returned to her notes, and she found herself looking at his hands, very elegant for a man, with pale short nails and a scattering of dark hair on the backs. She noticed the slim gold band on his wedding finger and found herself wondering about his wife, if she was Indian too, or Asian anyway, and if they had any children. There were no photographs on his desk, only the double-screen computer and various files. Maybe he had another office somewhere else where he kept his more personal things.

'OK, let's take a look at you, shall we?' he said, removing his glasses as he pushed the file away.

Though she went behind the screen to undress he left the room anyway, and was back a few minutes later with Yvonne, the nurse she'd met before. It was oddly like seeing an old friend, and from the way Yvonne greeted her it seemed she thought so too – except she was probably lovely with everyone who came here.

The examination and ultrasound didn't seem to take very long, and before she knew it she was sitting back next to his desk. 'So, is there a chance I might not have to have a mastectomy?' she asked, secretly crossing her fingers.

He brought his gentle brown eyes to hers in a way that made her heart turn over. 'No, you won't have to have a mastectomy,' he told her, and for some reason she didn't feel as relieved as she'd expected.

She continued to look at him, wondering why a sense of unreality was coming over her, a sort of effort to detach from where she was – probably because he was still speaking and the tone of his voice was making her feel stranger than ever.

'. . . the tumour has shrunk, as we'd hoped,' he was saying, 'but I'm afraid the results of your latest bone scan are showing that the cancer's spread.'

She blinked, unable, unwilling, to take it in. *Spread.* That meant . . . She felt suddenly panicked, and wanted to run as far away from here as she could get. 'I – um, does that mean . . .?' she stumbled. She looked at Yvonne, and the sorrow in the nurse's eyes brought a rush of frightened tears to her own.

She swallowed hard, and dug her nails into her palms. Her heartbeat was racing; there was an odd buzzing sound in her ears. She couldn't form the words she needed to say.

'Are you saying I've got secondaries?' she finally managed.

'I'm afraid so,' he confirmed.

The horror of it tore at her heart, ran through her like a deranged form of panic. 'So I'm going to die?' she whispered.

His eyes were still on hers, soothing and fathomless. 'Not for a very long time if we can help it,' he told her.

He hadn't said no. She'd wanted him to say no, that he could cure it, or that it was possible to operate and remove it, but she knew from what she'd read online that there was no cure for secondaries. She took a breath that was mangled by a sob. 'Sorry,' she said, pressing a hand to her mouth.

'It's OK,' he assured her. 'I know this has come as a shock, but I promise you, we're going to do everything we possibly can to slow its progress.'

Slow its progress, not stop it!

'So – so a mastectomy's no good?' She'd much rather have dealt with that than with what he was telling her now.

'We're going to continue with the chemotherapy,' he explained, 'followed by . . .'

'But if the tumour's shrunk and I don't have to have a mastectomy, why do I have to go on with the chemo?'

'Because we don't want it to grow again and risk it breaking through the skin.'

Shrinking from the very thought of that, she could only stare at him, wishing she'd never come here to find out what was wrong in the first place.

And what good would that have done you, Josie?

'At the end of this course of chemotherapy,' he continued patiently, 'we'll assess the situation again, but it's likely we'll start you on bisphosphanates.'

What were they when they were at home? 'Will I still be able to go to my daughter's wedding?' she mumbled, trying to think ahead and finding herself more frightened than ever as darkness began obliterating her dreams.

'Of course,' he smiled. 'You have my word on it.'

With no hair, but two boobs. Be thankful for small mercies, Josie.

She wanted to cry so badly it hurt, but she didn't want to be a nuisance, or to scare Lily when she went back to the waiting room.

He was offering her a tissue, and Yvonne's hand was on her shoulder. His eyes were so gentle, but they were kind of forceful too, in a way that made her feel as though she was being swept along safely to a place she didn't want to go.

Time to climb the wooden hill, Josie, her father used to say, and swinging her up in his arms he'd carry her up to bed, ignoring her protests. *It's for your own good. Early to bed, early to rise will make a little girl healthy, wealthy and wise.*

If he'd stayed around a bit longer it might have worked; as it was, after he'd gone her mother had never really seemed to mind what time she went to tuck herself in.

Remembering what Lily had insisted she put to him,

Josie said, 'My daughter was reading about a new technique . . . I think she said it was called a cell matrix graft, or something like that.'

'Acellular dermal matrix graft,' he told her. 'It's a form of reconstruction, so I'm afraid it doesn't apply in your case.'

What did, apart from goodbyes and funeral parlours, and what was it all about anyway?

'Sorry, I'm not handling this very well,' she told him, her voice choked with anguish.

'You're doing just fine,' he assured her.

She nodded, slowly, then more firmly. She wondered if she should be asking more about her prognosis, but maybe she'd found out enough for today – and she couldn't carry on sitting here taking up his time, feeling sorry for herself. He had other people to see who might be in an even worse state than her.

How could it be worse than dying? He hadn't used that word, but essentially it was what he was saying.

He'd also said they were going to do everything they could to make sure it wouldn't be for a very long time, *so pull yourself together, Josie, and try to be thankful for all the good things in your life.*

She couldn't remember what they were.

'I know it's difficult to think straight at the moment,' he said, 'but is there anything else you'd like to ask?'

He was right, it was hard to think, especially with Lily sitting outside. Although maybe having Lily there was a blessing, because she had to be strong now whether she felt it or not. 'It's good, isn't it,' she said, needing to carry some positive news out with her, 'that the tumour's shrunk?'

'It is,' he confirmed.

'And I don't have to have a mastectomy?'

He shook his head.

Grasping the useless straws as though they were lifelines, she stood up ready to leave. 'That's all right then,' she said. 'Thank you very much for . . . Well, for being so nice about it.'

Standing up too, he asked, 'Is someone here with you?'

'Yes, my daughter,' she reminded him, 'but I'd rather

she didn't know anything yet, if you don't mind. I'll tell her another time.'

'Of course.' He stood aside for her to go out of the room ahead of him, and escorted her back along the corridor.

'Aha,' he said, as they reached the waiting area, 'I'm guessing this is the daughter who's getting married?'

'Yes, that's my Lily,' Josie answered proudly as Lily stood up. 'And this is . . .'

'Bel!' he exclaimed in surprise.

'Harry,' Bel smiled. 'How are you?'

Josie watched them shake hands. It seemed to be happening in a dream.

'Are you together?' he asked, glancing at Josie and Lily.

'Yes, I've come to drive Josie home,' Bel informed him.

'I didn't realise you knew each other.'

'Bel's been . . . helping me to deal with things,' Josie told him, her voice sounding echoey in her ears.

'Then you're in very good hands,' he assured her.

She turned to Bel, who was regarding her curiously.

'Are you all right, Mum?' Lily asked.

'Yes, I'm fine. Never better,' Josie smiled.

'How's the flat purchase going?' Bel asked Harry.

'Yes, OK,' he replied. 'Our offer's been accepted. They want an early completion, so it could be ready to move into by the end of next month.'

'That's great,' Bel responded. 'Or is it?' she added doubtfully.

'It's good,' he assured her, in a tone that made Josie wonder if he meant it. 'Thanks for your expert guidance.'

Bel smiled. 'I didn't do anything, apart from agree with your choice.'

'Mr Beck?' the receptionist called out.

'I'll be right there,' he told her. 'It was good to see you,' he said to Bel. 'Take care, Josie, and be in touch if you need to be. You have the number?'

'I do,' she promised, and after watching him give Lily a smile, and Bel a second glance, she turned her attention to Yvonne who'd appeared with a prescription.

'So how did it go?' Lily wanted to know as they started for the pharmacy.

'Quite well actually,' Josie replied, feeling Bel's hand tuck into her arm. She was struck by how soothing it was to have her there. 'The tumour's shrunk,' she said, 'and they're giving me something to help with some of the side effects.'

'Thank goodness for that,' Lily sighed. 'You scared poor Dad out of his wits the last time, when you started screaming.'

'I know, I'm sorry about that, but the constipation . . . You've got no idea. I'd rather go through childbirth a dozen times than experience anything like that again.'

'So when does your next round of chemo begin?' Bel wanted to know.

'I'm presuming it's Wednesday of next week,' Josie replied, 'that's what I was told before, so I don't expect it's changed.' She put on a cheery smile. 'Which means,' she continued, 'if they stick to the same cycle, I could be up for doing the Pink Ribbonwalk.'

Bel didn't seem to be listening; she was regarding her too intently.

'Did I tell you Jasper's mum wants to join us?' Lily piped up.

'No, you didn't,' Bel replied. Her face was draining of colour; Josie wondered what she was seeing, reading in her eyes.

She looked away as Lily told Bel that Jasper's parents were coming to Kesterly this weekend to take Josie and Jeff for dinner, at the Crustacean, if Josie felt up to it. Josie was going to make sure she did. There was no point letting this spoil anything for anyone, least of all her precious girl.

Don't think about how much you love her now, it'll get the better of you.

'Did he say anything about a mastectomy?' Lily asked, as they joined a short line at the pharmacy.

'Oh, that's the other bit of good news,' Josie told her, avoiding Bel's eyes, 'I don't have to have one.'

Lily's face lit up with surprise and relief. 'That's brilliant,' she declared. 'Did you hear that, Bel? Isn't it fantastic?'

'Absolutely,' Bel agreed, but the way she tightened her hold on Josie's arm told Josie that she hadn't done so well at pulling the wool over her eyes.

*

An hour later, after dropping Lily at the station, Josie was at home, lying on the bed feeling drained and battered and afraid to think. Bel had wanted to come in with her, but she'd claimed tiredness and said she'd give her a call in a while. Bel knew, she could tell, but she couldn't talk to her about it, not yet. Probably not ever, because Bel had already been through this once; Josie wasn't going to put her through it again. It would bring back too many painful memories; remind her of how helpless they were in the face of a disease that destroyed lives and tore families apart.

It was going to happen to her family and she just couldn't bear it.

As panic welled in her chest she fought to make herself breathe.

She didn't want to miss out on her children's lives, all the small things that made them who they were, and the big things that marked their years passing. She had to be there for them, to share in their joys and hardships, to help them through whatever challenges came their way. She wanted to see her grandchildren, hold them in her arms and do what mothers did when their children became parents themselves.

Oh dear God, what if she didn't live long enough to see Ryan leave prison? She couldn't let that happen, she just couldn't. He needed her to help him start again, to keep him safe from any more mistakes, to ensure he made up with his father. Whether Lily was right about him being gay or not, she wanted to see him find a nice partner, someone who'd make him happy and feel loved. It would be easier to leave him if she knew he was settled and taken care of.

She didn't want to leave him at all.

Please God don't take me away before I get him back.

What would it be like for Lily no longer having her to turn to? She was more independent than Ryan, and would have a husband soon, but their closeness was as vital a part of her life as it was of Josie's. Never a day went by that they didn't speak or text; it was as natural to them as breathing. How was Lily going to cope when her phone fell silent, and her mother was never there when she came home?

She had to be here. Lily depended on it, and she did too.
Her children were her life.

Terrible, wrenching sobs were tearing through her body. She could barely catch her breath. She wanted to make this stop, to carry on seeing an endless road ahead of her instead of the wall that was starting to form. Faces of those she knew began coming and going, painted with sympathy, shock, confusion, even laughter. She wanted to reach out and hold on to them, as though they could pull her out of this despair and keep her here.

What was it going to mean to Jeff to lose her? After all the years they'd been together, the ups and downs they'd shared, the dreams they'd made come true or had to discard, how much was he going to miss her? Even if he still had feelings for Dawnie, she knew he still cared about her. He might not always show it, but she could sense it, and that was what really mattered. They were bound by the knowing of each other and the sharing of children and the day-to-day ordinariness of their lives. She couldn't imagine him without her, any more than she could imagine herself without him. Josie and Jeff. Even their names belonged together.

Would he go to Dawnie after she'd gone?

Hearing the front door close, she tried to pull herself together as she listened to him moving about downstairs. She wished he'd come and lie down with her, give her a cuddle and tell her everything would be all right.

Had he spoken to Lily yet? He was sure to have done, so he'd know by now that she didn't have to have a mastectomy, and that the tumour had shrunk. It was good to give them something to feel pleased about; they didn't need to deal with all this fear going round in her head. Plenty of time for that in the months to come, after the wedding, or even later than that, depending on how things progressed.

How was it progressing now, as she lay here? Was it creeping through her bones like a poison, eating away at them, destroying them and moving on to claim more?

What had she done to make her own body turn against her like this? Why couldn't she undo it?

Maybe they'd find a cure in time to save her.

She knew everyone in her position prayed for that, and now she was going to start praying for it too.

Jeff was going in and out of the back door by the sound of it, probably bringing his fishing gear in from the shed. He usually went off with his mates around Eastertime, so maybe they'd chosen this weekend. Though she desperately wanted him to stay with her, she also wanted him to go; it would give her more time to get herself under control ready to face the world again.

'Are you asleep?' Jeff whispered, cracking the door open.

Maybe she'd dropped off for a few minutes, because she hadn't heard him come up. 'No, I'm awake,' she told him, keeping her eyes closed so he wouldn't see she'd been crying. 'What are you up to down there?' she asked, as he sat on the end of the bed.

'I was just putting the washing out,' he said.

Surprise almost made her eyes open. He'd never done that in all the years they'd been married, or not that she could remember.

'How're you feeling?' he asked. 'Can I get you something? Nice cup of tea?'

'I'm all right,' she answered, 'just a bit tired so I thought I'd have a nap.'

'Yes, you do that. It'll make you feel better.'

'Are you going fishing this weekend?' she asked as he started to leave.

'No, I thought I'd give it a miss this year.'

She wondered why.

'It's good news, isn't it,' he said, 'that you don't have to go through that operation.'

She managed a smile as she nodded.

'I'll pop back in an hour to see how you are,' he told her.

'Thanks,' she whispered. It was lovely that he seemed so caring. Maybe he'd finally read the booklet for partners of people with cancer; or he could be feeling more able to cope now there had been some good news.

Feeling more tears stinging her eyes she willed him to leave the room, but her mobile was ringing and he was picking it up.

'It's Bel,' he said. 'Do you want to speak to her?'

'Not right now. Tell her I'm sleeping and I'll ring her back. Or no, let it go through to messages.' Though she couldn't imagine Bel telling him what she'd guessed, she didn't want her having to pretend there was good news when she knew there wasn't.

'I'll take it downstairs with me,' Jeff said, holding on to the phone, 'so it won't disturb you.'

She wanted to say he could just turn it off, but she was too close to tears to speak.

As the door closed behind him, she sobbed so harshly she was afraid he might hear, but he didn't come back.

She had to get a better grip on herself than this, and she would, she really would, just as soon as the shock wore off a bit and she found a way to stop herself thinking about the future she might not have.

Bel was sitting at the table with her head in her hands, feeling so agitated she barely knew what to do with herself. She couldn't go through it again, she just couldn't, but nor could she walk away from Josie as though she didn't care, when she could hardly care more.

Maybe she was wrong. Maybe she'd misread things, or her mind was playing tricks, projecting the past on to the present, and making it fit. History repeating itself: don't get too close to Bel or you'll end up dead.

She had to stop doing this or she'd drive herself mad.

The fact that Josie had been told she didn't need a mastectomy didn't necessarily mean the cancer had spread – except she'd seen the look in Josie's eyes, that same glazed shock that had come over Talia after Harry had broken the news to her. She'd tried to hide it too, not from Bel, because Bel had been in the room when Harry had told her, but from Nick, and the children, of course, and from all the friends who'd been so certain she'd end up beating it.

Hearing the entryphone buzz she forced herself to go

and find out who it was. Probably the postman, or a courier with some papers for her to sign.

At first she didn't recognise the car at the gates, but when the driver, who was standing next to it, turned to the camera she saw straight away that it was Harry. Her heart somersaulted as she tried to make sense of why he was there.

'Can I come in?' he asked over the intercom.

She didn't want to see anyone; she couldn't speak to him now, and yet she was already releasing the gates and opening the door.

She wasn't aware she was crying until he came up the steps, and taking her hands he pulled her inside.

'I was afraid I'd find you like this,' he said, using his fingers to push away her tears.

Her eyes closed. 'If you're here . . . If you thought . . . It must mean I'm right about Josie?'

He neither confirmed nor denied it; how could he, when he was Josie's surgeon?

She tried to speak, but only choked on a sob. She wanted to tell him she couldn't go through it again, but how could she make it about her when Josie was the only one who mattered?

'Come on,' he said, and slipping an arm round her shoulders he led her into the kitchen.

'I shouldn't have got involved,' she said, reaching for a tissue. 'I wasn't ready. I'm no good to her . . .'

'Ssh,' he came in gently. 'It's bringing back a lot of painful memories, it's bound to. I understand that, and so will Josie.'

She swallowed as she nodded. 'If I know her at all,' she said, blowing her nose, 'she'll try to push me away so I don't have to go through it again. I can't let her do that.'

'She has family,' he reminded her.

'Who she's trying to protect – you can't blame her for that. Her best friend slept with her husband so they're not in touch any more.'

He inhaled deeply, and she was reminded of his wife's affair. 'She can't keep it to herself for ever,' he pointed out.

Accepting that was true, Bel walked to the window and stared out at the milling clouds. The small patches of blue in their midst seemed like portals to the next world. She felt slightly nauseous and displaced, even from herself.

'Stop thinking about me,' Talia said. 'I'm nothing to do with this.'

'You're everything to do with it.'

'Only because you're telling yourself that. She's not your sister; her children aren't your niece and nephew. You're separate in a way you could never be from me. She needs you and you won't let her down.'

'How do you know?'

'Because who do you think's talking to you now? It's not me, it's you.'

Bel shivered as though someone had walked over her grave.

'Are you OK?' Harry asked. 'Can I get you something?'

She turned round, a faint smile on her lips. 'It's me who should be asking you that,' she said. 'I have tea, beer, wine . . .'

'I'm fine. I have to be going soon. I'm expected home, but I wanted to make sure you're all right.'

Staying where she was, with the table between them, she said, 'Thank you.'

'Are you?' he prompted.

'I think so. Yes, I am. I suppose I just panicked and . . . Everything seemed very muddled for a while.'

Nodding his understanding, he said, 'Will you call? If you feel muddled again?'

'I'm sure I'll be fine,' she replied. 'You don't need to worry about me.'

She hadn't meant to hurt his feelings, and wasn't entirely sure that she had, but the way he withdrew seemed to suggest she might have.

'I'll be going then,' he said. 'If you, or Josie, need to talk, you know where to find me.'

She waited until the front door closed behind him before going to release the gates. Her breathing was ragged again, her pulses racing as though a new kind of panic was setting in.

'He only wants to be friends. Why are you shutting him out?'

'You know why.'

'He's lonely, you can see that. He doesn't want his marriage to break up, surely that must make you feel safe.'

She had no answer to that.

'Take a chance, Bel.'

'Why?'

'Because not all men are the same.'

Chapter Twenty

'Are you out of your tiny mind?'

Considering where she was, and what she was doing, Josie had to admit that she possibly was. On the other hand, if she ended up achieving what she'd come for, no one would think she was mad; they might even wonder if she was some sort of magician.

Debbie Prince checked her mobile as she dropped her cigarette end into a cup. With her greasy grey hair, missing teeth and wizened complexion she was a bit of a fright to look at. Scarier even than her was what might be crawling in the sofa Josie was sitting on. 'Let me get this straight,' Debbie Prince sniffed, lighting another cigarette. 'You want me to get *my* son to cop for what *your* son did, so yours can pick up a get-out-of-jail-free card?'

Josie took a breath. 'Not exactly,' she replied, feeling her heart rate accelerating; but it was OK, she could do this. 'We both know that it was your son who hit the man with a baseball bat. So what I'm asking is that he owns up to it so my son can come home, where he belongs.'

Debbie Prince stared at her, apparently waiting for more. When she realised nothing was coming she cackled a laugh and tossed her mobile on to the mantelpiece. 'I got to hand it to you,' she declared in her raspy voice, 'you've got some front coming here with your crazy talk. There ain't many would have the nerve, and you're lucky I'm in a good mood, or I'd be kicking your scrawny ass out the door by now and telling you to fuck off, because you know that's where this is going to end, don't you?'

Josie was determined not to be cowed. 'My son,' she began, and stopped as Debbie Prince's mobile rang.

'What?' she barked into it. 'How the fuck do I know? All right, all right, I'll go and have a look,' and as though Josie wasn't even there she left the room.

Josie stared around at the yellowing wallpaper, cracked and crooked mirror over the brick fireplace and the scraps of Christmas trimmings still pinned to the ceiling. She couldn't imagine the place had seen a duster or a vac this side of the new millennium, or much in the way of fresh air, given the rank smell and half-boarded-up window. She wondered how anyone could live in such squalor, and felt worried about the child who owned the toys cluttered around a giant TV.

Remembering none of this was her business, she checked her own mobile to see if anyone was trying to be in touch. No one was, which wasn't surprising since she'd texted Jeff and Lily to say she was going to have a lie-down this afternoon, and they usually waited for her to contact them if she was napping.

It was a surprise, not to mention a profound relief, to find herself handling this course of chemo better than the last one. She'd started it three weeks ago and mercifully had overcome the worst of the side effects a bit quicker than she had before. She still suffered from dreadful fatigue though, and swells of nausea, and chronic constipation, and the sores in her mouth weren't healing all that well. However, she felt blessed to be getting off relatively lightly this time around – at least for now. She still had two more treatments to go, but if it carried on like this she'd be able to make the most of however much time she had left, which could be years, of course, but there again it might not.

Feeling fussed by the thought, she firmly pushed it aside and concentrated on more positive thoughts. What was surprising her most these days was how different the world had started to seem since she'd found out about her secondaries. Or maybe it was she who'd changed, because she didn't feel quite as panicked as she had the day she'd left Mr Beck's office, or as desperate and angry. In fact, once she'd found the wherewithal to start fighting her way past all the self-pity and black dread, it had been like stepping slowly out of a violent storm into a beautiful sunny day. Perhaps that was putting it a bit too strongly: the violent storm was right, but the beautiful sunny day was more of a break between downpours. Still, she'd definitely found an inner strength she hadn't been aware of before, and a way of speaking her mind that often left Jeff open-mouthed.

'I don't know what's got into you,' he'd tell her at times, 'it must be the stuff they're pumping into your veins, because you never used to be like this.'

'Like what?'

'I don't know, cheeky, a bit full of yourself. I'm not saying it's wrong, I'm just saying you're more upfront than you used to be.'

She hadn't told him yet why she'd changed, partly because she didn't really know how to put it into words, or if it was even going to last; and partly because no one needed to know how bad things were for her until after the wedding. The only person she talked to was Bel, who, in spite of how hard Josie argued, couldn't be persuaded to leave her to get on with it.

'You had your share of all this when your sister was ill,' Josie had told her firmly. 'I'm not going to make you go there again, but thank you very much for caring. I've loved having you as a friend. It's helped in ways you probably don't even know and made me feel very special, but it's time to start putting yourself first now.'

'I'm not listening to any more of your nonsense,' Bel had protested, and that was what she kept on saying every time Josie tried to tell her that she ought not to be worrying about someone who wasn't even her family.

In truth, Josie was relieved not to lose Bel. She had to admit that she didn't feel strong and brave the entire time, and it was lovely to have someone to talk to when the demons started crashing about like hooligans trying to do their worst. However, the instant she sensed it getting too much for Bel she was going to put her foot down, and that would be that.

She wondered if she might become friends with Miriam, Jasper's mother. Not that she'd ever dream of offloading her problems, but what a lovely person she had turned out to be, and her husband Richard. Lily was right, they weren't stuck up at all, quite a laugh, in fact, which had come as a surprise to her and Jeff. They'd been the last to leave the Crustacean on the night they first met, and Richard hadn't allowed Jeff to contribute a penny to the bill. One of these days they'd find a way to return the hospitality, but meantime Miriam was insisting on joining the Pink Ribbonwalk next month. Josie was thrilled about that, especially as she could imagine her getting along very well with Bel.

'You still here?' Debbie Prince snorted, seeming genuinely surprised as she came back into the room. 'So, where was we? Oh that's right, you want me . . .'

'What I was saying before you left,' Josie interrupted with much bravado, 'was that my son confessed to the assault, because your son threatened to harm his family if he didn't.'

Debbie Prince's eyebrows shot skywards. 'Is that right?' she drawled.

Josie nodded.

'Well, it seems to me,' Debbie Prince retorted, 'if your son confessed to something he didn't do then he's an even bigger fuckwit than you are for coming here expecting me to care.'

Josie took a breath. She wasn't going to allow this woman to get under her skin; if she did they'd end up in some shrewish slanging match which she definitely wouldn't win. So, remembering the moral high ground was hers, she put on a disbelieving tone as she said, 'You really don't care?'

Debbie Prince shook her head.

'You mean, you think it's all right for an innocent boy to serve a prison term for a crime your son committed?'

'Hang on, hang on,' Debbie Prince protested, 'your son was there that night, he got the key that let them into the place, so don't come the innocent boy with me. He's fucking guilty, that's why he's gone down.'

'He's not guilty of assault.'

Debbie Prince's eyes narrowed.

Suspecting the woman had known all along this was true, Josie said, 'It was his first offence; if he hadn't been forced to confess to the assault he might only have got probation.'

Reaching for her cigarettes, Debbie Prince lit another and inhaled deeply. 'You know what I don't get,' she said, smoke skittering about her mouth and nose as she spoke, 'is why you think, for a single minute, that I'd do what you're asking.'

'I'm appealing to you as one mother to another,' Josie replied.

Debbie Prince seemed to find that amusing. 'You've got to know,' she smirked, 'that even if I tried to get Shane to cop to it, he'd tell me to go and get my fucking head fixed. So maybe that's what you should do, little lady, because you definitely ain't thinking straight.'

'I want my son to come home,' Josie said quietly, 'because I'm not sure how much longer I have to live.'

Debbie Prince cocked an incredulous stare.

'I don't want to die,' Josie continued, 'without being able to hold him this side of a prison wall.'

Debbie Prince blew out two more lungfuls of smoke. 'Very touching,' she commented, 'but we're all going to die sometime. Could be tomorrow, could be next week, could be fifty years from now, so why should that make a difference?'

'I have an incurable cancer,' Josie told her, feeling surprisingly strengthened by speaking the words aloud. 'So in my case it's likely to be sooner rather than later.'

Debbie Prince grimaced as she nodded. 'You've got cancer,' she repeated. 'And I've got to believe that because?'

'Do you really think I'm lying?'

'You could be.'

Reaching up, Josie removed the scarf from her naked head and continued to look at her. It was rare she allowed anyone to see her like this, she didn't even look in the mirror if she could help it, so it came as a shock when Debbie Prince only shrugged.

'So you're bald,' she said. 'For all I know you shaved it off before coming here to make me feel sorry for you.'

She surely didn't believe that. On the other hand, she could have been thinking there were no lengths a mother wouldn't go to for a child. 'And my eyebrows and eyelashes?' Josie asked. 'Do you think I shaved them too?'

Debbie Prince took a lengthy pull on her cigarette and sucked it in sharply.

Josie waited, hating sitting here exposing herself like this, but if it worked, and she managed to get Shane Prince's mother on her side, it would have been worth every second.

'Do you know what I reckon?' Debbie Prince said eventually. 'I reckon it's time for you to cover up that head of yours and take yourself off home.'

Though she could have gone on arguing, Josie conceded that she was unlikely to get any further today, so getting to her feet she retied the scarf. 'Will you at least think about what I'm asking?' she prompted.

'Tell you what,' Debbie Prince replied, 'I'll do more than that, I'll tell my old man about it next time I visit, it'll give us a good laugh.'

Josie regarded her with pity. 'Are you really that cold-hearted?'

Debbie Prince didn't answer, merely walked out to the front door and tugged it open. 'Nice meeting you, Mrs Clark,' she said, as Josie passed. 'Hope you don't get run over by a bus on the way home,' and cackling through a cough at her tasteless joke she disappeared back inside.

Refusing to feel despondent, or even disheartened, Josie picked her way through the dumping ground of a garden, past an old BMW raised on bricks, and out through what would have been a gate if one had been attached to the rusted hinges. At least she'd tried, and in spite of how unpleasant Debbie Prince had been she might yet find a conscience and speak to her son.

Of course, even if she did, Josie had no idea if the authorities could then be persuaded to release Ryan, but they certainly wouldn't if she sat back and did nothing.

Who'd ever have thought a terminal diagnosis could be this empowering, she was thinking as she began the risky walk back through the northern part of the estate. Not her, that was for sure, but the way she was trying to make herself see it, with Bel's help, was that she had a few choices, and it was up to her which ones she went for. She could turn to God, who she didn't really know and who never seemed to have any worthwhile answers to the questions she put to him (no answers at all, in fact). Or she could become all spiritual and take up chanting and meditating, which would totally freak Jeff out. Or she could bury her head in the sand and pretend it wasn't happening (this was quite a good fallback now and again, she had to admit). Or she could NOT live her life as if it was all about cancer and dying. Come to think of it, she might be doing a bit of everything, because she'd started saying a prayer or two when she went to the church about the wedding (just a little request asking for courage and thanking him for all the good things she had, just in case he was in some way responsible for them). Plus she was reading some interesting books Bel had given her – *Chicken Soup for the Soul* and *The Power of Now* (she especially liked the second one). And when she wasn't pretending it wasn't happening, and she wasn't exhausted by the chemo, she could feel quite uplifted by the way she was able to go about her day with a confidence and appreciation of the world and its people that she'd never really had before.

In fact, it was like she was floating about on a cloud, while the rest of the world got themselves all jammed up in impossible traffic.

Taking out her mobile as it rang, she saw it was Bel and immediately clicked on. 'Great minds,' she announced, stepping back as a white van sped by, too close to the kerb, 'I was about to call you.'

'Where are you?' Bel asked, clearly picking up on the wail of a siren as it chased the van.

Waiting for the police car to pass, Josie said, 'In the north part of the estate. I've just been to see Debbie Prince.'

There was a beat of shocked silence before Bel said, 'You mean the mother of Shane?'

'That's her. A charming lady, if you measure charm by tattoos and rotting teeth.'

Sounding amused, Bel said, 'So what did you say to her?'

After recounting the details, Josie said, 'You know, I still can't quite believe she thought I'd lie about having cancer.'

'Whatever she thought, you are totally amazing, do you know that?' Bel told her.

Enjoying the praise, Josie said, 'I'd agree if I'd persuaded her to see things my way.'

'Never mind, at least you've left her with something to think about, and who knows, she might decide to do the decent thing.'

'Indeed, but I won't be holding my breath. I just feel better for having done it, that's all. It's good to be proactive, as you put it.'

'As *I* put it?' Bel cried. 'I think it's you who came up with the term, and it's definitely you who's living it. I just wonder what you're going to do next with this new lion heart of yours.'

'A ten-mile walk the weekend after next,' Josie reminded her, crossing the street to avoid a couple of hoodies on bikes. She didn't want them snatching her bag or her phone; it would only make her mad, and she was trying to avoid negative energy.

'The way you're carrying on I wouldn't put it past you,' Bel declared. 'Have you heard back about the fashion show yet?'

Josie's spirits took a dip. 'No, but I don't expect they've chosen me. I'm too short and we can't be sure I'll still be around by then.' Amazing how relaxed she could make herself sound about it, when it had just thumped a black hole into her heart.

'It's only a few months,' Bel protested, 'you're definitely not going anywhere before that.'

'Says you, and I hope you're right. Anyway, I expect they get loads of applicants.'

'Probably, but don't give up on it yet. You could still be in with a chance.'

'I have to admit I hope so, because I really fancy doing it if only to see Jeff's face when I come strutting down the catwalk. Not that we'll get him there, I'm sure, but I expect you or Lily would film it and we could show him when we got home. Anyway, that's not the only surprise I've got in store for him, but I won't tell you what the other is now, I want to do a bit of work on it first then see what you think.'

'I'm intrigued,' Bel laughed.

'So am I,' Josie confessed, 'and you'll see what I mean when you know what it is. Anyway, what's going on with you? Is your brother-in-law any better?'

Sighing, Bel said, 'He's over the flu, but he's still in a bad place where everything else is concerned.'

'So he hasn't been to see a counsellor yet?'

'He says he has, but I'm not sure I believe him.'

'Are the children still with you?'

'Yes, I'm about to go and pick them up from school, then we've got football practice, ballet, and something else I've forgotten, but I'm sure it'll come back to me.'

'Hang on,' Josie said, 'someone else is trying to get through. It might be Hollywood offering me a part,' and enjoying Bel's splutter of laughter, she clicked to the other line. 'Hello, Josie Clark at your service.'

'What?' Jeff exclaimed.

'Hello love, I knew it was you. Are you OK?'

'Of course I am, but where are you? I just came home to check on you and the house is empty.'

'Ah yes, well I thought I'd take myself for a little walk,' she explained. 'It's such a lovely spring day, and the sun was shining when I set out.'

'Well it's not now, it's starting to rain, so where are you and I'll come and get you.'

'Oh, there's no need. I'll be back before you can turn the car round. Why don't you just put the kettle on and we can have a nice cup of camomile or orange blossom when I get in.'

'I reckon those fruit teas are going to your head,' he grunted, and abruptly rang off.

'I'm back,' she told Bel. 'So what about the barn? Did you exchange today, like you were supposed to?'

'I haven't heard from my solicitor yet, but I can't see any reason why it wouldn't go through. Are we still on for coffee at the Seafront tomorrow?'

'Of course. I'm looking forward to it, and don't start going on about coming to pick me up. I'll be perfectly all right on the bus, or Jeff'll drop me off if he's going that way.'

'OK, if you're sure. Hang on, it's me who's got another call this time. Tell you what, I'll call you back, just in case it's the solicitor.'

After ringing off and pocketing her phone, Josie decided to drop into the health centre to check her blood pressure, just because she could, and finding everything pleasingly normal she carried on to the high street, where she ran into one of her mother's friends in the butcher's.

'Oh, Josie, how are you, love?' Sandy Tremble asked mournfully. 'I'm ever so sorry about what you're going through. Must be terrible, and you've lost such a lot of weight. Eileen's that worried about you. Well, we all are. You know if there's anything I can do . . .'

Like cheer up, Josie was thinking. 'That's lovely of you, Sandy,' she said. 'Thanks, but I'm doing really well.'

'I must say you look a bit better than I was expecting,' Sandy admitted, 'but you ought to get our Cheryl to show you how to hide those sores on your face. You know what she's like with make-up.'

'Oh, they'll go soon enough,' Josie assured her. She hadn't realised the sores were so conspicuous, and how typical of Sandy to remark on them. She'd never been known for tact.

'Josie? Is that you?' the butcher's wife called out. 'Yes it is. How lovely to see you up and about. And there's a pretty scarf you're wearing. That shade of blue really suits you. Goes with your eyes.'

Josie smiled. 'Thanks, Ellie.'

'Are you going to get a wig for the wedding?' Sandy asked.

'I'm thinking about it,' Josie replied.

'It's tragic, all your beautiful hair falling out like that,' Sandy sighed.

Ellie said, 'It happened to my cousin when she had it, but it grew back once the chemo was over.'

'Which cousin was that?' Sandy wanted to know.

Leaving them to it, Josie took her mobile outside to answer a call from Lily. 'Hi love,' she said. 'Everything OK?'

'No, it's not,' Lily cried wretchedly. 'I've just heard from the Kesterly Golf Club – apparently we can't have our reception there, because they've gone and double-booked and the other people were first. What are we going to do? I've told everyone now. It's on all the invitations.'

Josie was thinking fast. 'Who did you speak to?' she asked.

'Mrs Camber, the one we saw when we went for a look round.'

'OK,' Josie replied. 'Leave it to me.'

She picked up a couple of lamb chops for Jeff's tea, finding later that Ed, the butcher, had thrown in half a dozen bangers for free. As soon as she got home, Josie grabbed Jeff's car keys and handed them to him.

'What's going on?' he demanded, as she started for the door.

'We've got some business to sort out for Lily,' she informed him.

'Well, whatever it is,' he retorted, 'it'll have to wait, because you look all in, woman, and I've got to pick someone up from Maple Drive at quarter past.'

Accepting that she didn't actually have the energy for it now, and anyway Mrs Camber had probably already left for the day, Josie sank down in her favourite chair and felt it might be good if she didn't have to get up again for quite a while.

'So what's happening with Lily?' Jeff prompted.

As she explained, Josie felt her eyelids starting to droop.

'OK, let me deal with it,' he told her when she'd finished. 'You're doing too much these days and wearing yourself out.'

'I'll be fine tomorrow,' she assured him, 'and we should go there together.'

'Will you do as you're told for once in your life?' he cried.

Keeping her eyes closed, she smiled. She liked it when he put his foot down.

'I'm not joking,' he growled. 'You're not helping yourself, gallivanting around the place . . .'

'Ssh,' she interrupted, putting a finger to her lips.

'Are you going to answer that?' he asked as her mobile rang. 'It's Bel. I'll tell her you'll ring back . . .'

'No, it's OK,' and clicking on she said, 'So was it the solicitor?'

'It was,' Bel replied. 'Apparently there's some mix-up with the paperwork. I'll have to go and see him in the morning, so can we get together later in the day?'

'No problem, something's come up here as well, so why don't we speak on the phone around lunchtime and work things out from there?'

'You're kidding me,' Bel cried in outrage as Fliss brought a tray of drinks to the table. 'They can't do that.'

'Apparently they can, and so they have,' Josie told her, the dark circles around her eyes appearing more like bruises than shadows. How tired she looked today, Bel had thought the minute she'd seen her. Now she knew that the encounter at the golf club had knocked it out of her.

'She put up a good fight,' Jeff declared, patting Josie's hand, 'but the events co-ordinator, or whatever she calls herself, wasn't going to budge. Apparently the other booking's for the mayor's son, so I reckon we got shafted, not double-booked. Of course we can't prove it, so all we can do is accept our deposit back and start looking for somewhere else.'

Bel was having none of it. For almost a month now, since learning she had secondaries, Josie had been coping brilliantly, doing her best, to rise above everything life was throwing at her. Added to that, Lily was on tenterhooks waiting for her exam results while she held down a job at Sainsbury's. So no way was she, Bel, going to allow some jumped-up mayor and snooty events organiser to get away with slamming them down like this. 'I need to know the woman's name,' she told Jeff firmly, 'because someone has to pay for the invitations to be reprinted and resent, and if we're going to hold the reception in my garden, which I think we should, they're going to bloody well pay for the marquee.'

Josie blinked.

'We can't let you do that, Bel,' Jeff protested. 'I mean, it's lovely of you, but you . . .'

'Before you turn it down,' Bel interrupted, 'you need to come and see the place. As Josie knows, there's plenty of room, a terrific sea view and no golf balls flying about to take out your eye or crack your skull.'

'You're being too hasty,' Josie declared. 'You need to think about it, because I'm telling you, you won't want the likes of our lot trampling about your lovely home . . .'

'Don't be such a snob,' Bel scolded.

Josie had to laugh at that.

'Josie's right,' Jeff told her. 'We can't let you throw open your doors to people you don't even know, especially when it's Josie's family.'

'*My family!*' Josie cried, turning on him – and seeing the mischief in his eyes she slapped his hand. 'Well, I have to admit,' she said, 'I've already got visions of my mother chucking up in the garden and our Steve half-inching the silver. Honest, Bel, you really don't want to do this.'

'Yes I do,' Bel insisted, becoming keener on the idea by the minute, 'provided Lily and Jasper are willing, of course, and let's face it, the chances of finding somewhere else now, when August isn't much more than three months away, are almost non-existent. Everything will have been booked up ages ago.'

'We ought at least to look around,' Josie said, 'because I'd feel terrible if anything of yours got damaged . . .'

'I have insurance, and the few valuables I keep there can always be locked away. Why don't you take Josie home when we've finished here,' she said to Jeff, 'then come and have a look yourself?'

Josie seemed about to speak, but then remained silent. Probably, Bel decided, because she was too weary to form the words. Damn mayor and golf club. She was going to give that events organiser such a rollicking when she got hold of her. 'Did you sleep last night?' she asked Josie gently.

Josie glanced at Jeff. 'Yes, I think so,' she replied, but Bel could tell she hadn't, probably worrying about the venue for Lily's wedding, but also because it was one of the cruellest parts of chemo, making someone feel utterly exhausted, but not allowing them to sleep.

'What's happening about the barn?' Josie asked, trying to change the subject.

'Oh, it's being sorted,' Bel replied dismissively. She wasn't going to get into the fact that the farmer was considering a higher offer from somebody else. It wasn't Josie's problem, and she didn't much want to think about it right now anyway. 'So what time's your treatment tomorrow?' she wanted to know. 'I could probably come and pick you up after I've dropped the children at school.'

'Oh no, no, I don't want you putting yourself out like that,' Josie protested. 'You've got enough on your plate taking care of those kids . . .'

'It's OK, I'll go with her tomorrow,' Jeff announced, signalling Fliss for the bill.

Josie turned to him in surprise.

'What?' he said. 'My company not good enough for you now?'

'Don't be daft. I just thought you'd be working.'

'That don't mean I can't take my Mrs to the hospital. I'll fit everything in around it.'

Still amazed, Josie looked at Bel.

Smiling, Bel simply raised her eyebrows.

Turning back to Jeff, Josie squeezed his hand as she said, 'That'll be lovely.'

'All right, all right, you don't have to get carried away,' he told her, but he left his hand in hers as he dug into his pocket to pay for the drinks.

'It's OK, I'll do it,' Bel insisted. 'I was here before you, so I've had an extra cup.'

'It's all on the house,' Fliss declared rashly, having moved within earshot.

'You're not going to get rich that way,' Jeff protested. 'Come on, how much do I owe you, and make it quick because I have to get Josie home before I go for my next pickup.'

'Keep your money,' Fliss told him, turning back to the counter. 'Or give it to charity.'

'Is your phone ringing?' Josie asked Bel, nodding to where it was on the table.

Having forgotten it was on silent, Bel picked it up, and seeing who it was she turned the phone for Josie to look.

Josie's non-existent eyebrows arched with interest as Bel said, 'Hi Kristina, how are you?'

'I'm fine,' Kristina replied, sounding throaty and faint, 'well, actually I'm not. It's why I'm ringing. I was wondering if I could come to see you.'

Bel was looking at Josie as she said, 'Of course you can come to see me. Where are you?'

'In London. I can drive down tomorrow or the next day, whenever suits you.'

'How about tomorrow?' Bel suggested. 'Do you want to meet up somewhere, or will you come to the house?'

'I'll come to the house if that's OK. Unless . . . Is Nick . . . Is he staying with you?'

'No, but the children are, so if you can make it around eleven?'

'That's fine. I'll see you then. And . . . thank you.'

Feeling for how wretched she sounded, Bel clicked off the line and looked at Josie again.

'So she wants to see you,' Josie stated. 'I can't say I'm surprised.'

Bel shook her head. 'I don't suppose I am, either. I just wish I knew what I was going to say to her.'

'You'll have a better idea of that once you've heard what she has to say to you,' Josie pointed out, 'but remember, it's not your fault this is happening.'

Knowing that in large part it was, Bel said, 'It's time you were going home. You look shattered.'

'Do I?' Josie replied. 'I'm starting to perk up actually. See, that's the effect you have on me.'

Laughing, since she knew it was Jeff's offer to take her for her treatment that was providing the boost, Bel said, 'Let me know what Lily and Jasper think of my idea, and if they're up for it we'll arrange for them to come and see the garden.'

'I still reckon you ought to take some time to think it over,' Jeff advised, 'because it's a big thing to take on, especially when you're not going to know anyone, apart from us.'

'I'll cope,' Bel promised, packing up her bag to leave, 'and I'll call you as soon as I have some news from the golf club.'

'Are you sure about coming to the hospital tomorrow?' Josie asked, as Jeff got into the driver's side of their car.

'Course I'm sure,' he retorted, wincing at the way the engine turned over half a dozen times before catching, 'I wouldn't have said it otherwise. Or don't you want me there? I don't mind if you'd rather have Bel . . .'

'No, no, I want you to come. It's just, you and hospitals, I thought . . . Well, we don't want you passing out on us, do we?' she teased.

He cast her a glance that was just like his old humorous self.

Feeling a lovely catch in her heart at how handsome he was, she said, 'So why now all of a sudden, when you've only picked me up a couple of times before?'

He shrugged. 'Just thought it was time I did my bit . . . And our Lily told me if I didn't she'd divorce me.'

Josie had to laugh, even though she'd have preferred it to have been his own idea.

'Anyway,' he said, 'I don't want you coming out the end of this thinking I never did anything to help. I know I haven't been all that good about it up to now, but to be honest, I didn't know what to do. It really got to me, thinking you might . . . Well, you know what happens to people who have cancer . . . I know not all of them, but if you were going to be one . . . Anyway, you're not now, so we just have to get this next bit of chemo out of the way and then we can go back to normal. Although, I have to tell you, I'm getting used to the new you, the way you went at that woman in the golf club earlier, wow, that's my Josie, I thought. You can hang on to a bit of that if you like.'

Josie could feel her heart breaking. How was she ever going to be able to tell him the truth? 'It didn't get us anywhere though, did it?' she replied flatly.

'Maybe not, but at least you gave her what for, and I bet Bel don't have much trouble putting her in her place either.

She won't be dealing with the little people then, will she, stuck-up mare that she was? I'm telling you, if she'd been a bloke I'd have put one on her.'

'I thought you were going to anyway.'

His expression turned sardonic again. 'Maybe I should have. Anyway, you'd better save the next time you go off on one till all this is over,' he advised, 'cos it's worn you out.'

It was true, it had; she'd obviously taken on too much, going there after her visit to Debbie Prince yesterday. She wondered if she ought to tell him about that, but since she didn't have the energy the dilemma soon faded.

Still sounding upbeat, he said, 'Are you too tired to call Lily to tell her about Bel's offer? I reckon she'll be over the moon, myself, and I know you are. I don't mind admitting, it's done you the power of good having a posh friend like that, but I don't want it giving you airs and graces now, cos we ain't never going to be in that league, I hope you know that.'

'It doesn't matter,' she said, putting a hand on his as he changed gear, 'I'm happy the way we are.'

Entwining his fingers round hers, he said, 'That's what I hoped you'd say.'

They drove on in silence for a while, holding hands when they could, and occasionally glancing at one another. Josie wished she knew what to say, but whatever it was, it couldn't be the truth, not now when he was so happy to think he wasn't going to lose her.

'You know,' he said as they turned into their street, 'you being sick and everything, well, it really woke me up to how much you mean to me. I should have known it before, well I did, but something like this, it brings it all home to you, doesn't it?'

'Yes,' she agreed softly, 'it definitely does that.'

Chapter Twenty-One

'Yes, that'll be quite acceptable, thank you,' Bel was saying into the phone as she opened the door to Kristina. 'Sorry,' she mouthed, 'go on through, this won't take a minute. Yes, yes, I'm still here,' she told the events organiser at Kesterly Golf Club. 'You were saying you're prepared to cover the cost of a marquee, which is what we'd hoped for. And the stationery? Not good enough, you need to cover the cost of that too. I'd appreciate a satisfactory response from your company within the next twenty-four hours, or I'll start by posting details of this double-booking on your Facebook page, before I send it around Twitter and go to the local press. As I don't imagine anyone wants that, I'm sure you'll come back with an agreement to pay for the new stationery *and* postage. Thank you for your time, I'll wait for your call,' and clicking off the line she turned to Kristina.

'Wow, who was that?' Kristina asked, looking impressed, though as fragile as she'd sounded on the phone.

'It's a long story, and a battle I'm determined to win. So, how was the drive?' Bel asked, dutifully embracing her guest. 'Would you like a coffee?'

'That would be lovely, thanks.' As she unbelted her raincoat Kristina was looking at an open cookbook on the table. 'Bruce Bogtrotter's humongous chocolate cake,' she read out loud.

Bel wondered if she knew anything about Roald Dahl. Had she ever read *Matilda*?

'Have you made it yet?' Kristina asked.

'No, it's on the agenda for tonight,' Bel replied. 'Oscar wants to invite some friends over at the weekend, so it's supposed to be for them.'

Kristina nodded, and glanced at the paintings magnetised to the fridge as she took the coffee Bel was passing her. 'You're so good with them,' she said, taking her cup to the table. 'Maybe if I'd tried a bit harder . . .' She sighed and shook her head.

Feeling for how lost she seemed, Bel said, 'You mustn't blame yourself. It hasn't been easy for anyone.'

Kristina was staring into her coffee. 'No, it hasn't,' she agreed.

She'd lost weight, Bel was thinking as she sat down with her, and her hair and skin had lost their usual lustre. It was impossible not to feel sorry for her when she was clearly far more devastated than Bel had imagined.

'I need to know,' Kristina said, bringing her head up and fixing Bel with an imploring stare, 'if you're in love with him, because if you are . . .'

'I'm not,' Bel came in gently.

Kristina swallowed hard as tears rushed to her eyes.

'He's very mixed up,' Bel said.

'Aren't we all?'

'Have you spoken to him since you left?' Bel asked.

'Several times, but I never really get anywhere.' She took a breath and let it go shakily. 'One minute he's saying he still loves me, the next he's telling me I must get on with my life.' Her eyes went briefly to Bel's. 'That might be easier if I thought there was no hope.' She swallowed. 'Do you think there is?' she whispered.

Having guessed this might be the purpose of the visit, Bel had spent many hours through the night trying to decide how best to advise Kristina in a way that was fair, and didn't put Bel's own interests first by asking her to give up the idea of going to Sydney. Though she still wasn't entirely sure how to do it, she found herself saying, 'He more or less admitted to me that he loves you, but he's obviously finding it very difficult to be with you for now. He needs to sort himself out, to deal with his grief, and if you can give him the time, the space, to do that, I think there's a chance you could pull through.'

Kristina's eyes closed as her emotions swelled. 'That's what he says.'

Relieved she'd hit a right note, Bel said, 'Did you tell him you were coming here today?'

Kristina nodded.

Surprised, since Nick hadn't mentioned it when he'd called in to spend some time with the children last night, Bel said, 'If that's what he feels, I can't see there's a problem, unless you're not prepared to wait.'

'No, I am,' Kristina assured her, 'or I would be, if I thought it might get us somewhere. The trouble is, he's never going to be able to take the children away from you, he's said as much, and if he can't do that, I just don't know where, how I'd ever fit in.'

Having feared this, Bel searched for the right words, but she could find nothing to give that Kristina would want to hear.

Kristina was biting her lips, staring down at the mangled tissue in her hand. 'When he was offered the job in Australia,' she said, 'he seemed so excited at first. It was exactly what we needed, he told me, a fresh start, some-where a long way from the memories so we could make new ones of our own. He thought it would be a great place for the children to grow up, for me to bond with them, but then . . .' Her voice trailed off, and Bel knew why she didn't want to go any further.

'But then he spoke to me?' she said.

Kristina nodded. 'He knew it wasn't going to be easy, breaking it to you, but he didn't have any idea of the effect it would end up having on him. Neither of us did. He could see you had a point, that it wouldn't be good to tear the children away from you so soon after losing their mother, and he didn't want to hurt you either. He was so conflicted, he didn't know what to do, so he started getting drunk and saying he'd made a terrible mistake, he should never have married me. It wasn't fair to keep me hanging on, he said, when he'd probably never be able to separate the children from you.'

Feeling utterly wretched for being the cause of so much heartache, Bel wished there was something she could say to defend herself, but no matter what she said, the harsh reality would always remain that she didn't want to let the children go. But they weren't hers, and this woman who loved their father, who would do almost anything to try to create a new family for them, was their stepmother. Surely that gave her more rights than an aunt.

'I don't know what to tell you,' she said in the end. 'I can't change the bond I have with the children, it was there even before Talia died . . .'

'Of course, I understand that. You mean the world to them, to Nick too, though he's obviously horribly muddled about how he really feels about you.'

'I don't think he's in love with me,' Bel told her.

'But he feels a loyalty to you, or a connection, or something that he can't let go of, and until he does . . .' She turned her head towards the window, as if somewhere in the strange yellowy light threading through the metallic sky were the words she was seeking. 'I want to ask you,' she said, 'if you'll try to persuade him to take the job in Australia.'

Bel became very still. She hadn't expected this, or anything like it.

'I truly believe,' Kristina turned back to her, 'that the only way he'll make the break from you, is if you tell him it's all right to go.'

Though she didn't move, Bel's mind was racing: panic was rushing to shield her from a request she simply couldn't comply with. Yet she needed to think straight, to make Kristina understand that while she appreciated how important it was for her to save her marriage, it was every bit as important for Bel to have regular access to the children.

'Will you do it?' Kristina asked.

Bel swallowed drily as she shook her head. 'I'm sorry,' she replied, 'they're my sister's children, my own flesh and blood. I can't just give them up, nor can I believe it would be good for them to be so far away from me that we'd never see one another.'

Kristina looked away again; her face was pinched, her head tilted up as though to sink back the tears.

'I'm sorry,' Bel repeated. 'I know how much this means to you . . .'

'Do you?' Kristina cut in, her eyes bright with the challenge. 'How can you know what it's like to lose the man you love, when you've never even had a proper relationship?'

Bel flushed hotly.

'You have no idea how it feels to be where I am,' Kristina ran on angrily, 'watching my life falling apart and knowing there's nothing I can do to save it, apart from beg you to set my family free so they can be mine.'

My family. She was right, they were hers.

But it wasn't as simple as that.

'And you have no idea,' Bel countered, 'what it's like to lose a parent the way they have, but this isn't a contest. I promise you, I do understand how difficult this is for you, and I want to help you get back with Nick, I swear it, but asking me to persuade him to take the children away . . .' She shook her head helplessly. 'I just can't do it. I'm sorry.'

'If you'd find a man of your own, you might not be so dependent on Nick,' Kristina cried. 'You could have children of your own, a life with someone who loves you, a world that belongs to you two and nobody else. Like this, you're hanging on to what belongs to Talia, and if you ask me, it's *you* who hasn't got over losing her, not Nick.' Her hand went up. 'OK, he's still in a bad way over it too, but we both know you've got issues that go way back, that have nothing to do with Nick, or the children, but rather than confront them you're trying to live your sister's life now instead of your own.'

Stunned, not only by the words, but by the fact that Nick must have told her what had happened in the past, Bel got up from the table and went to pour herself more coffee. Her hand was shaking, she realised, while her mind was still recoiling from the attack.

In the end, Kristina was the first to break the silence. 'I'm sorry,' she said, dashing a hand through her hair, 'I shouldn't have said all that . . .'

'It's OK,' Bel interjected. 'You're right in most of what you say, it's just not very pleasant hearing it.'

Kristina's eyes were regretful, but ringed with hope as she looked at her.

'I need some time to think,' Bel told her, 'but please don't leave here imagining that just because you've carried out your own amateur analysis on me it's going to change anything.'

Kristina was about to reply when the telephone rang.

Needing the distraction, Bel snatched it up. It turned out to be the lawyer dealing with the barn. Apparently the farmer had received another offer amounting to seventy thousand more than he'd agreed with her, and wanted to know if she'd care to match it.

'How can I trust him not to do this again?' Bel demanded.

'You can't.'

'Then tell him the deal's off.'

As she put the phone down she took a steadying breath in an effort to stop herself shaking. No barn, no children, no Nick, no Talia, no mother . . . A father she'd rather die than ever see again . . .

'I should go now,' Kristina said, reaching for her raincoat. 'I'm sorry for some of the things . . . I didn't mean to hurt you, I guess when you're hurting yourself . . . Will you at least think about what I've said?'

Knowing she wouldn't be able to get it out of her mind, Bel replied, 'Of course.'

As they walked to the door, Kristina said, 'Will you call me?'

Bel nodded. 'When are you driving back?'

'I'm not sure. If Nick'll see me maybe I'll stay with him tonight.'

'You know,' Bel couldn't stop herself saying, 'neither of you helped the situation by going away so often. If you'd put the children first, and not constantly given them to me to take care of, you might already have a relationship with them.'

'Your criticism might be more justified if you hadn't done your best to shut me out from the start,' Kristina replied.

Accepting she had no defence for that, Bel opened the door, and kept her eyes down as Kristina stepped outside.

'Time's not on our side now,' she said, 'the job in Sydney

won't be open for ever,' and pulling her raincoat more tightly around her she went to get into her car.

After waiting for the gates to close, Bel shut the door and leaned against it. It wasn't so much Kristina's parting words that were resonating in her mind, though God knew they were there, it was the ones she'd thrown at her about never having been in a proper relationship.

Why was the shame and loneliness of that hurting so deeply now, when she'd never denied, at least to herself and Talia, that she had a problem? Maybe it was knowing that Nick had discussed it with Kristina. Or maybe it was the fact that everything seemed to be slipping away, exposing her for what, or who she really was – a woman who had nothing to feel proud of, and no right to claim anything or anyone as her own.

'You're not feeling sorry for yourself, are you?' Talia asked.

'Nor for myself, for what I did,' she replied.

'You didn't know it was going to turn out that way.'

It was true, she hadn't known, could never have known; if only she had.

'You have to let go of the past.'

'How can I, when it's made me who I am?'

'No, it's made you afraid, and you don't need to be any more.'

Bel wanted to believe that so badly.

'I know how often you think about Harry, how you long to take a chance and trust him.'

'He's married; he'll probably end up going back to her.'

'Maybe, but why not take a risk for once in your life? Losing me should have taught you that we have to make the most of the time we're given, but you still haven't learned it.'

'Is that why you brought Josie into my life?'

'Do you think I did that?'

Bel only knew that was how it felt.

Pushing herself away from the door, she returned to the kitchen, where Kristina's scent was lingering like a reminder. 'How can I give up your children?' she asked Talia, knowing she'd almost rather die than never be able to hold their precious little bodies in her arms again, or watch their faces light up when they saw her, or listen to their funny chatter. Her world would be completely empty without them, and she couldn't bear to think of how confused and devastated they'd be if they thought she was turning away from them. *'Answer me, Talia.'*

'You know the answer,' Talia told her, *'you just don't want to hear it.'*

'Oh my word,' Josie exclaimed as she realised what she was reading. 'Jeff! Jeff!' she called out, before remembering he'd left ten minutes ago.

Taking the stairs slowly, she went back to the bedroom for her phone. 'Lily,' she said into the voicemail, 'call me when you get this. I'm fine, don't worry. I just need to speak to you.'

Sitting on the edge of the bed she waited for a wave of dizziness to pass. If they were going to carry on using chemo to keep her alive, she might start wondering if it was worth it.

Don't say that, Josie, you know you don't mean it.

'Hi, it's me,' she said when Bel answered her phone. 'Are you all right?'

'Yes, I'm fine,' Bel assured her. 'How are *you*?'

'You sound a bit down,' Josie commented.

'No, honestly, I'm fine. In fact, I have some good news. The delightful events manager rang from the golf club just now: apparently they're going to pay for a marquee, *and* for the reprinting and postage of new invitations.'

Josie was amazed, impressed and hugely relieved. 'Jeff felt sure they'd listen to you,' she told her.

'I'm just sorry they didn't have the manners to treat you a bit better,' Bel responded with feeling. 'Anyway, how did the treatment go yesterday?'

Sighing, Josie said, 'Same as ever, but it was nice having Jeff there.' Her eyes closed as more aching exhaustion swept through her. 'We played a game of Scrabble,' she went on. 'I think he let me win.'

'You sound tired.'

'I am, but I have to tell you my news,' she announced with a smile in her voice. 'I've had a letter inviting me to go and have my measurements taken for the fashion show.'

Bel gave a cry of triumph. 'I felt sure you'd get through,' she declared.

'They'll probably change their minds when they see me.'

'Don't talk nonsense. When do you have to go?'

'Just under two weeks. Will you come with me?'

'Of course. No way would I let you jaunt off to London on your own.'

'That's good,' Josie said weakly. 'I'll see you tomorrow then?' She had to ring off now, or she might start groaning and retching down the phone.

The following afternoon Bel was sitting at one end of Josie's sofa, her feet curled under her, a cup of peppermint tea going cold on the floor in front of her. She could hardly believe how much talking she'd done in the past half an hour, and was embarrassed and concerned now about loading her problems on to Josie's worryingly frail-looking shoulders. 'I'm sorry,' she said, pushing her hands through her hair, 'I didn't mean to . . .'

'There's nothing to apologise for,' Josie interrupted, managing to sound far stronger than she looked. 'You obviously needed to get it all off your chest, so it's good that you did.'

'Not good, selfish,' Bel protested. 'The trouble is you're an amazingly patient listener and I'm going round and round in circles . . .'

'It's no wonder, when you're facing such a dilemma. Have you spoken to Kristina again since?'

Bel shook her head. 'She texted to say she's gone back to London, but I don't know how things went with Nick when she saw him.'

'Does he know what she's asked you to do?'

'I shouldn't think so.'

Josie let a breath go slowly as she thought, or was it, Bel wondered, to give some inner discomfort time to pass. 'OK, let's deal with the other things first,' Josie decided, 'then we'll come on to the children.'

Confused, Bel said, 'What other things?'

'The barn? Are you sure you want to give up on it?'

Going with the subject change, Bel said, 'No, but I don't

like being blackmailed into upping my offer when we shook on a deal.'

'I understand that, and I don't blame you, but this farmer's obviously a bit of a charlatan, or greedy b— as Jeff would call him, so now you have to ask yourself, is the property, as it stands, worth seventy grand more?'

Since she'd already given this some thought, Bel was able to say, 'Depending on how the property market's looking after the conversion, it could be.'

'In which case you could say you were getting a bargain, and now you're being asked to cough up full price?'

That was one way of putting it.

'So why don't you do that, look at it as paying the going rate, but make a promise to yourself that it stops there? Unless you want to get into a bidding war with this other buyer, but I don't imagine you do.'

'No, of course not.' Bel sighed irritably. 'I think I'll sit on it for a couple more days, just in case the other guy pulls out. If not, I'll do as you say and match the offer.' Her smile was weak as she said, 'If I'm going to let the children go, I have to have something to help fill the gap.' The mere thought of it was making her want to force Kristina to go away and never come back into their lives – as if she could!

Josie's lashless, red-rimmed eyes were dark with earnestness as she said 'You can't let them go. It wouldn't be right for them, or for you.'

Bel took a breath. Though it was what she wanted to hear, she knew in her heart that Josie was just being loyal.

'What you should do,' Josie continued, 'is call Kristina and say you're sorry you haven't made things easy for her, but if she's prepared to abandon the idea of Sydney for now, and give you another chance, you'll work much harder to accept her as the children's stepmother and Nick's wife. In fact, it sounds to me as if you all need to try a bit harder. You're grown ups, after all, and there's no reason why you shouldn't get along, and the best place to start is with you forgiving her, and Nick, for getting married so soon after your sister's death.'

Bel was quietly stunned. This wasn't what she'd expected

from Josie, and for the moment she wasn't sure how to react.

'Of course, she might not go for it,' Josie ran on, 'but if she's that keen to save her marriage I'm sure she'll be willing to give it a try. Naturally she'll have to feel convinced you really will accept her into the family.'

Bel was regarding her in disbelief. 'You're a bit of a genius really, aren't you?' she murmured, meaning it.

'That would be me,' Josie agreed with a twinkle.

Still adjusting to the possibility that she might not have to give up the children, Bel said, 'Do you think I should go and see her to talk it through?'

'You could, but if I were you I'd have a chat with Nick first, and if he's in agreement he can ask her to come back to Kesterly so the three of you can sit down and discuss it together.'

Finding herself completely taken by the idea, Bel was tempted to call Nick right away.

'Do it,' Josie urged, when Bel voiced her thoughts.

Taking out her phone Bel scrolled to his number. Given the time of day she wasn't surprised to find herself going through to voicemail. 'Nick, it's me,' she said, her eyes on Josie, 'I'd like to have a chat with you this evening, if you can stay on after the children have gone to bed. It's quite important and might take a while, so . . . Well, I hope you can make it.'

After ringing off she regarded the genius again. 'I'm starting to wonder if you're hotwired to my sister,' she told her, 'because I'm sure this is exactly what she'd have advised.'

'It wasn't so difficult really,' Josie responded.

'Maybe not from where you're sitting, but I'm only just seeing how complicated I've made things, and how difficult I've been, not to mention possessive and protective of the children, even of Nick, and all the time Kristina was trying to be my friend. Oh God, what a horrible person I am, trying to shut her out when she's very sweet really, and I know she longs to be a good mum.'

'So you can show her how,' Josie said.

Bel's eyebrows rose. 'I'm a good aunt, not mother,' she corrected.

341

'Call yourself what you like, the point is you have a longer history with the children than she has, so you can share that history and make her feel a part of things in a way you clearly haven't up to now.'

Noticing the way her hands were clenched in her lap, possibly reacting to pain, Bel said, 'Are you OK? Would you rather I left so you can lie down for a while?'

'I'm fine,' Josie assured her. 'Another tea would be lovely though, then maybe we ought to get down to the other issue Kristina raised.'

'The other issue?' Bel echoed.

'About you not having any proper relationships.'

Bel's heart turned over. She really ought not to have mentioned that, and seriously wished now that she hadn't.

'Is she right?' Josie asked. 'It's hard for me to imagine when you're so lovely, but she must have said it for a reason and I can see from the way the light went out in your eyes that she definitely hit a nerve.'

'It's not . . . I don't think we should get into it,' Bel replied shakily. 'I know it's something I have to sort out, but I can promise you, it's not as straightforward as the issue with the children. In fact, it's not straightforward at all.'

'You didn't think the one with the children was,' Josie reminded her, 'so now I'm going to be cheeky enough to tell you that I thought I noticed a spark of something between you and Mr Beck when we were at the clinic . . . I can see your colour coming up, so I'm right.'

'It's really not what you think,' Bel insisted.

'Whatever it is, and whatever I might think, I know it's not unusual for women who have issues from the past to get themselves into relationships that are almost bound to fail, and I'm worried that you might be attracted to him because he's married. Married can make people with commitment issues feel safe.'

'Actually, his marriage is breaking up,' Bel admitted. 'He's moving into a flat on the Promenade as soon as the sale goes through.'

Josie's eyes widened. 'Well, if that's the case, there's not quite so much to worry about. Unless . . . Do you know what went wrong with the marriage?'

'He's a workaholic, and I believe his wife met someone else.'

'Oh dear, poor Mr Beck. Is he upset about it? I'm sure he must be.'

'Yes, I think he is, but we haven't really discussed it.'

'I see. So you could say he's on the rebound. I'm not sure that's very good either. Has he . . . Well, has he ever made a pass at you?'

Bel had to laugh at that. 'Not as such,' she replied, 'but I think he'd like to be friends. The trouble is, if it leads to anything else . . .' She put up a hand to show that she wasn't prepared to let it.

'We all need friends,' Josie pointed out, 'and knowing what a very lovely one you are, I can only applaud his good sense.'

'Thank you for that,' Bel said, 'but believe me, it would be better for him if he found somebody else.'

Apparently Josie wasn't going to be budged. 'I take it your sister was aware of whatever your problem is,' she stated.

Bel nodded. 'Yes, of course.'

'So did she think you were dealing with it the right way?'

Bel couldn't lie. 'No, she didn't, but . . .'

'So what would she say if she was here with us now?'

Bel had no problem finding the answer to that. 'Very probably what you want to say,' she conceded.

'OK, then I'll say it for her, why don't you give it a try? What harm can it do to have a drink or a meal with him once in a while?'

Bel sighed. 'When you put it like that it sounds very easy, but . . .'

'No buts,' Josie scolded. 'If your sister can find the courage to face all that she went through, I'm sure you can find enough to reach out a hand of friendship to someone who deserves it.'

How could she possibly argue with that?

'Unless,' Josie continued, 'you really do want to spend the rest of your life alone, and somehow I don't think you do.'

Bel's eyes went down as she heard Talia urging her to

understand how important it was to take her advice. *I've told you this so many times, will you please start listening?*

Setting her troublesome subconscious aside, she said, 'I'll go and make that tea. Then, if you're feeling up to it, we can have a look through the list of caterers I've brought with me. Did Lily tell you that she rang me last night to say she doesn't need to see the garden, she'd love to accept anyway?'

'Yes, she called me after,' Josie replied. 'What she said to me was fab, fab, fab, Bel is amazing and we have to make sure we let her invite someone too.'

Realising exactly where Josie's mind was going with that, Bel had to smile, even though she knew how unlikely it was that she'd end up asking Harry.

'Speak of the devil,' Josie declared, as her mobile rang. 'Hello my love,' she said to Lily. 'Any news yet?'

'Oh Mum! You're never going to believe this,' Lily cried. 'I've only got a first.'

Tears rushed to Josie's eyes. 'Oh my goodness, my goodness,' she spluttered. 'Oh Lily, I'm so proud of you. Bel, she got a first. My girl has *got a first.*'

Bel couldn't have felt more thrilled. 'That's fantastic, Lily,' she called out. 'Well done. You're amazing!'

'How about Jasper?' Josie remembered to ask.

'He got a first too,' Lily told her. 'We're going to get wasted tonight, that's for sure. Oh Mum, I love you so much. I can't wait to tell Dad. Let me ring him, will you?'

'Of course, but make sure he's not driving or he might go off the road.'

Laughing, Lily said, 'We'll have to get his wedding suit early so he can wear it to the cathedral for my graduation.'

'Oh, I think we can manage that. I might even treat myself to a new dress for the occasion.'

'You definitely have to. I'm going to ring off now, but I'll call again later, OK?'

'OK. Love you, best and cleverest girl in the world.'

'Love you too, best and most beautiful mum in the world.'

As Josie rang off, her throat was tight with emotion. What she wouldn't give to have some good news about her boy.

*

Though Nick was looking as exhausted and unkempt as Bel had ever seen him, she could sense the first stirrings of hope and relief starting to lighten his despair as he listened to what she was saying.

By the time she'd finished he was close to smiling, though still appearing cautious. 'Do you think you can do that?' he asked. 'I know it hasn't been easy . . .'

'I'm willing to give it a try,' she assured him.

He sat back, almost as though he couldn't believe this was happening. 'I think it's a great idea,' he told her. 'I'm sure she'll go for it.'

'I am too, provided you can convince her that you don't have feelings for me.'

He nodded and looked embarrassed as he pulled a hand over his unshaven chin. 'I guess I've misunderstood a lot of things,' he confessed, 'or tried to make something out of nothing. Not nothing, exactly, but you know what I mean. I've been very mixed up, worse than I realised, but I think the counselling is helping. And now this . . .'

So he was seeing someone.

'I had no idea what she'd come here to talk about,' he murmured. 'She never said a word when I saw her.'

'I know you're in love with her,' Bel said, 'and I'm sorry I couldn't accept it.'

His eyes searched hers, as though needing to be certain she meant it. 'Will you say that to her?' he asked.

'Of course.'

He smiled, and had to swallow a lump in his throat as he said, 'Thank you.'

Touched by how emotional this was making him, and still fighting the loyalty to Talia that was making her want to pull back, Bel steeled herself to continue. 'You won't be able to bring the children here quite so often,' she told him, 'or when you do you should all come. No more escaping for weekends, that's just running away, we need to work on this together.'

'Of course, and we will.'

His eagerness was so moving, it reminded her of Oscar. 'Do you mind about Sydney?' she asked.

He shook his head. 'This is a much better solution.'

Getting up from the table she went to put her glass in the sink. She could ask why he'd told Kristina about her past, but she'd already decided she wouldn't. It wouldn't change anything, nor would it help them to go forward.

'I'll say goodnight now, and leave you to call Kristina,' she said. 'You know where everything is, and if you decide to stay over the bed's already made up.'

'Thanks, I think I will,' he replied. 'Is there a time that suits you for us all to get together?'

'Any time will work for me,' she assured him.

As she took herself upstairs, stopping at the children's rooms to make sure they were sleeping, she was experiencing an unsettling mix of relief and profound unhappiness. Of course, she knew why there was so much sadness in her heart, and knew too that it would never go until she confronted it, but she wasn't ready to do that tonight.

'So when will you be ready?' Talia asked.

'I'm not sure.'

'Remember what Josie said about courage?'

How could she forget, it had barely left her mind, but she hadn't heard from him since the day he'd come to check on her after Josie's news.

'You surely can't be surprised by that. He did it out of kindness, a genuine concern, and you ended up blocking him in a way that was almost cold. Think of how vulnerable he's feeling right now. His marriage is over, he's having to move out of the home he shares with his children . . . All he wants is a friend, someone who's not a part of his past, and think how good that would be for you too.'

It was just after nine when she finally made herself dial his number.

'Bel,' he declared, sounding surprised. 'What a coincidence, I was just thinking about you.'

'Oh, only good things I hope,' she countered.

'Actually I've just exchanged on the apartment today. Or I should say, my mother has with me as her proxy.'

'That's good. I'm glad it's working out.'

'Yes, I guess it seems to be.'

There was an awkward silence until they spoke at once.

'You first,' she insisted.

'I was wondering how Josie is,' he told her. 'Have you seen her recently?'

'Actually, I was with her today. She was weak after the chemo, but determined not to show it.'

'And how are *you* coping?'

Feeling guilty for even being a concern, she said, 'Much better than I expected. She's a wonderful person to be around.'

'I imagine she probably says the same about you.'

Bel smiled at the compliment. 'I wouldn't be surprised, she never has a bad word to say about anyone.'

'Are you still thinking of taking her on the Pink Ribbonwalk?'

'She's insisting on going, even if she only manages the first mile. Her daughter's future mother-in-law is going to be on hand to take care of her if need be, while Lily, the daughter, and I cover the ten miles in her honour. Will you be there, with The Medics?'

'I shall. My cousins Sameena, Joel and Ozzie, whom you've met, are all doing the walk.'

'And your wife?'

'No, she's pulled out this year.'

'I see.' She wondered how hurt he was by that.

'Were you ringing for anything in particular?' he prompted.

She took a breath.

'Say it,' Talia urged. 'It's not difficult. Just speak the words out loud.'

'I was wondering,' she said, digging her nails into her palm, 'if you might be free for a drink one evening next week.'

With no hesitation, only surprise and pleasure, he said, 'Of course. I don't have anything on apart from Thursday when I'll be taking the boys to football, so whenever suits you.'

'OK, shall we say Friday?' she suggested, reminding herself that it was nothing more than two friends catching up over a glass of wine. All very normal, it was happening all the time. 'We can meet at the Grape Escape again, if you like.'

'Fantastic. Would seven thirty be good for you?'

'Seven thirty it is.'

You see, it wasn't so difficult, was it? she asked herself as she rang off, and it wasn't until she'd finally emerged from the relief and satisfaction of doing it that she realised she hadn't attributed the words to Talia.

Chapter Twenty-Two

At last the chemo was over. They had started her on radiotherapy now, targeting the place in her spine that the cancer had reached to help reduce the pain and stop it from fracturing. She was terrified it was going to end up crippling her. Sometimes, in the black of night when the fear really took hold, she wanted to scream and scream and crawl out of her horribly diseased body to get away from it all, but that would be the same as dying and she wasn't ready for that yet.

Not by a long shot.

There were all kinds of things she wanted to do before that happened – and drugs they could give her to keep her going. She was reading a lot more of the information she'd been given now, which she hadn't before, and following various forum threads on the BCC website, so she wasn't feeling quite so alone. It turned out people could survive a very long time with secondary breast cancer in the bones, so she had no need to be pessimistic; and the way everyone was doing their best to be helpful was just lovely. Of course they all thought she was getting better; her mother had even thrown a party at the pub to mark the end of the chemo, and the amount of cards she'd received wishing her well! It was like Christmas in their living room. People could be so kind, she'd discovered, especially with some of the things they wrote – and stunningly stupid too, the way a couple of her neighbours would cross the street to avoid having to speak to her, probably because they didn't know what to say, while others blurted out things about someone they knew who'd been diagnosed one day and were dead inside a week.

Really cheerful that, thanks for sharing!

What had touched her deeply was how many people had signed up for the Pink Ribbonwalk back in May and trudged ten miles in her honour. Lily had been behind it all, knocking on doors, making calls, and getting the neighbours out for training. She and Bel had ended up with about twenty women from around the estate on their team, and almost as many young students from UWE. What a day it had been, up there at Blenheim Palace with Mr Beck and his band playing everyone off at the start, and Miriam, Jasper's mother, waiting with the car at the first rest stop to bring her back. She'd have dearly loved to go all the way round, not only to see more of the beautiful grounds with all their lakes and pastures and history, but because the women who'd come from all over the country, a lot of whom were in the same boat as her, had turned out to be so friendly. Kelly had been there, the girl she'd met during the early days of chemo. How lovely it had been to see her again, and to find out that she was in remission. It had really touched Josie's heart to see how happy she was.

While the walk was under way Josie had spent a magical hour touring the palace with Miriam, who'd told her about the Dukes of Marlborough and Winston Churchill, and all sorts of shenanigans that had gone on there over the years.

What a wonderful woman Miriam was with her sparkly green eyes, smart salt-and-pepper hair and wicked sense of humour. They'd attracted some very stern looks from a couple of the stewards as they burst into giggles at a portrait of some sorry soul with a head too big for his body, and a bedside implement that Miriam had decided was an early sex toy.

By the time the walkers returned to base camp, played in by The Medics, Josie had rested for an hour in Bel's car, so she was able to join 'Team Josie' as Lily had named it, for a picnic on the grass. With so many stalls serving drinks and food it didn't matter that they hadn't brought anything with them, there were more than enough burgers, hot dogs, chips and Pimm's to go round. For Josie, two of the abiding memories from that day would be having her picture taken with Kelly and one of the professionals from *Strictly Come Dancing*, who'd dropped in to cheer everyone on. And watching Lily and Bel start off the impromptu dancing when all the walkers were back. It had done her heart so much good that she'd summoned the energy to join them, and before they knew it a hundred or more women were on their feet bopping and boogieing to Mr Beck's swing jazz band. What a wonderful day, and how blessed she'd felt to know Bel, because without her she'd never have been a part of it.

And now here she was, in St Mark's church on the hill overlooking Temple Bay, watching Lily and Jasper, still flushed from the heady triumph of their graduation ceremony at Bristol Cathedral, tying the knot to become husband and wife. If it were possible to feel any happier, or prouder – *her girl had a first in history and politics and was marrying a wonderful lad who adored her* – she truly didn't know how. There was no fear hanging about her today, only the joy of being there for the most important event of Lily's life. Mr Beck had promised she'd make it, and she had. What she'd never have expected was that he'd be a part of it too: though he wasn't in the church, he was coming to the reception later. Fancy that, Mr Beck at Lily's wedding. She could only wish that he and Bel had managed to get beyond being friends by now, but as it seemed to suit them the way they were who was Josie Clark to start telling them to get a move on?

'I, Jasper,' her almost new son-in-law was saying, 'take you, Lily, to be my wife, to have and to hold from this day forward; for better, for worse, for richer for poorer, in sickness and in health . . .'

Feeling Jeff's hand reach for hers, Josie smiled secretly to herself as a huge surge of love laid claim to her heart. The daft old thing had cried when he'd seen Lily in her dress earlier, and when he'd said he wished Ryan could be there, Josie had had to get out a hankie too. If only her letter to the prison had received a more positive response, but she hadn't really expected them to let him out for the day, she'd just had to try. Poor love, sitting there all alone today with no visitors and wishing he could be here for

Lily. She hoped Chaplain Paul was with him; he'd said he would be and she had no reason to doubt him.

She'd never heard another word from Debbie Prince who'd no doubt forgotten all about her by now, or was still having a laugh at her expense. Though Josie tried never to think badly of anyone these days, she didn't mind making an exception for the Princes.

'In the presence of God,' the vicar was saying, 'and before this congregation, Lily and Jasper have given their consent and made their marriage vows to each other. They have declared their marriage by the joining of hands, and by the giving and receiving of rings. I therefore proclaim that they are husband and wife.'

'That was us once,' Jeff whispered, tightening his hold on her hand, as Jasper and Lily turned to each other.

As Josie's heart swelled she couldn't avoid the spike of reality that was trying to make the joy bleed. The cancer had spread again, to her ribs, upper arm and breast bone. Bel knew, but no one else. There would be time for that after the wedding; she wasn't going to spoil anything for anyone now, least of all Jeff and her beloved girl.

'Twenty-two years ago come next month,' she whispered in Jeff's ear, finding it hard to believe that so much time had gone by.

Bel had organised for them to go up in a hot-air balloon as an anniversary treat which they were both really looking forward to, though feeling the way she did today, so full of happiness and goodwill towards the world (except Debbie Prince), Josie didn't think she'd need any help flying.

'Wow, look at you,' Jeff had exclaimed earlier when he'd come into the bedroom to check if she was dressed yet. 'Apart from our Lily you're going to be the most beautiful woman there.'

Josie had glowed. He hadn't given her compliments like that in so long she could barely remember the last, and she'd been able to tell from the way he was looking at her that in spite of how thin and haunted she was, he'd really meant it.

She had so much to thank Bel for, including this very

elegant pale blue silk dress with matching shoes, along with a wig that was so like her own hair even she could hardly tell the difference. They'd bought it the day they'd gone to London for her to be measured up for the fashion show. Bel had known about the shop because it was where her sister had bought her wig, and talk about expensive! Josie was still waiting for the NHS to refund some of it so she could pay Bel back; meantime she was donating five pounds a week from her benefits to Breast Cancer Care, since Bel was refusing to take the money.

Her own hair had started growing back over the last few weeks, but it wasn't very long and though she quite liked the pixie cut, as Bel called it, she'd wanted to look more her old self for the wedding. After all, Lily was going to be looking back on the photos in years to come, and it wouldn't be very nice for her to be reminded every time she did that her mother had had cancer.

Everyone was now singing 'And Did Those Feet', one of the hymns she and Jeff had chosen for their wedding. How long ago that seemed, and yet it could almost have been yesterday. Glancing across the aisle she saw Miriam taking a peek her way, and they both smiled. Apparently Miriam and Richard had had the same hymn at their wedding, which was why Lily and Jasper had chosen it, to please both sets of parents.

Feeling her mother nudging her, Josie turned to see what she wanted.

'Got a tissue?' Eileen whispered through her tears.

Digging into her purse for the Kleenex, Josie passed one over and touched a hand to her fascinator to make sure it was straight. She'd never before worn such a pretty outfit, apart from her own wedding dress and veil which she'd bought, at great expense, from a bridal boutique in Exeter. She'd had it cut up later to make a christening gown for her children, which was what Lily had said she was going to do with hers when the time came.

Lily's dress was an absolute dream. She looked like a princess or a movie star in the glittering waterfall of lace and silk that hugged her slender frame to the knees and fishtailed with a lavish swish around her ankles. It had cost a packet but was worth every penny of the fifteen hundred pounds Jeff had given her to pay for it. Quite where he'd got the money from Josie still didn't know, but she had a suspicion he'd borrowed it from her cousin, Steve, who was never short of a bob or two.

The hymn was so rousing everyone was singing their hearts out, even those who hadn't been invited but had made their way to the church anyway, eager to watch Lily Clark arrive on her dad's arm, and leave with her handsome new husband. Steve was their chauffeur, having talked someone into lending him a Rolls-Royce for the day, and Bob, from the karaoke bar, had driven the four bridesmaids in his nearly new Honda Hybrid. Josie, Eileen and Carly were travelling with Bel, who'd picked them up in her brother-in-law's BMW because, she'd decided, it was more appropriate for them to arrive in a saloon car than an estate, even if it was a Mercedes.

Bel was sitting in the row behind looking an absolute treat in her tangerine dress with its lacy drop waist and low-cut back, like someone out of the twenties. Everyone had turned to look at her when she'd arrived at the church. Being so tall and obviously sophisticated, it was only natural she'd turn heads, but she hadn't seemed to notice. Sitting in the same row were some of the bridesmaids' relatives, most of whom had known Lily since she was born. Three of the bridesmaids were Lily's friends from school; the fourth was Elodie, Jasper's fourteen-year-old sister. Such a pretty name that, Elodie. It was French, apparently, because that was where she'd been conceived.

Experiencing a sharp twinge in her upper arm Josie gave it a gentle rub, as if telling it not to worry, she'd take some more painkillers soon. She was taking bisphosphonates now, so was having to get used to their side effects, but on the whole they weren't too bad, at least not so far. Even if they got worse it didn't matter, she'd cope, and she definitely wasn't going to worry about it today.

Another wave of happiness swept over her as she and Jeff were invited to come forward to sign the register.

'Are you all right, Mum?' Lily whispered, as they arrived in the vestry.

Surprised, Josie said, 'Of course. Don't I look it?'

Lily laughed. 'Actually, you look so happy I was wondering if you might be on something, then I remembered you are.'

Josie laughed too, and felt the next few minutes trickling over her like sunshine as she added her name to Jeff's and ignored the stiffness in the small of her back. It didn't hurt too badly, thank goodness, because that was definitely the worst of the pain when it got going. Apparently she'd have to be careful in the future about spinal collapse, but that was still a long way off and right now she was too wrapped up in the utter bliss of the moment to care.

'Are you all right?' Eileen asked, as she edged in next to Josie for the family-group shot.

'Why does everyone keep asking me that?' Josie wanted to know.

'OK, no need to bite my head off,' Eileen grumbled, 'I was just making sure.'

'Sorry,' Josie whispered, and tucking her purse under her arm she reached for her mother's hand.

'What's all that about?' Eileen protested, pulling her hand free.

Remembering they didn't do lovey-dovey, Josie said, 'I just thought it might be nice for once.'

'Daft old sod,' Eileen muttered, but a moment later Josie felt her hand being taken. 'Glad you're over all that nonsense now,' Eileen whispered, 'did my head in good and proper it did, thinking of you with all that going on inside you.'

Smiling into the lens, Josie squeezed her mother's hand and leaned in a little closer to Jeff. Nothing was going to spoil today, not even the fact that Ryan would never feature in the shots of his sister's wedding. What a sweet boy he was, the way he'd kept insisting that Lily shouldn't change anything for him.

'Everyone looks so gorgeous,' Bel commented, as the bridesmaids, in their purple satin halter necks and glittering hair pieces, grouped around the bride.

'Isn't it the most perfect day?' Josie beamed, gazing out at the sparkling waters of the bay and pristine blue sky.

'You've done her proud,' Bel responded.

'She did most of it herself, and the rest was down to you,' Josie reminded her.

Smiling softly as she touched a hand to Josie's cheek, Bel said, 'I used to think I had the world's best mum, but now I know that Lily does.'

Surprised by this rare mention of her mother, Josie rolled her eyes, but before she could comment, Bel went on, 'I'm going to head back to the house now, make sure things are ready for when everyone arrives.'

Since it had already been arranged for Miriam and Richard to take Josie and Jeff to Stillwater in their car, Josie said, 'I guess it's a bit late now to ask if you're sure about hosting it, but remember, you were warned. Everyone might be on their best behaviour now, but heaven only knows what they'll be like when they've got a few drinks inside them.'

It was close to nine in the evening by now, the sun was setting in a golden blaze over Westleigh Bay and Bel couldn't imagine how the day could have gone more perfectly. In spite of Josie and Jeff's concerns everyone had been on their best behaviour, at least up to now. Jeff had made her smile, however, a few minutes ago with a reminder that the night was still young, so he'd be keeping a close eye on the likeliest candidates for shame and disgrace as the music got going.

The garden looked spectacular, thanks in part to having no need of the marquee, also to Kristina's management of the caterers who'd arranged everything beautifully. In all there were fourteen round tables full of guests, and one long top table for the wedding party, each covered in starched white linen with exquisite orchid and lily arrangements at the centre, and silver and glassware glinting like jewels in the evening sun. It wouldn't be long now before Kristina and Nick began lighting the candles they'd spread about the lawns and terrace, and Bob from Chanter Lysee was already setting up his station for some interactive entertainment, as he liked to call it. Until now the music had been provided by a harpist Lily had met at a friend's wedding, and Jasper's cousin, a gifted flautist.

Since it was a special occasion Oscar and Nell were being allowed to stay up late, though Bel could see that after all the excitement and crafty sips of wine they were beginning to struggle. Once she'd have whispered to Nick that it was time to start taking them up, but that was Kristina's role now and Bel had to admit she was playing it well. Watching her and Nick finding their way back to each other over the last couple of months had occasionally made her ache inside, as she saw the happy family evolving without Talia at the heart of it.

'It's not that anyone's forgotten her,' Nick had promised during one of their rare heart-to-hearts, 'that's never going to happen, but we can't go back. We can only go forward.'

He was right, of course, and though she might not be settling into this new situation as quickly as he was, she felt glad for him that his counselling was evidently helping so much.

Besides, the alternative, of watching him and Kristina break up, wasn't one she wanted even to consider, especially when she cared for Nick so deeply – and when her friendship with Kristina was starting to put down roots. The most difficult part was stepping back from the children, but hopefully she was doing it gradually enough for them not to notice too much. And it wasn't as though she was being shut out of the family in any way. Far from it, as Nick and Kristina were careful to include her on all sorts of weekend jaunts, school sports days, visits to the zoo, and donkey rides on the beach. The greatest treat for everyone was sailing with Harry and his sons.

'More wine?' Harry asked.

Turning to find him with the bottle poised over her glass, she smiled and nodded. Though they didn't see each other often, his friendship had already come to mean a great deal to her, and she felt sure it was special for him too. He'd been the first to turn up with champagne the day she'd completed on the barn – for her original offer after the other buyer pulled out – and along with his cousins Semeena and Joel she'd helped him move into his mother's new apartment. He was so easy-going, undemanding and full of fun in ways that could make her laugh with a light-heartedness she hadn't known for too long. It was also thanks to him, now the summer was upon them, that her terrace was becoming a popular place to meet for drinks at the end of a busy day as the sun went down.

'Have you chosen your karaoke songs yet?' he asked, sitting back in his chair to see her better. He was looking particularly handsome today, she was thinking, in his pristine white shirt and the tie he'd unfastened to hang loosely either side of his open collar.

'Have you?' she countered, her eyes sparkling with mischief.

He laughed and grimaced. 'I swear you don't want to hear it,' he assured her. 'Whereas you, I'm reliably informed, have a voice like Edith Piaf.'

She choked on a laugh, knowing he was making it up. 'Apparently Josie and Jeff are going to serenade the happy couple with "We've Only Just Begun",' she told him.

'Sounds appropriate,' he commented. 'Maybe you and I could put ourselves down for a duet. How about "I've Got You Under My Skin"?'

Her eyes shot to his, wondering if he'd meant anything by it, but detecting nothing in his manner to suggest he did, she said, 'Or what about . . .' she was about to blurt out the old karaoke classic, 'Don't Go Breaking My Heart', but quickly switched it to, '"How Much Is That Doggie in the Window?" I'll do the woofs.'

Laughing, he said, 'Is it on the list?'

'No idea.'

'If it is I'm going to hold you to it. What do you think Josie's mother's put herself down for?'

Looking over to where Eileen was wobbling on her heels as she kept embracing Jasper, she said, 'Oh, I know that, because it's her party piece, apparently. "I Will Survive".'

Slapping a hand on the table, he said, 'I should have guessed. And Lily and Jasper?'

'The last I heard it's between "Crazy in Love" and "It Had to Be You".'

He looked impressed. 'Maybe they should do both.'

'I daresay they will,' and getting to her feet as Kristina carried a sleepy Nell over for a kiss goodnight, she wrapped Nell's little body in a big embrace as she said, 'You've been a very good girl today.'

'I want to stay up and sing,' Nell wailed.

'We've agreed,' Kristina said, 'that you'll get ready for bed, and if you still want to come back down you can.'

Nell gazed at Bel imploringly.

'Sounds like a good idea to me,' Bel told her.

Yawning, Nell nodded and let her head drop on to Kristina's shoulder.

'Are you going to say goodnight to Harry?' Kristina suggested.

'Goodnight Harry,' Nell responded, giving him a little wave. 'Where are Josh and Neel today?'

'They're with their mummy,' he smiled.

She nodded and yawned again. 'Can we go sailing with them tomorrow?' she wondered.

Rolling her eyes, Kristina said, 'Let's get today over with first, shall we?'

Oscar was next, riding on Nick's back. 'I'm just pretending to go up,' he informed Bel, 'so Nell will think I'm going to bed, but I'm not.'

'Oh, I see,' she smiled, tousling his hair. 'Well just in case you decide to stay, can I have a kiss?'

Releasing his father's neck, he threw his arms round Bel and planted a giant smackeroo on her cheek. 'Will everyone still be here when we get up in the morning?' he asked.

'I hope not,' Bel laughed, 'but we might have to scour the bushes to make sure no one got left behind.'

Turning to Harry, he said, 'Me and Neel found a really good hiding place the last time he was here. I bet you'll never be able to find us. Daddy couldn't this morning, could you, Daddy?'

'And I searched high and low,' Nick assured him. 'Come on now, it's time for bed.'

'But only pretend,' Oscar reminded him as they started inside.

'Aha, here he is, the dishiest bloke at the party,' Eileen slurred, sinking down in the chair Nick had vacated, 'apart from my new grandson-in-law, of course. Got yourself a real looker there, my girl,' she told Bel. 'If I was ten years younger I'd be giving you a run for your money.'

Torn between embarrassment and laughter, Bel said, 'But I know you'd win, Eileen.'

'Well, I'm not so sure about that,' Eileen mumbled, 'because you're a bit of a classy bird, but I've had a few lookers in my time, I can tell you. Anyway, hasn't it been a lovely day? Our Lily's a proper picture, isn't she, and she couldn't have found a better bloke.'

'What are you rattling on about over here?' Josie demanded, coming to join them. 'I hope you're not showing yourself up,' she said to her mother.

'I wouldn't be having a good time if I wasn't,' Eileen retorted.

As Harry and Bel laughed, Jeff and his brother Phil rolled up, followed by Richard, Jasper's dad, and another man Bel thought was Jasper's uncle. It seemed everyone wanted to talk to Harry, so leaving them to it for the moment she went inside to check everything was OK with the caterers.

'This is the best wedding ever,' Lily announced, appearing, Bel presumed, from the downstairs loo. Though she'd obviously downed several glasses of champagne by now, she still looked as radiant as the sunbeam her mother called her. 'I feel so lucky to be having our reception here,' she hiccuped. 'It's much better than the golf club, with all those crusty old blokes and toffee-nosed Marjories strutting about with their silly bats and balls.'

Bel had to laugh. 'We don't have quite as much space here,' she said, returning Lily's hug, 'but I think we're doing OK.'

'More than,' Lily insisted. 'I swear I've never been this happy in my entire life, I just wish my brother was here to share it, but he's not so there's no point going on about it. What really matters is that Mum's OK now, or getting better anyway, and she looks so gorgeous today, doesn't she?'

'Absolutely,' Bel agreed, turning to where Josie was laughing at something Harry was saying. He was always so good with people, she was thinking, and to look at the two of them now no one would ever guess how they'd come into each other's lives. *Please Lily, don't ask me anything about your mum's condition. I don't want to lie, but there's no way I can get into the truth today, and definitely not without Josie's permission.*

'Oh my God, listen to Nan,' Lily groaned, as Eileen gave a raucous shriek of what was probably laughter. 'She's had way too much, as usual, bet Mum and Dad end up carrying her home. Unless you've got room for her here?'

Catching Lily's mischievous twinkle, Bel raised her eyebrows. 'Where are you and Jasper spending the night?' she asked. 'Or is it a secret?'

'No, we're booked into the the Grand, down on the seafront, until Monday, then we're going to look at a new flat in Bristol before flying off to Tenerife for a week.'

'So you're staying in Bristol?'

'For the time being, yes. Jaz is up for an internship with the MOD at Filton, which'll be brilliant if he can get it, and I've got an interview with the Crown Prosecution Service at the beginning of September. They're taking on apprentices at sixteen grand a year, an amazing amount when just about everyone we know is having to work for nothing. Fingers crossed I get it. Oh my God, what is Jasper doing? Excuse me,' and lifting up her dress she went charging back to the top table, where her new husband and his best man were attempting to hoist two bridesmaids on to their shoulders to begin some sort of bunfight.

Returning to her own table, Bel slipped an arm round Josie's shoulders as Eileen said, 'So what are the chances of you getting us all tickets to this fashion show, Bel?'

'Mum,' Josie protested.

'Well, we don't want to be missing your big day, do we?' Eileen pointed out.

Amused by the thought of Eileen at the Grosvenor House Hotel, Bel said, 'I was thinking I'd find out how much they want for a table . . .'

'It's about ten grand or more,' Josie cried.

'Well, Eileen's right,' Bel responded, 'we all have to go, so if there are ten of us . . .'

'We can get ten people together,' Eileen piped up.

'There's me, you, Lily, Carly . . . I expect Miriam will want to come, and our Steve's wife, Mandy . . . How many's that so far?'

'Six,' Josie told her, 'and I hope you're not forgetting Jeff, because I definitely want him there . . .'

'Where?' Jeff demanded, breaking off a football chat with Harry.

'At the fashion show where she's modelling,' Eileen told him. 'You're coming, aren't you?'

Jeff looked doubtful.

'You have to go,' Harry insisted, 'it's a really big deal for Josie.'

'I don't want to be the only bloke there,' he protested.

'You won't be,' Bel laughed. 'Lots of men go to support their wives, girlfriends, mothers, sisters, in some cases husbands or brothers . . . Nick came when Talia took part and if you talk to him, he'll tell you he wouldn't have missed it for the world.'

'What's that?' Nick asked, bringing a fresh bottle of wine to the table.

When Bel enlightened him he immediately said to Jeff, 'Don't even think about not going, mate. It wasn't at all what I was expecting. I mean, it's dead glamorous and glitzy and everything you'd expect from that sort of event, but the women that take part . . . Well, go, see for yourself and you'll know why I'm telling you you have to be there.'

'I'll come with you, Jeff,' Lily's new father-in-law offered.

Clearly surprised and pleased, Jeff held up a hand to high-five. 'You're on,' he told him.

Glowing with pleasure, Josie said to Harry, 'And what about you, can we invite you to join our table?'

Glancing at Bel, he said, 'I'll have to check my schedule. When is it?'

'October 2nd,' she provided. She'd enjoy having him there; he might even be prevailed upon to give a short talk, as he sometimes did on these occasions.

'It's during Breast Cancer Awareness month,' Josie announced, in case anyone had forgotten, 'which obviously is what it's all about.'

'But you don't have it any more,' Eileen pointed out.

Ignoring her, Josie said to Bel, 'Do you think Kristina would like to join us?'

Feeling guilty that she hadn't thought of it herself, Bel said, 'If she can find someone to look after the children, I'm sure she would.'

As Nick began to speak a sudden blast of music drowned him out, and even when the volume was brought under control it was still difficult to make himself heard. In the end he gave up and went to help Kristina, who'd started lighting the candles.

A couple of hours later, with the karaoke in full throat and the dancing powering on, Bel and Harry were smooching to one of the few lazier numbers being performed by Jeff's brother. It was the first time, she couldn't stop herself thinking, that they'd actually touched, apart from swift kisses on meeting and parting, and either because she'd had a bit to drink, or because the atmosphere was so romantic, she was wishing he'd hold her even closer.

Did he have any idea, she wondered, how attractive she found him? Was it possible he might feel the same way? He'd never given any sign of it, but there again, nor had she. Indeed, they'd gone out of their way to avoid anything at all of an intimate nature, whether a touch, a look, or even the slightest innuendo. Yet there was a chemistry between them that she couldn't deny, and this evening it felt particularly insistent.

Earlier in the day she'd promised herself that if he tried to initiate something tonight she wouldn't allow herself to pull back, and if he didn't she might indicate that she wasn't averse to a relationship developing between them. She wondered if he could already feel it in the heat between their bodies and the gentle sway of their hips. His fingers were loosely in hers; the male scent of him, mingled with the warm, salty air, was as heady as wine.

As he moved in closer to her she felt her breath flutter inside.

'I have some news,' he murmured in her ear. 'I don't know if you'll be happy for me. I think you will.'

Trying to imagine what it was, she waited for him to continue.

'My wife wants to try again,' he said.

The words hit her like blows.

Somehow she managed to go on dancing, to smile and say, 'That's wonderful. Of course I'm happy for you. The children will be pleased.'

'Yes,' he agreed, 'yes, I'm sure they will.'

Chapter Twenty-Three

Jeff's face was taut, ashen, as he watched Josie settling into her chair. They were in the living room, just the two of them, after spending the afternoon barbecuing with a few neighbours.

She could tell from the look on his face that he had an idea what was coming, and she'd have given anything to be able to prove him wrong.

'You're going to tell me it's back, aren't you?' he blurted, before she could begin.

Back, spread, what difference did it make? She nodded and watched the colour flush across his neck. 'I bloody knew it,' he said tightly. 'I've been watching you . . .' He smacked a hand on the arm of his chair. 'I bloody well knew it!'

'I'm sorry, love, I wish it wasn't happening . . .'

'What are you sorry for?' he snapped. 'It's not your fault, is it?'

'It's no one's fault,' she replied, though she wished there was someone to blame, if only to allow them a rant against something more accountable than God, or fate, or whatever the heck was driving this wretched disease. 'It's gone into my bones,' she told him, 'which is why I've been getting a lot of backaches.'

He stared at her hard, clearly thinking of the Pilates board, the change of mattress that had never happened . . . 'So what are they doing about it?' he demanded, almost belligerently.

What, indeed? 'Well, you know they've changed my medication,' she began. 'I'm taking these bisphosphonates now. It's a lot better than chemo.' The side effects were still bad, especially the headaches and nausea, but at least she

365

didn't have to keep going to the hospital for treatment, only for blood tests and scans.

'And what are they supposed to do, these bisphopherates or whatever they're called?'

Taking a booklet she'd secreted down the side of the chair, she put it on the coffee table. *Secondary Breast Cancer in the Bone, Factsheet.* 'It'll tell you all about it in there, but basically these pills help to slow things down.'

His eyes were sharp as they came back to hers, his face still pinched. 'I thought you were getting better,' he said, accusingly.

Though he was doing his best not to show it, she knew the bluster was to hide how scared he was; she was, too, but she needed to stay strong or they'd both end up in a mess.

'What's our Lily going to say?' he growled. 'This isn't what she's going to want to hear when she gets back from honeymoon.'

'Of course she won't, but we'll have to tell her.'

Getting to his feet, he walked into the kitchen and grabbed a beer from the fridge.

Josie looked up as he came back, and reached for his hand as he passed. 'It'll be all right,' she said.

Using the back of a hand to wipe his mouth, he continued staring at nothing as he said, 'Will it?'

Her heart contracted. No, it wouldn't, but she couldn't bring herself to destroy what little hope he might have flickering under his fear.

'You have to be honest with him,' Bel had told her yesterday. 'Try not to hold back this time, because you need his support every bit as much as he needs yours. More, in fact.'

'It says in that factsheet,' she said to Jeff, 'that people can go on for a long time, years, with a secondary cancer in the bones, and I've been chatting to people online who have it and they're doing really well.' She wouldn't bother mentioning those who were having a rough time, because she wasn't one of them. In fact, apart from the headaches and nausea, she hadn't felt this up together in months. Physically, that was; mentally she'd been a bit all over the place since the wedding, but Bel was probably right when she'd said she was coming down from an emotional high.

'We can go on with our lives like normal,' she told him as he sat down again. 'Nothing's changed, not really. I might even be able to go back to work.'

He glared at her as if she'd gone mad. 'Don't talk daft,' he snorted. 'I'm not having you out looking for jobs when you've got all that going on inside you.'

Since they had more income now she was on the social than when she'd worked she didn't argue, though she felt tempted to ask where he'd got the money he'd given to Lily for her dress. It could wait for another time, but she needed to know, especially if he'd gone to one of those payday loan sharks. It would end them up in a whole heap of trouble, never mind debt, if he had, so hopefully he'd had the sense to borrow it from Steve.

'Shall we watch a bit of telly?' she suggested after a while. He probably needed some time to adjust to what she'd told him, then they could talk again later, if he wanted to.

It turned out that he didn't, although he did take the factsheet up to bed with him, and by the time he switched off the light he seemed to be breathing a bit easier.

'Come here,' he said, raising an arm for her to rest her head on his shoulder. 'You're going to be all right,' he told her, once she'd snuggled in. 'We're not going to have it any other way, so I don't want you worrying yourself silly. We'll get through this.'

Loving the words almost as much as she loved him, she curled a hand into his and found herself remembering the surprise she wanted to give him. She still hadn't done anything about it yet, but she would, probably after they'd been up in the balloon. Come to think of it, it might be a good idea to wait till after the fashion show, given how busy she was going to be between now and then. It was probably going to take it out of her, travelling up and down to London for the fitting and rehearsals, but Bel was insisting on driving her so they could stop any time she liked, whenever she liked.

Thinking of Bel got her worrying again about the effect

Harry returning to his wife was having on her. Though Josie understood he had to put his family first, she couldn't help wondering if he knew how much courage it had taken for Bel to enter into their friendship in the first place. Josie was willing to bet he had no idea how emotionally vulnerable, fragile even, Bel really was. Even if he had, Josie guessed there was nothing he could do about it; whatever had happened to Bel in the past wasn't his fault, nor was it really his problem to try and help fix. He shouldn't have led her on though, and he had, whatever Bel said to the contrary, because Josie had seen them together enough times lately to feel as convinced by the chemistry between them as Bel had been. In fact, the night of the wedding Josie had fully expected a proper romance to spring into blossom; it had certainly looked as though it would. Instead, Harry had ended up killing Bel's hopes with news that might be good for him, but was utterly devastating for her, and now Josie could only wonder if Bel was ever going to find it in herself to trust a man again.

Bel could hardly believe that more than six weeks had passed since Lily and Jasper's wedding. In many ways the time had seemed to fly, yet in others it had dragged like a weight she couldn't shake free. Keeping her mind off Harry and how much she missed him didn't seem to get any easier – sometimes it felt as though it was becoming a whole lot worse. She hadn't heard from him at all since the night he'd told her he was giving things another try with his wife, but though she longed to talk to him, or simply to hear his voice, she had no idea what she wanted to say, nor would she ever be able to reveal what was going on in her heart.

How could she have fallen so hard without realising it? How could she have allowed it to happen at all?

'*You had to take the risk,*' Talia kept telling her. '*If things had turned out differently you'd have been great together.*'

But they hadn't turned out differently, they'd gone precisely the way she'd feared, and now here she was constantly trying to pretend to herself that it didn't matter, when it seemed to be mattering more and more. Every time the phone rang her heart leapt with the hope it might be him, and the disappointment when it wasn't felt as crushing as the loneliness she was left with. She'd become so used to him calling, or dropping in, or meeting her at the Grape Escape for drinks, sometimes dinner, that without the regular contact and the humour they'd shared she felt as though she'd been cut brutally adrift.

'He shouldn't have led you on,' Josie or Kristina would say, but Bel honestly didn't feel that he had. Not once had he made a pass, or uttered a word to make her think he was interested in anything more than a friendship, and though she still felt the chemistry between them had been real, he'd never attempted to act on it. So she couldn't blame him for the way she was feeling now. It was her fault, and hers alone.

'You might say that,' Josie had protested during one of their journeys to London, 'but your relationship must have meant more to him than just friendship, otherwise why wouldn't he be in touch now?'

Nick often said the same, so did Kristina, and Bel never had a good enough reply.

Oddly, this gap in her life seemed to be bringing her and Kristina closer together, maybe because Kristina felt there was something she could do for Bel now, when there had never been anything before. She was always ready to listen and offer what advice she could, without telling Bel she had to get over it and move on. Bel was very good at telling herself that, so there was no need for anyone else to be so brutal – she only wished she could make herself do it. It was like she was stuck in a place she could find no escape from.

Thank God for the barn. If it weren't for the problems it was kicking up all over the place, she'd be wallowing in even more despair. Rarely a day went by when she wasn't having to source more stone or roof tiles, or sort out a foundation or structure issue, and while she was doing that at least she wasn't thinking, wondering about Harry.

'The problem is,' she'd said to Josie only yesterday, on their way home from a fashion-show rehearsal, 'I can't wish he'd come back, because that would be like willing his marriage to break down.'

'Which would be OK if the marriage isn't any good,' Josie had pointed out. 'Since we don't have any idea what's going on there . . .'

'We have to assume that it's all wonderful,' Bel interrupted. 'If I start telling myself anything else I'll be setting myself up for more disappointment, and believe me, this is already enough.'

'You can't let him make you afraid to trust again,' Nick had told her last night. 'The way things turned out is unfortunate, that's for sure, especially given your history, but he didn't know anything about it . . .'

'Even if he did, he was hardly going to turn his back on his wife to spare me, his *friend*, the experience of having everything that's gone wrong in my life suddenly rise up again like some horrible nemesis. He's not responsible for me, any more than I'm capable of being the right woman for him.'

'You have to stop telling yourself these things,' Nick protested. 'You're perfectly capable of being the right woman . . .'

'No! It was different for Talia, she didn't have to live with the guilt . . .'

'And you don't either. You have to let it go, Bel, or it really will destroy you.'

How easy it was to say the words 'let it go', how impossible to make them happen when she was as trapped by her past as she was by the inability to change it. It was always going to govern her, because it would always be there, a quiet undertow of truth sucking all the promise from her world. Never a day passed when she wasn't forced in some way to remember; even standing here, on the terrace of her house, gazing out to sea, could make her think of the home she'd shared with Talia and their mother. Were they somewhere in that pristine sky now, watching her, reading her mind, waiting to see what she would do next? Why didn't her mother speak to her, tell her what she needed to hear, instead of staying silently beside Talia, always there, and yet nowhere.

Hearing the shriek of her name she lowered her eyes to find Kristina and the children coming across the meadow with fishing nets and jam jars. Thankful they were there so she wouldn't have to spend the evening alone, she gave them a wave and started across the lawn to meet them. They'd been digging about in rock pools for the past half an hour, searching for crabs, cockles, blennies, gobies, pipefish and no doubt all kinds of shells to add to the collections at their own home as well as Bel's. Since Friday was the only day of the week they didn't have an after-school activity of some sort, Kristina had fallen into the habit of bringing them here on that day, and more often than not Nick would join them later.

'What, no marine life!' Bel cried when she saw the jam jars were empty.

'I caught a crab,' Oscar told her, 'but then I let it go again.'

'Because it pinched him,' Nell piped up, her creamy complexion reddened by the sun, 'and he screamed.'

'I did not.'

'Yes you did, and all the seagulls started screaming too. We found a nest with some eggs in, but we didn't touch them in case the mummy seagull came back and didn't want to sit on them any more. Is Daddy home yet?'

'No, it's far too early for him,' Bel smiled, pushing open the gate for Kristina to come through, while the children scrambled over the stile. 'Your biscuits are out of the oven though, and should be cool enough to eat by now.'

'Yay,' they cheered, and thrusting their cargo at Bel they shot off towards the house.

'No more than one each,' Kristina called after them, 'and take your sandy shoes off before you go inside.'

'We will,' Nell called back.

With a roll of her eyes Kristina took the nets and jam jars and went to put them in the shed. 'Any news yet?' she asked, coming out again.

Feeling a catch in her heart, Bel shook her head. The question wasn't about Harry and she knew it, nevertheless he'd come to her mind as quickly as Josie had. 'There must have been a longer wait than usual at the hospital,' she said, finding she didn't mind too much when Kristina linked her arm to wander across the lawn. Mostly she welcomed the friendship, but there were still odd times when she'd feel Talia watching and her conscience would fall prey to a sickening sense of disloyalty. 'If I don't hear by five thirty I'll call myself.'

'I'm sure she'll be all right for the fashion show,' Kristina commented as they mounted the steps to the terrace.

'She's been on good form lately, so I don't see any reason why she wouldn't be. You should see the way she struts up and down the catwalk, like she was Kate Moss herself.'

Laughing, Kristina said, 'Is she coming over at the weekend?'

Wishing the mere word 'weekend' didn't conjure an instant memory of the days they'd spent sailing with Harry and his sons, Bel replied, 'I'm not sure yet. I think tomorrow's a visiting day so she'll probably go up to Bristol. Maybe I'll invite them for lunch on Sunday. Would you like to come too?'

'I'm sure we would if we weren't going to see my parents.'

'Of course. Sorry, I'd forgotten.' Why wouldn't this blasted wretchedness leave her alone?

Inhaling the warm salty air as she turned to gaze out over the bay, Kristina said, 'I wonder how much longer this Indian summer's going to last? It's so beautiful today, isn't it?'

There went her mind again, straight to Harry and how wonderful it would be if she could invite him for a drink this evening to watch the sun set. Where was he now? At the hospital poring over a problem with a patient? On his way home after a stressful day? Flying to a conference somewhere in Europe? With his wife and children, taking advantage of this spell of warm weather? He'd be making more of an effort to spend time with them now, considering what his workaholic tendencies had almost cost him before. She wanted to feel pleased for him that things were working out, and a part of her did, but the other part seemed incapable of lifting her out of this awful decline.

'Do you think it might be an idea to speak to the doctor?' Kristina said gently.

Bel turned to her curiously.

'I'm afraid you might be falling into a depression,'

Kristina explained, 'and there's probably something they can give you.'

'You mean like Prozac?'

'Whatever helps you get past this sadness.'

Bel's eyes followed the rise and swoop of a gull. Yes, it was a sadness, so deep and so consuming it seemed to be swallowing her alive.

'Or what about talking to the counsellor Nick's been seeing?' Kristina suggested. 'We know what a difference it's made to him.'

Yes, the change in him was impressive, but he had Kristina at his side making his efforts worthwhile, and no shadows from the past to darken his tomorrows.

'Auntie Bel, your phone,' Oscar called, bringing it to her.

Seeing it was Jeff she quickly clicked on. 'Hi, how did it go?' she asked worriedly. As she listened to the answer her eyes went to Kristina. A moment later her face turned white. 'Where is she now?' she demanded. She was still looking at Kristina. 'OK, I'll be right there.'

As she rang off Kristina caught her hands. 'It's gone to her brain,' Bel said shakily, and tearing herself free she ran to the car.

Josie had taken a little wander around the church for a while, enjoying the cool air and musty smell, the sun streaming through the stained-glass windows and the roses someone had arranged on the altar. The scent of the flowers had transported her back to when she used to make perfume from the petals as a child. Lily had done the same when she was small, dabbing the rosewater on her neck and wrists before wiggling off down the garden in Josie's high heels.

During her brief tour of St Mark's she'd paused every now and again to read the faded lettering on a memorial stone, wondering about the person and where they were now. For a few moments she'd sat in a pew, waiting to see if something unusual or extraordinary might occur. Having received such fateful news it seemed that something ought to happen even if she couldn't say what she expected it to be, but the air had remained still and no one had come.

She was outside now, sitting on a bench overlooking the

glittering sweep of the bay. Those who lived on her side of the hill always said you had to be rich or dead to get the best views from Temple Fields, and they weren't wrong. Apart from their natural beauty, there was something mesmerisingly mysterious about the endless expanses of sky and sea stretching quietly, sometimes stormily out to a far horizon.

The laden branches of a maple were lending her some shade from the sun, and what sounded like a family of turtledoves was purring and cooing nearby. She watched a pair of gulls riding the thermals, freely trusting to something they could neither see nor understand. How exhilarating it must feel to fly and float as though nothing could weigh you down. When the time came, would she be able to let go like that?

It was a pity she and Jeff hadn't managed to go for their hot-air balloon ride. The weather had turned against them that day, then Jeff had gone down with flu, and the next available date had turned out to be today. How fortunate she would consider herself if she and Jeff were drifting across the bay now, thrilling at the views below, and having no thought for anything beyond how lucky they were to have chosen such a perfect day.

It was strange how the colours around her seemed brighter, richer, deeper, while every sound was music of one variety or another.

She watched a group of surfers paddling out of the waves, not enough wind for them today, although a flurry of white sailboats was bobbing and fluttering between the headlands, caught in a lively sea breeze. A rib sped away from a landing stage, towing a water-skier behind, while devoted sun-worshippers spread towels on the rocks and shale beach to catch some rays. The fine weather had brought everyone out to make a quick last grab at summer before autumn set in.

She'd come here thinking she might have a chat with the vicar, ask her if there was anything she ought to do during the time she had left to help her with the hereafter, but she didn't seem to be around. It didn't matter, she wasn't sure she wanted to talk to her anyway. She might think it was a bit of a cheek, a non-believer turning up looking for answers when she'd never done anything to earn them.

Was she a non-believer? It was hard to say when she hadn't given it much thought before. She supposed on some level she must think there was something, or why would she have got married and had the kids christened in this very church? It was a different vicar now to when she and Jeff had walked down the aisle, and to when Lily and Ryan had been baptised. They didn't seem to stay very long at St Mark's, which was surprising when it was such a lovely spot – and there was no shortage of sinners down on the estate, so plenty of outreach opportunities for a man or woman of the cloth.

Easily able to imagine the short shrift the likes of Debbie Prince would give anyone seeking to save their souls, she sighed quietly to herself, and tried to unravel the tangled thoughts in her mind. Some were in the past, caught up in her children's births, and precious moments along the way: small fingers making daisy chains, beach rides on donkeys, bluebell and blackberry picking, presents at Christmas, guinea-pig grooming, shoulder rides at school fetes, chubby arms and smiling faces bringing more happiness into her world than she could ever have believed possible.

Other thoughts were turning to the future, only to vanish into the empty space where she would no longer be: the living-room chair she'd always sat in; the side of the bed she usually slept; the kitchen where she'd cleaned, cooked, had cuddles with Jeff and the children; their table at the karaoke bar; the visitors' room at the prison. She wouldn't be in those places any more; Jeff, Lily, Ryan would carry on alone. Would she be able to watch, from wherever she was, when Jeff lifted their first grandchild in his arms? Would he feel her presence, and think of how happy this moment would have made her? Would her arms long to hold the baby too? Would she know when Ryan was set free? Would she be able to do anything at all to help him on his way? They'd all be going forward into the future, those she loved and who loved her, and her heart ached to think of how much of their lives she was going to miss, and of how they would miss her.

If you are out there God, she said in her mind, *and you know what's happening, I have to ask why you chose me. I know you won't answer, but I'm wondering it anyway, when I'm such an ordinary person with not a lot going for her, so why on earth would you want me over there? It's not going to serve much of a purpose for anyone, as far as I can see, whereas if you let me stay here I could carry on being the best mother and wife I'm able to be, and granny too one of these days. Don't get me wrong, I'm not feeling sorry for myself, well, I suppose I am in a way, but I understand it's far worse for those who've got small children. I've never been able to work out why you have to take them. At least I've seen my two grow up, which I'm very thankful for, but there's still so much I can do for them, and it's making me feel terrible to think of them trying to go on without me. I don't think it'll be easy for Jeff either . . .* Tears welled in her eyes as she pictured him coming home to an empty house at the end of the day, wanting with all his heart to find her there, while knowing this would never happen.

She wondered what he was doing now. If Lily hadn't come with them to the hospital today she'd never have left him alone to deal with the news, or with the letter that had arrived from the council telling them they had to move so a family could have their house. Jeff's temper had flared, rightly so since they'd paid the bedroom tax. They really hadn't needed this cock-up today. Lily had taken charge, saying she'd sort it out, and because she'd needed to get away from them for a while, Josie hadn't argued. Later, once she'd had some time to come to terms with the cancer being in her brain, she'd be stronger and able to take on the council, or social services, or whoever else gave them grief. She'd also have it in her to show Jeff and Lily how important it was to make the most of the time they had left together.

Oh God, she cried silently, *how am I going to get through this without letting them see how afraid I am to leave them? I don't want them to have to witness what this disease is going to do to me. I don't even know if I have the courage to face it, except what choice do I have? I feel so alone, and yet that's how we all are really, alone, so it's not just me. Thank you for sending Chaplain Paul to Ryan, I know he's going to be a big comfort to him in the weeks and months ahead. I wish you'd find a way to let him come home before I go. I think it would be easier for us both if we could be together for a while before the time comes.*

She took a deep, shuddering breath and turned her watery eyes to the sky. *I don't know if you're listening, or if you even care, but I'm talking to you anyway, because there isn't anyone else I'd want to burden with all this cowardliness I'm feeling, and anger, and fear that I'm not going to know my family by the end.*

Though she wasn't expecting a sign to say she'd been heard, she still felt let down, abandoned even, when nothing changed in the sky, or the sea, or anywhere around her. The world, God, the whole universe appeared impervious to her plight. She watched a rabbit hop between the gravestones, and a butterfly flit around a colourful cluster of verbena. Everything seemed so beautiful, vital and special in a way she'd never taken the time to notice before.

As a shadow fell over her she looked up, half expecting it to be the vicar, but her heart gave a leap of gladness when she saw it was Bel. She tried to blink back her tears, but Bel was crying too, and as she sat down with her and took her in her arms Josie started to sob.

Minutes ticked by as they held one another, and Josie felt Bel's strength stealing into her heart.

'I'm sorry,' Bel whispered, smoothing Josie's newly formed curls. 'I'm so, so sorry.'

'It's me who should be sorry,' Josie told her, 'putting you through all this.'

'Oh Josie, please don't think about me,' Bel cried, hugging her tighter, 'you're the only one who matters now.'

Josie sat back, attempting to dry her eyes. 'That's not true,' she said, 'you matter too, and I'm worried about you. I want you to be happy, Bel, and all I'm doing is bringing you more sadness.'

'You make me happy too,' Bel insisted. 'Knowing you is the best thing that's happened to me in a very long time.'

Josie smiled through her tears. 'I can't believe that,' she chided, 'but I certainly don't know where I'd be without you. You've been my rock in so many ways, and here you are now, letting me lean on you again when surely to God you've had enough of trying to be strong for . . .'

'Sssh,' Bel whispered, putting a finger over Josie's lips. 'You've been my rock too, and there's still a way to go yet. We're going to carry on being there for each other right up until you don't need me any more.'

'Oh Bel, you can't go through it . . .'

'Yes I can. I'm not letting you push me away, so please don't try.'

More tears flowed down Josie's cheeks. 'If I believed in God,' she said brokenly, 'I might think he'd sent me an angel when he sent me you.'

Bel smiled. 'My mother used to say that we're all angels in our way, just not for everyone, and not always for long. And do you know what I think? I think you're my angel, because knowing you, going through this with you is forcing me to face up to things that I was afraid to when I went through it with Talia.'

Josie gazed at her anxiously. 'I want to help you,' she said softly. 'Whatever happened before . . .'

'You have enough to worry about.'

'I'd like not to have to think about it,' Josie admitted wryly, knowing there would probably come a time when it was impossible to think about anything else, if indeed she was even capable of thinking by then. 'You're saying I'm some sort of catalyst for you, but I think Harry was that too.'

Bel didn't disagree. 'It seems the way forward for me is learning to let go, and I'm afraid I'm still not very good at it.'

Josie's eyes were searching hers. 'Have you heard from him?' she asked.

Bel shook her head. 'But don't let's talk about that now. We have more important matters . . .'

'But this is important, to me as well as to you. I know I'm not all that knowledgeable about things, but it seems to me that releasing yourself from whatever happened in the past would be a good way to start dealing with the future.'

Bel took a breath as she gazed into Josie's eyes. 'No,' she said, 'I'm not letting you do this . . .'

'You don't have to tell me what it was,' Josie interrupted softly, 'but it might help if you talked to someone.'

Bel's expression seemed to dull as she turned towards the horizon. 'I think it would,' she agreed, 'but not today, Josie. I can't let you make today about me.'

'But don't you understand, helping you would be the best thing I could do right now, because I don't want to talk about me. I realise that sounds like I'm going into denial, but reality's going to catch up with me soon enough and there'll be plenty of time then to feel scared and sorry for myself, and all the other things that go with being where I am. You know better than I do about most of it, so let's leave it until it can't be avoided and take the advice you're always giving me to deal with the here and now.'

Bel said nothing, but Josie could sense how torn she was.

'Why don't you start by telling me about your mother?' she suggested. 'I can tell by the way you talk about her that you loved her very much, but you say so little.'

Bel's head went down, and for several moments it seemed she was going to say nothing at all. 'It's actually very simple really,' she said in the end, 'she died because of me and I know I'm never going to forgive myself.'

Reaching for her hands, Josie said, 'Why are you blaming yourself? What happened to make you think it was your fault?'

Bel's smile was faint. 'I don't think, I *know* it was my fault,' she replied. 'My father's too, but he doesn't seem to carry the burden of guilt in quite the same way.'

Having already guessed there was something terrible in the past concerning her father, Josie said, very gently, 'What did he do?'

Bel's eyes turned cold as she looked back towards the past. 'What didn't he do?' She took a breath and released it so slowly it was as though she was afraid to let it go. 'It started when Talia and I were eight,' she began, 'and it never stopped.' Her eyes went to Josie. 'I expect you know what I'm talking about?'

379

Josie nodded, though God knew she wished she was wrong.

'It was like we were his property in every imaginable way,' Bel continued, using the chill of her tone to separate her from the pain of the memory. 'Not just his daughters, his muses, his pride and joy, we became . . .' She shook her head abruptly. 'You won't want the details, no one would. Suffice it to say we were terrified of him, but he was never put off by our pleas for mercy. If anything they seemed to excite him, so we learned over time to accept what he was doing, to show no emotion at all, but he never stopped. If our mother hadn't loved him so much in spite of how brutal he could be with her, we'd have spoken out, but we were afraid of what he might do to her if she knew the truth, and what he might do to us. His tempers were violent, uncontrolled, he often beat my mother, but it didn't seem to make a difference to how she felt. She called it his artistic temperament. So we kept the abuse to ourselves, carried on suffering it right up until we were sixteen and about to go to college. This was when we decided we would never see him again. Talia didn't want to tell Mummy the reason, but I couldn't see how it was possible not to. I guess a part of me was angry with her for not knowing what he'd been doing for so long, or at least not acknowledging it. So I told her about it in detail, made her accept it was true, and three weeks later she killed herself.'

'Oh Bel,' Josie gasped, clutching Bel's hands. 'Oh my God, what a terrible thing for her to do. How could she? Oh Bel, I understand now why this has been so hard for you, but it wasn't your fault. Please, you have to see that.'

'If I hadn't told her, she'd still be here,' Bel stated, as if there was no other way of seeing it.

'But you had to tell her. How else were you going to explain not seeing your father again?'

Bel only shook her head.

'Bel, please, you have to listen to me,' Josie said urgently. 'I know you loved your mother, but what she did was wicked. She was only thinking about herself, not about her girls, and you should have come first. So she's the one to blame, not you. And your father for the terrible things he did. If it weren't for him there would never have been anything to tell your mother.'

'I know you're right, but it doesn't make the guilt go away. It's because of me that she couldn't face carrying on, that Talia lost her mother . . .'

'No, *not* because of you, because of your father, and because she couldn't cope with her own guilt for not realising it was happening. Did Talia blame you?'

'Maybe, at first, I'm not sure, but eventually she was able to handle it much better than I was. Meeting Nick made all the difference. He helped her to overcome her fears, and to understand what love was really about.' Her head went down. 'She never suffered from the kind of guilt I do. There was no reason for her to, when she hadn't even wanted to tell our mother what was happening.'

Feeling for the terrible burden she was carrying, Josie said, 'Did your mother leave a note?' Surely to God the woman had left her daughters something to help them forgive her actions, perhaps even, to a degree, understand them.

'Yes, she did,' Bel answered, 'but all it said was, *Just because you can't see me doesn't mean I'm not there. I love you my darlings, and I'm sorry.*'

Unable to imagine how devastating it must have been to have read those few short words, Josie put a hand to Bel's cheek. 'If I know anything at all,' she said softly, 'I know she wouldn't want you to torment yourself the way you do.'

Bel swallowed hard. 'Maybe not,' she conceded, 'but she never talks to me. Talia does, all the time . . . Obviously, I know it's my subconscious speaking, or my conscience, whichever is in charge that day, but I've never been able to connect with my mother the way I do with Talia. It's like she's holding back from me, perhaps even punishing me for telling her the worst imaginable thing for her to know.'

Josie was shaking her head. 'She's not punishing you, not if she loved you as much as I'm sure she did. More likely you're shutting her out rather than risk hearing things you won't be able to bear, but even if you did hear them, you said yourself it's your own subconscious speaking, or your conscience, so it wouldn't be her blaming you, it would be you blaming yourself.'

Taking a breath, Bel gazed deeply into Josie's eyes. 'You're just like my sister,' she told her, 'she'd always find excuses for me, do her best to persuade me it wasn't my fault.'

'I only wish she'd had more success. And what about your father? I take it you never see him now?'

Bel's jaw tightened. 'Never,' she replied. 'Our only contact, which isn't really contact at all, comes from an ex-policeman who lives on the same island, who I'm paying to watch him. He writes to me every six weeks or so to let me know that there's nothing to report. The instant there is I'll go straight to the authorities, naturally, but until then . . . It's a part of my life I never want to revisit if I can help it.'

'Of course not,' Josie concurred, thinking what a terrible shame it was that Harry wasn't able to do the same for Bel as Nick had for Talia. She desperately needed someone to help her move on from the tragedies of her past, someone who could show her what a beautiful, sensitive, worthwhile and wonderful young woman she was. 'You've kept it bottled up for too long,' she said gently. 'You need to speak to someone who knows how to deal with these issues.'

There was a hint of irony in Bel's eyes as she surveyed her friend. 'I'm talking to you,' she countered.

Josie smiled. 'You can always do that, any time you like, but I'm probably not the best person.'

'In my book you're always the best person, but you don't need to be shouldering my problems . . .'

'You mean the way you don't need to shoulder mine?'

Bel couldn't help but laugh.

'I'm here for you,' Josie whispered. 'I'll always listen and help you in any way I can.'

Tears glistened in Bel's eyes as she said, 'I know you will, and I also know that you share my sister's gift for turning the subject away from herself to make it about the other person.'

Josie's expression was wry. 'It seems a good idea to me

to talk about things we can change, rather than those we can't.' Even as she said the words her heart gave a twist of fear. She couldn't alter the course for herself now, but she could at least try to do some good while she was still here.

'Jeff and Lily are going to worry if we don't head back soon,' Bel reminded her.

Josie nodded, but made no attempt to move. 'I can't help wishing,' she said, 'that things could have worked out for you with Harry. He's the kind of man you deserve. He'd understand what you've been through, and being as clever as he is he'd be able to advise you much better than I can.'

'Even if you're right, it's neither his, nor your job to advise me, and I refuse to let you carry on talking about me.'

'You can refuse all you like . . .'

'Josie!'

'OK, just as long as we don't get started on what happened at the hospital today.'

'You'll have to deal with it sometime.'

'I know, and I will, but I read somewhere online, written by someone in the same position as me: "The cancer and treatment are only the staples holding things together, the pages are for the story of my life and I intend to keep filling them." I thought I'd take a leaf out of that book, pardon the pun.'

Bel's eyes filled with admiration.

'Does that make me like your sister too?' Josie teased.

Bel nodded.

'I like having her as a role model. I don't expect I'll make quite the same sort of impact on the catwalk as she did, though.'

'I think you'll be marvellous,' Bel assured her, 'as long as you feel up to it. No one's going to think any the worse of you if you decide you have to pull out.'

'What? It's only a couple of weeks away,' Josie declared, 'so I shall be taking part in that show even if it's the last thing I do.'

Bel's eyes narrowed as the words resonated between them.

'I probably shouldn't say things like that, should I?' Josie grimaced.

Bel shook her head. 'No, you really shouldn't,' and loving the way Josie laughed, she slipped an arm round her shoulders to begin the walk home.

Chapter Twenty-Four

'Mum, are you sure about this?'

Lily was having to shout to make herself heard above the cacophony of the dressing room. There was so much excitement in the commotion of stylists, choreographers, make-up artists, hairdressers, runners and other models, that it was impossible not to feel electrified simply by being there.

'Please stop asking me that,' Josie replied, keeping her eyes fixed on the multi-bulb mirror and the glamorous young girl who was turning her into a supermodel. Already she was looking sophisticated enough for a front cover, and they hadn't even dressed her yet. 'I'm fine, honestly. Now go away.'

Lily turned to Bel. 'What do you think?' she asked, her violet eyes tormented with worry. 'Should she be doing this?'

Concerned herself, since Josie had suffered two seizures in the past week, Bel said, 'I think we have to let her make the decisions.'

'That's right,' Josie informed them from under her rollers. 'I've got all my costumes sorted out now, and shoes and hats and belts, so no way am I backing out.'

'Hold still,' the make-up artist cautioned, skinny brush poised ready to apply more liner.

Seeing how happy, and apprehensive, and determined Josie was, Bel said to Lily, 'I guess the best thing we can do now is go and join the others at the tables.'

Lily looked at her mother and broke into an exasperated smile. 'I don't know if I love you because you're stubborn, or because you're just so damned lovely.'

'It'll be all of the above,' Josie laughed through the side of her mouth. 'You won't forget to film it, will you, cos Ryan'll want to see me strutting my stuff?'

'Kristina's brought a proper camera,' Bel told her, 'so we don't have to rely on our phones.'

Josie's eyes shone.

'OK,' Lily said, attempting to hug her, 'I'd say break a leg if I weren't afraid you might act on it, so go for it, best mummy in the world. I already know you'll look fabulous and we're all going to be dead proud of you.'

'She's the star of the show,' Kelly, her ex-chemo mate and fellow model, called out. 'You wait till you see some of her frocks.'

'Yours are fantastic too,' Josie shouted back. 'And you've got all the moves, not like me, but I'm doing my best.'

'You'll be brilliant,' Bel assured her, speaking in unison with the stylist who was circling around with last-minute notes.

Laughing, Bel said, 'I rest my case,' and squeezing Josie's hand she was about to pull away when Josie tugged her in closer.

'You won't go saying anything to Jeff about his surprise, will you?' she whispered.

'Of course not,' Bel assured her, 'but it's not happening today, is it?'

'Oh no, definitely not, but I thought I might tell him about it later, when we're on our way home.'

Though Bel wasn't convinced the surprise was a great idea, she understood where Josie was coming from, so all she said was, 'Don't worry, your secret's safe with me,' and giving Josie's movie-star reflection a wink in the mirror, she linked Lily's arm to steer her through the crowds to a door marked Exit.

Moments later they were in the opulent ballroom of the Grosvenor House Hotel, where dozens of large round tables were set out around a twenty-metre-long catwalk, and enormous video screens had been installed behind the stage. The noise was every bit as cacophonous out here, with models' families and friends, corporate and celebrity sponsors, the hierarchy of Breast Cancer Care, and journalists from all over having turned up to support this very special event.

By now the meal had already been served, so most were on their coffee and petits fours, apart from Eileen and Carly who were only just getting started on their dark chocolate mousse desserts.

'Haven't you finished yet, Nan?' Lily scoffed, taking her place between Bel and Eileen. Since their table was right at the end of the catwalk, they couldn't have asked for a better view.

'They've been going round getting their photos taken with celebrities,' Kristina whispered to Bel.

Unsurprised, Bel laughed. They had a right to enjoy themselves, and if a celebrity didn't want to be photographed he or she could always say no.

'How's she getting on back there?' Jeff wanted to know. 'She was that nervous when we got up this morning,' he told Miriam, who was sitting next to him.

'She's doing great,' Bel assured him, 'and she's going to look sensational.'

Though he nodded, showing it was the answer he'd hoped for, he still looked strained.

'Honest, Dad, she'll be fine,' Lily called across to him, making Bel smile at the way she was bolstering him, when only moments ago she was the one who'd needed the reassurance. Bel remembered only too well how she and Nick had tossed that ball between them when Talia was here; she knew how vital it was to try and keep it in the air.

'Have you had a gander at what's in these goody bags?' Eileen demanded of Lily. 'Bloody lovely stuff it is, all sorts of make-up and chocolates and shower gel and tokens for health spas; there's even a book by some author I've never heard of, but Carly reckons she has.'

'Oh, yeah, I read her all the time,' Carly piped up. 'You wouldn't,' she told Eileen, 'because you don't ever read.'

'I might now I've got a book,' Eileen retorted. 'This mousse is bloody delish, innit? You've done us right proud here, Bel my girl. Never been anywhere like this in our lives, have we, Carl, and now here we are, hobnobbing with the rich and famous, drinking champagne, and my

387

girl's only going to be up there putting on a show. I hope she remembers to give her old mum a wave when she passes.'

'Don't bank on it,' Lily told her. 'And whatever you do, don't call out to her. You'll only show yourself up and put her off her moves.'

'What do you take me for?' Eileen protested. 'I know how to behave meself, you wait and see.'

Catching Lily's sceptical eye, Bel had to laugh. Though neither Josie nor Jeff had been wild about Eileen coming today, no one had had the heart to tell her she couldn't, and Bel was glad about that. She was Josie's mother, after all, so it was only right she should be a part of this special day, and if anyone had a problem with how raucous she could be, as far as Bel was concerned it was theirs to deal with. Unless, of course, Eileen got completely out of hand, but now the alcohol had run out there was hopefully far less chance of that.

'What happened to your doctor friend?' Richard asked Bel. 'Couldn't he get away in the end?'

Remembering that Richard had been at the table when it was suggested that Harry might like to join them, Bel felt her heart twisting as she said, 'He's always very busy.'

Richard nodded knowingly. 'Shame, he was a nice chap. I'd like to have seen him again.'

'And very good-looking,' Miriam added, as if Bel might have forgotten.

'Bloody drop-dead if you ask me,' Eileen put in passionately. 'I told him he could examine my . . .'

'Nan, no,' Lily cried, clapping a hand over Eileen's mouth. 'Totally inappropriate, especially given where we are.'

Eileen looked puzzled. 'What do you mean, where we are?'

'This event is to raise money for Breast Cancer Care,' Lily reminded her in a heated whisper, 'so it's not on to make light of what Harry does, when some of the women here could be his patients.'

'You're too sensitive, that's your trouble,' Eileen grumbled. 'I was only meaning it as a bit of fun.'

'My point exactly. There's nothing fun about it, now finish your coffee, the show's about to start.'

Picking up her empty glass, Eileen said, 'Do you reckon they'd serve us more vino if we asked?'

'No,' Bel said firmly.

'What is she like?' Lily muttered.

'You're getting yourself too many airs and graces, my girl,' Eileen told her, 'but I suppose that's a good thing, we want you going up in the world. Oh, here we are,' she declared, as the compère came on to the stage to thunderous applause.

'Are you OK?' Kristina whispered to Bel.

Suspecting she was concerned about the mention of Harry, Bel said, 'Yes, I'm fine. Honestly,' she added when Kristina didn't look convinced. Actually, what she was finding far more difficult at the moment was the constant reminder of Talia. However, she wasn't going to dwell on her own issues on Josie's big day, and besides, since the chat she'd had with Josie in the churchyard, she hadn't been feeling quite so down. It was as though putting her past into words, instead of harbouring it like a lead weight inside her, had started to unlock at least some of the angst.

Whether it was temporary, or she really had taken a first step forward, she still didn't know, but she'd find out over time. Meanwhile, what mattered most of all today was that she held it together for Josie's family, since she knew from experience how emotional the next hour was going to be.

'Isn't he the chap off *The X Factor*?' Eileen asked Lily, as a young lad came on to sing.

'That's what they just said,' Lily told her. 'He won a couple of years ago.'

'I thought he was runner-up.'

'Does it matter?'

'Shut up talking,' Jeff hissed at Eileen.

Poking out her tongue, she reached across the table and seized the rest of his wine.

Catching his eye Bel gave him a smile, and almost received one in return. He was so tense, poor guy. He'd hardly eaten or drunk a thing, and she understood why:

he was terrified Josie might have another seizure in the midst of things.

Praying that wasn't going to happen, she sat back to enjoy the performance, not only from the singer, but from Eileen and Carly who were arm-bopping in their chairs like a couple of teenagers, while Lily hid behind her hand pretending not to know them.

'Here, have you seen the brochure?' Eileen demanded, as the applause died down. 'Our Josie's only in it! Lovely photo it is too, and have you seen what she wrote?'

Since Bel had helped Josie put together the short piece about her diagnosis, how life had been since and why she was so grateful to Breast Cancer Care, she was able to smile and nod.

'And she's not the youngest model,' Eileen went on, 'not by a long shot. There's one poor girl here only thirty-one and mother of three. That's bloody wicked, that is, innit, someone like her having cancer.'

'Kids get it too,' Carly reminded her.

'I know, but all the same. Anyways,' she carried on to Bel, 'there's some full-page articles in here what a couple of the models wrote, and I reckon our Josie ought to do one next year. She can talk about how brilliant you've been with her, and how she wouldn't of known you if it weren't for Breast Cancer Care. You know, stuff like that.'

'Ssh,' Lily whispered, as one of the celebrity guests took the mike.

Glad to let the subject drop, Bel wondered how much of Josie's illness Eileen had actually taken in. Surely she must understand there was a chance Josie wouldn't make it to this time next year. On the other hand, who was she, Bel, to rule out the possibility of a miracle, or to doubt the strength of Josie's will?

The celebrity was being thanked and applauded now, and after the compère explained about the raffle and silent auction another famous face stepped on to the stage – an actor from one of the soaps, they were told. Though Bel had never seen him before, it was clear from Eileen's and Carly's ooooohs that they had.

'Have you got the camera ready?' Bel asked Kristina,

experiencing a flutter of nerves for Josie as the opening music began. She'd be in the wings by now, adrenalin pumping into her veins as she prepared, with three others, to open the show.

'Right here,' Kristina assured her, bringing the camera out of her lap.

'They ought to be playing "I Will Survive",' Eileen declared. 'It'd be very fitting, that.'

'It would,' Carly agreed.

'Did you get that?' Bel whispered to Kristina. 'It'll make Josie laugh.'

'Cringe, more like,' Lily corrected. 'Oh my God, look, look, here she is.'

Kristina immediately rose to her feet capturing a wide shot of all four women as they emerged, before zooming in tighter to Josie who was second down the catwalk wearing a netted petticoat skirt from George at Asda, a white silk blouse also from George and four-inch stilettos from Next.

'Blimey, she looks gorgeous,' Lily gasped. 'I've never seen her in anything like that before.'

'She's a bloody marvel,' Eileen declared, and promptly let rip with a piercing whistle. 'That's it, Jose, go girl,' she cried.

Choking back a laugh, while hoping Josie hadn't heard above the music, Bel joined in clapping to the beat, loving the way Josie was sashaying confidently towards them, swinging her shoulders and smiling fit to burst.

Looking as though he couldn't believe this was his wife, Jeff sat staring at her, his eyes never leaving her as she gave a sassy little hip swing in front of them before swivelling round to start back up the catwalk.

Moments later she was gone and Kelly, with two more models, was parading along the runway, designer jeans tucked into leather biker boots, tweed jackets over skimpy silk dresses or fur gilets over vivid sequinned tops. The fact that every single one of them was at one stage or another of breast cancer – Kelly thank God in remission – would never have been known from how confidently and rhythmically they moved. The atmosphere in the room was so powerfully charged with the women's exultation that many onlookers already had tears running down their cheeks.

Then Josie was back onstage, a heart-stopping vision in a red full-length evening dress, strappy gold sandals and matching gold feather boa, all from QVC. Only Bel knew what difficulty she'd had with the shoes, but there was no staggering or flinching today as she slunk like a panther towards them, earning herself a cheer from the crowd and a burst of laughter from Lily and Bel. At the end of the catwalk, right in front of their table, she treated Jeff to an outrageously saucy wink, beckoning with one finger before tossing her head and turning back to the stage. Whether she heard Eileen's second whistle only she knew, but she surely caught Jeff's shocked expression before he broke into an uneasy chuckle.

'Never knew she had it in her,' he announced, finally starting to clap his hands.

'Isn't she fabulous?' Lily cried, tears streaming down her face. 'I'm so proud of her.'

More models were swarming down the ramp now, three men this time, six women in various shades of blue, and all moving like professional dancers to the beat.

'I can't believe how brilliant this is,' Lily said to Bel, as Kristina panned the camera round the table. 'It's like a proper show.'

'That's because it is a proper show,' Bel laughed.

'Bloody hell, is that her?' Eileen demanded, when Josie returned to the stage all kitted out like a sixties girl in black and white mini dress from Wallis, black slingback shoes from M&S and a black bob-cut wig from Natural Image.

'Yes, it's her,' Bel smiled, tears blurring her own eyes as Josie, one hand on her hip, the other clicking to the beat, wiggled down the catwalk, her inner glow making her so radiant it caught hard at Bel's heart. *In years to come*, Bel was thinking, *this is how I'm going to remember her.* Not all dressed up and acting her heart out, but happy, thrilled to be taking part and proud for her family to see her.

As she reached them they cheered and applauded with

all their might. Everyone was weeping now; it was impossible to remain dry-eyed in the face of so much resilience and courage, particularly when more than one woman on the stage was terminal.

It wasn't until Josie disappeared for the final change that Bel noticed how pale Jeff had become. Before she could ask if he was all right he was getting up from his chair and leaving the room.

She found him in a deserted hallway, leaning against a wall, his arms circling his head as he sobbed so hard he could barely stand. 'Josie, Josie, Josie,' he was gasping. 'Josie, please don't leave me.'

'Oh, Jeff,' Bel murmured, moving swiftly to hold him.

'I can't lose her, Bel, I just can't,' he choked wretchedly.

'It's not happening yet,' she assured him, tears starting from her own eyes.

'Oh God, I don't want to go on without her,' he sobbed. 'Nothing's going to be worth it. She's my life, Bel. She means everything to me.'

'I know, and you mean the same to her.'

Pushing the heel of his hand into his eyes, he said, 'Why can't it be happening to me? Everyone loves her, the kids, our mates, everyone . . .'

'They love you too.'

'Not like they love her. She's special, Bel, you know that.'

'Yes, I do, and I wish to God I knew how to change things, but all we can do is make the most of the time she has left. That's what she's doing in there today, and knowing you're watching means the world to her. Please don't miss her finale, Jeff. It's amazing and she's been rehearsing so hard to get it right, just for you.'

Nodding as he struggled to catch his breath, he took her already sodden tissue to try and dry his eyes. 'I'm sorry,' he gasped, 'it all just got to me, seeing her up there like that and . . . Oh Christ, it's so bloody hard.'

'I know, but you can do it.'

'Dad! Bel!' Lily cried, running towards them. 'Oh God, Dad, it's Mum. You have to come.'

Jeff moved so fast that he was through the door and following Lily round to the back of the stage in seconds.

Bel was right behind him. They found Josie, collapsed on the floor in the dressing room, surrounded by two BCC nurses.

Jeff quickly took her in his arms. 'It's all right, my love,' he murmured against her cheek, 'I'm here, I've got you.'

'What happened?' Bel asked one of the nurses.

'It seemed like she had some sort of seizure,' the girl replied. 'The paramedics are on their way.'

Kneeling down next to Jeff, Bel took Josie's hand. 'Can you hear me, sweetheart?' she asked.

Josie's eyes flickered open. 'Jeff?' she murmured.

'I'm here, baby,' he said brokenly. 'You're all right, just a bit of a turn, nothing to worry about.'

'No, nothing to worry about,' she assured him weakly. 'Got to finish the show.'

Bel looked up at the stylist and both women shook their heads. Heartbroken though Josie would be to miss the finale, she simply wasn't strong enough to go back out there now.

'Stop fussing,' Josie scolded, as Jeff and Lily helped her in through the front door. 'I'm not an invalid. I can manage on my own, thank you.'

'Do you want to go straight up to bed?' Jeff asked worriedly, 'or would you rather sit in the chair for a while?'

'What I want is for you two to go on with whatever you're supposed to be doing, so I can do the same.'

'I'll put the kettle on,' Lily told her father, and headed for the kitchen.

'Then Dad'll take you to the station so you can get back to that husband of yours,' Josie called after her.

'Will you stop being so bossy?' Jeff chided, plumping up the cushions for her to sit down. 'You've been in hospital for two days, and they told you when you left you had to take things easy for a while.'

Josie regarded him askance. 'So what, I've got to sit around here feeling sorry for myself? It's not going to happen. I've got things to do, people to see.'

'Like what, and who?'

'Never you mind. Now give me a bit of peace, please. I

need to make some phone calls, and you ought to be out earning a living, especially after spending all that time in a five-star hotel. Honestly, what are you like? We can't let Bel foot the bill, you know, so we have to find a way of paying her back.'

'Don't worry, I will.'

She regarded him suspiciously. 'How? The same way you managed to pay for our Lily's dress?'

His face darkened. 'I borrowed that from your Steve, all right, and he gave me some good terms, so let it drop.'

Deciding she would, since she was more worn out than she was admitting after the long drive, when Jeff had gone off to the kitchen she sank down in her chair and took out her phone. Lots of texts, mostly from her beautiful fellow models wishing her well, bless every one of them; one from her mother saying she wouldn't sleep a wink until she knew Josie was home; and one from Bel asking her to call when she got in.

'Hi, it's me,' she said, when Bel picked up. 'Are you all right?'

'I'm the one who should be asking that,' Bel protested.

'Oh, I'm fine,' Josie assured her. 'No more fits and raring to go once I've had a cuppa. When did you get back?'

'About an hour ago. I don't suppose you've had a chance to check your emails?'

'No, but I will as soon as no one's looking over my shoulder.'

'So you haven't told Jeff about his surprise yet?'

'I couldn't with Lily in the car.'

'Good, because I honestly don't think it's going to work, Josie. I'll come over later, if you like, and we can talk it through . . .'

Worried, Josie said, 'I thought you were all for it?'

'What I said was I understand why you want to do it, but I think we should discuss it some more. By the way, when you go online you can check out the footage Kristina got of the fashion show. She's already uploaded it and you, my wonderful friend, are an absolute star.'

Josie chuckled. 'Apart from the extra bit of dancing I did backstage at the end. Never mind, at least I got to do most of the show, and everyone's been sending really lovely messages. Jeff's going to pay you back for the rooms, by the way. Who does he think he is, swanning about the Grosvenor House living the life of Riley while I get stuffed into scanners and hospital beds?' Her arms were still bruised from all the blood they'd taken, and she'd been warned she would probably have to have more radio-therapy. Dr Pattullo would tell her more when she went to see her next week.

'I don't want paying back,' Bel was saying, 'and I'm not going to argue about it either. I just want you to rest after the journey and unless you call to tell me not to, I'll come over around four. Will Lily still be there?'

'I hope not. She's got her own life to lead, and . . .'

'I'm not going anywhere until after you've seen Dr Pattullo,' Lily interrupted hotly as she brought a liquorice tea in from the kitchen. 'Do you want something to eat? Dad's making cheese sandwiches.'

'I'm all right,' Josie assured her, 'but you should have a bite *before you go*.'

'Not listening,' Lily retorted, head in the air as she returned to help her father.

'Children, who'd have 'em?' Josie sighed, and feeling as though she'd like to sleep for a week, she allowed her eyes to flutter closed.

Whether she spoke to Bel again after that she had no idea, she only knew, when she woke up, that her tea had gone cold and someone had turned off her phone. There didn't seem to be any sign of anyone, either.

Turning her mobile back on, she forced herself up to her feet and looked outside for Jeff's car. Seeing it wasn't there, she called out for Lily and got no reply.

Satisfied she was alone, she went through to the kitchen and found a note telling her that Lily had popped over to Asda and would be back in half an hour. Since she hadn't said what time she was leaving, that could be any minute, so Josie quickly set up her laptop to check her emails.

Floods of them, again mostly from her new friends at Breast Cancer Care who she was determined to stay in touch with, a couple about her hospital appointment next

Wednesday and one from Kristina containing the link to the video.

Nothing from Dawnie.

Disappointed, and more downcast than she ought to have been, she spent a few minutes watching the video, which cheered her up no end. She'd had such a lot of fun that day, and all the rehearsal days leading up to it, but now it felt very depressing to know she probably wouldn't be able to do anything like it again.

Still, the important thing, she reminded herself forcefully, was that she'd done it at all, and all thanks to Bel.

'I'm awake now,' she announced when Bel answered the phone, 'but you don't have to come all the way over here, you've done enough driving today, all the way back from London.'

'If you're saying that because you're still tired, I won't come,' Bel replied.

'I am, a bit,' Josie admitted. She always was, no matter how hard she tried not to be. 'She hasn't emailed back,' she stated flatly. 'I thought she would have by now. I wonder if my message got spammed.'

'It might have,' Bel conceded, 'but what you're asking of her isn't easy, and to be honest, I really don't think it's going to be what Jeff wants.'

'It'd be better than having to live on his own,' Josie pointed out, 'and they were in love back then. For all I know they still are, so I just want them to know that I forgive them and they can have my blessing if they want to be together. I told her that in the email.' She was starting to cry; it was hard thinking of Jeff growing old with somebody else, when she wanted to be that person.

'Oh, Josie,' Bel said soothingly, 'I know you mean well, but you can't organise their lives for them. Talia tried with me and Nick, and it got us into a terrible muddle. You just have to let them find one another, if it's what they want, and as I said just now, I don't think Jeff will want it at all.'

Josie didn't know what to say.

'During the show,' Bel continued, 'before you collapsed, he completely broke down. Not in front of anyone, he took himself out of the room, but I followed. He really loves you,

Josie. Whatever happened with Dawnie . . . Call it a mistake, an aberration if you like, but there's no doubt in my mind that you're the one he loves – always has, and always will.'

Josie's tears were coming so fast now she couldn't speak. She had to try and pull herself together before Lily came back, but she just didn't know how.

'Are you still there?' Bel asked softly.

'Ye-es,' Josie sobbed. 'He's a daft old sod, isn't he, but I love him so much and I can't bear to think of him on his own.'

'The only advice I can give you is to try to pull your thoughts back from that, and stay in the present. I know I keep saying it, but the value of today is so much greater than the value of a tomorrow you can only imagine, so it doesn't have any actual truth.'

'I know you're right,' Josie sniffed, 'it's just that some-times it comes over me in a way I can't do anything about. I'll be all right in a minute. Lily'll be back and we can watch the video together. Kristina did a lovely job, didn't she? She ought to be a professional.'

'I'll tell her that.'

Josie tried to think of something else to say, but she was afraid if she opened her mouth she'd just sob.

'Will you call me if you need to talk?' Bel asked gently. 'You know I'll come over any time, or we can chat on the phone.'

Hardly able to get the words out, Josie said, 'You have to stop being kind to me.'

With a smile in her voice, Bel replied, 'They say what goes around comes around, so with all the kindness you dish out, I'm afraid you have to expect some back.'

'Then you have to be in for a good helping of it too,' Josie insisted. 'Here's our Lily coming in now, so I'll let you go. Thanks for taking care of Jeff. You're a good person, Bel Monkton. My very own angel.'

Lily was no sooner in the door than she was at Josie's side, wanting to know why she was crying.

'Oh, it's you lot, on the video,' Josie told her, waving a hand at the computer, 'when I saw how you were all blub-bing, it got me going too.'

Hugging her, Lily said, 'So you've seen it. Isn't it fantastic? You were so brilliant. I'm dead proud of you.'

'I have to admit, I feel quite proud of myself.' Josie was thinking it was something Lily would be able to show her children one day, but it probably wasn't a good idea to say so. 'Where's Dad?' she asked, going to help put the shopping away.

'I'm not all that sure,' Lily replied. 'He got a call from someone and said he had to go out, so maybe he's gone to work.'

Thinking of him breaking down at the show brought more tears flooding back to Josie's eyes. It seemed she couldn't stop today, so maybe it would be best if she let Lily carry on down here while she went to tuck herself up in bed.

Chapter Twenty-Five

Bel had just arrived home after a long, rainy morning at the barn when Lily called her mobile to ask if they could meet.

'I thought you were going to the hospital with Mum,' Bel replied, shrugging off her dripping raincoat.

'That's where I am,' Lily told her, 'but Dad's here too, so I thought, if I got the bus to yours . . . There's something I need to ask you.'

'Of course. I'm planning to be here all afternoon, so come when you like.' After ringing off, she immediately clicked on again to take a call from Kristina.

'Are you still at the barn?' Kristina asked.

'Just got home. It's a quagmire out there today, and not a lot's happening.'

'But the good news is,' Kristina announced, 'they're delivering the trailer tomorrow, so we'll have an office.'

'Fantastic,' Bel exclaimed in relief. Since Kristina had joined the project on a part-time basis, she'd found herself way more organised. She was even considering taking on another, smaller barn, over on Exmoor, now she had someone besides the builder to bounce ideas off.

Perhaps Kristina was her and Nick's angel; she just hadn't wanted to see her that way.

By the time they'd finished discussing various other matters concerning roof lights, gable ends and the square metreage of an oak floor, she'd made herself a bowl of soup and was just sitting down to enjoy it when the gardener turned up. With autumn now well under way there was plenty she needed to discuss with him, so abandoning her lunch she grabbed a dry coat and went outside to give instructions.

She was still there when Lily arrived, looking cold and worried and, Bel thought, very, very young.

'Come on, let's go in,' she urged, leading the way. 'It's a miserable day, isn't it?'

'You're telling me.' Lily shivered, drawing her jacket more tightly around her. 'Thanks for letting me come over.'

'Would you like some soup?' Bel offered, ushering her through to the kitchen. 'It won't take a moment to heat.'

'No, I'm fine thanks,' Lily assured her. 'I had something earlier.'

Deciding to save hers for later, Bel emptied the bowl back into the saucepan and put the kettle on. 'How's it going at the hospital?' she asked.

Josie shrugged. 'They were still waiting to go in when I left, but Mum seemed OK. You know what she's like, she'll always tell you she's fine, even when she's not, but she hasn't been too bad these last few days.'

'She's sounded quite up when we've spoken on the phone,' Bel agreed. 'She's amazing, the way she's coping with it all.'

Lily nodded, but her expression was glum, reminding Bel of how down she used to get when Talia was having a good spell. It was the only time she could allow her energy to wane. 'So what would you like to talk about?' she asked, waving Lily to a chair.

As she sat down at the table, Lily said, 'I've discussed it with Jasper, and we decided you were the best person to ask.'

Intrigued, Bel went to sit with her. This surely couldn't be about Josie's funeral arrangements, it was far too soon for that – unless Josie had come up with some wacky idea that had her family worried. Bel wouldn't put it past her: after all, the attempt to contact Dawnie Hopkins had been pretty out there, and she was afraid Josie might not have given up on that yet.

'The thing is,' Lily said, twisting her fingers, 'well . . . I'm going to have a baby.'

Though Bel broke into a smile, she understood right away why Lily wasn't looking thrilled. 'That's wonderful news,' she said softly. 'Congratulations.'

'Thanks,' Lily whispered. 'We're really pleased, even though we didn't plan on it happening so soon. The trouble is, we can't decide whether or not to tell Mum. It'll be horrible for her, having to deal with the fact that she might never see the baby, and so I was wondering . . . Well, do you think it might be easier for her if she didn't know anything about it?'

Bel inhaled deeply. 'How far along are you?' she asked carefully.

'Only a month. So there's ages to go yet, and if she . . . If she doesn't make it . . .'

'Oh, Lily,' Bel murmured, going to hug her as she started to sob.

'It's so awful,' Lily wept. 'I love her so much and I can't bear to think of being without her.'

'I know,' Bel murmured, hardly able to think about it herself.

'It's going to be terrible for Dad. He'll be so lonely, and when Ryan comes out . . . He's always been lost without Mum and he might not even see her properly before she goes. Oh God, I'm sorry,' Lily choked, 'I promised myself I wouldn't break down . . .'

'Ssh,' Bel soothed, stroking her hair. 'You cry as much as you need to. It's a very difficult thing you're going through, probably one of the worst you'll ever face.'

As more tears streamed down her cheeks, Lily wailed, 'She'd be the world's best granny, just like she's the world's best mum. It's so unfair, Bel. Why is it happening? It's just not right.'

'No, it isn't,' Bel agreed, 'she's too young, and so are you. I don't know why it has to be like this, I wish I did, perhaps then we could make some sense of it.'

Trying to catch her breath, Lily said, 'Do you reckon, if we went to church, it would help?'

'You could definitely try,' Bel replied. 'A lot of people find a great deal of comfort in turning to God.'

Lily nodded. 'I think Ryan will. He says his prayers all the time about Mum.' Her eyes turned desperate. 'It doesn't seem to be doing any good, does it?'

How could Bel tell her otherwise? 'Maybe things happen on a level we don't understand,' she ventured.

Lily nodded, seeming to want to believe that. 'Did you turn to God when it was happening to your sister?' she asked.

Bel sighed. 'Not really. I tried for a while, so did Nick and Talia herself, but we'd none of us grown up as believers, so we never really got much from it. That isn't to say you wouldn't, because there's every chance you would.'

Lily shook her head. 'We only got married in church because we thought it was what our parents would want,' she said. 'Maybe that's wrong. I suppose it is, really.'

'I like to think, if there is a God, that he'd be willing to forgive our lack of understanding, considering how little evidence of himself he's given us to go on.'

Lily smiled distantly. 'Ryan, or Chaplain Paul, would say that he shows himself all the time, if we just cared to look. Like in nature, or near misses, or people we meet. I've been reading about miracles online, and they do seem to happen.'

Not doubting that for a minute, Bel said, 'We just have to hope that God, or fate or whatever, decides to perform one for Mum.'

Lily was looking thoughtful. 'If we believe passionately enough that she'll get better, maybe we could make it happen for her?' she suggested.

Knowing how difficult that was in the face of medical science, Bel said, 'There's certainly no harm in trying.'

'She has to believe it too. And Dad. Maybe knowing about the baby will make her fight so hard that she'll turn things around for herself?'

Bel smiled. 'In which case, you'll need to tell her.'

Lily smiled too. 'I will,' she declared, glancing over her shoulder as someone knocked on the front door.

'Wait there,' Bel said, 'it's probably the gardener about to leave.'

To her surprise, it turned out to be Josie and Jeff, and the brightness of Josie's smile, contrasting so starkly with the shell-shocked look on Jeff's face, made Bel's heart turn over.

'Is our Lily here?' Josie asked. 'She said she was coming.'

Bel nodded and gestured for them to go through. 'What is it?' she asked as Josie hung back.

'Liver and lungs,' Josie told her matter-of-factly. 'Not much they can do now. A few weeks, they reckon, and it'll all be over.'

'Oh my God,' Bel gasped, pressing a hand to her mouth.

'There, there,' Josie said, giving her arm a pat. 'It'll be all right. At least it won't be happening right on Christmas. It'd spoil it for everyone if it did.'

'Oh, Josie,' Bel choked, unable to imagine any time of year feeling right without her.

Hearing Lily cry, 'No! Mum!' Josie blanched as she said, 'Jeff's told her,' and opening her arms as Lily ran into the hall she caught her hard.

'There, there,' Josie murmured, rubbing her back.

'No, Mum, no, no, no,' Lily sobbed. 'You can't let them be right, you just can't.'

Holding her tighter, Josie turned her own teary eyes to Bel. 'Sorry about loading all this on you,' she apologised.

'Oh Josie, please don't say that,' Bel urged.

Josie smiled, but Bel could see the fathomless depths of her sadness. 'We ought not to leave Jeff on his own,' she said.

Leading the way through, Bel found Jeff standing at the window staring out at the bleak afternoon sky. She wished she had some words to offer that might make a difference, but knew that none existed. Hope was turning to dust, dreams were fading to nothing.

If only Talia could offer some comfort now, some sort of reassurance that Josie would be fine on the other side and no one was to worry.

'I'm going to tell her,' Lily whispered to Bel. 'I think I have to.'

Bel nodded in agreement. If anything could make Josie fight, this would be it.

Josie was regarding them curiously. 'Tell me what?' she asked.

Turning to her, Lily took her hands as she said, 'I'm going to have a baby.'

Josie's face lit up. 'Well there's a lovely piece of news,'

she declared, as if this was all it would take to make everything else go away. 'Just what we need to cheer us up. Jeff, did you hear that? We're going to be grandparents, my love.'

Though Jeff nodded, he kept his back turned.

Going to him, Lily put an arm round his shoulders and rested her head against his.

'He'll be a very good granddad,' Josie told Bel.

And you, Bel was thinking, *would be the world's best granny.*

As though reading her mind, Josie twinkled. 'Come on, let's get that kettle on,' she said. 'We've got some celebrating to do,' and before Bel could make a move she headed off for the teapot.

A week later Josie was sitting in her chair at home, glad to be alone for five minutes, though keen for Jeff to come back. She wasn't sure where he'd gone. He'd probably said on his way out and she'd forgotten or hadn't heard – it was hard to know when her brain might not be acting properly. Not that she was aware of any glitches, she felt the same as she always had, but then she might not know if things had changed, and chances were no one wanted to tell her. Although she reckoned the palliative care team would, even if Jeff and Lily wouldn't.

What a lovely bunch of people they were, so kind and thoughtful – it was always a pleasure to see them. They never seemed to mind taking the time to explain about the treatment they were giving her, although she had to admit she didn't listen all that closely. As long as she wasn't in any pain, or making a nuisance of herself with fits and the like, she was happy to let all the medical jargon wash over her. It was enough for her to know she was in good hands, and she didn't doubt that for a minute.

She'd just finished five sessions of radiotherapy in as many days, so she was quite tired today. Her back ached, so did her head, but on the whole she wasn't as bad as she'd been expecting, and luckily not nearly as down as she'd been yesterday.

She was finding that the panic came and went, a bit like the pain. While steroids and radio got rid of one, she had to rely on herself to deal with the other, and though she wasn't always up to beating it she never stopped trying. She didn't want to be someone who went out screaming, scaring her loved ones half out of their wits and leaving them feeling even more traumatised than they already were. She wanted to go quietly, preferably at home, but if it all got too much for Jeff she was OK about going to the hospice. They'd gone for a look round the other day and it was really quite nice.

It was all very well people taking care of her, and she was glad of it, but what she wanted to know was who was going to take care of Jeff after she'd gone? Where would he go, what would he do if they took this house away? Chances were they would, because without her benefits boosting their income he wouldn't be able to afford the bedroom tax so everything in his life would change, and she could hardly bear to think of him having to set up home on his own. Of course Lily would help, but if they put him in one of the high-rise flats on the north side it would likely be the end of him.

'You have to stop getting yourself in a state over me,' he kept telling her. 'I'll manage, all right? I'm not an invalid and work's picking up, so for all we know I might be able to afford the tax.'

'But even if you can, who's going to cook and clean for you, make sure your clothes are washed and ironed, go to the supermarket, the . . .'

'Josie, you're not doing yourself any good.'

'But you've never done any of it, and you'll be too tired if you've been at work all day.'

'Then I'll get myself a butler,' he decided, and that was when she had to laugh.

The other thing that was tearing her up, apart from having no chance of seeing her grandchild, which was breaking her heart over and over, was the fact that she was hardly ever able to make it to the prison now, and she still hadn't been able to persuade Jeff to go in her place.

'This is my dying wish,' she'd cried only yesterday, 'to know that you and Ryan have made up. How can you deny me that when he's your own son? You have to forgive him now, Jeff. Please, do it for me.'

'If I've told you once, I've told you a thousand times,' he retorted, 'I am never going to set foot inside a prison.'

'Then write to him. Let him know that you'll be there for him when he comes out. It'll mean the world to him, especially now.'

'I'll deal with it when the time comes,' he replied, 'so let's leave it there.'

She ought to put her foot down even harder, she knew that, but she didn't always have enough fight in her. She'd make him do it though, she really would, even if it was the last thing she did.

Smiling and feeling her heart churn as she recalled the time she'd said that to Bel the day they'd sat together in the churchyard, she considered calling Bel now, just for a chat. Not since Dawnie had she found it so easy to talk to someone, and though she didn't like to make comparisons, especially when Dawnie and Bel were from such different worlds, she couldn't imagine Bel ever letting her down the way Dawnie had. If she didn't want to be forgiven and get back together with Jeff that was one thing, but to ignore the fact that she, Josie, had cancer – she could hardly believe Dawnie would do that.

'It just goes to show,' she said to Bel when she got through to her, 'you never really know someone until the chips are down. Having said that, we still don't know if I got spammed, so I'm not going to think badly of her. I'm just going to hope she's happy wherever she is, and that she forgives me for taking Jeff away from her, because that might be the way she sees it.'

'And only you would ever be that generous,' Bel said fondly. 'Whoever, wherever she is, she never deserved a best friend like you, but speaking selfishly, her loss is my gain.'

Josie glowed. 'Oh go on with you,' she chuckled, 'you've got far more . . .'

'Josie, don't you dare deny being my best friend or I'll have to come over there and throttle you. True, there aren't many contenders for the position, but I've told you this before, and I'll tell you again, you're the best thing that's happened to me since Talia died. Actually, even before that.'

Though thrilled, Josie couldn't help wishing Bel was saying that about Harry – or at least someone else she might be falling in love with.

'It's funny how different our conversations are now, isn't it?' she remarked. 'Or is it only me who feels that?'

Because she understood, Bel said, 'Talia used to say they were more honest, because they had to be, so I'm going to be honest with you, Josie . . .'

'No, before you do that,' Josie cut in, 'please let me speak first. I reckon they've got it all wrong . . .' Hearing Jeff's car pull up outside, she groaned. 'Jeff's just come back,' she said, 'but that's OK, because I'd rather see your eyes when I tell you what's in my mind. I know you'll think I'm crazy, but I also think you'll understand. Now I'd better go, because his key's just gone in the door,' and clicking off the line, she tilted her head to one side as though she was sleeping.

'All right, go quietly,' she heard Jeff whispering. 'Take your stuff upstairs . . .'

Josie opened her eyes.

'Hello love,' Jeff said, coming into the room. 'Are you all right? I thought you were asleep.'

'Just dozing,' she told him.

'Do you want me to leave you alone?'

'Don't be daft. Who's with you?'

He gave a quick glance over his shoulder. 'It's someone to see you,' he said, turning back. 'Now, don't go having a heart attack on me, we've got enough problems without that, but anyway, here he is . . .' and standing aside he left an empty space behind him – until Ryan stepped into it.

Josie gasped and cried, 'Oh, my love, my boy.' She was out of her chair, pulling him into her arms. 'Ryan,' she sobbed. 'My baby.'

Wrapping her frailness gently, he said, 'Mum, you're going to get through this, OK? You're not going anywhere yet. The Good Lord already told me so, and if you don't believe in miracles it's about time you did.'

She drew back to look at him, her dearest little guinea

pig, standing here in her living room, as large as life and twice as bold. 'I believe in them now,' she whispered, cupping his face in her hands.

Ryan turned to his father. 'Come here,' Jeff growled, and pulled him into a giant bear hug. 'This is what your mother wants to see,' he said, and as father and son clung to one another Josie could only laugh through her tears.

'How can this be? What happened?' she implored.

Keeping an arm round Ryan's shoulders, Jeff said, 'There's been a lot of to-ing and fro-ing with the lawyers and the cops – I didn't want to tell you in case it didn't come good, but it turns out Debbie Prince grassed up her boy. She told them he was the one who'd coshed the bloke, and that our Ryan was only the lookout.'

Josie's eyes were wide with awe.

'So they decided,' Ryan continued, 'that I'd served enough time for that and so I could be released.'

'According to the lawyer,' Jeff added, 'you being sick was taken into consideration, and so it all went through as quickly as they could make it and I got the call yesterday to say he'd be on his way home today.'

Josie's hands were pressed to her cheeks. She could hardly believe it, and yet there he was, her precious boy, looking a lot more grown up than he had before he went in, with his rusty beard and beautiful piercing blue eyes. Reaching out her arms, she said, 'We've got a lot to talk about, but right now all I want to do is keep hold of you so I can make myself believe my dreams are really coming true.'

Two days later, with Jeff waiting outside in the car, Josie was in Debbie Prince's front room, staring at the tattooed woman and thinking of Bel's mother's words that everyone had it in them to be an angel. She'd never have imagined one coming from the north side of the estate, much less the notorious Prince family, but it just went to show how wrong she could be.

'I've come to thank you,' she said softly.

Debbie Prince sucked on her cigarette and regarded her through slit eyes.

'What made you do it?' Josie asked.

Debbie Prince started to cough. 'What do you think? It was you, coming round here with your sob story.'

'I didn't think you believed me.'

Debbie shrugged. 'Yeah, well, I did a bit of asking around and it turns out you was on the level. So I got to thinking and I decided it wasn't fair for your boy to be taking the rap for what I knew mine had done.'

So she had known. 'You went to the police?'

'No, I contacted the law firm you used and they sorted it.'

Josie shook her head in amazement. All this had been happening without her having any idea. Did they owe the lawyers now? It didn't matter; whatever they had to pay would be worth it, and they'd find it somehow. 'What's happening to your son?' she asked. 'Have they extended his sentence?'

'That's still in the works. There might have to be another trial.'

Though Josie baulked at the thought of Ryan being involved, she simply said, 'Maybe they'll decide to leave things as they are.'

Debbie Prince shrugged and coughed again as she ground out her roll-up. 'The world's better off with him behind bars,' she wheezed. 'He's an evil little bastard, got no morals, beats up his sisters and me, his own mother, if he don't get his way. Even his father's ashamed of him and Bob's no saint, I can tell you, but he's never gone round threatening little kids, or thieving from people he knows. The bloke Bob offed was asking for it, but that's another story.'

Not sure what to say to that, Josie decided it was time to leave. She wasn't feeling all that special, and the last thing she wanted was to pass out on Debbie Prince's carpet.

'Oi, Mrs,' Debbie Prince shouted, as Josie reached the missing garden gate.

Josie turned round to find her unlikely angel standing in the doorway.

Seeming uncomfortable, Debbie waved a hand as she said, 'Good luck.'

Josie smiled. 'Thank you,' she responded. 'To you too,'

and feeling perversely sad that she'd probably never see this woman again, she got into the car.

'All right?' Jeff asked as they pulled away.

Josie nodded. 'I'm glad we came.'

'Did she wonder why Ryan wasn't with you?'

'If she did, she didn't ask. Have you heard from him?'

'Yeah, he's back at home now and the news is, he can start college at the beginning of next term. He'll have to earn while he's studying, he knows that, but he's already made an appointment at the jobcentre so at least he's starting off the right way.'

Thank goodness for that, but Josie couldn't help worrying how long it would last when one of the biggest losses of Ryan's life was on such a close horizon. It just about broke her heart to think of him falling apart as he tried to carry on without her.

'Have faith, Mum,' he kept saying. 'You don't have to listen to what the doctors are saying. God's in charge, he's the one you should talk to.'

She didn't argue, she simply did as he said, because for all she knew he was right, and she wanted to see her boy settled almost as badly as she longed to hold Lily's baby in her arms and to know that Jeff was going to be all right. She couldn't go now, she wasn't ready, none of them were, but how could she make it stop?

'What are you thinking about?' Jeff asked as they pulled up outside the house.

Josie shook her head. 'Oh, nothing,' she replied dismissively. 'I think I'll give Bel a call when we get in, she'll be waiting to hear how it went with Debbie Prince.'

Bel was wearing a hard hat and goggles as she climbed the scaffold at the back of the barn, when one of the workmen called out that there was someone to see her.

Feeling her heart sink at the prospect of another run-in with the farmer, who seemed bent on interfering with the project, she made her way back to ground level and clicked on her phone as it rang. 'Hi Josie,' she said, deciding the farmer could wait. 'How did it go with Debbie Prince?'

411

'OK,' Josie replied. 'She's an oddball, that's for sure, but as far as I'm concerned she's definitely one of your mother's angels.'

Bel smiled, and stepped out of the rain into the shelter of a work tent. 'Where are you now?' she asked.

'We've just got home. Our Ryan's been accepted for college.'

'That's marvellous news. I can't wait to meet him.'

'He wants to meet you too. He'll be looking for a job, so if there's anything going at your barn . . .'

'I'm sure we can find something . . .'

'He's going to be studying in the day,' she heard Jeff saying.

'Oh yes,' Josie responded. 'Well, it was a thought. I expect he'll find something in a pub, or maybe Fliss can give him some shifts at the caff if I teach him to cook.'

'You and your ideas,' Bel heard Jeff grumble. 'You're trying to run the world, when what you ought to be doing is taking care of yourself. That's what we want to hear, isn't it Bel, that she's putting herself first for once.'

'Absolutely,' Bel responded, 'but I'm not sure we'll have much luck with it.'

'How's it going over there?' Josie asked. 'I was thinking we might take a drive out to have a look one day next week.'

'If you're feeling up to it, you'll be very welcome,' Bel assured her. 'Try to pick a day when it's dry though, it's pretty filthy underfoot when it isn't.'

'We're not worried about a bit of mud, are we Jeff? Oh, I think our Lily's trying to get through so I'd better go.'

Clicking off her end, Bel started round to the site office, preparing to do battle with the farmer. It was a dismal day and though they were more or less on schedule with the build, the forecast for the next week was making it unlikely they'd stay that way. Still, at least Kristina was on top of the paperwork, and a recent problem with the foundations was in the process of being solved.

Having Kristina on board was proving even more of a godsend than Bel had expected. Being an archaeologist by trade, she knew all about digging and foundations and the restoration of old relics, which the barn most certainly was. She was also a bit of an admin fiend, which suited Bel no end, given how much she detested paperwork. Just yesterday they'd signed for another, smaller barn, to start building up their portfolio of properties ripe for conversion or renovation. So perhaps Bel could finally say she was managing to move on with her life.

'OK, where is he?' she asked the workman who'd summoned her.

He looked around, and nodded towards the gaping entrance to the barn. 'He should have a hat on if he's going in there,' the workman commented.

Bel barely heard him. She was too stunned to register anything beyond the fact that someone who looked very like Harry appeared to be surveying the barn's interior.

Her first thought was for Josie – he'd come to break some awful news – but that made no sense when she'd only just got off the phone with her, and anyway she wasn't Harry's patient now. He'd surely have been kept informed of her progress though, but even so . . . Maybe his mother wanted to buy another apartment, and he was hoping to enlist Bel's help. Or he could simply have been passing and thought he'd drop in to find out how things were going. Since that was by far the most likely scenario, she quickly quashed all others, and began making her way through puddles and builders' debris towards him.

'Harry?' she said, as she reached him.

Turning, he broke into a smile and she felt her insides floating. Apparently her attraction to him hadn't diminished at all over the months; if anything, it was as strong as ever.

'Hi, how are you?' he asked.

'Yes, I'm fine,' she replied. 'And you?'

Nodding, he drew a hand over his jaw as he glanced back inside the barn. 'It seems to be coming along,' he remarked.

'Slowly.'

After a moment he turned to look at her again, and afraid her feelings might show, she glanced ahead, saying, 'Would you like to have a look round? There's still not much to see, I'm afraid . . .'

'Actually, I was hoping we could talk,' he said.

Her heart gave a brutal jolt. 'Of course,' she responded, too quickly, and felt herself blush. She turned towards the office. 'It's a bit warmer and drier inside,' she said, 'and I might be able to rustle up a coffee, if you have time.'

'Sounds good,' he smiled.

Feeling the scrutiny of the workforce as she led the way across to the trailer, she pushed open the sticky door and held it for him to go in ahead of her.

'You're not at the hospital today?' she queried, going to the kitchenette as he gazed at the plans and photographs covering the walls.

'I've just got back from Milan,' he replied, 'and I'm not due in again until tomorrow.'

'Were you on holiday?'

'Medical conference.'

'Sorry, it's not great,' she grimaced as she handed him a coffee.

He took a sip of the viscous brew, and the way his eyebrows rose made her smile. *Could he feel the chemistry, or was it just her?* She was going to hate it when he left; this meeting was likely to set her back months.

Putting the mug down, he said, 'I guess I ought to come to the point of why I'm here.'

Tense though she was, she managed to nod.

'Well, I . . . I'm back at the apartment,' he announced.

Registering the words, she became very still.

'Things didn't work out with my wife.'

She could feel herself quietly reeling. Was he thinking he could pick up with her again as though no word for months didn't matter at all? 'I'm sorry to hear that,' she said evenly.

His eyes went down. 'I don't know if you're going to want to hear this.' He paused. 'But the problem this time was that I couldn't stop thinking about you.'

She suddenly couldn't breathe.

'I'm sorry if I've got it wrong,' he went on quickly, 'I was never sure if you felt the same way about me . . .'

'I did,' she blurted.

His eyes darkened with humour. 'You did?'

She nodded.

'Then you made a good job of hiding it.'

She couldn't deny that. 'So did you,' she countered.

'Because I thought you weren't . . . That you didn't . . .' He laughed and dashed a hand through his hair. 'Why didn't you ever tell me?' he asked.

'I thought you were trying to get over your wife. Why didn't you ever tell me?'

He shook his head. 'I guess I sensed a distance, a line I shouldn't cross, and so I thought maybe . . .' He threw out his hands. 'I don't know what I thought, I just knew I wanted there to be more between us, but I wasn't convinced it was what you had in mind. Then my wife said she thought we should try again, and for the children's sake . . .' He shrugged.

Understanding, Bel asked, 'How long did you stay?'

'A couple of months. I kind of knew even before I moved back that it was doomed, but I had to give it a go.'

'Of course.'

'I wanted to stay in touch with you, so badly,' he said softly, 'but I knew if I did the reconciliation would be over before it began. It was anyway, because like I said, I couldn't stop thinking about you. I picked up the phone so many times, but it wasn't the right thing to do when I was still with my wife. After I moved back to the flat . . . Well, I could never convince myself you'd want to hear from me.'

'I did, all the time,' she confessed.

'As a friend?'

'Not only that.'

His eyes seemed to be melting into hers. 'Can we . . . ? Do you think we can . . . ?'

'Yes,' she nodded.

He smiled and they both laughed. 'Do you know what I'd like to do now?' he said.

She waited.

'I'd like to kiss you, if I may.'

'I'd like that very much.'

415

'So maybe,' he murmured, more humour shining in his eyes, 'you'd like to take off the hat and glasses?'

Spluttering on a laugh, she quickly removed them and stepped into his arms.

The feel of him against her, the taste of his mouth, was so wonderfully consuming she wanted it never to end. And it didn't for a very long time, until he finally said, 'Are you doing anything tonight?'

Still dazed from the kiss, she told him, 'I think I am now, but there are things you should know about me . . .'

'That I'm looking forward to finding out about,' he interrupted, 'but we have plenty of time.'

As he kissed her again, she felt more happiness than she could contain sweeping through her, and could hardly wait to tell Josie.

Chapter Twenty-Six

Josie couldn't be sure what happened to turn things around, or when exactly it began taking shape. There wasn't any sort of epiphany as such, it was something that came about more subtly and powerfully, as the threads of her family's love caught around her heart and bound it with a fierce determination to stay with them.

It helped too that Lily had shown her an article about five women who'd been told they were terminal, and years later every one of them was still going strong. Ryan was telling her about miracles all the time, and even Jeff seemed to believe in them – and why wouldn't he, when the few weeks the doctors had given her passed quietly by and she remained with them all?

No one could explain why the cancer had stopped growing, but it had, and as far as she was concerned that was all that mattered. She didn't even need to take much medication now, and her hair had completely grown back after she'd lost it a second time thanks to the radio. The really weird thing was that the cancer was still there in her body; it just didn't seem to be doing anything.

'Everyone's different,' Harry had told her, 'and you're not the first to defy medical science. It happens more than you might think, and believe me, no one is happier when it does than us so-called experts. We just wish we could distil the reasons into a treatment to share with everyone.'

Josie was loving watching Bel and Harry together. They were such a good-looking couple, and the way they made each other laugh always made Josie laugh too. She knew, because Bel had told her, that Harry was now aware of everything that had happened in the past and was carefully, lovingly helping Bel to dispel the demons that had held her captive for too long. There was still a way to go, Bel admitted, but she was seeing a therapist now, although it was having Harry in her life that was making the biggest difference of all.

Though they were too busy to see Josie and Jeff very often, Bel always stayed in touch by phone, and, bless their hearts, she and Harry had treated her and Jeff to a weekend at a hotel in Devon for Jeff's birthday in March, and they'd come too. Josie had never been to a place with such charm, set as it was on an island just off the south coast. When the tide was out it was possible to walk across the beach to the mainland, but they'd never bothered. The place was too special to want to leave it for a minute. They'd drunk cocktails each evening, all dressed up in the twenties- and thirties-style dresses they'd bought specially, and danced to a jazz band that was nearly as good as The Medics. Jeff had looked so handsome in his tux that Josie was sure she'd fallen in love with him all over again, and he must have felt something too, because they'd started talking that weekend about renewing their marriage vows. She'd found out on the way home that Harry and Bel had decided to move in together, so romance had certainly filled the air during those couple of days.

She and Jeff still hadn't got round to the vows business yet, but it didn't matter. What did was that she was still here and he was doing really well these days in his new job as a chauffeur. He'd gone into partnership with her cousin Steve, who'd got him a two-year-old Merc for a knock-down price, and Jasper had taken care of promoting the new business. Quite soon the better-off people of the area started using Jeff to get to the airports or various functions. Local companies were hiring him too, to ferry directors or important clients around. If it went on like this he might have to take on another driver.

It was lovely having Lily and Jasper living in Kesterly. They were renting for the moment, but now that Jasper had landed himself a good job with the MOD in Exeter they were looking around for somewhere to buy. They especially liked the Newton area, just outside the old town, where Ryan and Chaplain Paul, who was no longer a chaplain, had recently set up home. Paul was teaching special needs children at a school not far from the Temple Fields estate, and when he had the qualifications Ryan was hoping to do the same. Funny how Jeff had never batted an eyelid about Ryan being gay; it just went to show that even after all these years of being married he could still surprise her.

It had been a marvellous ten months since that awful time when they'd told her she only had a few weeks to go. Every day felt more special than the last, even when things didn't go right. She wasn't as big a worrier as she used to be; she'd learned, partly from books and partly from the BCC forum, how to control it, and she was sure Jeff had a different perspective on things these days too. Not that he was into the universe, the same as her, but he definitely seemed more relaxed and appreciative of what they had. It helped having a bit more money, of course; they might even be in a position soon to put a deposit down on a small place of their own.

It was amazing how powerful her meditation sessions were turning out to be. Bel had got her into them, and yoga; Josie also often went up to the churchyard to be quiet and alone while she tuned out of everyday stresses and petty worries. Lately she'd found herself going into a whole other dimension where she seemed to understand the language of animals and birds, and could hear the sound of trees growing or unborn babies crying. She never told anyone about it, they'd think she was barmy, but during those spiritual journeys it was as though she was somewhere outside time, halfway between here and there, drifting in the quiet beauty of simply being. She had no doubt now that heaven was right here on earth; that miracles were everywhere and angels were in everyone.

Her mother had taken up cosmic ordering, so was claiming responsibility for keeping her daughter alive. She preached its power to anyone who'd listen, though she still hadn't had any luck with finding a decent bloke or winning big on the lottery, her other two regular orders.

'It might help if you bought a ticket,' Ryan told her. He was very into Josie's new relationship with the universe, though he preferred to call it God, and was always on at his nan for being irreverent.

'I do when I can afford it,' Eileen assured him, 'but most I've ever won is a couple of hundred quid which don't go anywhere. Maybe I'm not asking for enough, but I don't want to be greedy, do I?'

'Never let it be said,' Jeff muttered.

Bel and Kristina – or Monkton and Lambert, as they were calling their new company – had recently sold Clementine barn to a famous musician, who was turning one of the outbuildings into a recording studio. Josie knew it had been a wrench for Bel to let the place go, since it was where she and Harry had shared their first kiss, although technically speaking that had happened in the trailer, which was now acting as an office at another barn. So their special location could be transported about the countryside along with them.

With Jasper being so well paid Lily was able to work from home as a fund-raiser for Breast Cancer Care, which she threw herself into wholeheartedly, ably assisted by Josie. They'd put on all sorts of events over the last few months, from strawberry teas, to bad-hair days, to battles of the bands, which The Medics had won by raising just under two thousand pounds. They didn't have anything else planned for a while though, since they had other important matters to deal with, like the beautiful little bundle Josie was holding now. This was her first grandchild, Joella, a joining of her and Bel's names that made Josie's heart sing simply to hear it.

'You're the best little miracle of all,' she whispered, tears of joy shining in her yellowing eyes. 'Granny's precious girl, that's what you are.' She hadn't felt so happy since she'd brought Lily and Ryan into the world, and was quietly sure she wouldn't feel like this again. She hadn't told anyone yet that the cancer was on the move again; they didn't need to know on Joella's christening day.

They'd left the church half an hour ago and driven to Bel's for the party. It was a beautiful day, very warm for October, with sunlight sparkling over the waves and not a cloud in the sky. In various towns and cities around the country two dozen or more women would be getting themselves ready for the fashion show next week. Josie could feel their joy in her heart, and wished them well. She wouldn't be taking part this year, but she and Bel had tickets to go and watch.

'She's got her mummy's and granny's violet-blue eyes,' Bel smiled, coming to put an arm around her.

'Yes, she has,' Josie said proudly, 'and our colour hair.' *Thank you, thank you, thank you for letting me see and hold her. Nothing could ever matter more than this.*

'Is the robe from Lily's wedding dress?' Bel asked, touching the lace.

Josie nodded. 'Lovely, isn't it? Just like my precious girl.'

Joella gave a little burp and a yawn, making them smile.

'What about going to your godmother?' Josie whispered, needing to hand her over. She wasn't strong enough to hold her for long.

'Oh, yes please,' Bel smiled, and taking the baby she pressed a kiss to her forehead.

Joella's pretty eyes gazed up at her curiously, before she yawned again and closed them.

'She's worn out from all that screaming at the church,' Lily announced, coming to join them. 'Shall I lie her down?'

'If you must,' Bel responded, reluctantly letting her go.

As they watched Lily settling her on the sofa, Bel slipped an arm through Josie's. 'Are you OK?' she asked.

Josie smiled as she looked around the room. How could she not be OK when the universe, God, or whatever controlled these things had allowed her to be a part of this day? Everyone she loved was here, Jeff, Lily, Jasper, Ryan, Paul, Bel, Harry, her mother, Miriam and Richard, Nick, Kristina and the children, and of course Joella. Fancy her thinking she'd never get to hold her, when she'd had no idea what the future might have in store. She still didn't, though she knew in her heart that it wouldn't be long now. Whether she'd made these last ten months happen simply by believing they could, or whether something else had been responsible, she would never know. The important thing was that she'd had them, and so had been given the time to write to everyone she cared about to thank them for the parts they'd played in her life, for the happiness they'd given her, and the love. She'd told them what she hoped for their futures, and assured them that they would always have her love. But because she knew with a certainty that filled her heart with joy that they would all meet again one day, she would never say goodbye.

ACKNOWLEDGEMENTS

It's hard to find enough words to thank Dr Emma Pennery, the Clinical Director of Breast Cancer Care, for all the incredible support and advice she gave to this book. It is no exaggeration to say that I really couldn't have done it without her. Thank you, Emma, thank you, thank you, thank you.

I would also like to thank Lynn Butteriss, Lauren Smith, Suzi Copland, again from Breast Cancer Care, for their own generous contributions to the research.

Another huge thank you to Mr Simon Cawthorne, breast surgeon at the Breast Care Centre of Southmead Hospital in Bristol for patiently explaining the process of diagnosis and treatment. Also very many thanks to oncologist Dr Jeremy Braybrooke for so much invaluable guidance through the challenging journey of chemotherapy.

Much love and thanks to Ann Ruddle who was generous enough to share her personal experience of chemotherapy.

Also a big thank you to Steph Harrison who not only brought us all together, but who has successfully reached the fantastic stage of remission!! Congratulations Steph, everyone is so happy for you.

I would be completely remiss if I didn't acknowledge with much affection and gratitude the tremendous support of my editors in the UK, Susan Sandon and Georgina Hawtrey-Woore, and in the US, Kara Cesare and Hannah Elnan. Not forgetting, of course, the wonderful publishing teams both sides of the Atlantic: Jenifer Doyle, Sarah Page, Louise Page, Jennifer Hershey, Elizabeth Maguire, Kristin Fassler, Susan Corcoran, Lindsey Kennedy, Andrew

Sauerwine and the incredible sales teams who do such a marvellous job in taking the book on its lengthy journey from me to you, the reader.

Lastly, I want to thank my very own romantic hero, James Garrett, who made my dreams come true during the writing of this book when he became my husband.